PRAISE FOR SEA SERPENT'S HEIR

"...a masterful blend of political high fantasy and gritty, other-worldly pirate lore that I highly recommend to anyone looking for a new adventure."
-MICHELLE FUS (AVA'S DEMON)

"What a gorgeous, dark fantasy tale that Mairghread Scott and Pablo Tunica have created! I want to follow every alley and turn over every stone in this saltwater and magic soaked world."
-IRMA KNIIVILA (EVERYDAY HERO MACHINE BOY)

"...A thrilling adventure set in an enthralling, magical world filled with pirate armies, evil knights, and of course... sea serpents. I was hooked (hehe) from beginning to end!"
-TRI VUONG (EVERYDAY HERO MACHINE BOY)

"A beautifully crafted world that takes every opportunity to twist your expectations in new directions. Not afraid of showcasing the darker sides of its characters while dazzling the reader with visuals of the most amazing creatures and world-building."
-JORGE CORONA (*The Me You Love In The Dark, Middlewest, Batgirls*)

"Action and intrigue and secrets and battles and magic and more. Adventure rings high on every single page with a delicious richness, which promises excitement after excitement."
-BOOKWORM FOR KIDS

"This engaging story will most likely resonate with readers who enjoy stories with strong female protagonists."
-THE GRAPHIC LIBRARY

"Enchanting, and dreamy. This book feels like a mash up between Hayao Miyazaki and Guillermo del Toro with its heart, mystery, and adventure."
-TILLIE WALDEN (*Spinning, On A Sunbeam*, CLEMENTINE)

MAIRGHREAD SCOTT
PABLO TUNICA

SEA SERPENT'S HEIR

BOOK ONE: PIRATE'S DAUGHTER

SKYBOUND
COMET

SEA SE
HEIR™

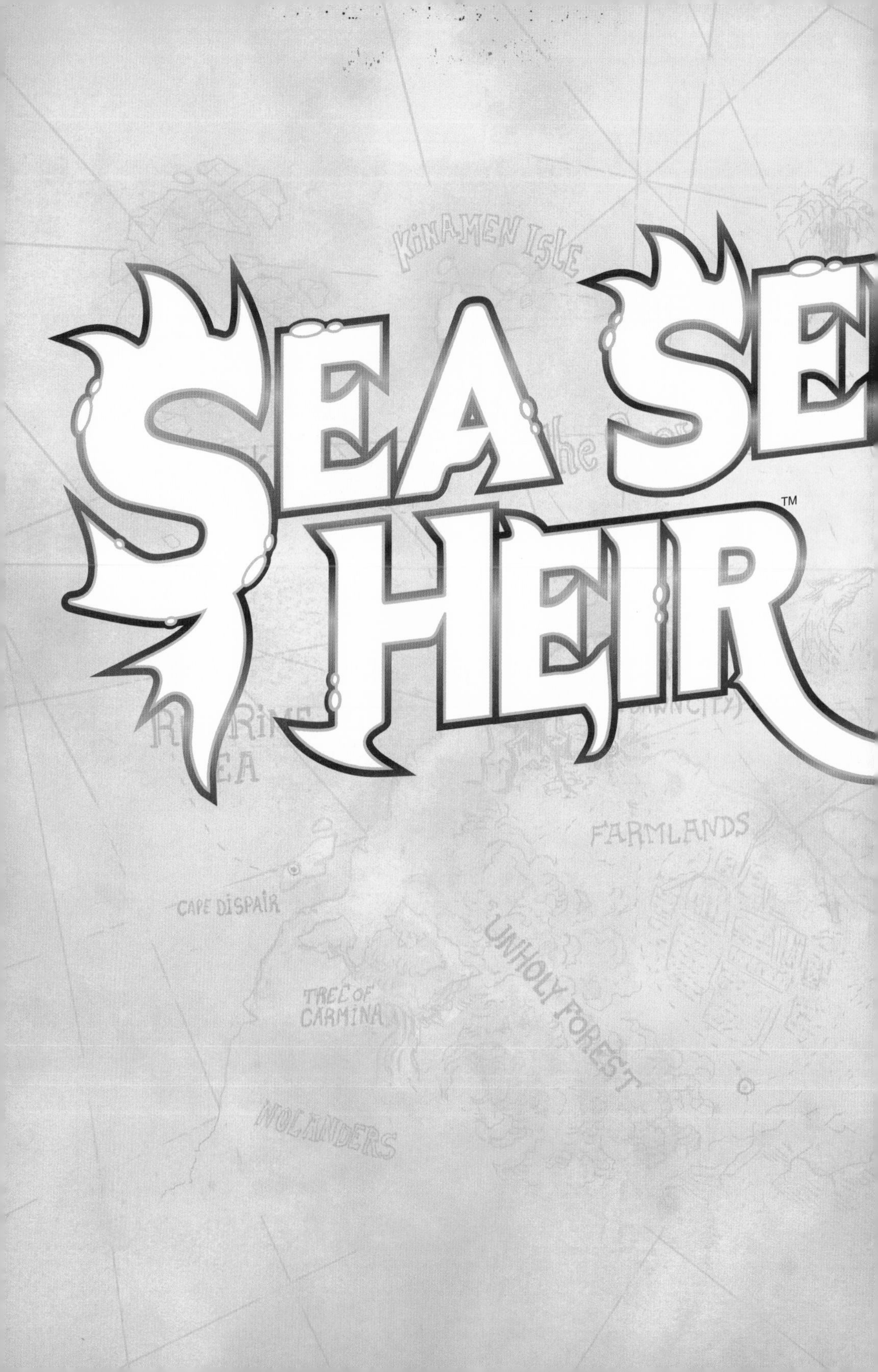
KINAMEN ISLE
FARMLANDS
CAPE DISPAIR
UNHOLY FOREST
TREE OF
CARMINA
NOLANDERS

RPENT'S

BOOK ONE: PIRATE'S DAUGHTER

Written by

MAIRGHREAD SCOTT

Illustrated by

PABLO TUNICA

Lettered by

ARIANA MAHER

Created by

MAIRGHREAD SCOTT & PABLO TUNICA

To Jason and Corran,
With all my heart.

Mairghread Scott

For Ludmila and Catalina.
Tiny now, but destined to
find hidden treasures in
the ocean.

Pablo Tunica

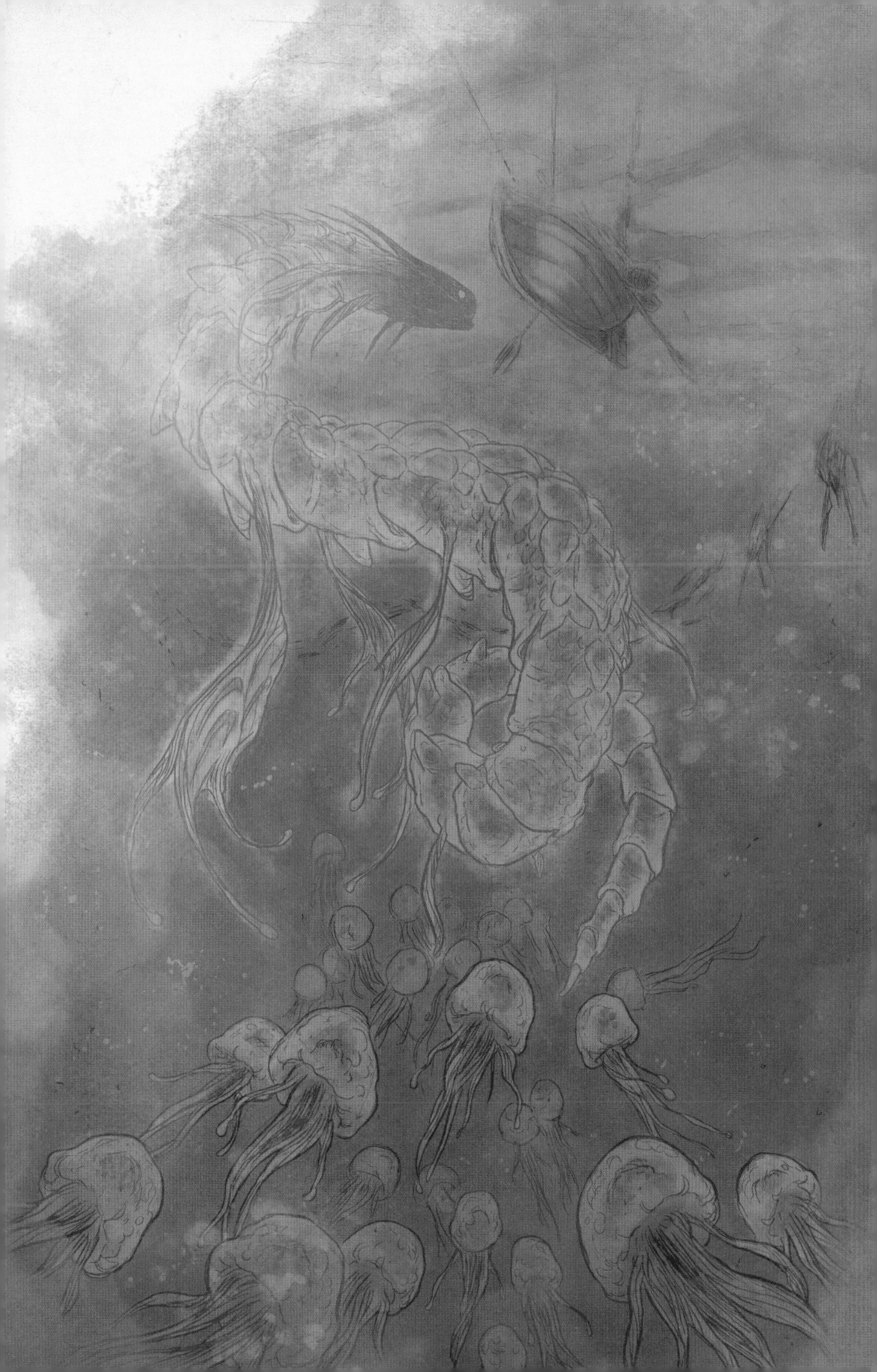

Prologue

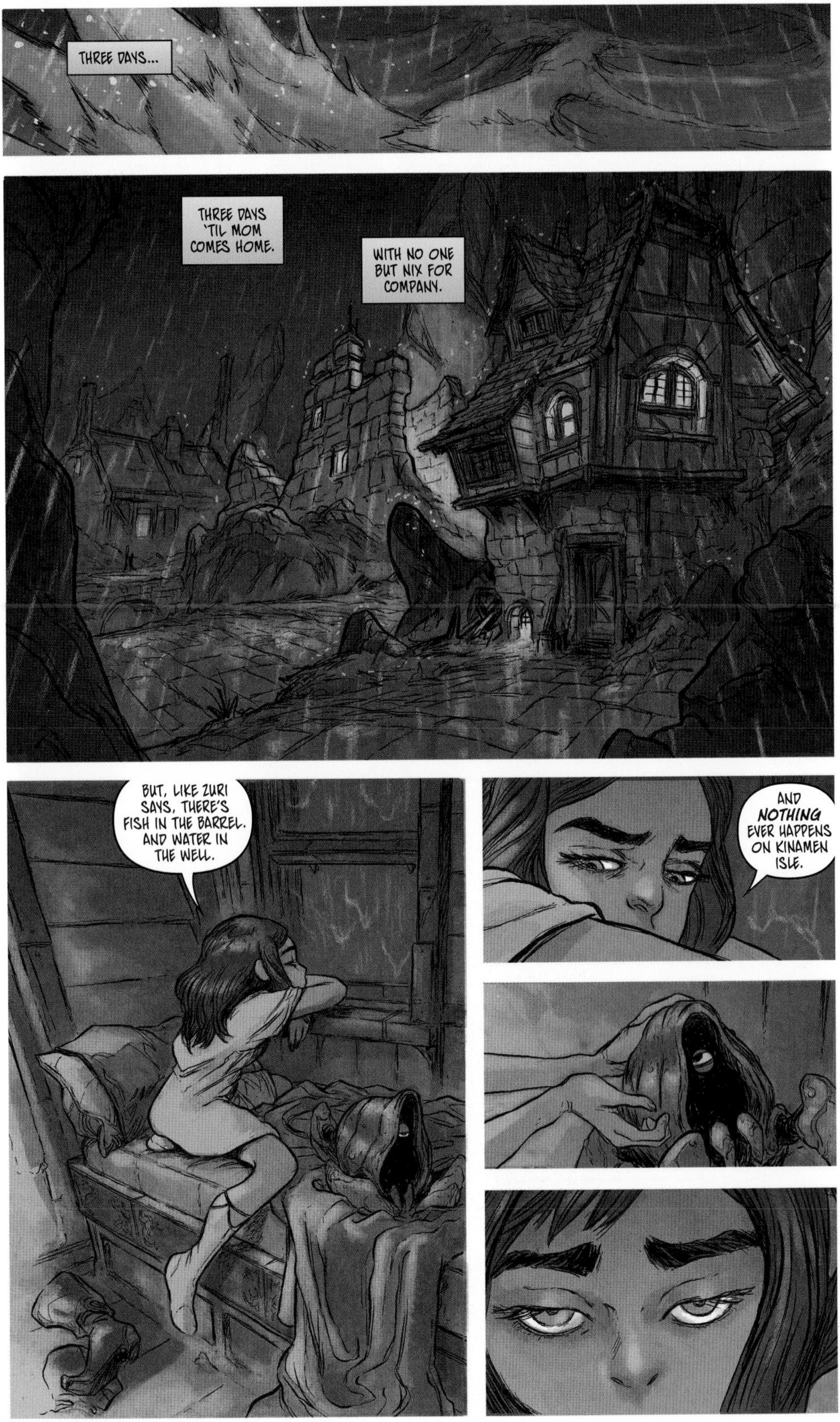
THREE DAYS...
THREE DAYS 'TIL MOM COMES HOME.
WITH NO ONE BUT NIX FOR COMPANY.
BUT, LIKE ZURI SAYS, THERE'S FISH IN THE BARREL. AND WATER IN THE WELL.
AND *NOTHING* EVER HAPPENS ON KINAMEN ISLE.

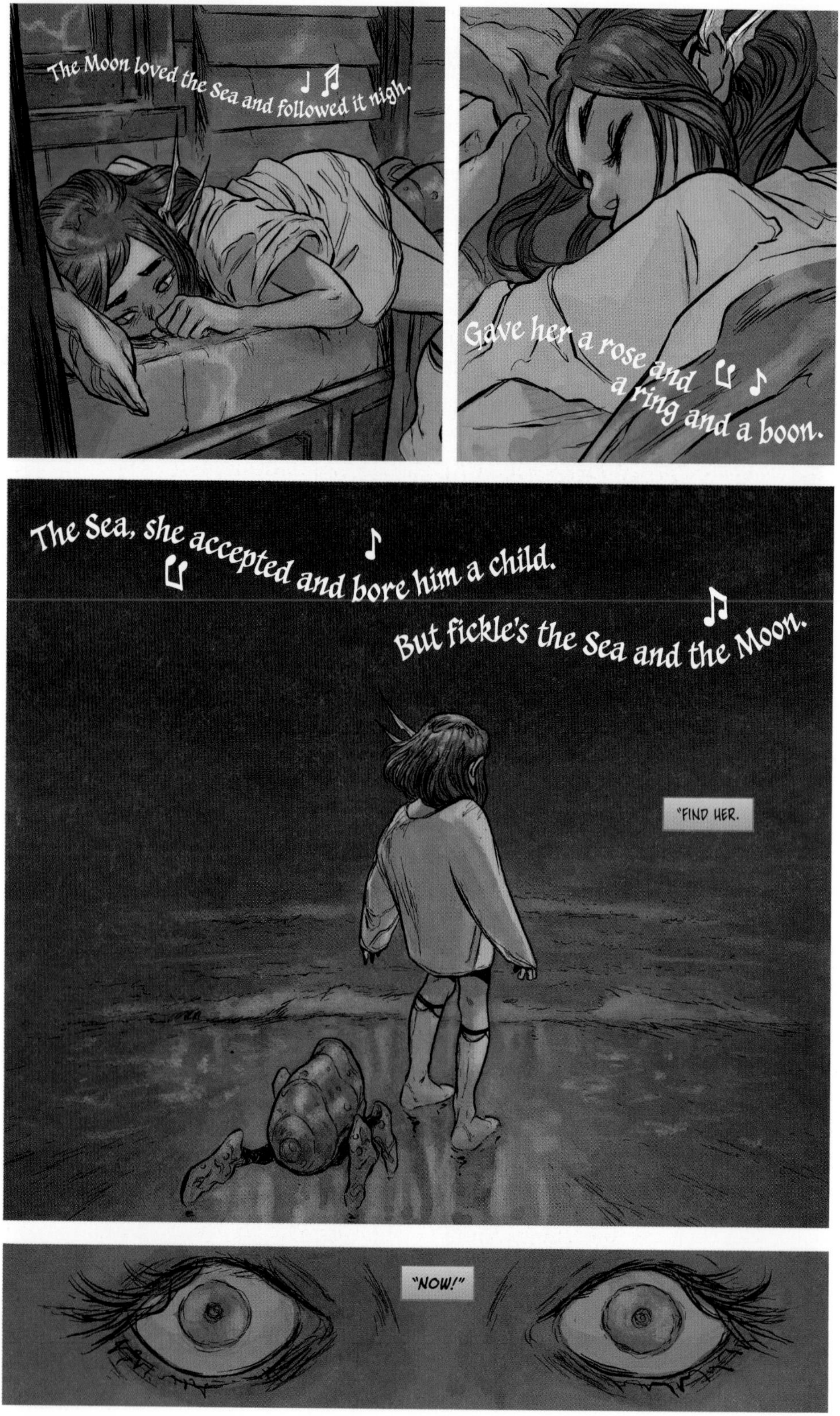
The Moon loved the Sea and followed it nigh.
Gave her a rose and a ring and a boon.
The Sea, she accepted and bore him a child.
But fickle's the Sea and the Moon.
"FIND HER.
"NOW!"

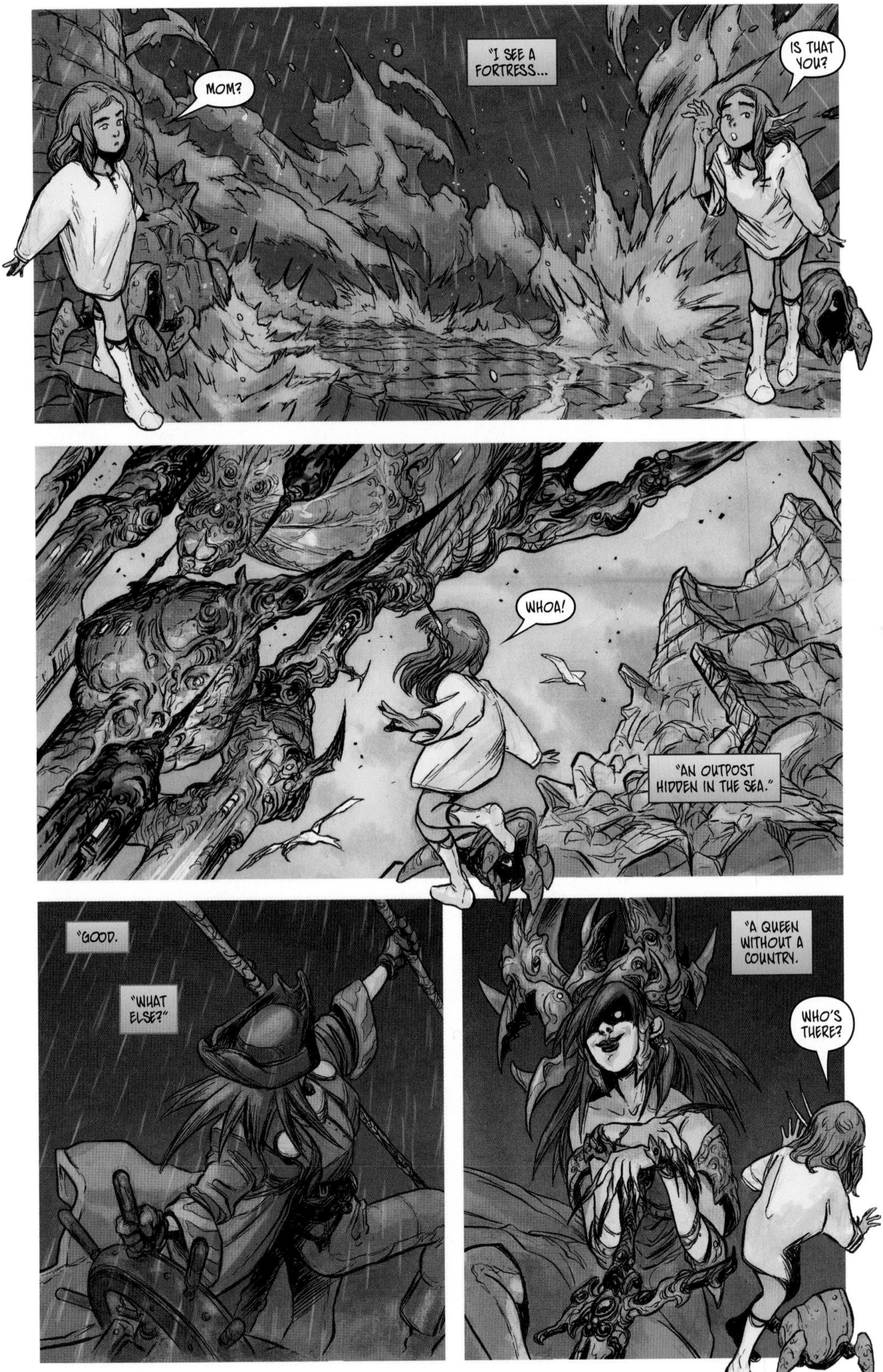
MOM?
"I SEE A FORTRESS...
IS THAT YOU?
WHOA!
"AN OUTPOST HIDDEN IN THE SEA."
"GOOD.
"WHAT ELSE?"
"A QUEEN WITHOUT A COUNTRY.
WHO'S THERE?

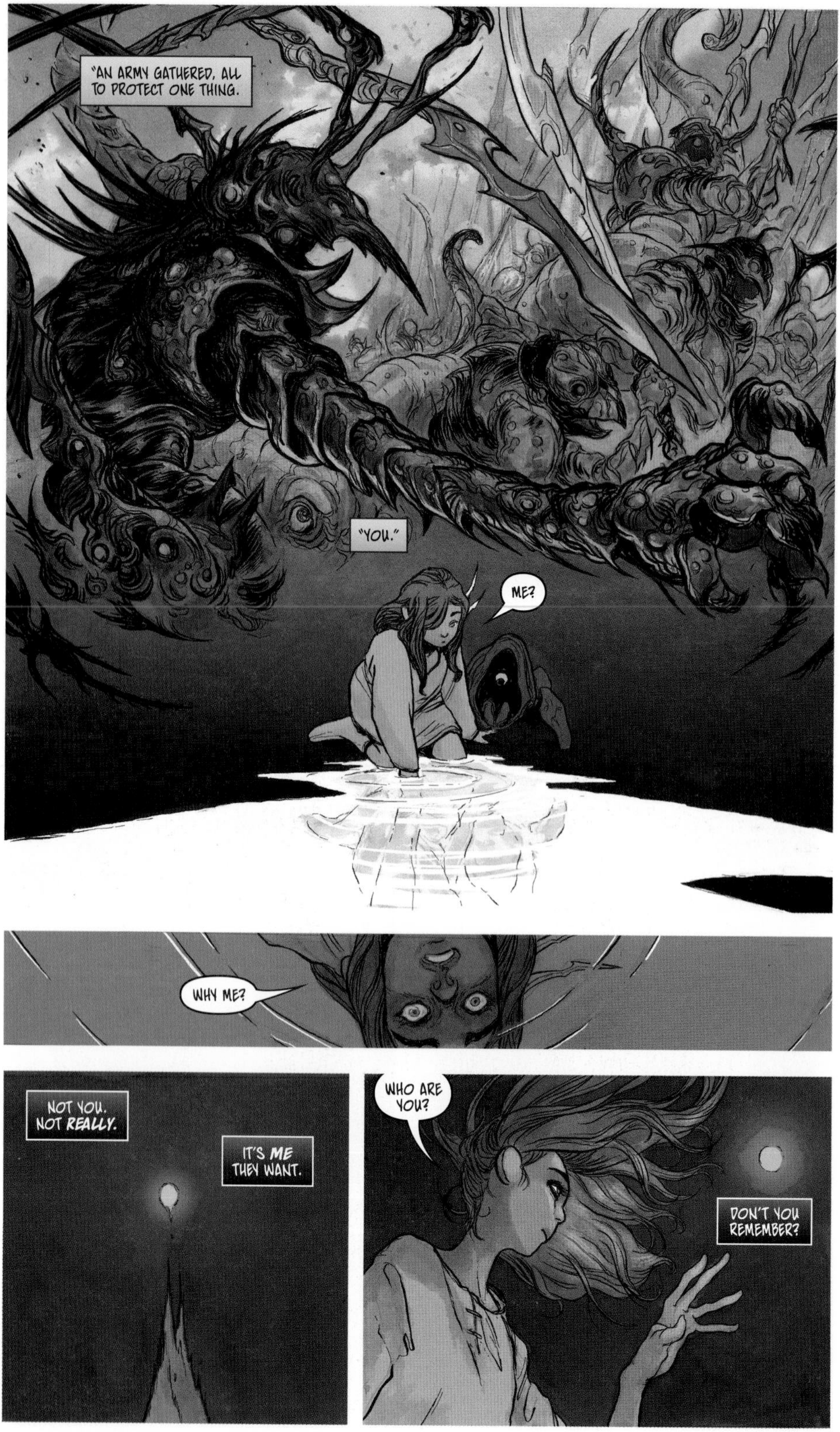
"AN ARMY GATHERED, ALL TO PROTECT ONE THING.
"YOU."
ME?
WHY ME?
NOT YOU. NOT REALLY.
IT'S ME THEY WANT.
WHO ARE YOU?
DON'T YOU REMEMBER?

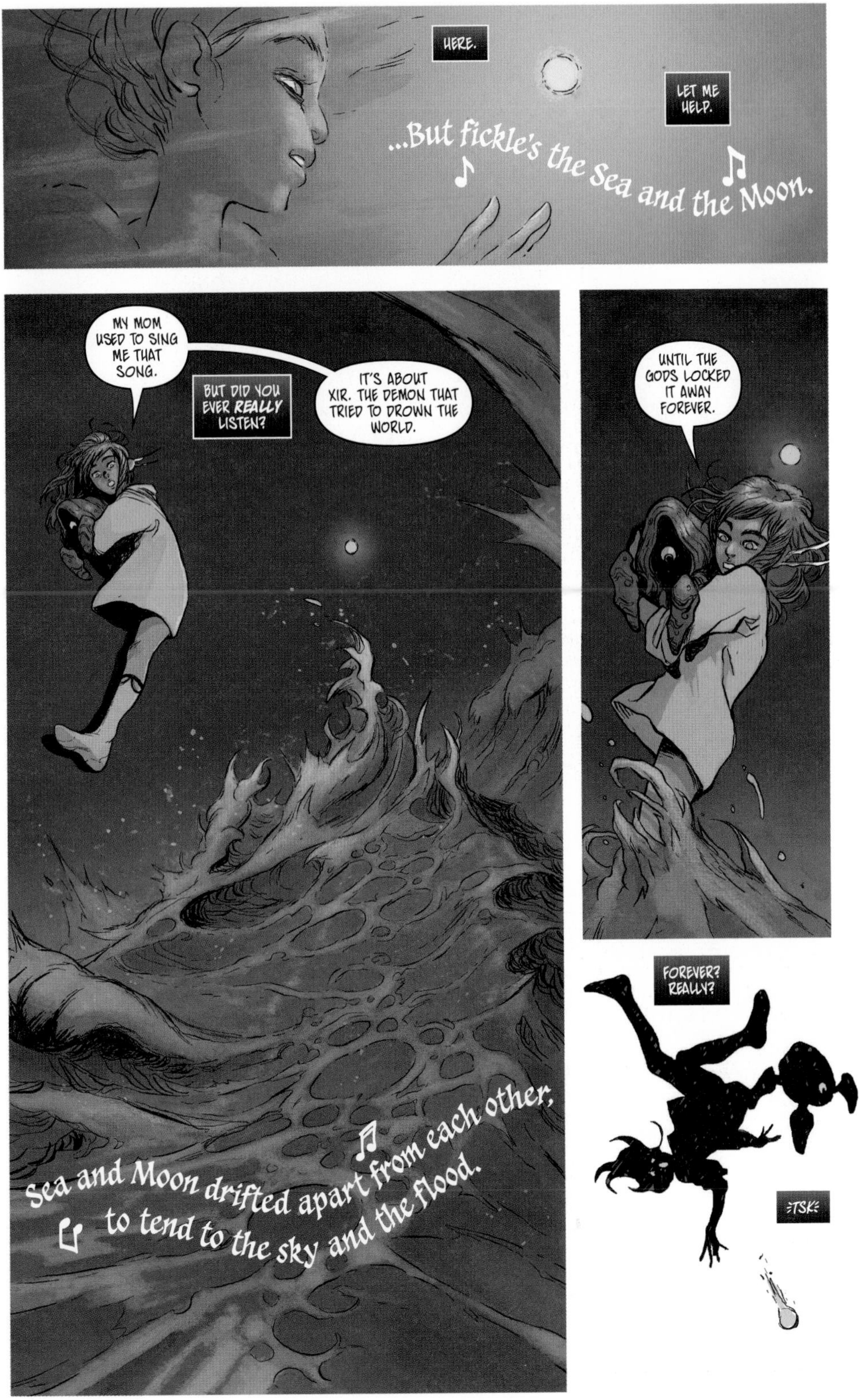
HERE.
LET ME HELP.
...But fickle's the Sea and the Moon.
MY MOM USED TO SING ME THAT SONG.
BUT DID YOU EVER REALLY LISTEN?
IT'S ABOUT XIR. THE DEMON THAT TRIED TO DROWN THE WORLD.
Sea and Moon drifted apart from each other,
to tend to the sky and the flood.
UNTIL THE GODS LOCKED IT AWAY FOREVER.
FOREVER? REALLY?
TSK

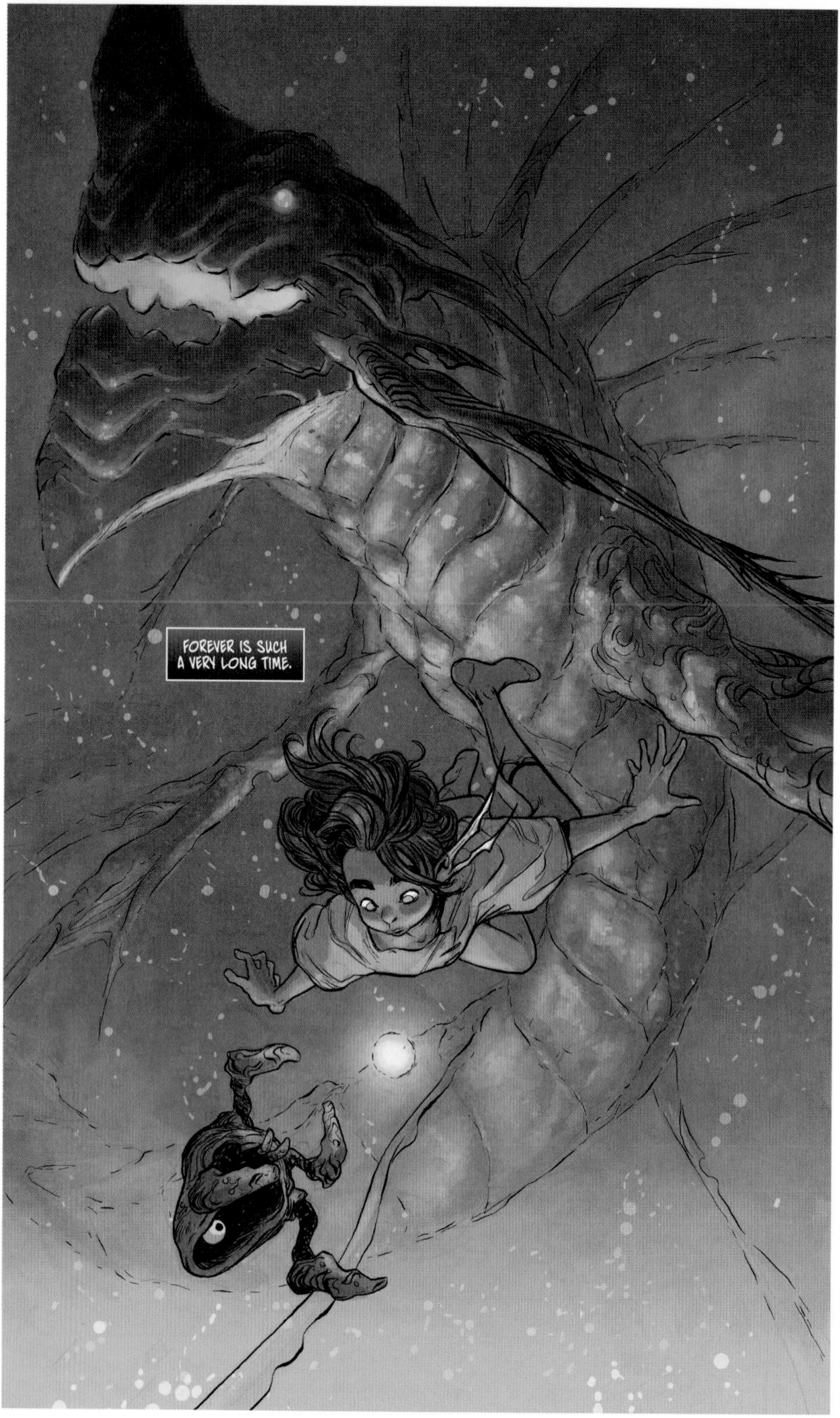
FOREVER IS SUCH A VERY LONG TIME.

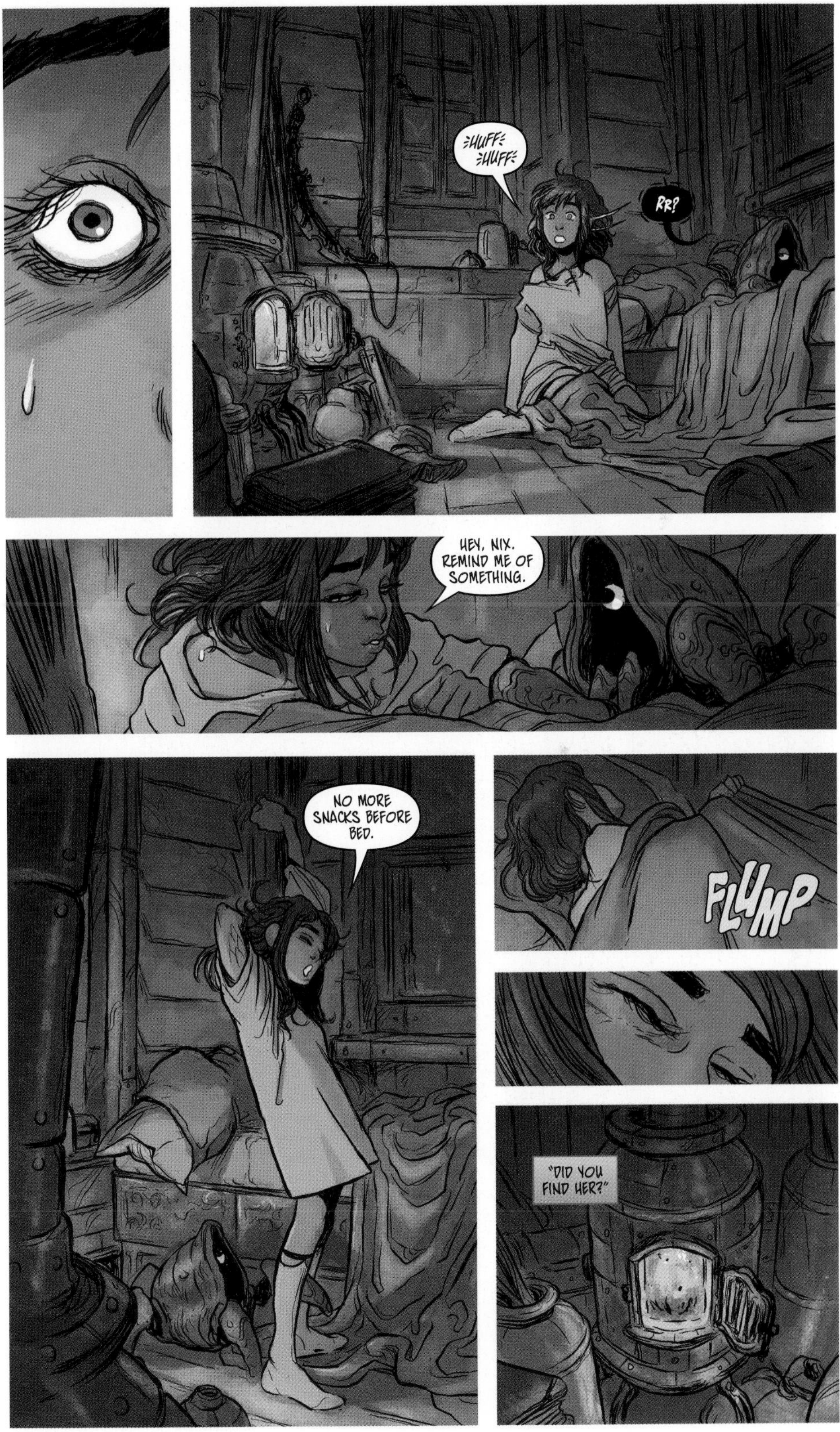
HUFF HUFF
RR?
HEY, NIX. REMIND ME OF SOMETHING.
NO MORE SNACKS BEFORE BED.
FLUMP
"DID YOU FIND HER?"

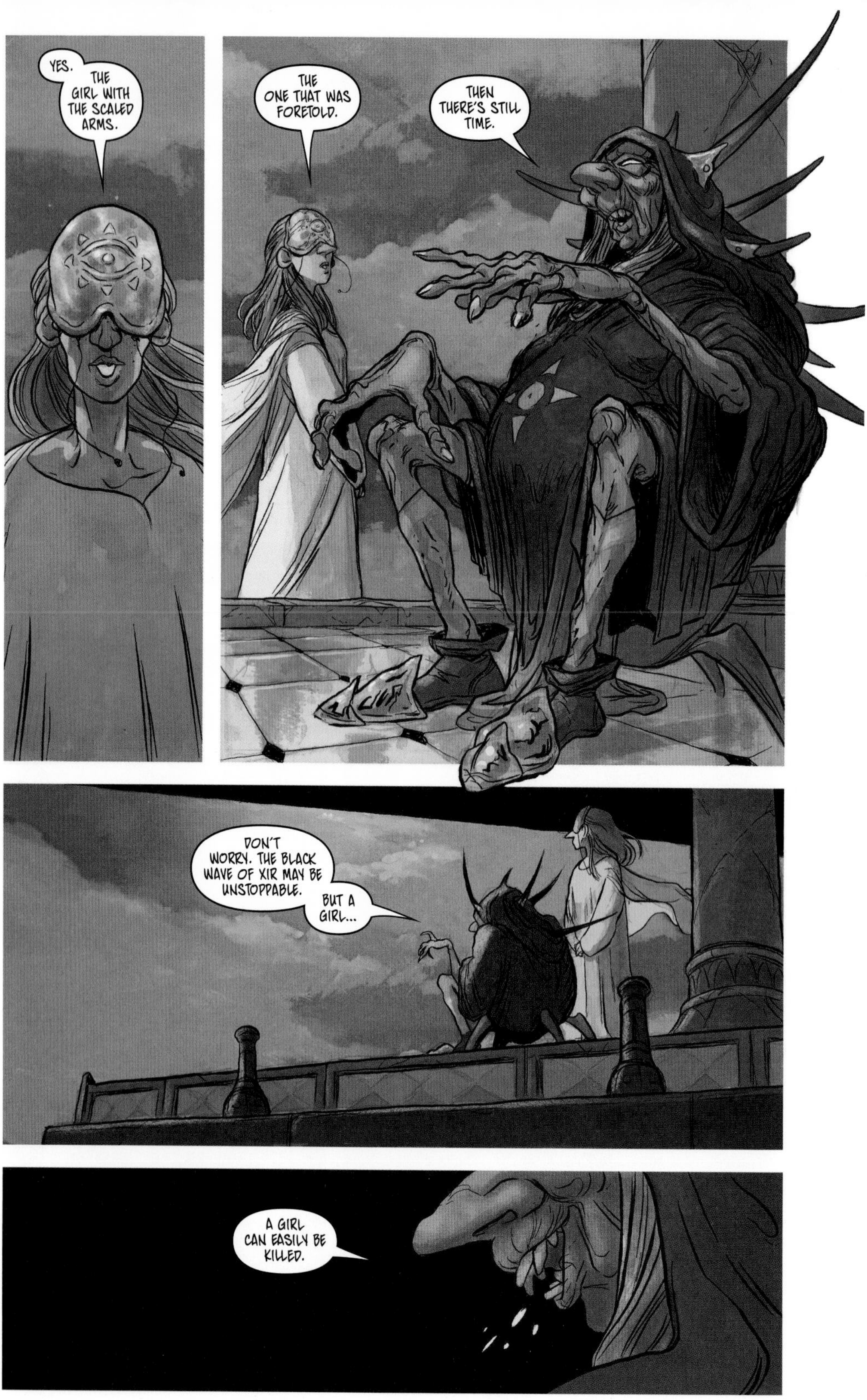
YES. THE GIRL WITH THE SCALED ARMS.
THE ONE THAT WAS FORETOLD.
THEN THERE'S STILL TIME.
DON'T WORRY. THE BLACK WAVE OF XIR MAY BE UNSTOPPABLE.
BUT A GIRL...
A GIRL CAN EASILY BE KILLED.

Chapter One

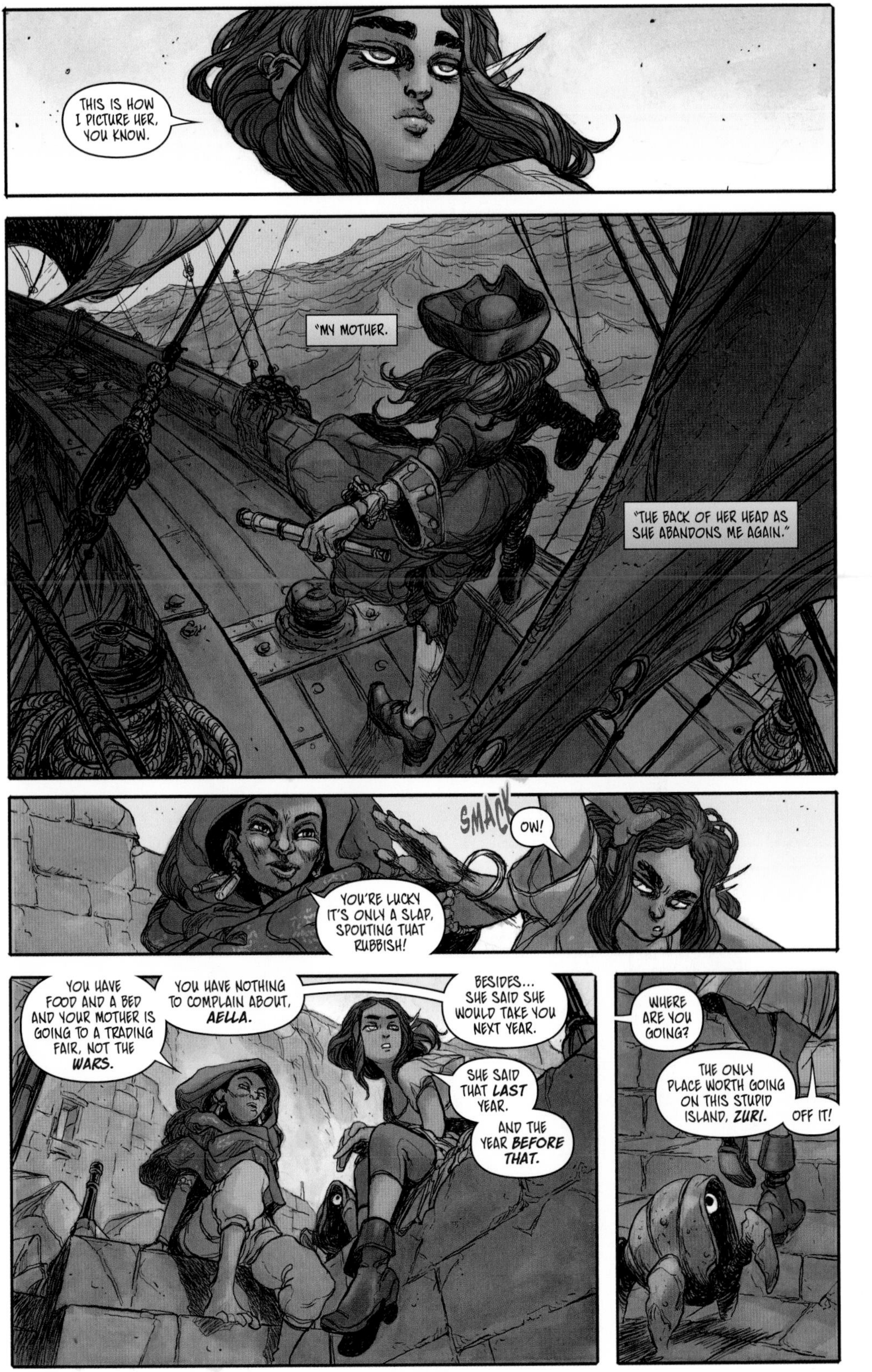
THIS IS HOW I PICTURE HER, YOU KNOW.
"MY MOTHER.
"THE BACK OF HER HEAD AS SHE ABANDONS ME AGAIN."
SMACK
OW!
YOU'RE LUCKY IT'S ONLY A SLAP, SPOUTING THAT RUBBISH!
YOU HAVE FOOD AND A BED AND YOUR MOTHER IS GOING TO A TRADING FAIR, NOT THE **WARS**.
YOU HAVE NOTHING TO COMPLAIN ABOUT, **AELLA**.
BESIDES... SHE SAID SHE WOULD TAKE YOU NEXT YEAR.
SHE SAID THAT **LAST** YEAR.
AND THE YEAR **BEFORE THAT**.
WHERE ARE YOU GOING?
THE ONLY PLACE WORTH GOING ON THIS STUPID ISLAND, **ZURI**.
OFF IT!

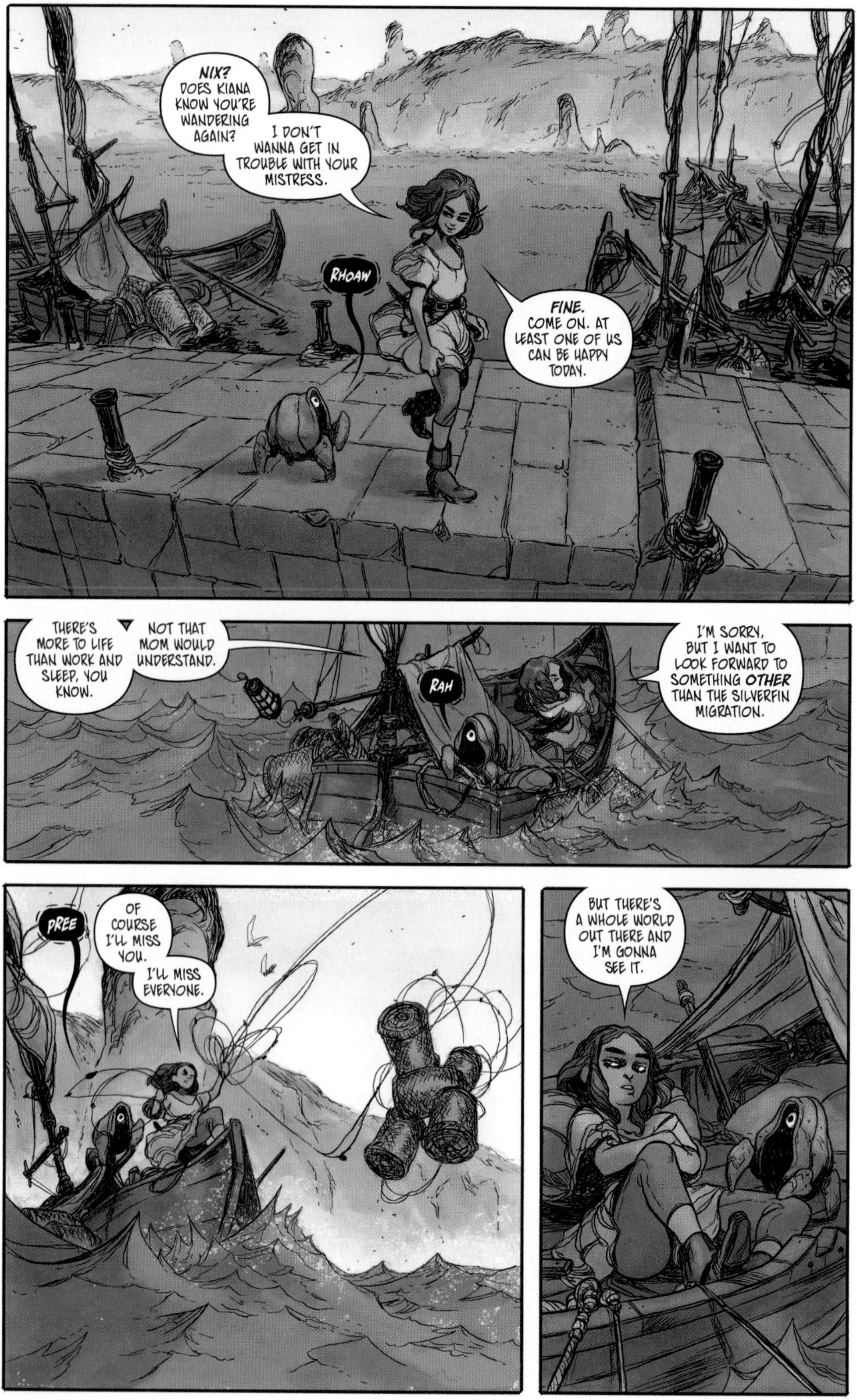
NIX? DOES KIANA KNOW YOU'RE WANDERING AGAIN?
I DON'T WANNA GET IN TROUBLE WITH YOUR MISTRESS.
RHOAW
FINE. COME ON. AT LEAST ONE OF US CAN BE HAPPY TODAY.
THERE'S MORE TO LIFE THAN WORK AND SLEEP, YOU KNOW.
NOT THAT MOM WOULD UNDERSTAND.
RAH
I'M SORRY, BUT I WANT TO LOOK FORWARD TO SOMETHING OTHER THAN THE SILVERFIN MIGRATION.
PREE
OF COURSE I'LL MISS YOU.
I'LL MISS EVERYONE.
BUT THERE'S A WHOLE WORLD OUT THERE AND I'M GONNA SEE IT.

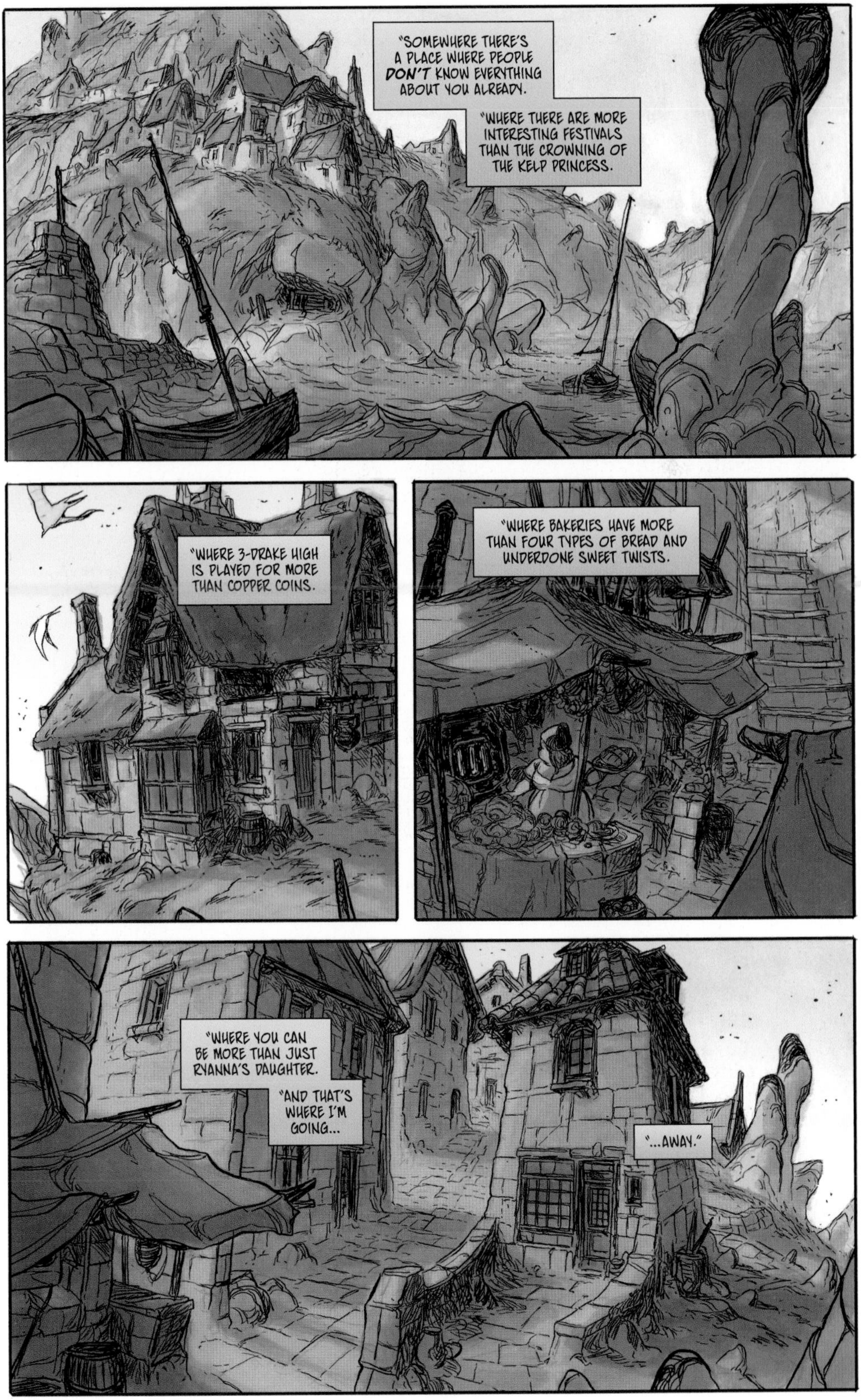
"SOMEWHERE THERE'S A PLACE WHERE PEOPLE **DON'T** KNOW EVERYTHING ABOUT YOU ALREADY.
"WHERE THERE ARE MORE INTERESTING FESTIVALS THAN THE CROWNING OF THE KELP PRINCESS.
"WHERE 3-DRAKE HIGH IS PLAYED FOR MORE THAN COPPER COINS.
"WHERE BAKERIES HAVE MORE THAN FOUR TYPES OF BREAD AND UNDERDONE SWEET TWISTS.
"WHERE YOU CAN BE MORE THAN JUST RYANNA'S DAUGHTER.
"AND THAT'S WHERE I'M GOING...
"...AWAY."

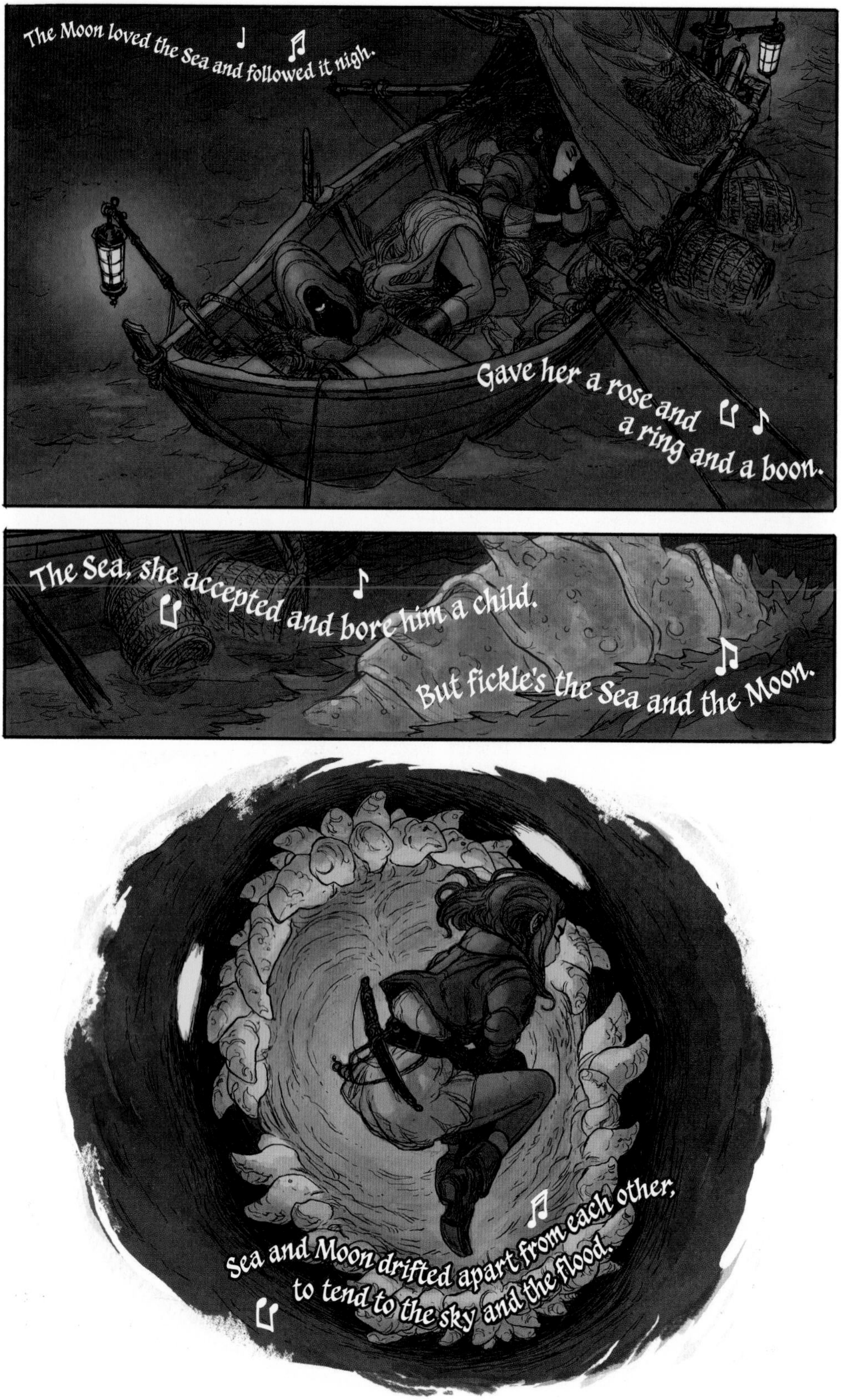
The Moon loved the Sea and followed it nigh.
Gave her a rose and a ring and a boon.
The Sea, she accepted and bore him a child.
But fickle's the Sea and the Moon.
Sea and Moon drifted apart from each other, to tend to the sky and the flood.

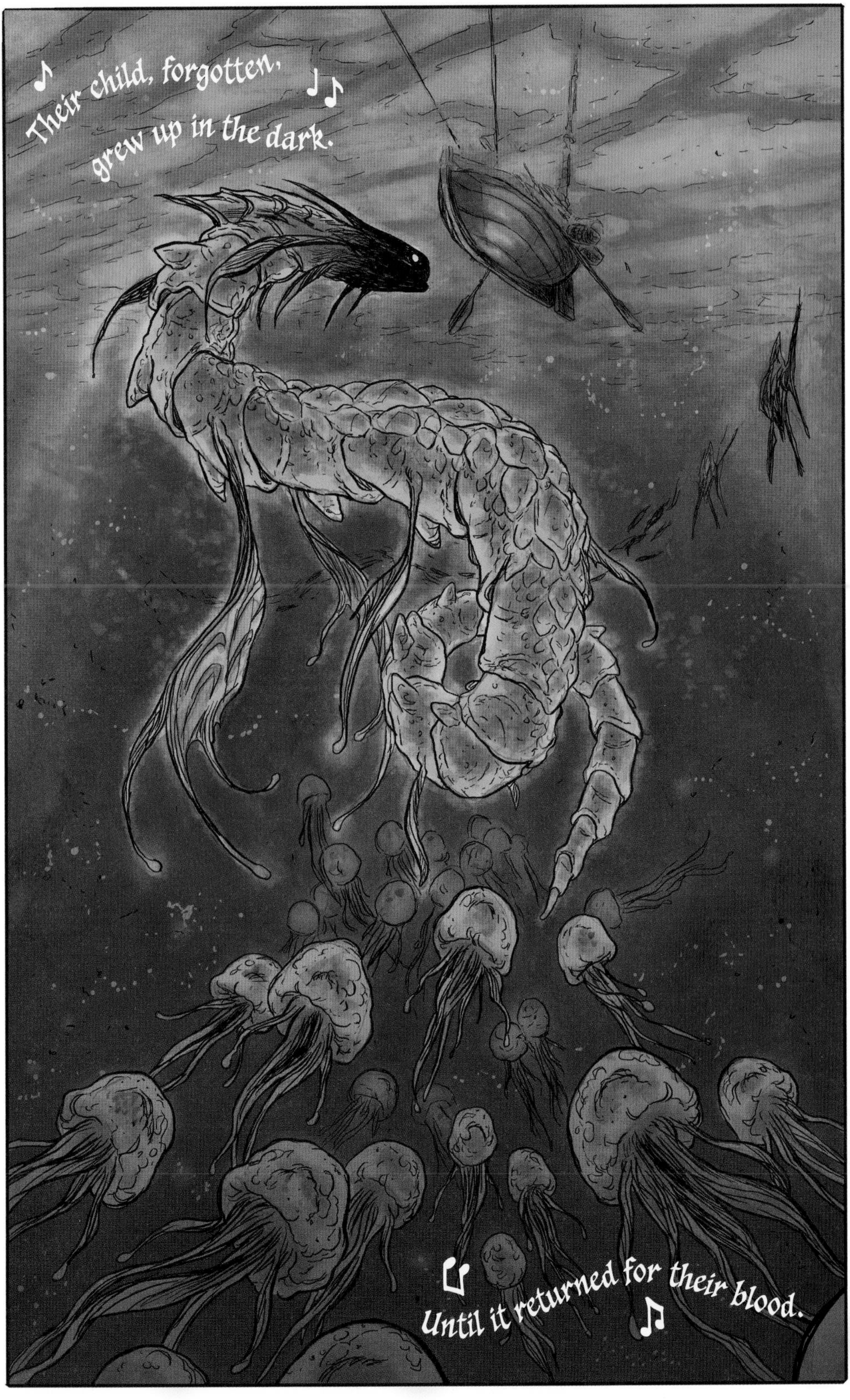
Their child, forgotten,
grew up in the dark.
Until it returned for their blood.

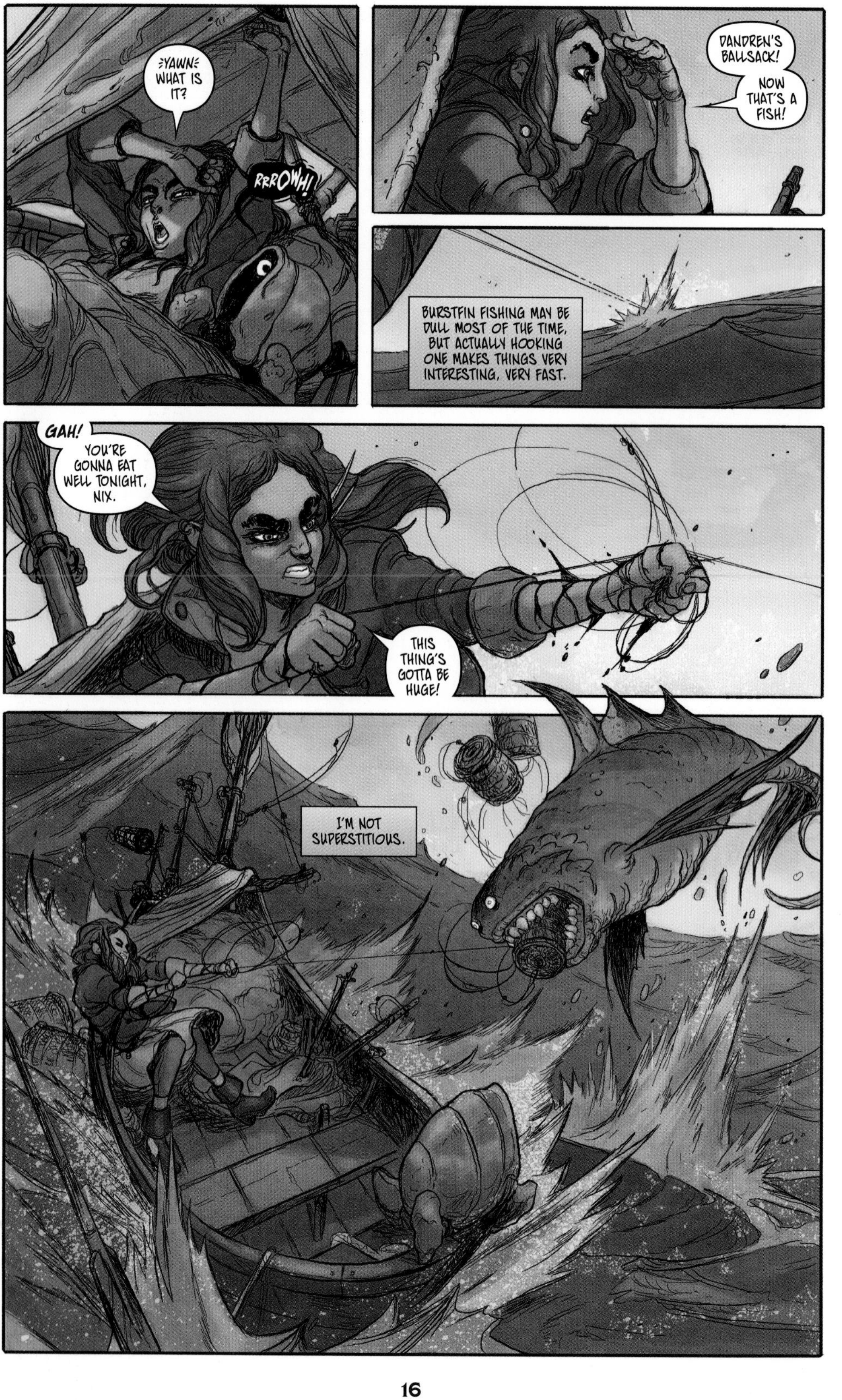

:YAWN: WHAT IS IT?
RRROWH!
DANDREN'S BALLSACK!
NOW THAT'S A FISH!
BURSTFIN FISHING MAY BE DULL MOST OF THE TIME, BUT ACTUALLY HOOKING ONE MAKES THINGS VERY INTERESTING, VERY FAST.
GAH!
YOU'RE GONNA EAT WELL TONIGHT, NIX.
THIS THING'S GOTTA BE HUGE!
I'M NOT SUPERSTITIOUS.

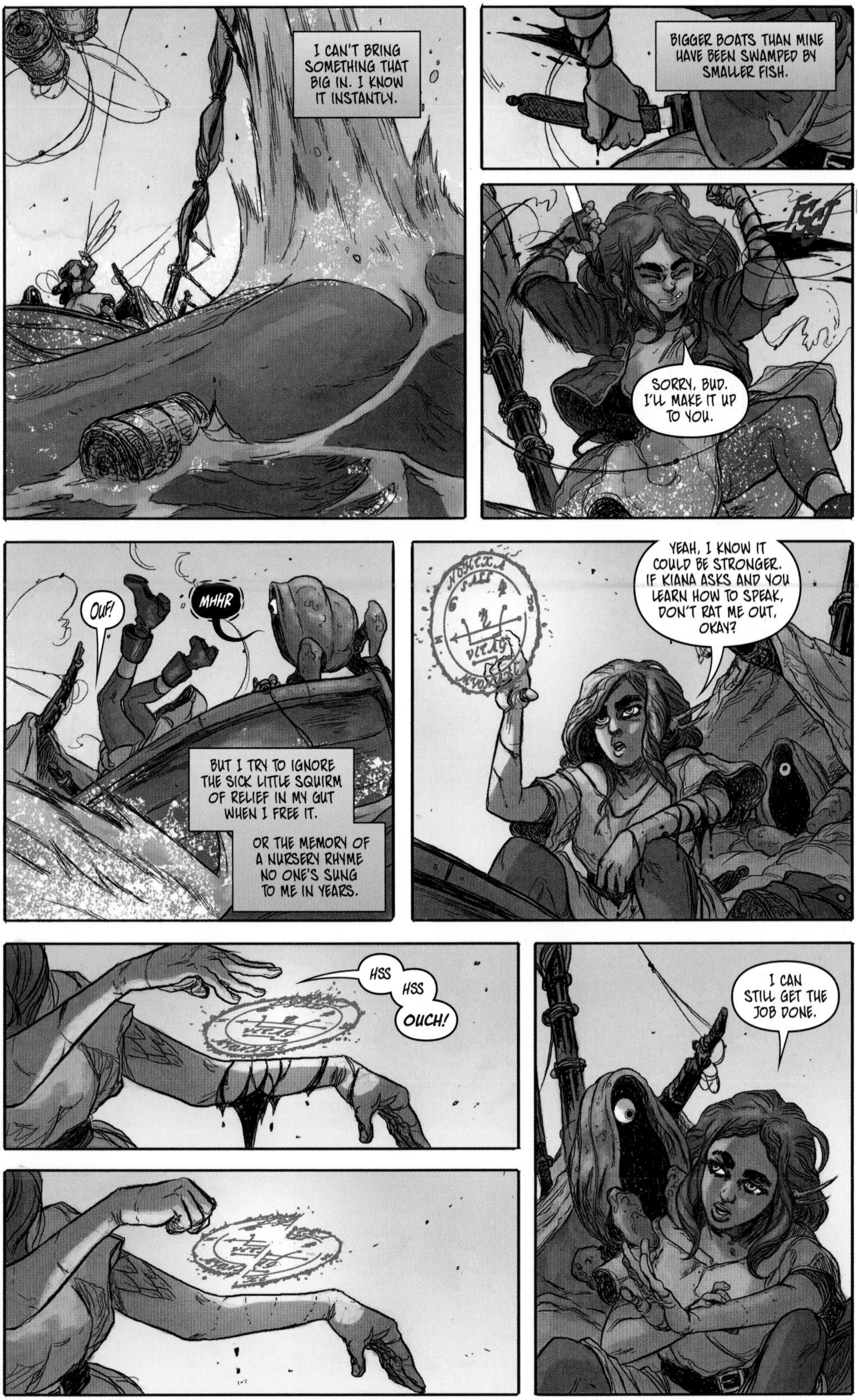
I CAN'T BRING SOMETHING THAT BIG IN. I KNOW IT INSTANTLY.
BIGGER BOATS THAN MINE HAVE BEEN SWAMPED BY SMALLER FISH.
SORRY, BUD. I'LL MAKE IT UP TO YOU.
OUF!
MHHR
BUT I TRY TO IGNORE THE SICK LITTLE SQUIRM OF RELIEF IN MY GUT WHEN I FREE IT.
OR THE MEMORY OF A NURSERY RHYME NO ONE'S SUNG TO ME IN YEARS.
YEAH, I KNOW IT COULD BE STRONGER. IF KIANA ASKS AND YOU LEARN HOW TO SPEAK, DON'T RAT ME OUT, OKAY?
HSS
HSS
OUCH!
I CAN STILL GET THE JOB DONE.

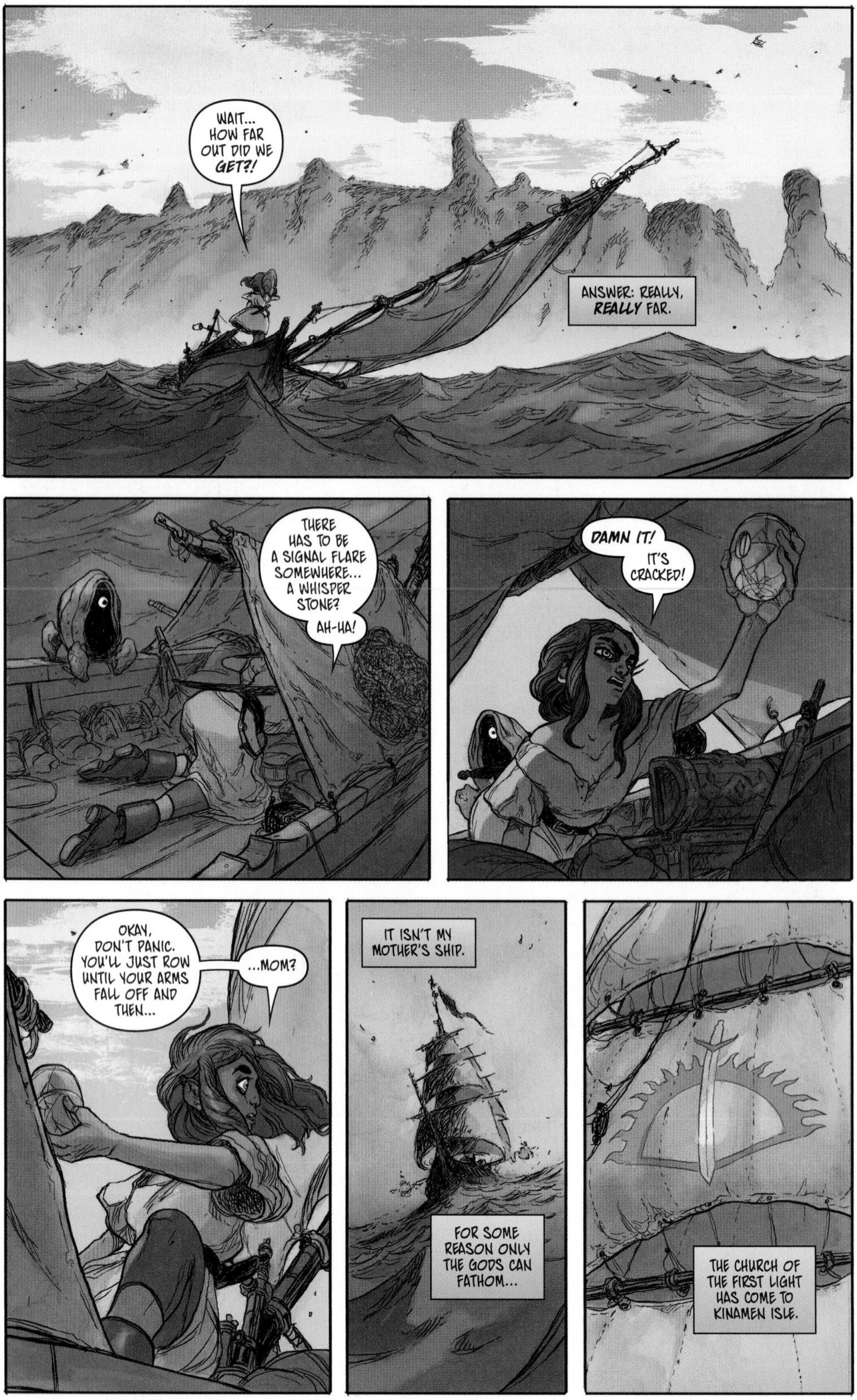
WAIT... HOW FAR OUT DID WE GET?!
ANSWER: REALLY, REALLY FAR.
THERE HAS TO BE A SIGNAL FLARE SOMEWHERE... A WHISPER STONE?
AH-HA!
DAMN IT!
IT'S CRACKED!
OKAY, DON'T PANIC. YOU'LL JUST ROW UNTIL YOUR ARMS FALL OFF AND THEN...
...MOM?
IT ISN'T MY MOTHER'S SHIP.
FOR SOME REASON ONLY THE GODS CAN FATHOM...
THE CHURCH OF THE FIRST LIGHT HAS COME TO KINAMEN ISLE.

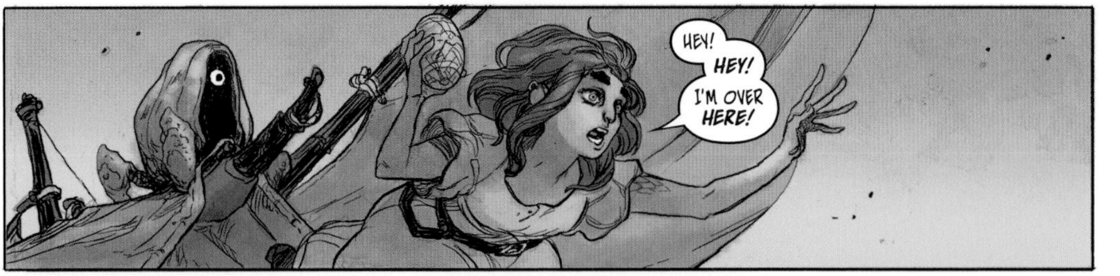
HEY!
HEY!
I'M OVER HERE!

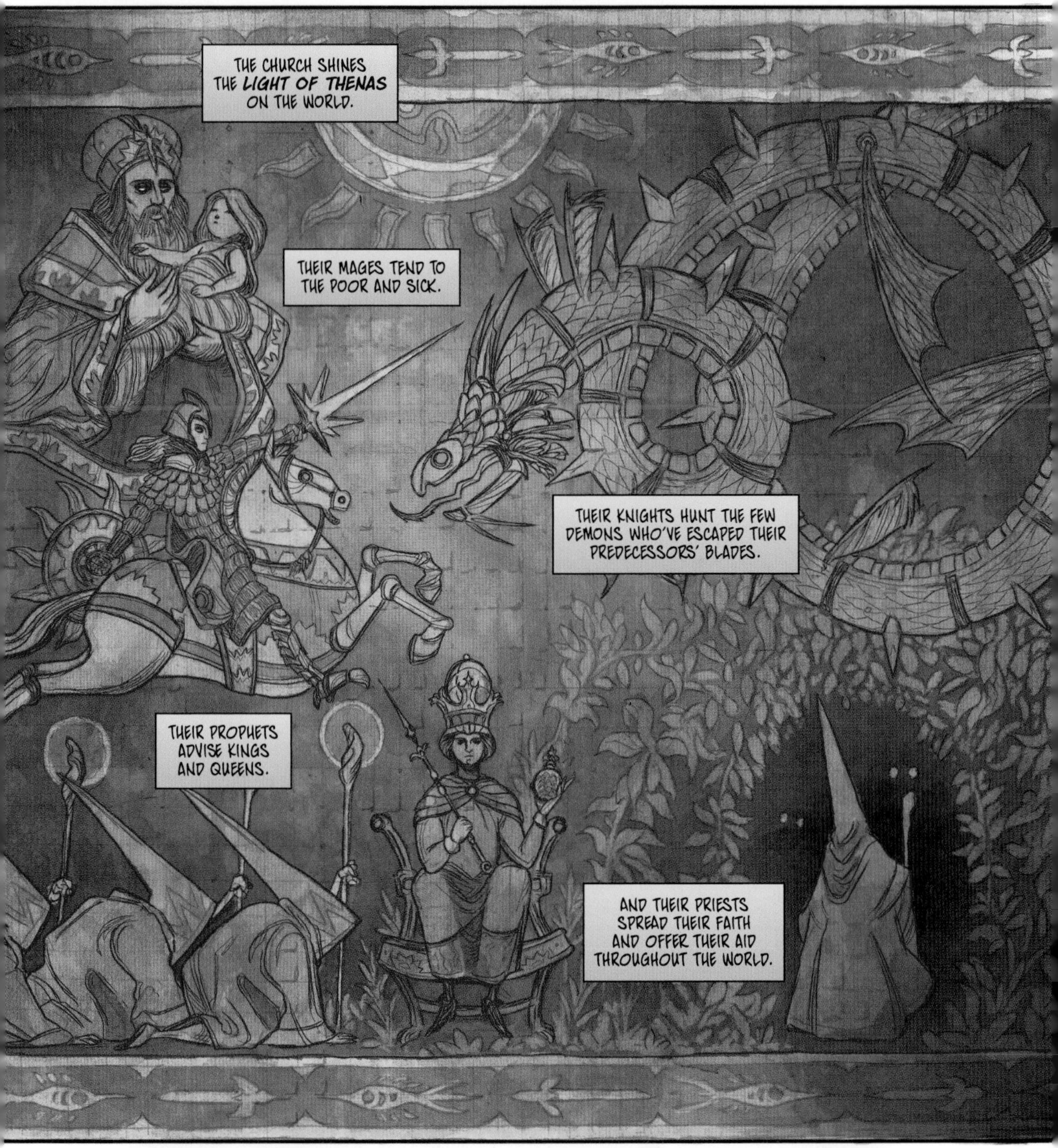
THE CHURCH SHINES THE LIGHT OF THENAS ON THE WORLD.
THEIR MAGES TEND TO THE POOR AND SICK.
THEIR KNIGHTS HUNT THE FEW DEMONS WHO'VE ESCAPED THEIR PREDECESSORS' BLADES.
THEIR PROPHETS ADVISE KINGS AND QUEENS.
AND THEIR PRIESTS SPREAD THEIR FAITH AND OFFER THEIR AID THROUGHOUT THE WORLD.

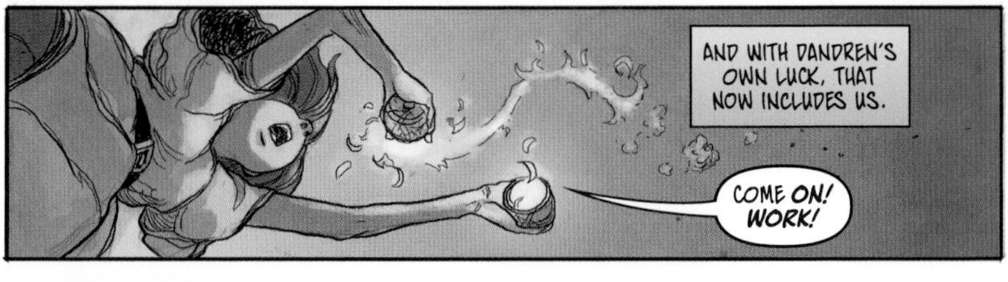
AND WITH DANDREN'S OWN LUCK, THAT NOW INCLUDES US.
COME ON! WORK!

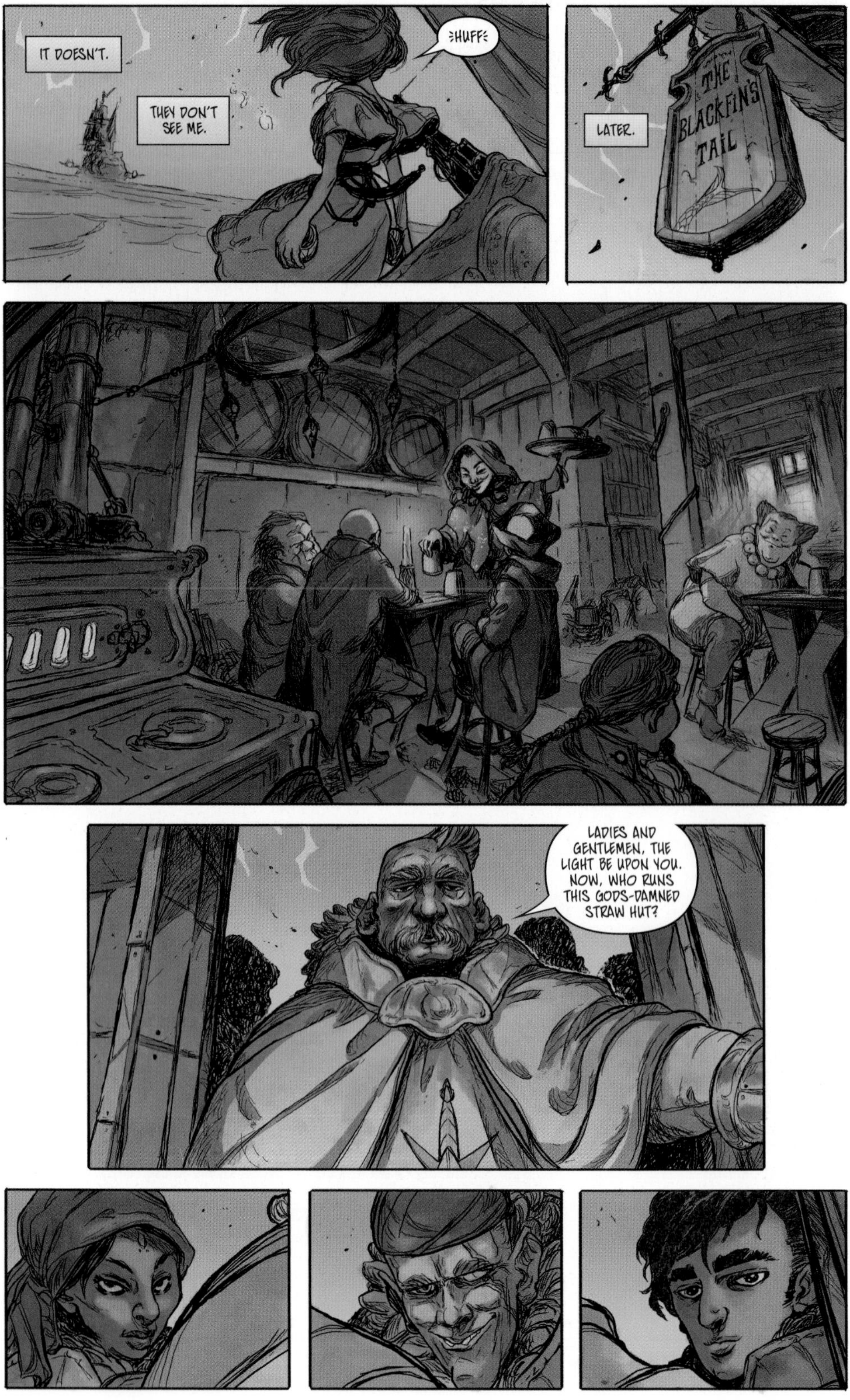
IT DOESN'T.
THEY DON'T SEE ME.
HUFF
LATER.
THE BLACKFIN'S TAIL
LADIES AND GENTLEMEN, THE LIGHT BE UPON YOU. NOW, WHO RUNS THIS GODS-DAMNED STRAW HUT?

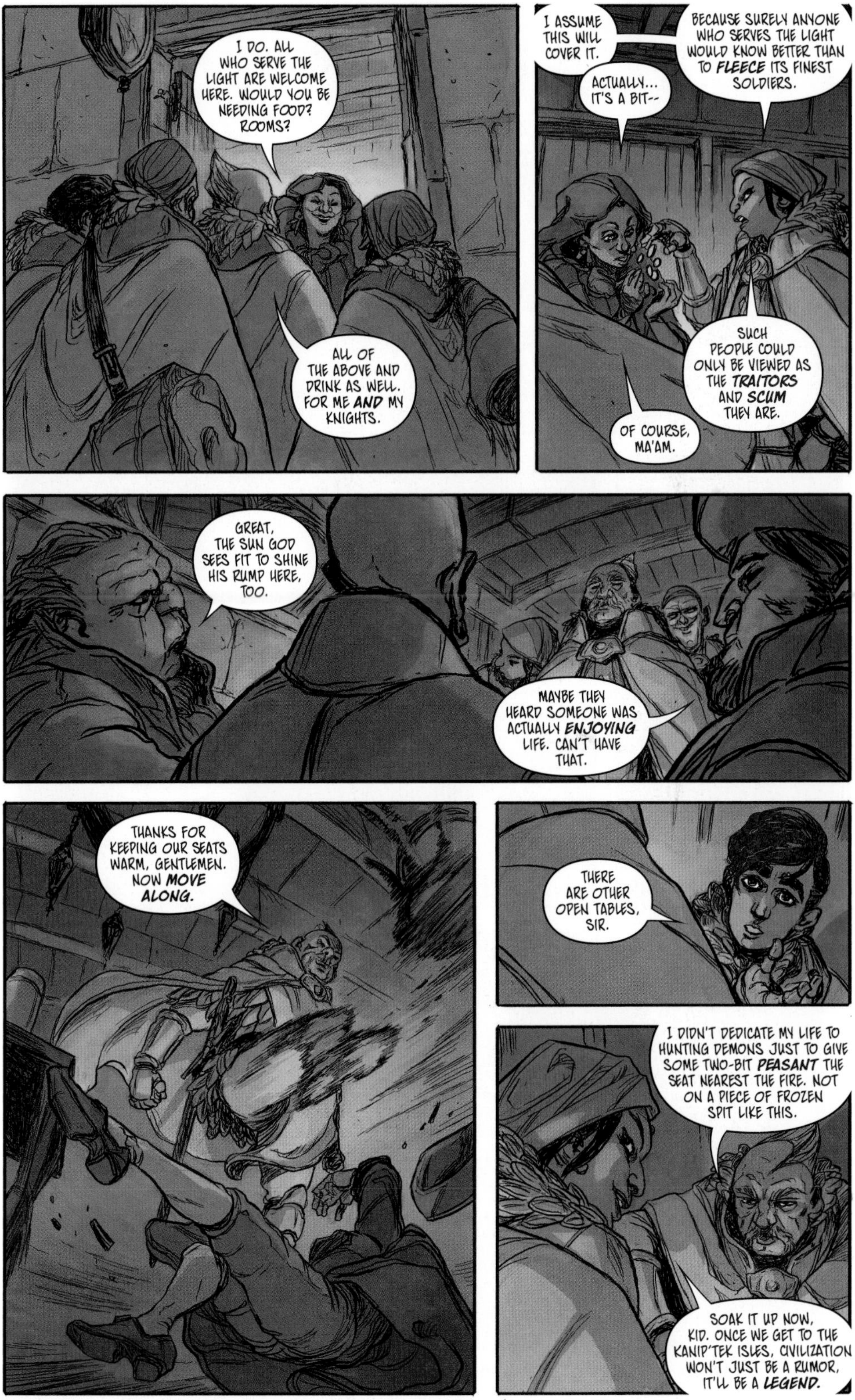
I DO. ALL WHO SERVE THE LIGHT ARE WELCOME HERE. WOULD YOU BE NEEDING FOOD? ROOMS?
ALL OF THE ABOVE AND DRINK AS WELL. FOR ME AND MY KNIGHTS.
I ASSUME THIS WILL COVER IT.
ACTUALLY... IT'S A BIT--
BECAUSE SURELY ANYONE WHO SERVES THE LIGHT WOULD KNOW BETTER THAN TO FLEECE ITS FINEST SOLDIERS.
SUCH PEOPLE COULD ONLY BE VIEWED AS THE TRAITORS AND SCUM THEY ARE.
OF COURSE, MA'AM.
GREAT, THE SUN GOD SEES FIT TO SHINE HIS RUMP HERE, TOO.
MAYBE THEY HEARD SOMEONE WAS ACTUALLY ENJOYING LIFE. CAN'T HAVE THAT.
THANKS FOR KEEPING OUR SEATS WARM, GENTLEMEN. NOW MOVE ALONG.
THERE ARE OTHER OPEN TABLES, SIR.
I DIDN'T DEDICATE MY LIFE TO HUNTING DEMONS JUST TO GIVE SOME TWO-BIT PEASANT THE SEAT NEAREST THE FIRE. NOT ON A PIECE OF FROZEN SPIT LIKE THIS.
SOAK IT UP NOW, KID. ONCE WE GET TO THE KANIP'TEK ISLES, CIVILIZATION WON'T JUST BE A RUMOR, IT'LL BE A LEGEND.

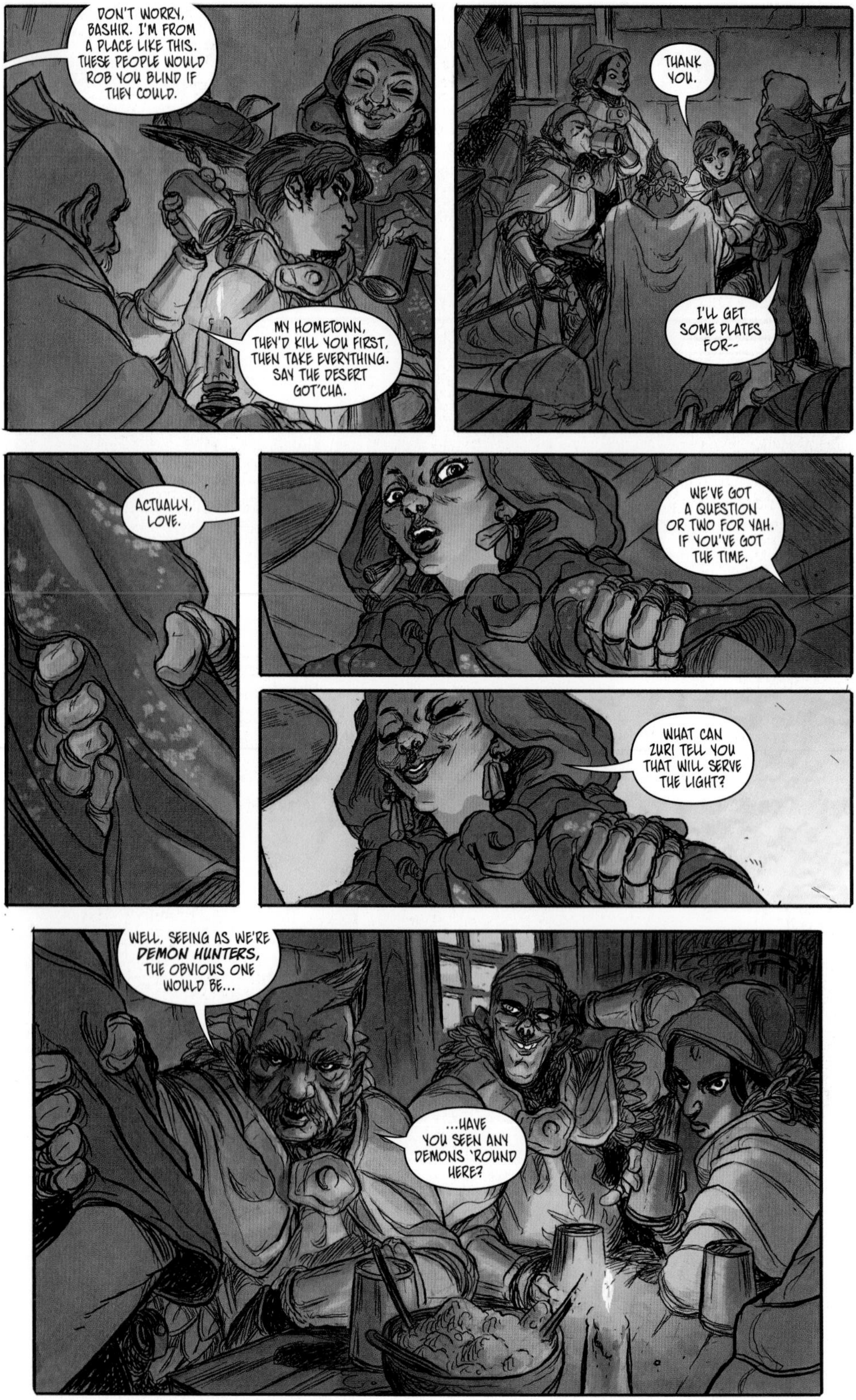
DON'T WORRY, BASHIR. I'M FROM A PLACE LIKE THIS. THESE PEOPLE WOULD ROB YOU BLIND IF THEY COULD.
MY HOMETOWN, THEY'D KILL YOU FIRST, THEN TAKE EVERYTHING. SAY THE DESERT GOT'CHA.
THANK YOU.
I'LL GET SOME PLATES FOR--
ACTUALLY, LOVE.
WE'VE GOT A QUESTION OR TWO FOR YAH. IF YOU'VE GOT THE TIME.
WHAT CAN ZURI TELL YOU THAT WILL SERVE THE LIGHT?
WELL, SEEING AS WE'RE ***DEMON HUNTERS,*** THE OBVIOUS ONE WOULD BE...
...HAVE YOU SEEN ANY DEMONS 'ROUND HERE?

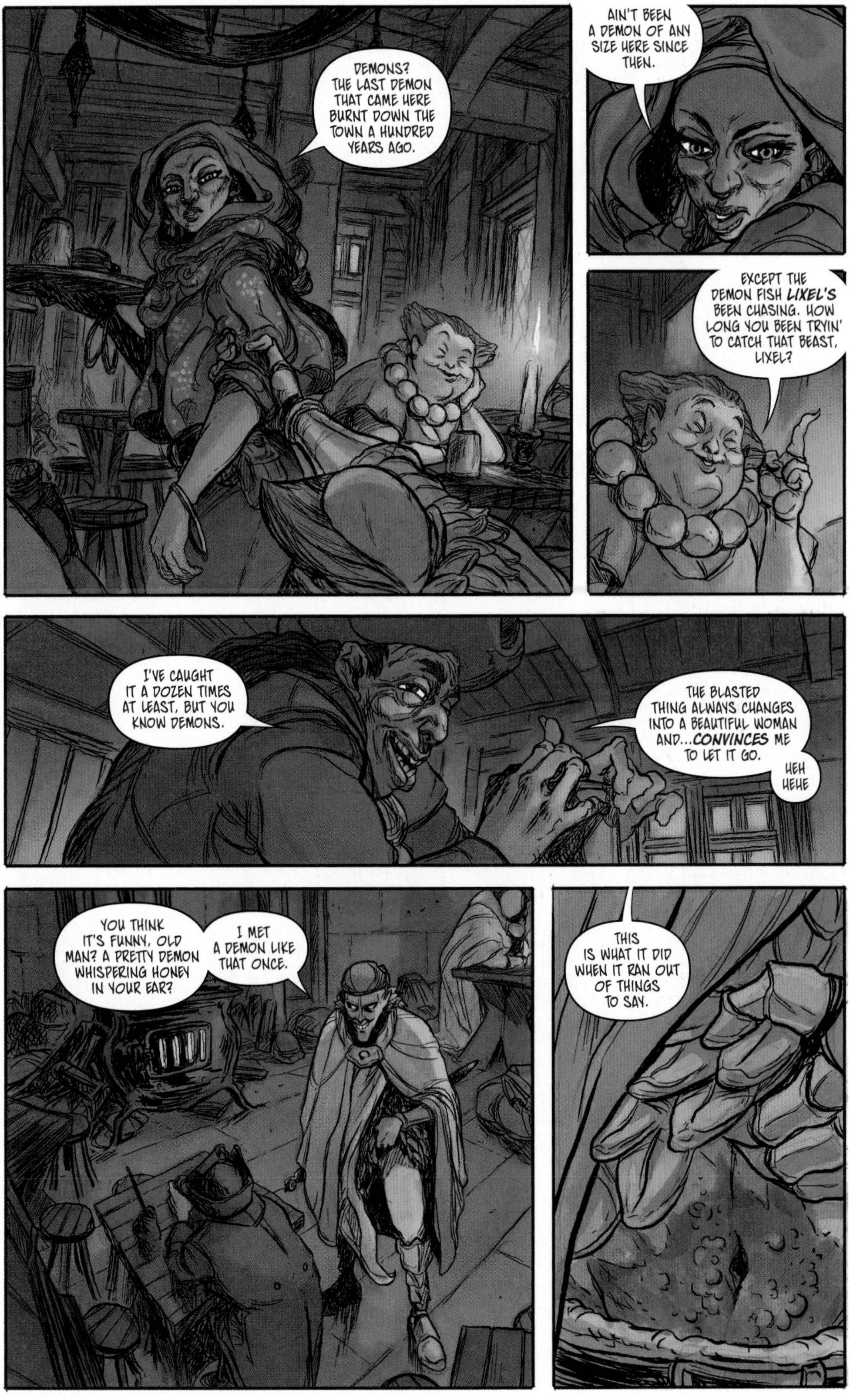
DEMONS? THE LAST DEMON THAT CAME HERE BURNT DOWN THE TOWN A HUNDRED YEARS AGO.
AIN'T BEEN A DEMON OF ANY SIZE HERE SINCE THEN.
EXCEPT THE DEMON FISH LIXEL'S BEEN CHASING. HOW LONG YOU BEEN TRYIN' TO CATCH THAT BEAST, LIXEL?
I'VE CAUGHT IT A DOZEN TIMES AT LEAST, BUT YOU KNOW DEMONS.
THE BLASTED THING ALWAYS CHANGES INTO A BEAUTIFUL WOMAN AND...CONVINCES ME TO LET IT GO.
HEH HEHE
YOU THINK IT'S FUNNY, OLD MAN? A PRETTY DEMON WHISPERING HONEY IN YOUR EAR?
I MET A DEMON LIKE THAT ONCE.
THIS IS WHAT IT DID WHEN IT RAN OUT OF THINGS TO SAY.

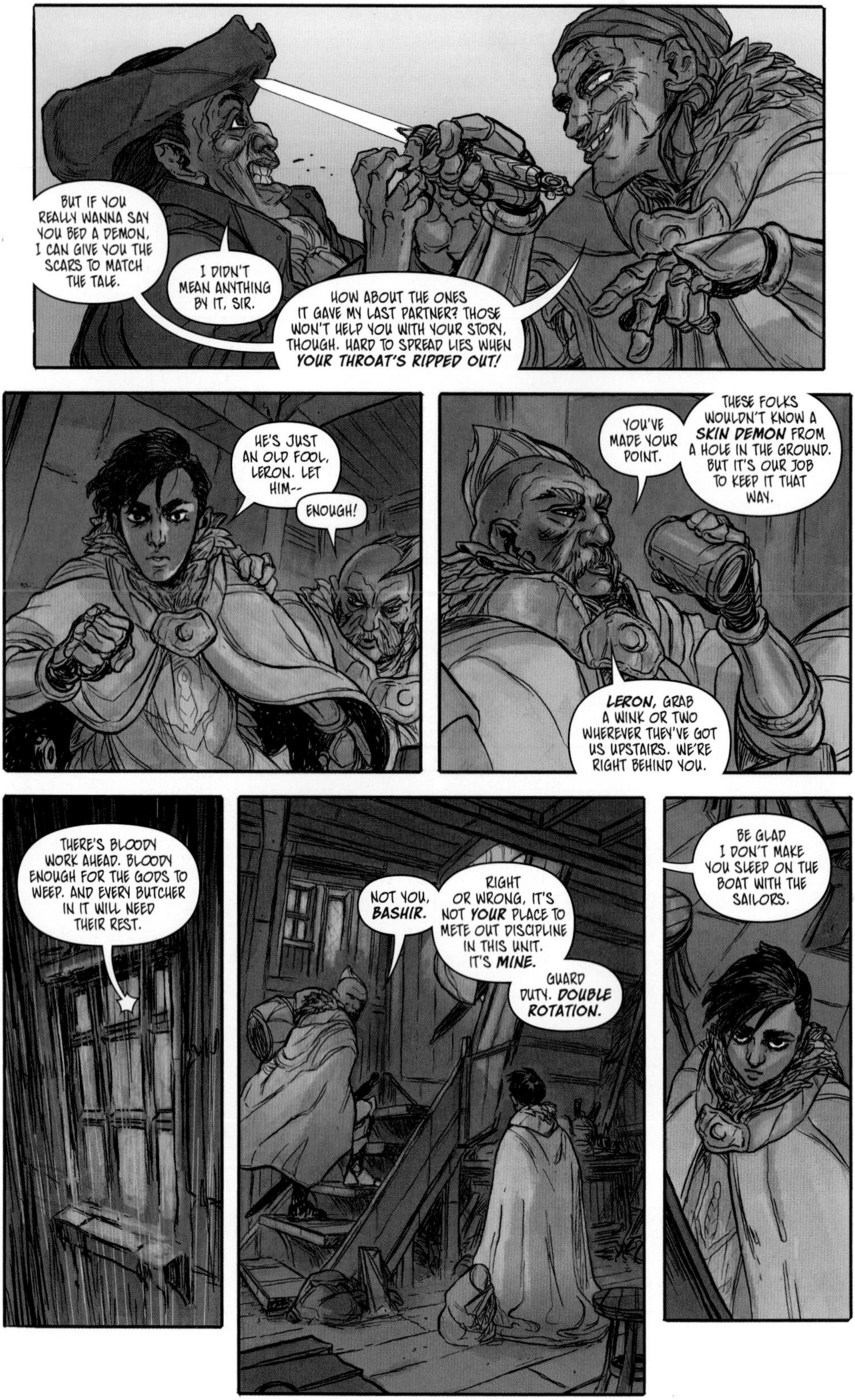
BUT IF YOU REALLY WANNA SAY YOU BED A DEMON, I CAN GIVE YOU THE SCARS TO MATCH THE TALE.
I DIDN'T MEAN ANYTHING BY IT, SIR.
HOW ABOUT THE ONES IT GAVE MY LAST PARTNER? THOSE WON'T HELP YOU WITH YOUR STORY, THOUGH. HARD TO SPREAD LIES WHEN YOUR THROAT'S RIPPED OUT!
HE'S JUST AN OLD FOOL, LERON. LET HIM--
ENOUGH!
YOU'VE MADE YOUR POINT.
THESE FOLKS WOULDN'T KNOW A SKIN DEMON FROM A HOLE IN THE GROUND. BUT IT'S OUR JOB TO KEEP IT THAT WAY.
LERON, GRAB A WINK OR TWO WHEREVER THEY'VE GOT US UPSTAIRS. WE'RE RIGHT BEHIND YOU.
THERE'S BLOODY WORK AHEAD. BLOODY ENOUGH FOR THE GODS TO WEEP. AND EVERY BUTCHER IN IT WILL NEED THEIR REST.
NOT YOU, BASHIR.
RIGHT OR WRONG, IT'S NOT YOUR PLACE TO METE OUT DISCIPLINE IN THIS UNIT. IT'S MINE.
GUARD DUTY. DOUBLE ROTATION.
BE GLAD I DON'T MAKE YOU SLEEP ON THE BOAT WITH THE SAILORS.

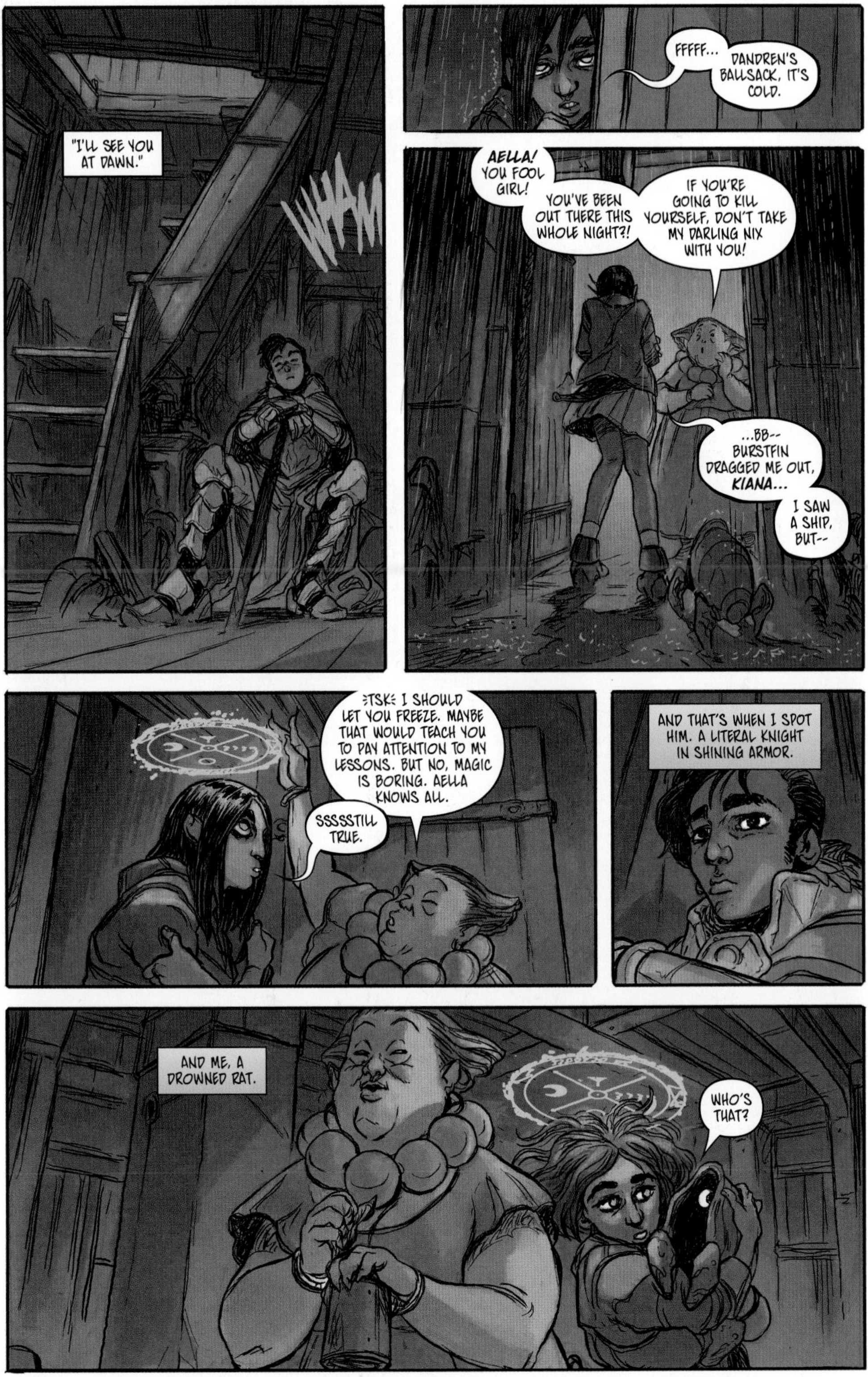
"I'LL SEE YOU AT DAWN."
WHAM
FFFFF... DANDREN'S BALLSACK, IT'S COLD.
AELLA! YOU FOOL GIRL!
YOU'VE BEEN OUT THERE THIS WHOLE NIGHT?!
IF YOU'RE GOING TO KILL YOURSELF, DON'T TAKE MY DARLING NIX WITH YOU!
...BB-- BURSTFIN DRAGGED ME OUT, KIANA...
I SAW A SHIP, BUT--
TSK I SHOULD LET YOU FREEZE. MAYBE THAT WOULD TEACH YOU TO PAY ATTENTION TO MY LESSONS. BUT NO, MAGIC IS BORING. AELLA KNOWS ALL.
SSSSSTILL TRUE.
AND THAT'S WHEN I SPOT HIM. A LITERAL KNIGHT IN SHINING ARMOR.
AND ME, A DROWNED RAT.
WHO'S THAT?

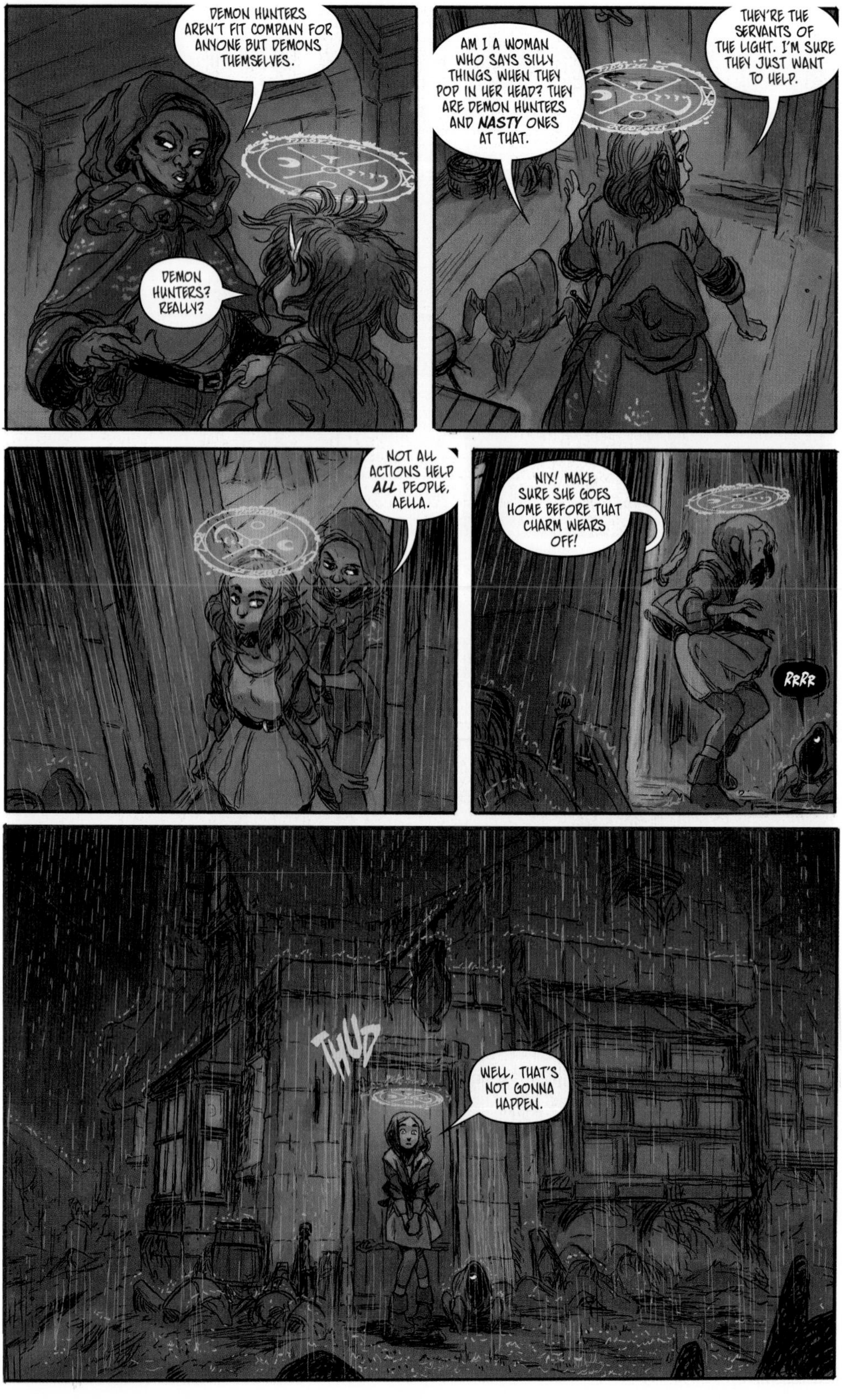
DEMON HUNTERS AREN'T FIT COMPANY FOR ANYONE BUT DEMONS THEMSELVES.
DEMON HUNTERS? REALLY?
AM I A WOMAN WHO SAYS SILLY THINGS WHEN THEY POP IN HER HEAD? THEY ARE DEMON HUNTERS AND NASTY ONES AT THAT.
THEY'RE THE SERVANTS OF THE LIGHT. I'M SURE THEY JUST WANT TO HELP.
NOT ALL ACTIONS HELP ALL PEOPLE, AELLA.
NIX! MAKE SURE SHE GOES HOME BEFORE THAT CHARM WEARS OFF!
RRRR
THUD
WELL, THAT'S NOT GONNA HAPPEN.

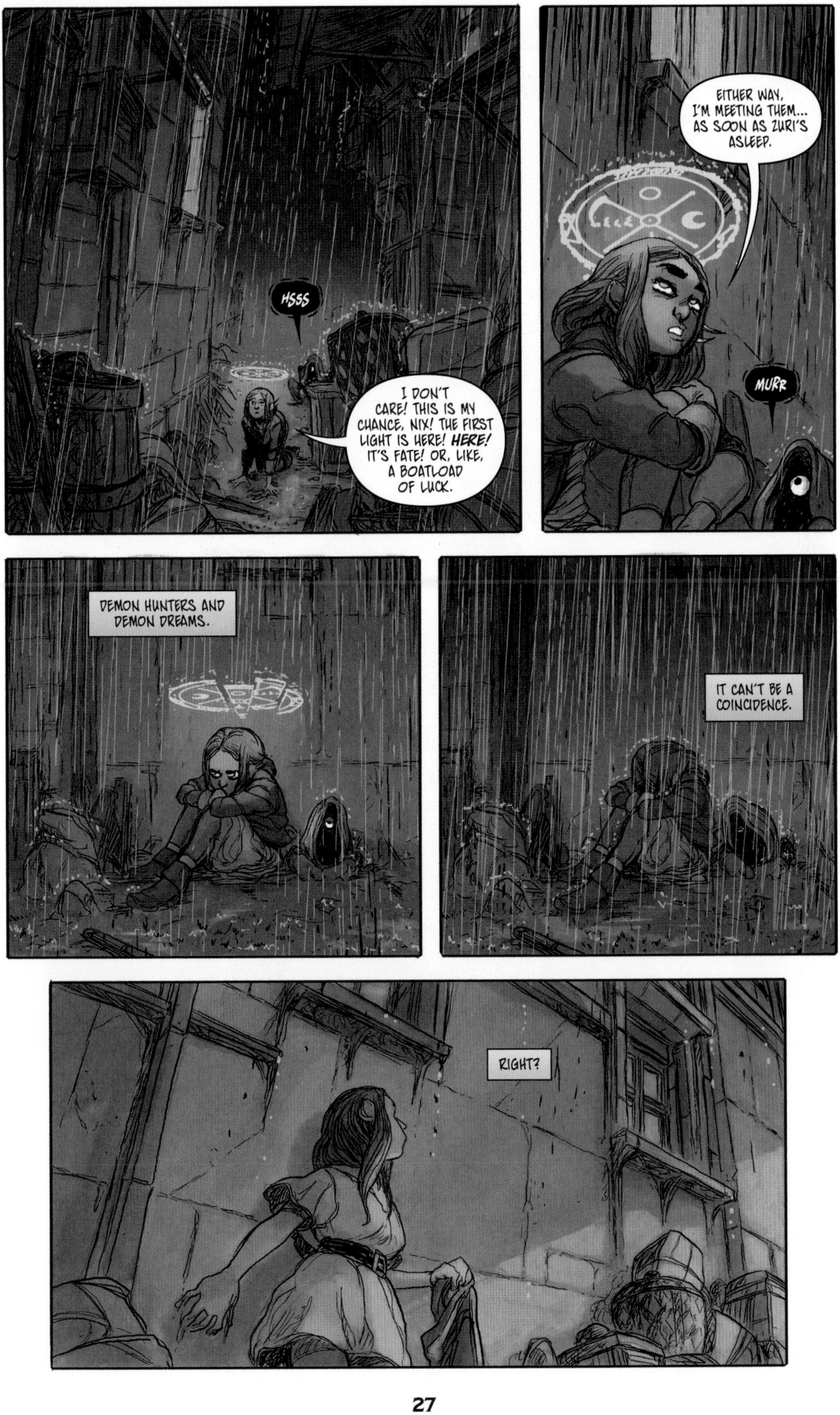
HSSS
I DON'T CARE! THIS IS MY CHANCE, NIX! THE FIRST LIGHT IS HERE! **HERE!** IT'S FATE! OR, LIKE, A BOATLOAD OF LUCK.
EITHER WAY, I'M MEETING THEM... AS SOON AS ZURI'S ASLEEP.
MURR
DEMON HUNTERS AND DEMON DREAMS.
IT CAN'T BE A COINCIDENCE.
RIGHT?

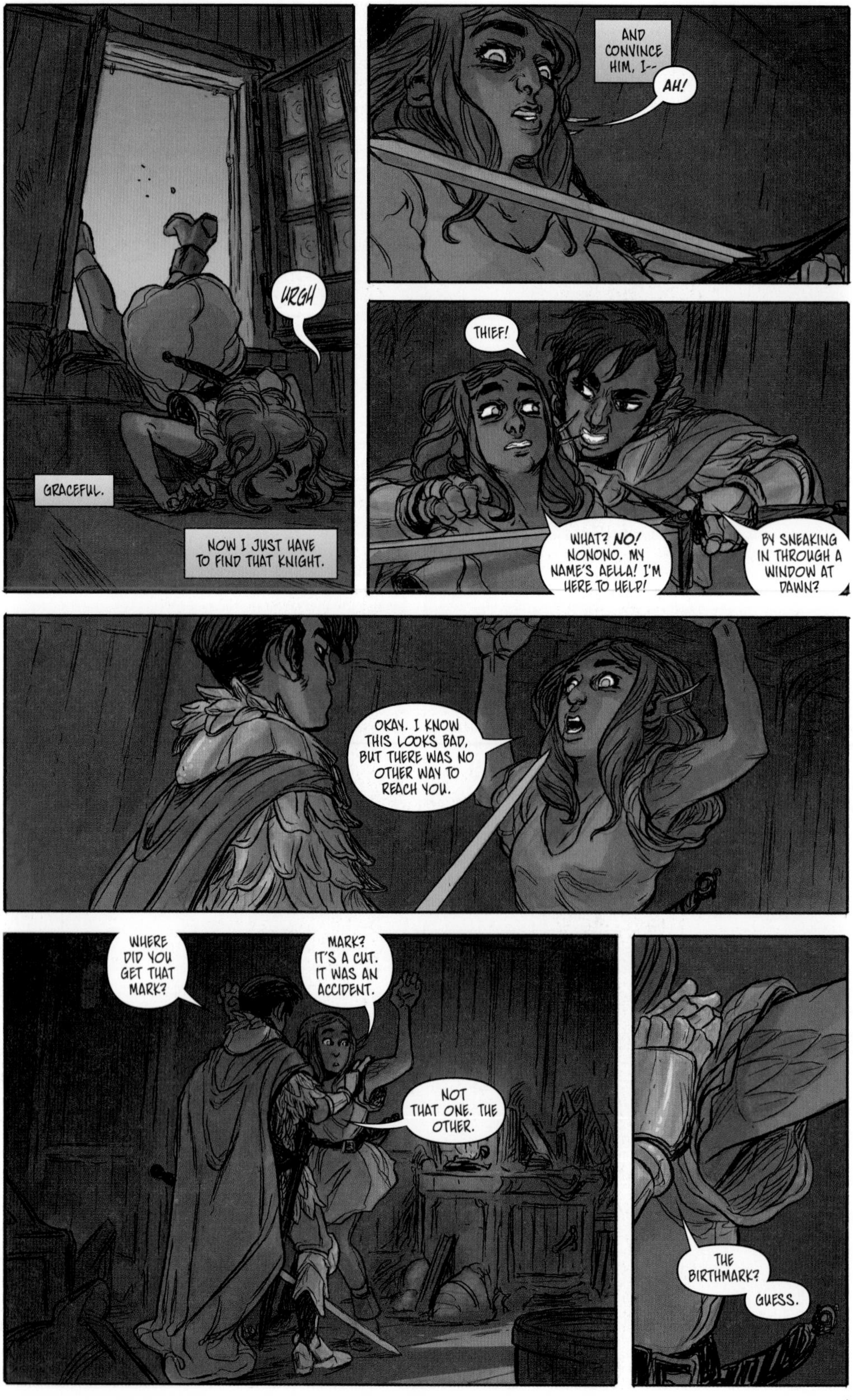
URGH
GRACEFUL.
NOW I JUST HAVE TO FIND THAT KNIGHT.
AND CONVINCE HIM, I--
AH!
THIEF!
WHAT? NO! NONONO. MY NAME'S AELLA! I'M HERE TO HELP!
BY SNEAKING IN THROUGH A WINDOW AT DAWN?
OKAY. I KNOW THIS LOOKS BAD, BUT THERE WAS NO OTHER WAY TO REACH YOU.
WHERE DID YOU GET THAT MARK?
MARK? IT'S A CUT. IT WAS AN ACCIDENT.
NOT THAT ONE. THE OTHER.
THE BIRTHMARK?
GUESS.

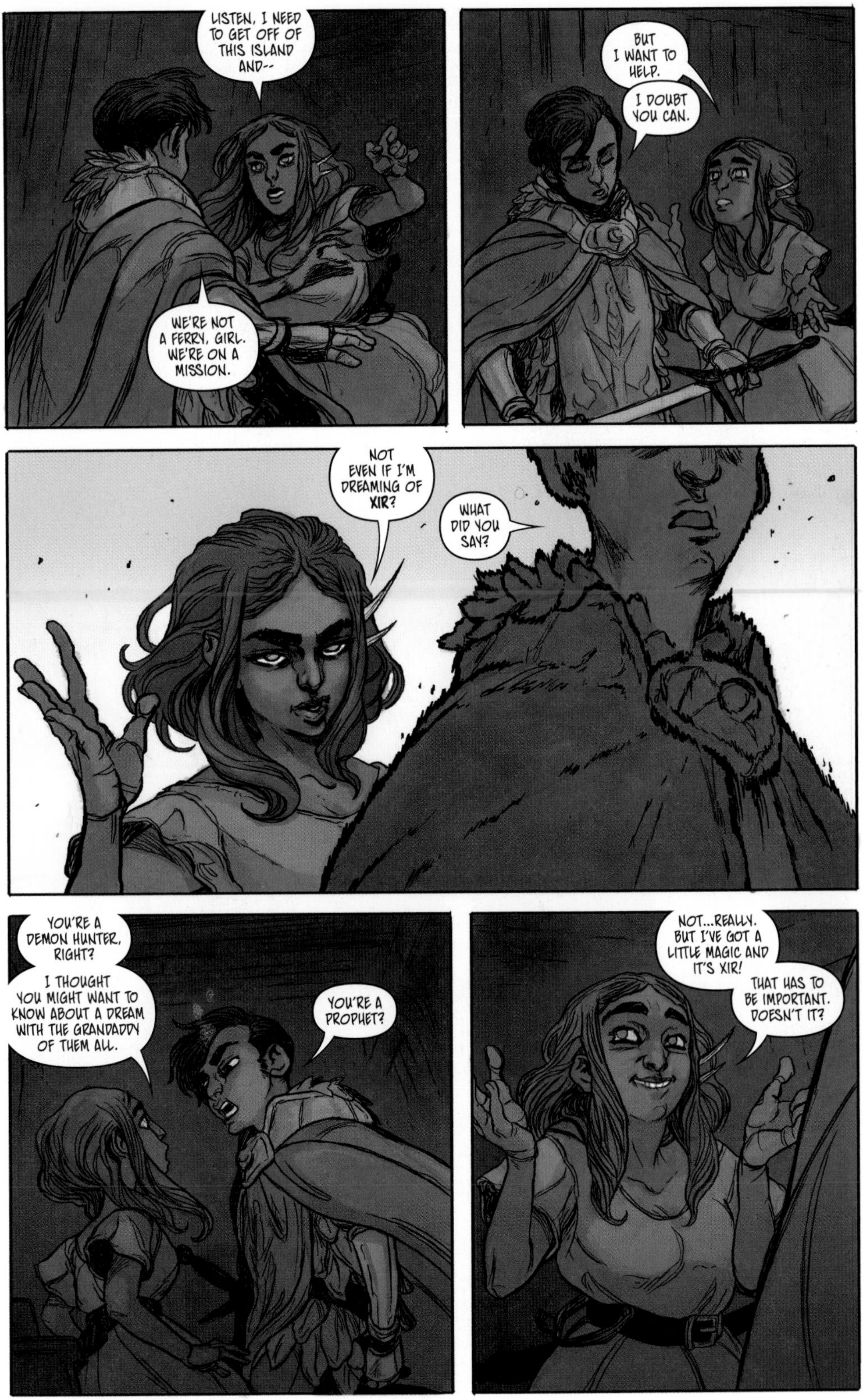
LISTEN, I NEED TO GET OFF OF THIS ISLAND AND--
WE'RE NOT A FERRY, GIRL. WE'RE ON A MISSION.
BUT I WANT TO HELP.
I DOUBT YOU CAN.
NOT EVEN IF I'M DREAMING OF **XIR**?
WHAT DID YOU SAY?
YOU'RE A DEMON HUNTER, RIGHT?
I THOUGHT YOU MIGHT WANT TO KNOW ABOUT A DREAM WITH THE GRANDADDY OF THEM ALL.
YOU'RE A PROPHET?
NOT...REALLY. BUT I'VE GOT A LITTLE MAGIC AND IT'S XIR!
THAT HAS TO BE IMPORTANT. DOESN'T IT?

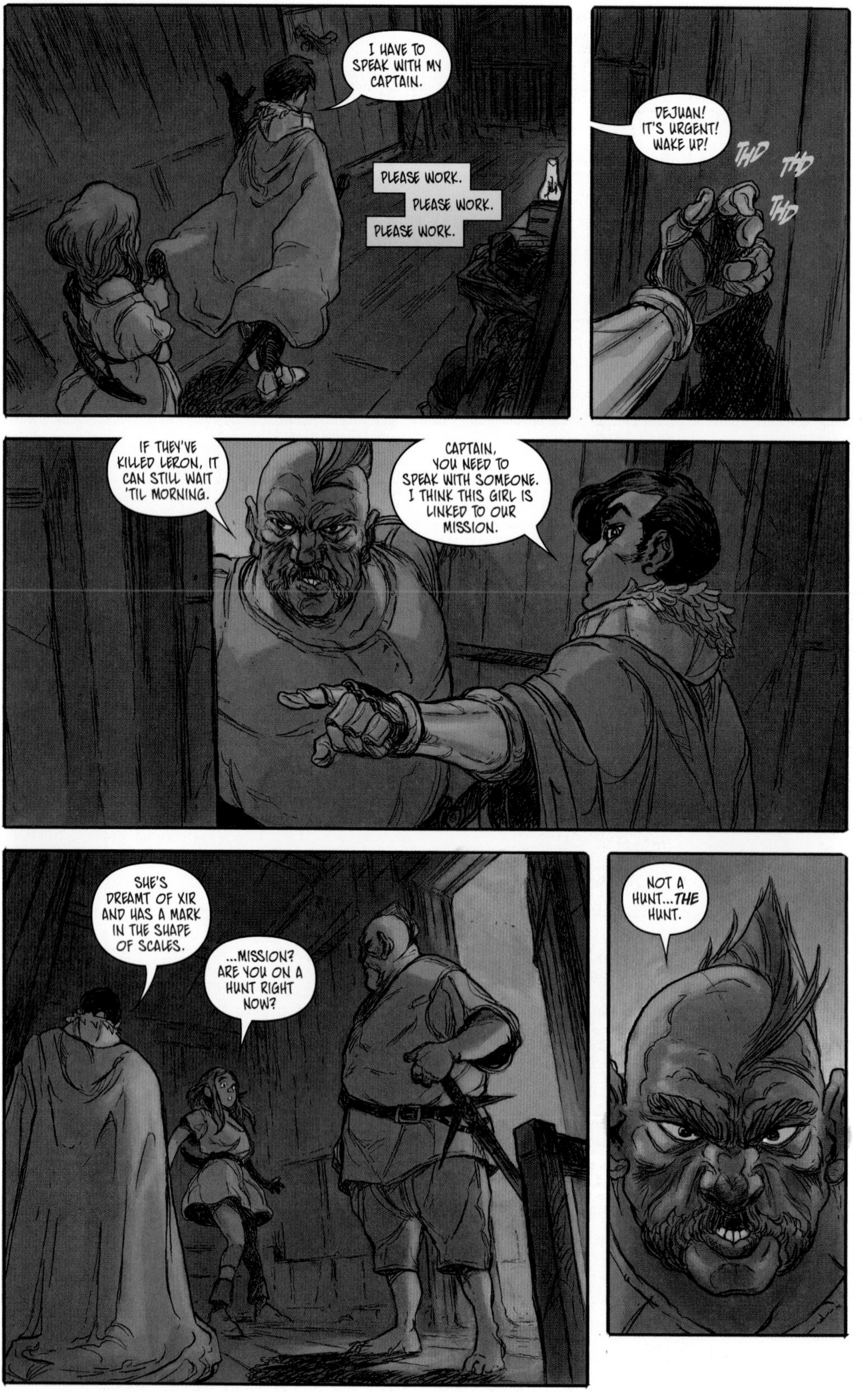
I HAVE TO SPEAK WITH MY CAPTAIN.
PLEASE WORK.
PLEASE WORK.
PLEASE WORK.
DEJUAN! IT'S URGENT! WAKE UP!
THD
THD
THD
IF THEY'VE KILLED LERON, IT CAN STILL WAIT 'TIL MORNING.
CAPTAIN, YOU NEED TO SPEAK WITH SOMEONE. I THINK THIS GIRL IS LINKED TO OUR MISSION.
SHE'S DREAMT OF XIR AND HAS A MARK IN THE SHAPE OF SCALES.
...MISSION? ARE YOU ON A HUNT RIGHT NOW?
NOT A HUNT...*THE* HUNT.

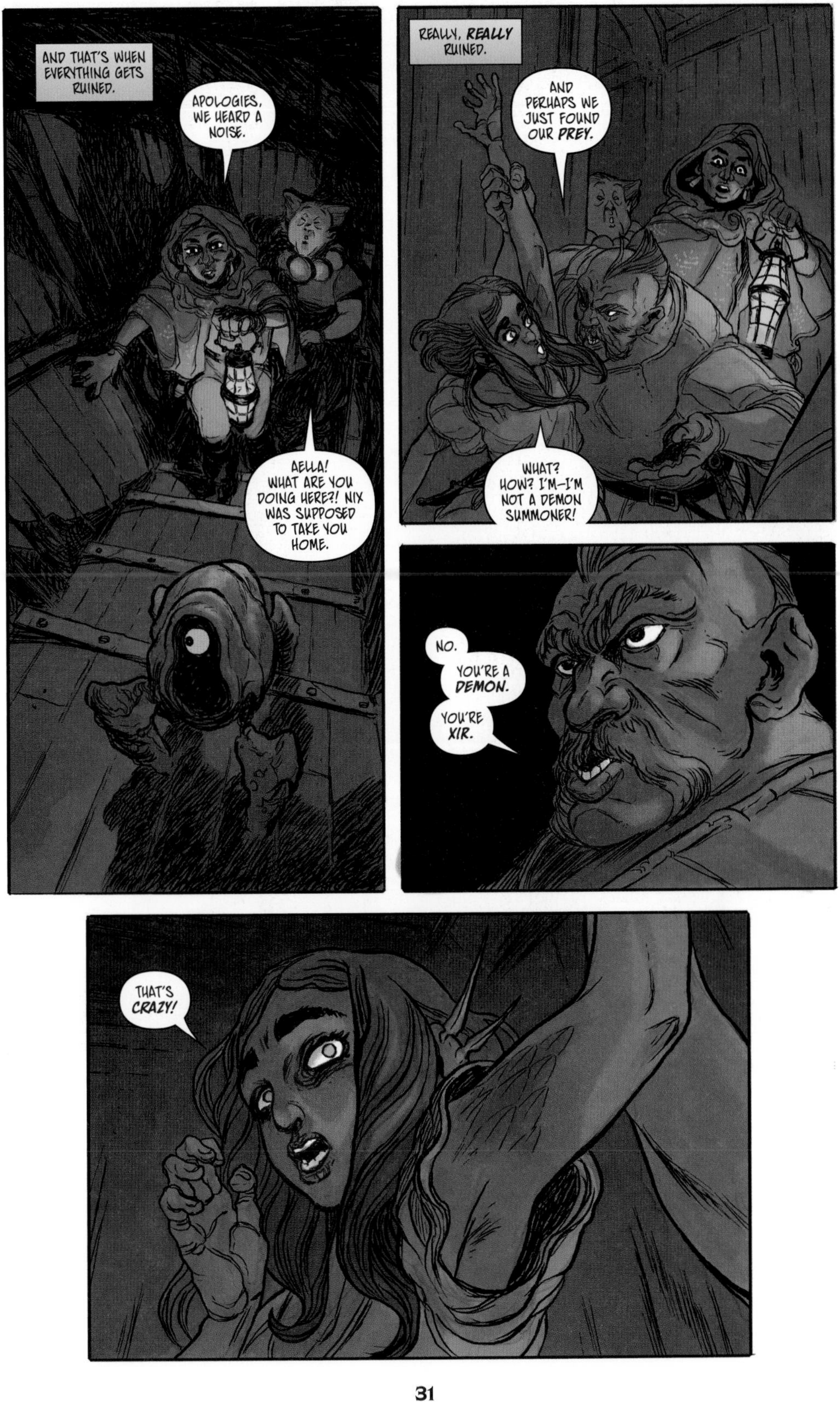
AND THAT'S WHEN EVERYTHING GETS RUINED.
APOLOGIES, WE HEARD A NOISE.
AELLA! WHAT ARE YOU DOING HERE?! NIX WAS SUPPOSED TO TAKE YOU HOME.
REALLY, **REALLY** RUINED.
AND PERHAPS WE JUST FOUND OUR **PREY.**
WHAT? HOW? I'M–I'M NOT A DEMON SUMMONER!
NO.
YOU'RE A **DEMON.**
YOU'RE **XIR.**
THAT'S **CRAZY!**

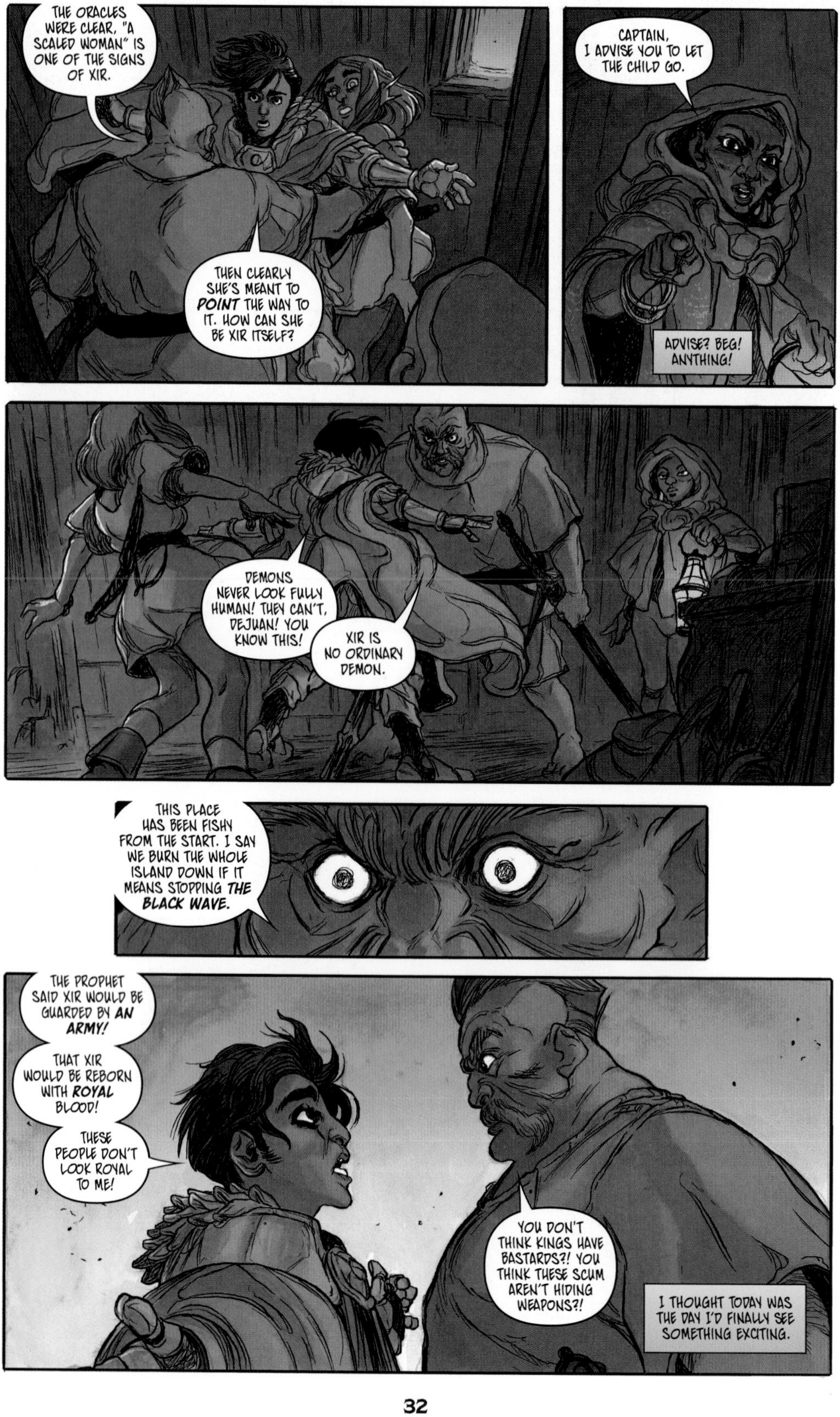
THE ORACLES WERE CLEAR, "A SCALED WOMAN" IS ONE OF THE SIGNS OF XIR.
THEN CLEARLY SHE'S MEANT TO **POINT** THE WAY TO IT. HOW CAN SHE BE XIR ITSELF?
CAPTAIN, I ADVISE YOU TO LET THE CHILD GO.
ADVISE? BEG! ANYTHING!
DEMONS NEVER LOOK FULLY HUMAN! THEY CAN'T, DEJUAN! YOU KNOW THIS!
XIR IS NO ORDINARY DEMON.
THIS PLACE HAS BEEN FISHY FROM THE START. I SAY WE BURN THE WHOLE ISLAND DOWN IF IT MEANS STOPPING **THE BLACK WAVE.**
THE PROPHET SAID XIR WOULD BE GUARDED BY **AN ARMY!**
THAT XIR WOULD BE REBORN WITH **ROYAL** BLOOD!
THESE PEOPLE DON'T LOOK ROYAL TO ME!
YOU DON'T THINK KINGS HAVE BASTARDS?! YOU THINK THESE SCUM AREN'T HIDING WEAPONS?!
I THOUGHT TODAY WAS THE DAY I'D FINALLY SEE SOMETHING EXCITING.

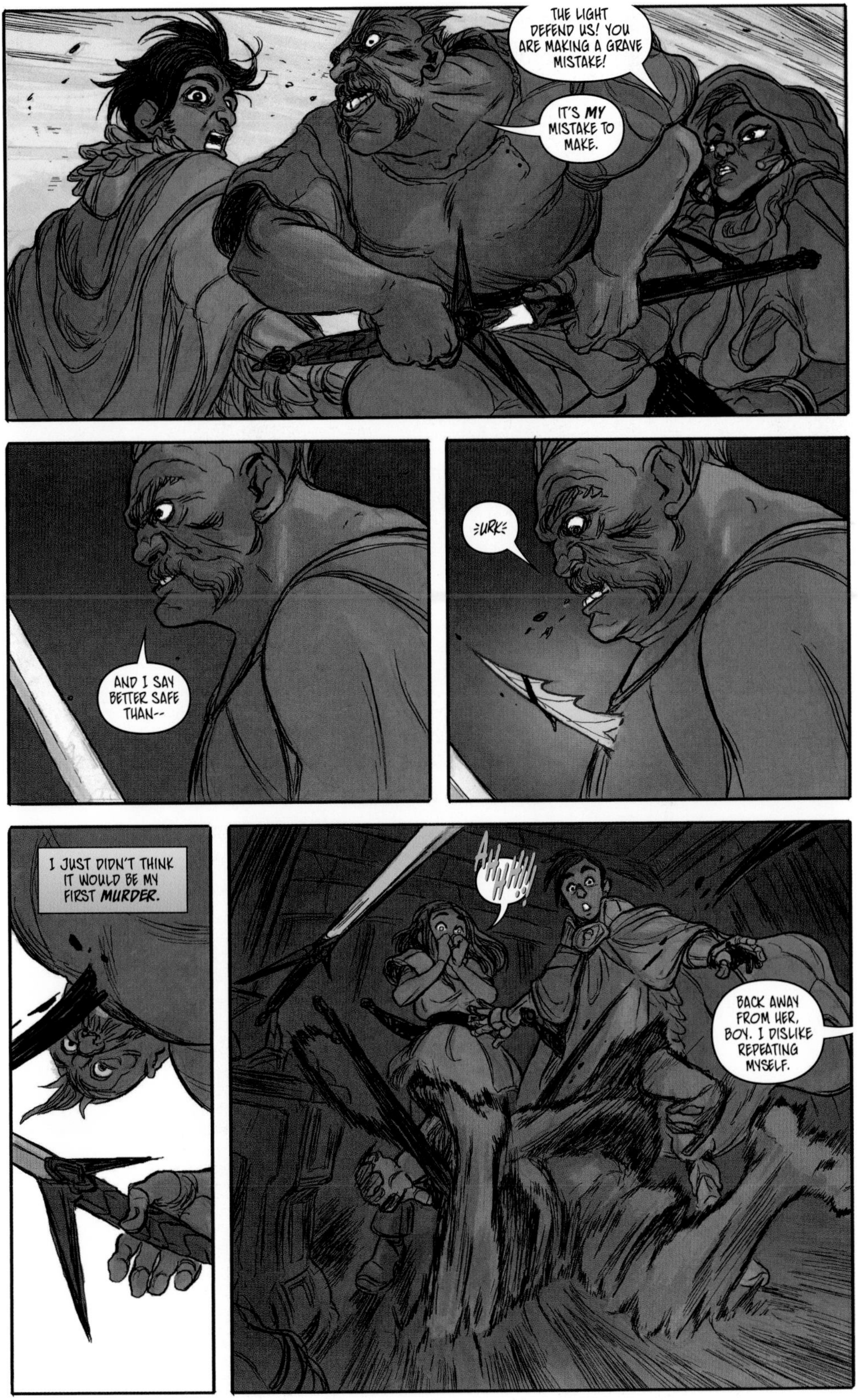
THE LIGHT DEFEND US! YOU ARE MAKING A GRAVE MISTAKE!
IT'S MY MISTAKE TO MAKE.
AND I SAY BETTER SAFE THAN--
URK
I JUST DIDN'T THINK IT WOULD BE MY FIRST MURDER.
AHHH!!
BACK AWAY FROM HER, BOY. I DISLIKE REPEATING MYSELF.

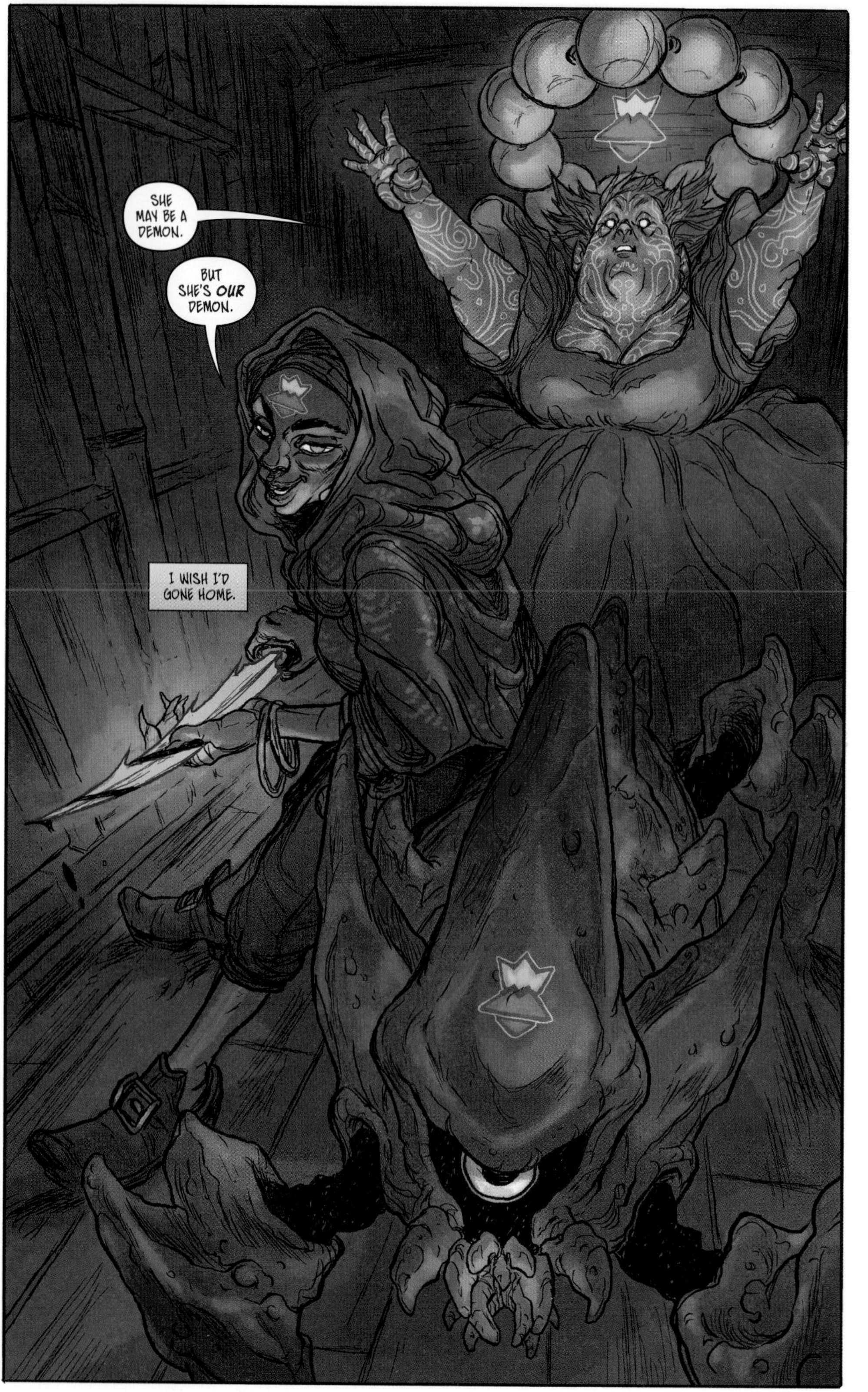
SHE MAY BE A DEMON.
BUT SHE'S OUR DEMON.
I WISH I'D GONE HOME.

Chapter Two

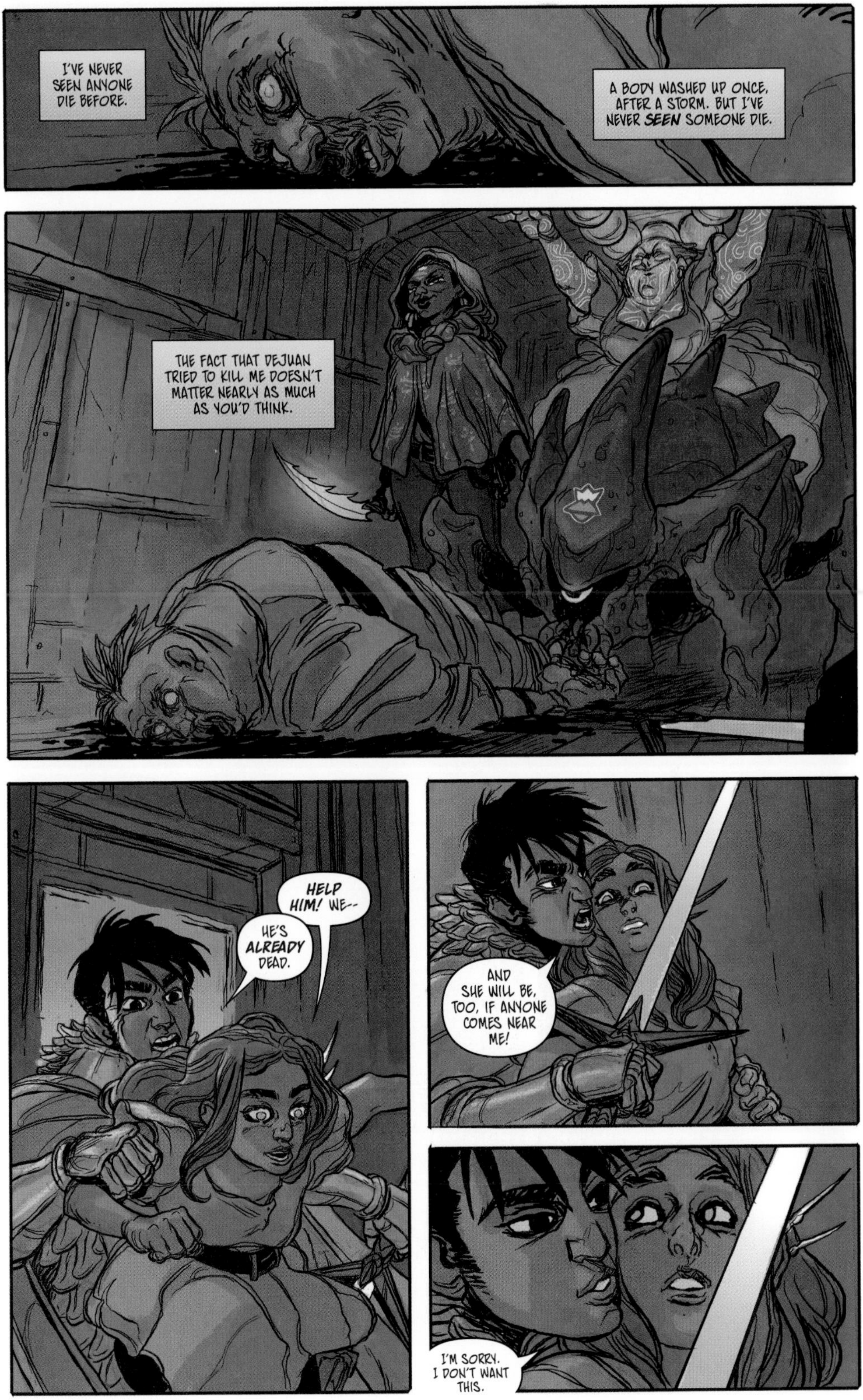
I'VE NEVER SEEN ANYONE DIE BEFORE.
A BODY WASHED UP ONCE, AFTER A STORM. BUT I'VE NEVER SEEN SOMEONE DIE.
THE FACT THAT DEJUAN TRIED TO KILL ME DOESN'T MATTER NEARLY AS MUCH AS YOU'D THINK.
HELP HIM! WE--
HE'S ALREADY DEAD.
AND SHE WILL BE, TOO, IF ANYONE COMES NEAR ME!
I'M SORRY. I DON'T WANT THIS.

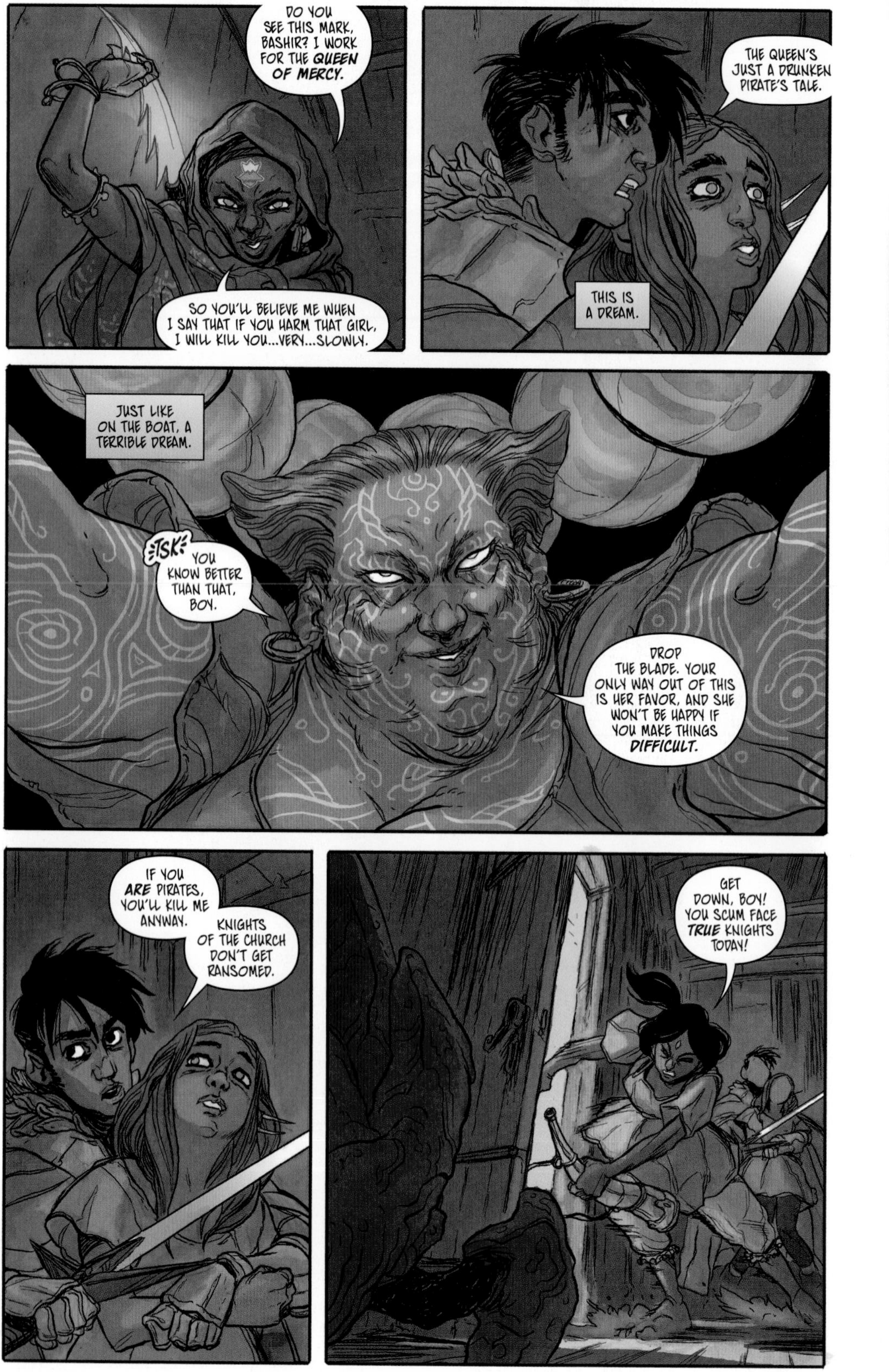
DO YOU SEE THIS MARK, BASHIR? I WORK FOR THE QUEEN OF MERCY.
SO YOU'LL BELIEVE ME WHEN I SAY THAT IF YOU HARM THAT GIRL, I WILL KILL YOU...VERY...SLOWLY.
THE QUEEN'S JUST A DRUNKEN PIRATE'S TALE.
THIS IS A DREAM.
JUST LIKE ON THE BOAT, A TERRIBLE DREAM.
TSK
YOU KNOW BETTER THAN THAT, BOY.
DROP THE BLADE. YOUR ONLY WAY OUT OF THIS IS HER FAVOR, AND SHE WON'T BE HAPPY IF YOU MAKE THINGS DIFFICULT.
IF YOU ARE PIRATES, YOU'LL KILL ME ANYWAY.
KNIGHTS OF THE CHURCH DON'T GET RANSOMED.
GET DOWN, BOY! YOU SCUM FACE TRUE KNIGHTS TODAY!

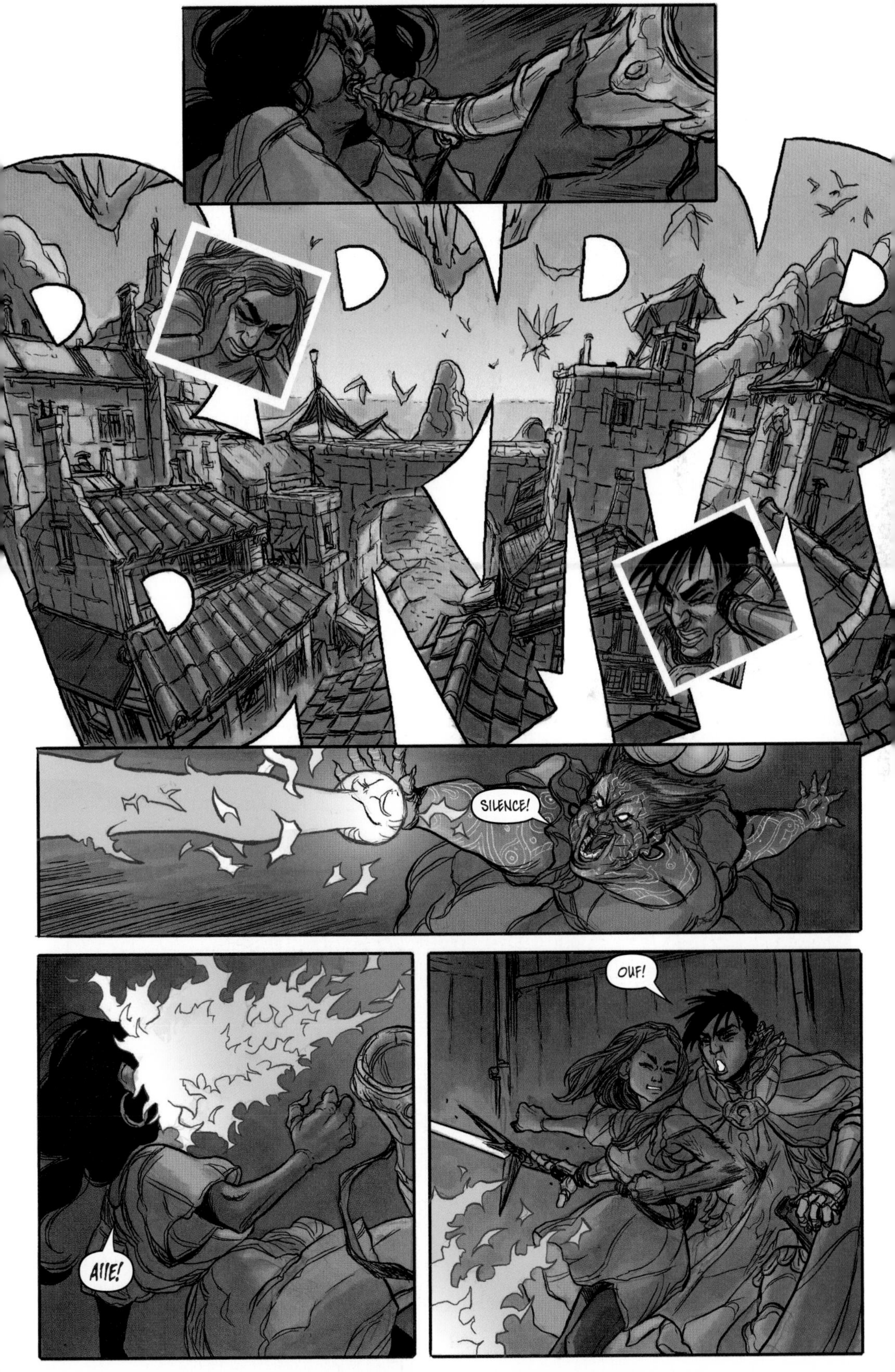
SILENCE!
AIIE!
OUF!

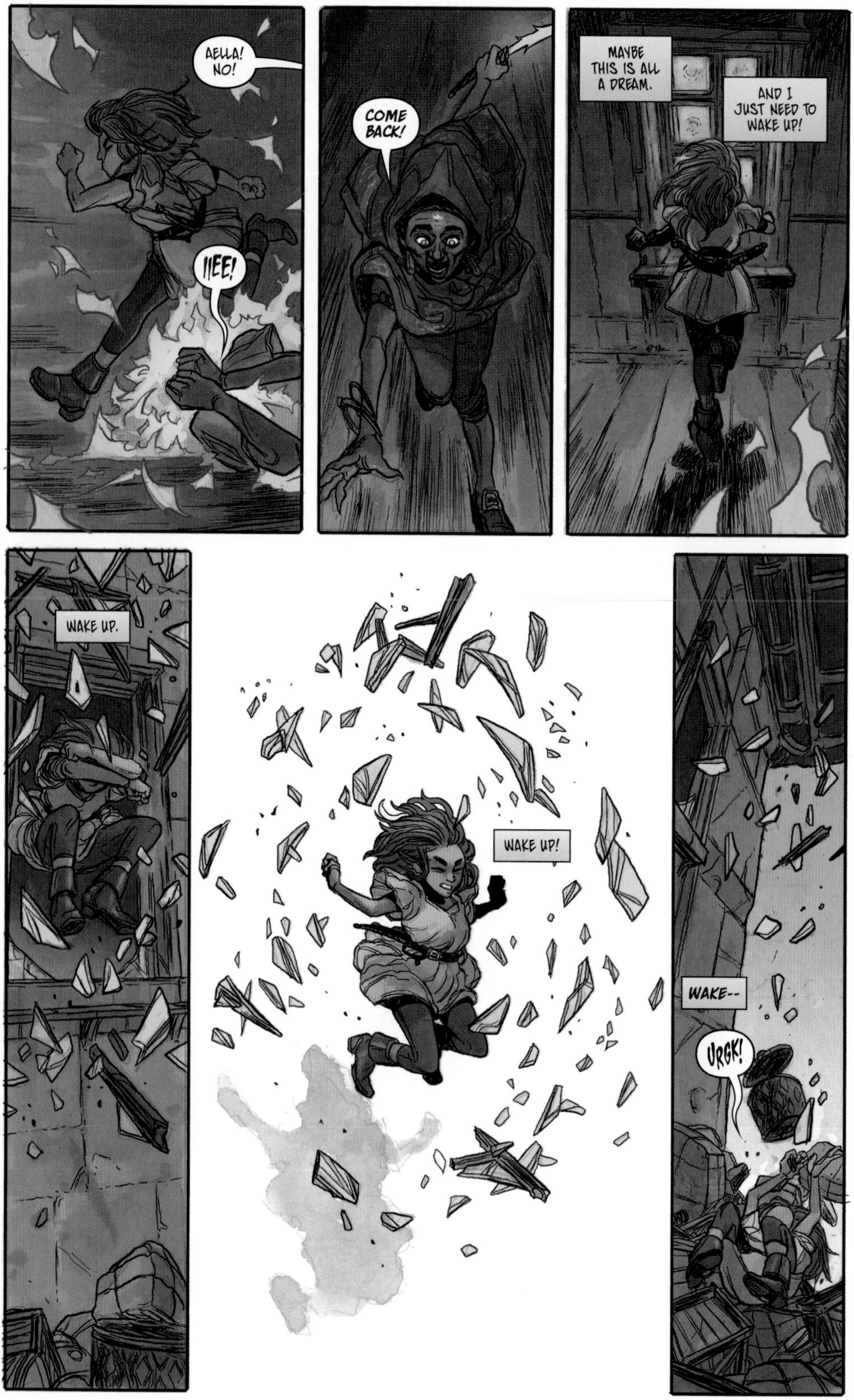
AELLA! NO!
!IEE!
COME BACK!
MAYBE THIS IS ALL A DREAM.
AND I JUST NEED TO WAKE UP!
WAKE UP.
WAKE UP!
WAKE--
URGK!

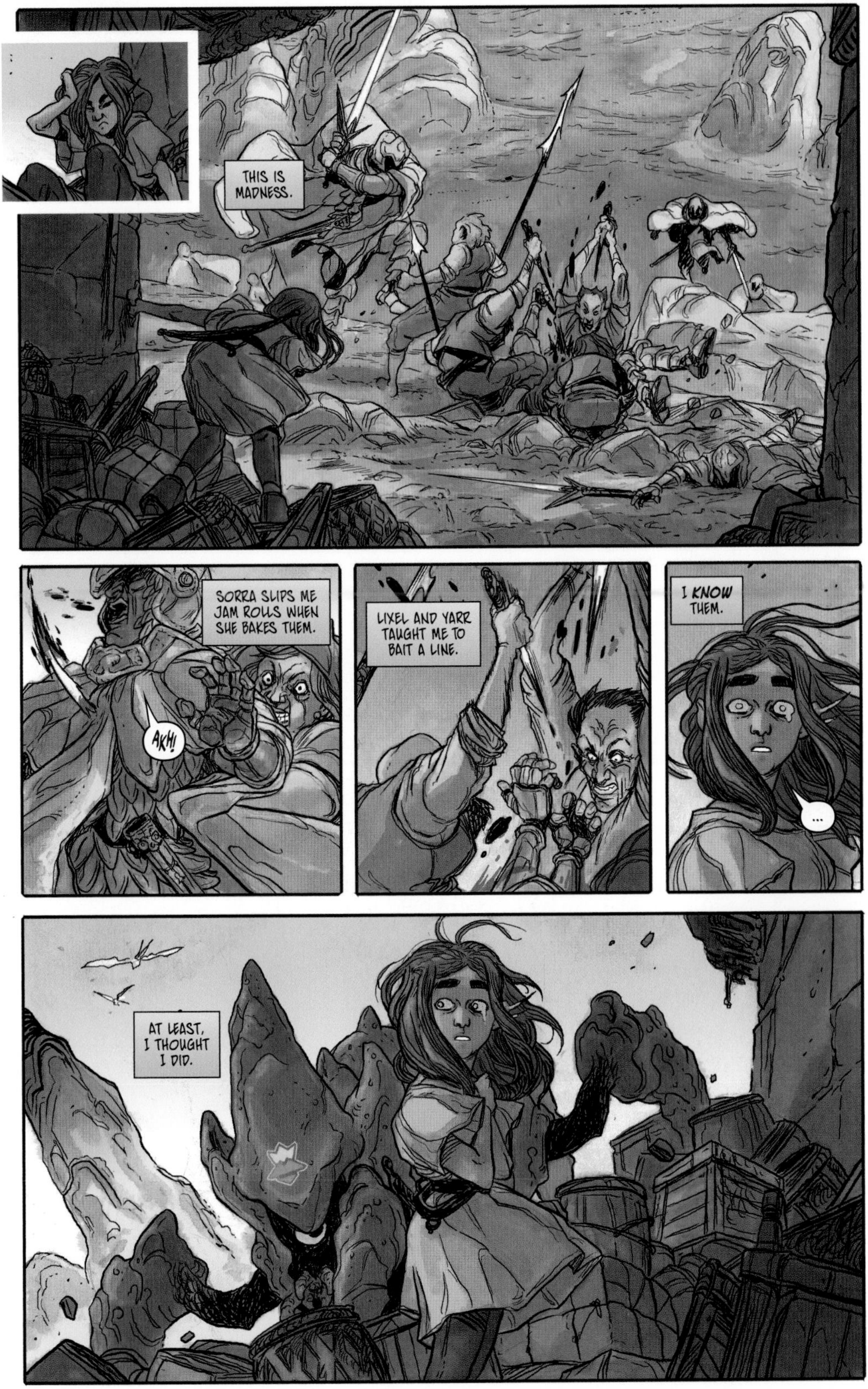
THIS IS MADNESS.
SORRA SLIPS ME JAM ROLLS WHEN SHE BAKES THEM.
AKH!
LIXEL AND YARR TAUGHT ME TO BAIT A LINE.
I KNOW THEM.
...
AT LEAST, I THOUGHT I DID.

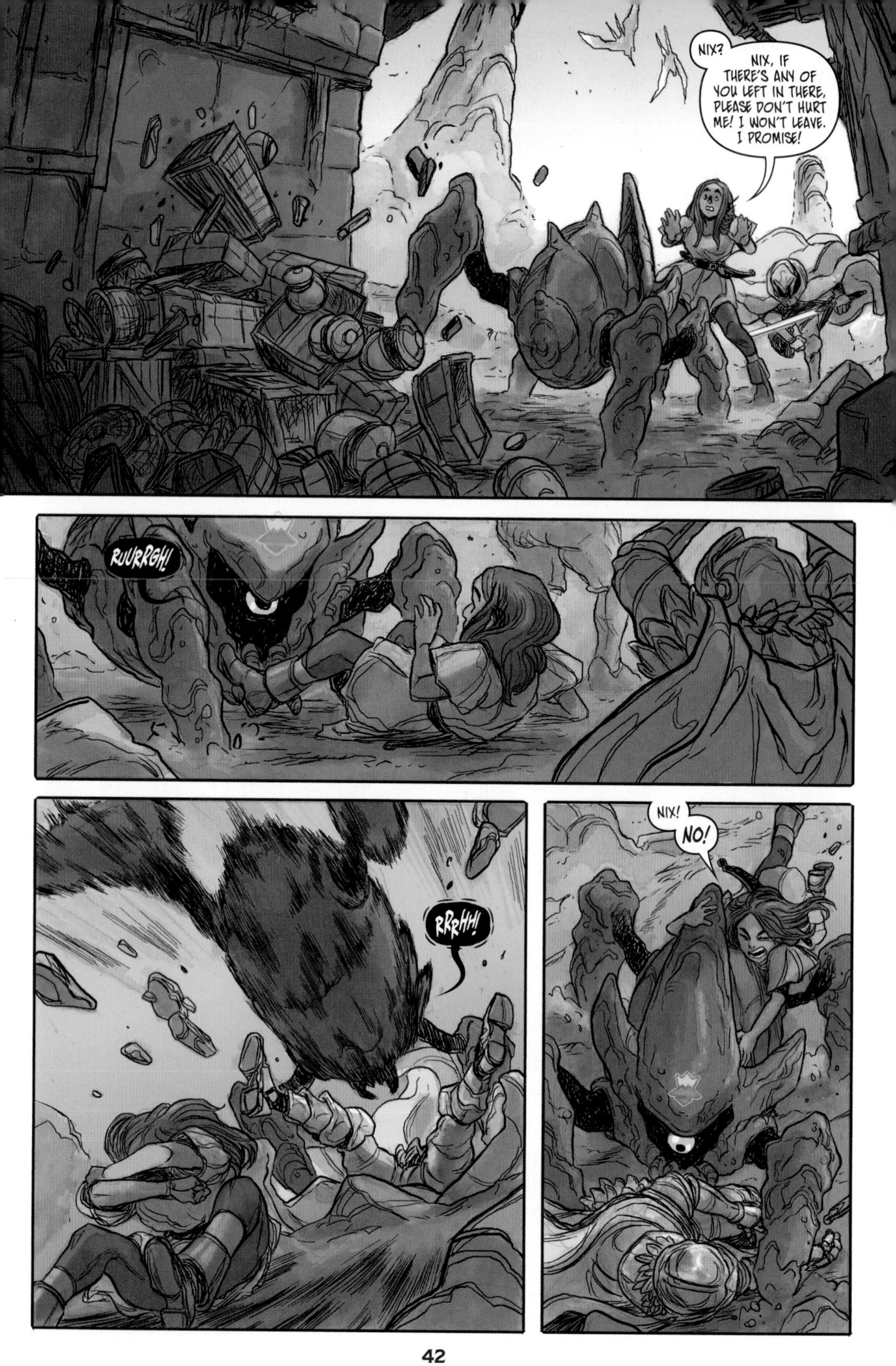
NIX?
NIX, IF THERE'S ANY OF YOU LEFT IN THERE, PLEASE DON'T HURT ME! I WON'T LEAVE. I PROMISE!
RUURRGH!
RRRHH!
NIX!
NO!

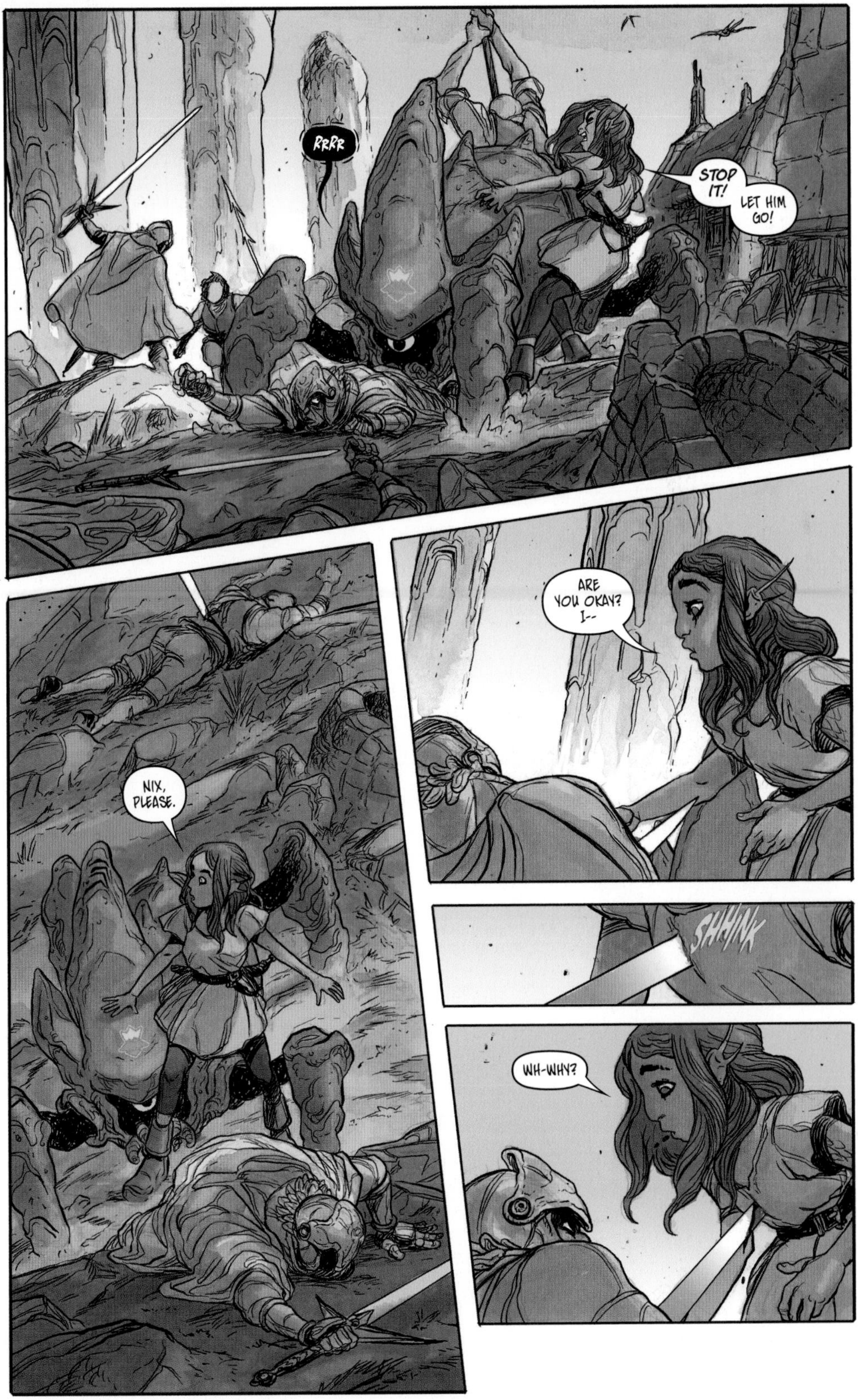
RRRR
STOP IT!
LET HIM GO!
NIX, PLEASE.
ARE YOU OKAY? I--
SHHINK
WH-WHY?

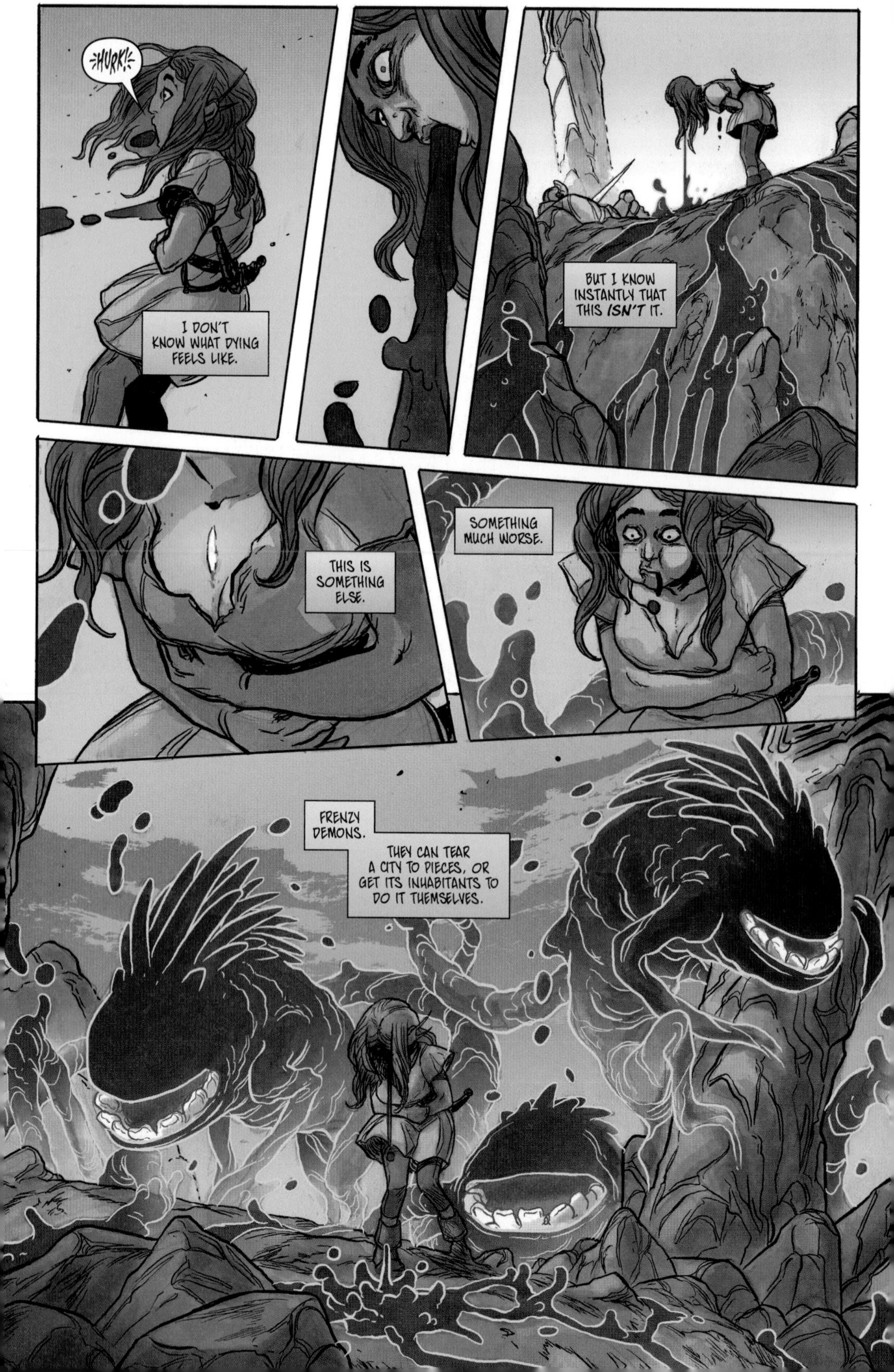
HURK!
I DON'T KNOW WHAT DYING FEELS LIKE.
BUT I KNOW INSTANTLY THAT THIS *ISN'T* IT.
THIS IS SOMETHING ELSE.
SOMETHING MUCH WORSE.
FRENZY DEMONS.
THEY CAN TEAR A CITY TO PIECES, OR GET ITS INHABITANTS TO DO IT THEMSELVES.

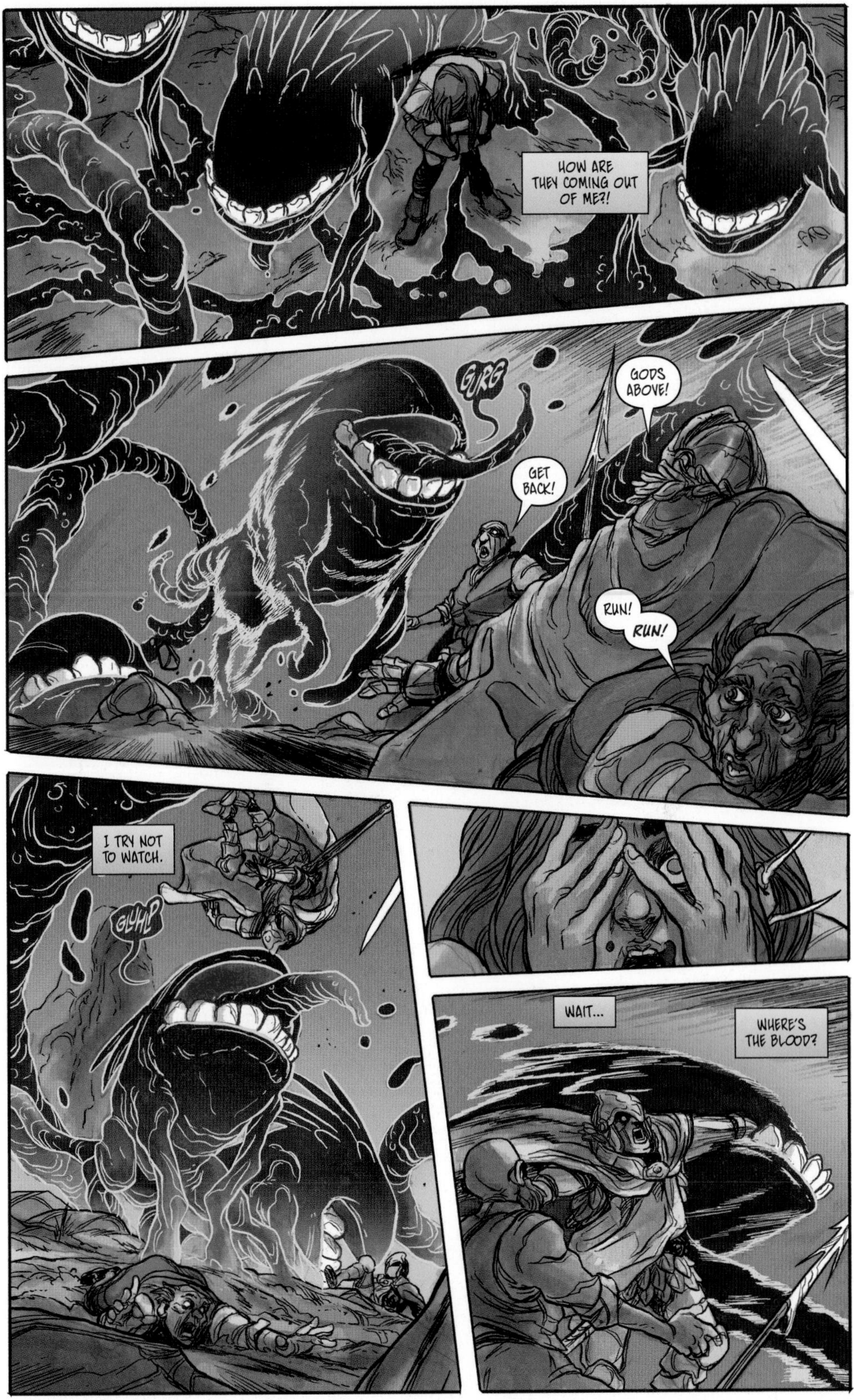
HOW ARE THEY COMING OUT OF ME?!
GURG
GODS ABOVE!
GET BACK!
RUN! RUN!
I TRY NOT TO WATCH.
GLUHLP
WAIT...
WHERE'S THE BLOOD?

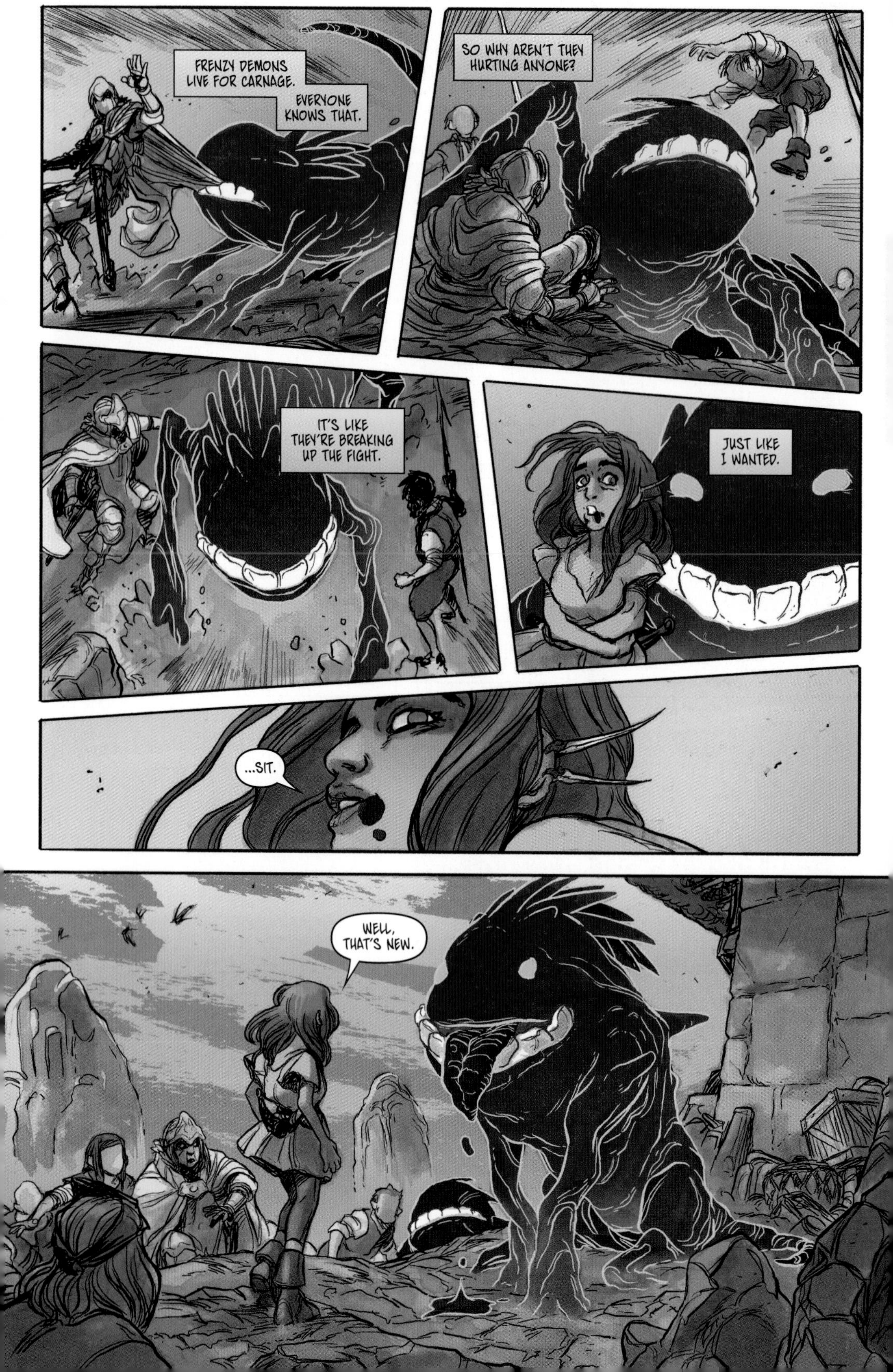
FRENZY DEMONS LIVE FOR CARNAGE.
EVERYONE KNOWS THAT.
SO WHY AREN'T THEY HURTING ANYONE?
IT'S LIKE THEY'RE BREAKING UP THE FIGHT.
JUST LIKE I WANTED.
...SIT.
WELL, THAT'S NEW.

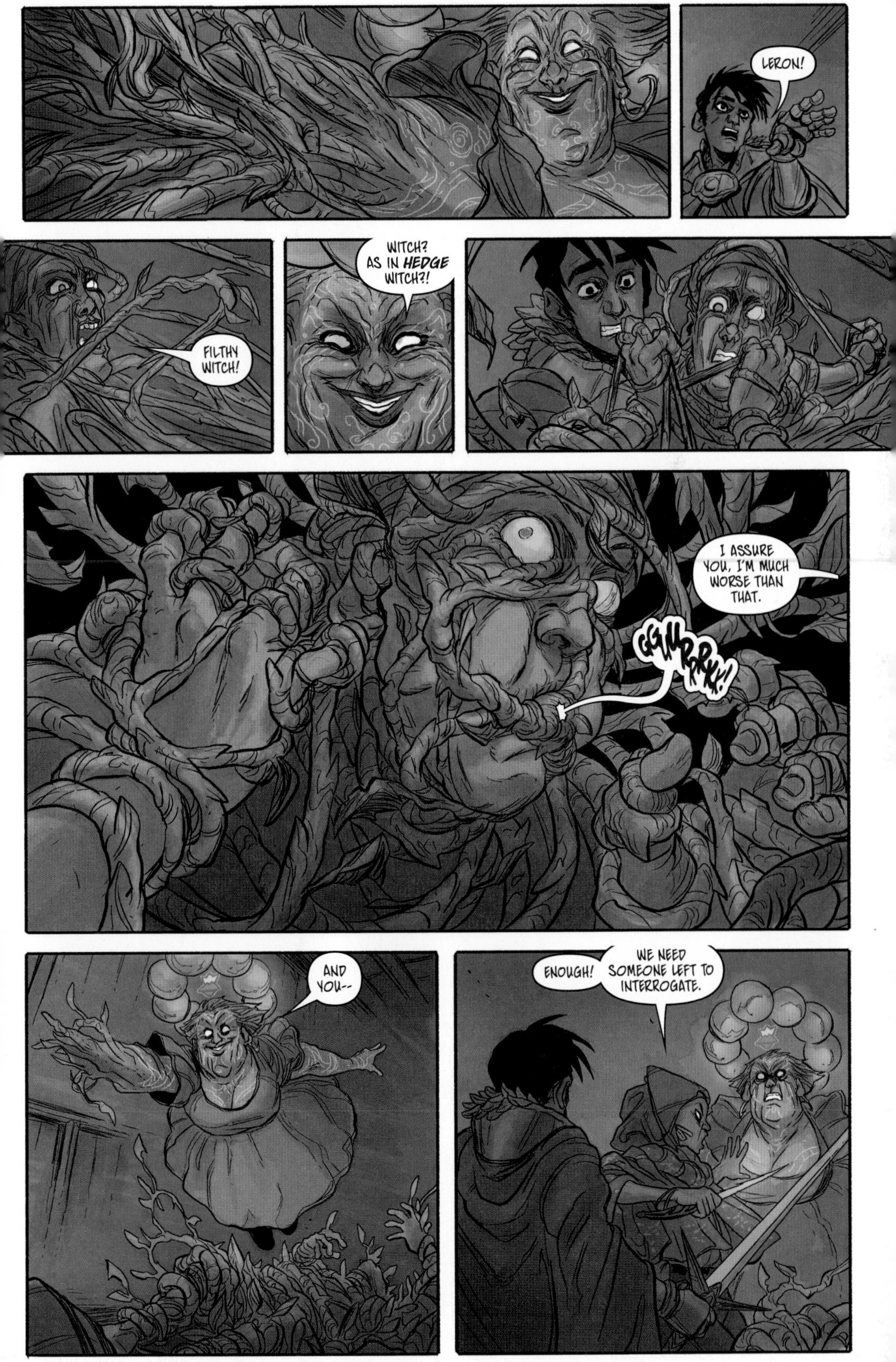
LERON!
FILTHY WITCH!
WITCH? AS IN HEDGE WITCH?!
I ASSURE YOU, I'M MUCH WORSE THAN THAT.
GGUMRRRK!
AND YOU--
ENOUGH!
WE NEED SOMEONE LEFT TO INTERROGATE.

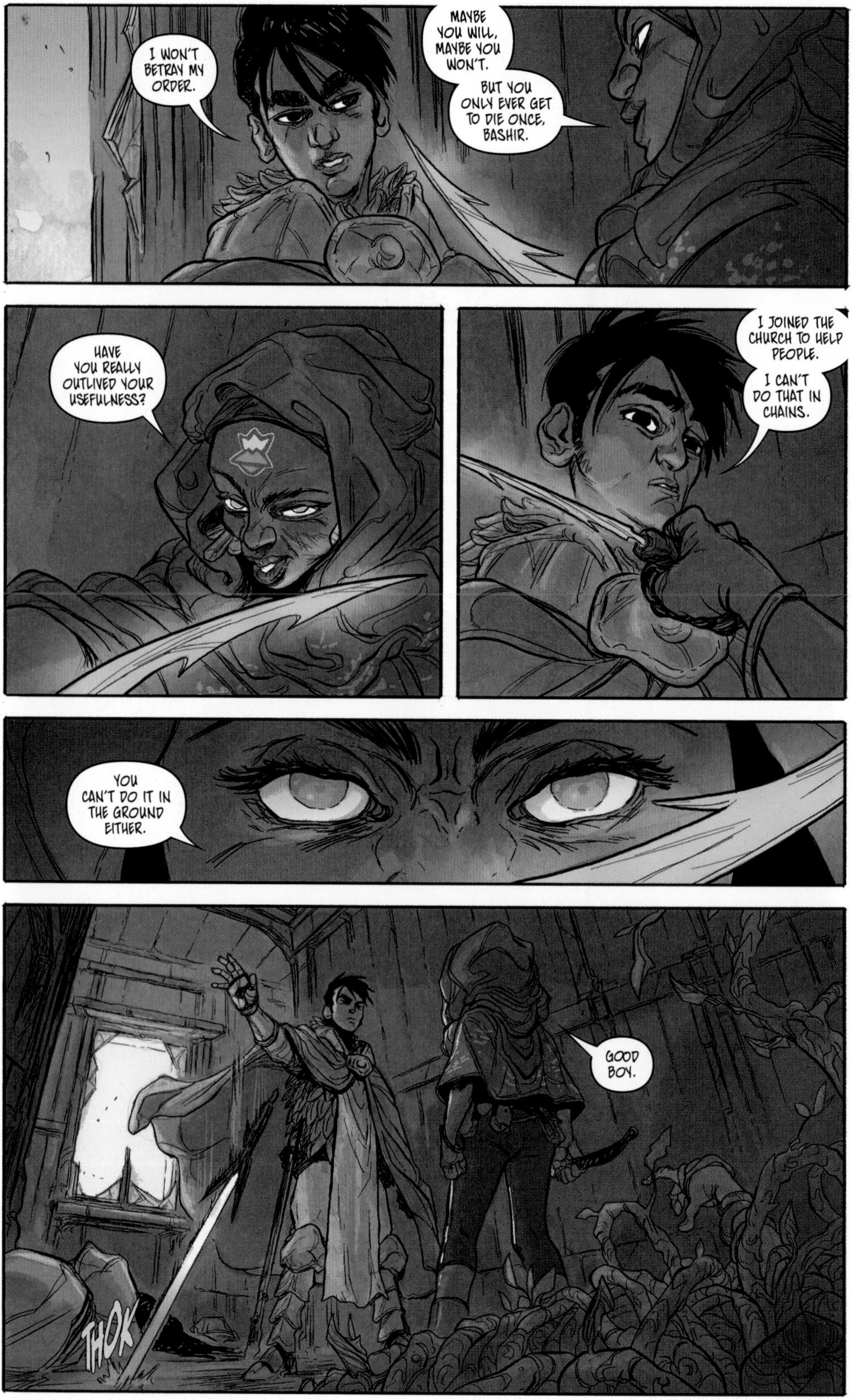
I WON'T BETRAY MY ORDER.
MAYBE YOU WILL, MAYBE YOU WON'T.
BUT YOU ONLY EVER GET TO DIE ONCE, BASHIR.
HAVE YOU REALLY OUTLIVED YOUR USEFULNESS?
I JOINED THE CHURCH TO HELP PEOPLE.
I CAN'T DO THAT IN CHAINS.
YOU CAN'T DO IT IN THE GROUND EITHER.
GOOD BOY.
THOK

HURRY! IF THEY'VE HURT AELLA...

THEY'D HAVE TO CATCH HER FIRST, AND THE GIRL'S RUNNING SCARED.

I TOLD HER MOTHER SHE NEEDED TO KNOW THE TRUTH SOONER.

SHE SHOULD HAVE BEEN ABLE TO DEFEND HERSELF!

GODS ABOVE!

KIANA?

I WAS *HURT* ANDTHEYCAMEOUT OFMEAND--

I DIDN'T MEAN IT.

RRRRRUUH

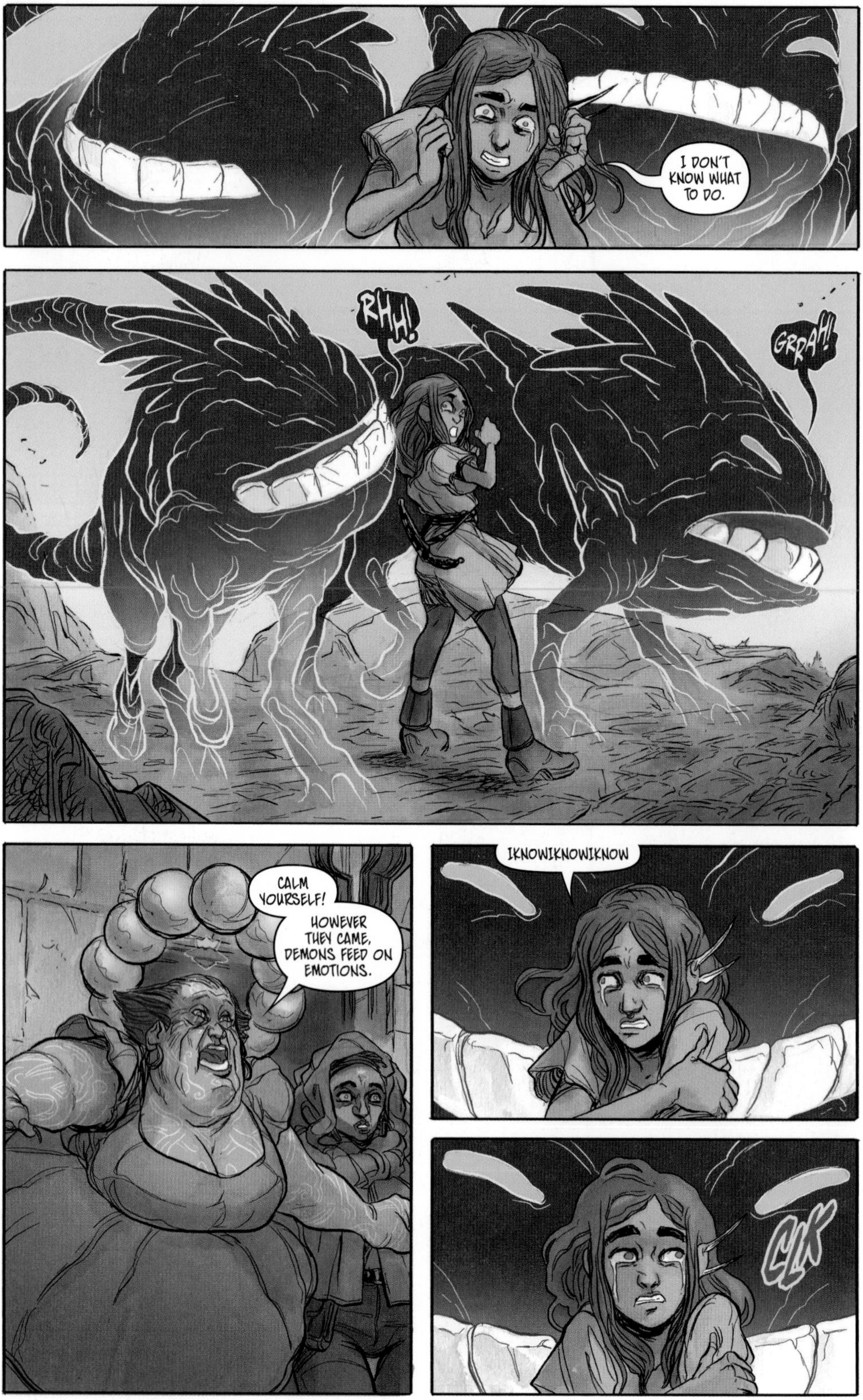
I DON'T KNOW WHAT TO DO.
RHH!
GRRAH!
CALM YOURSELF!
HOWEVER THEY CAME, DEMONS FEED ON EMOTIONS.
IKNOWIKNOWIKNOW
CLK

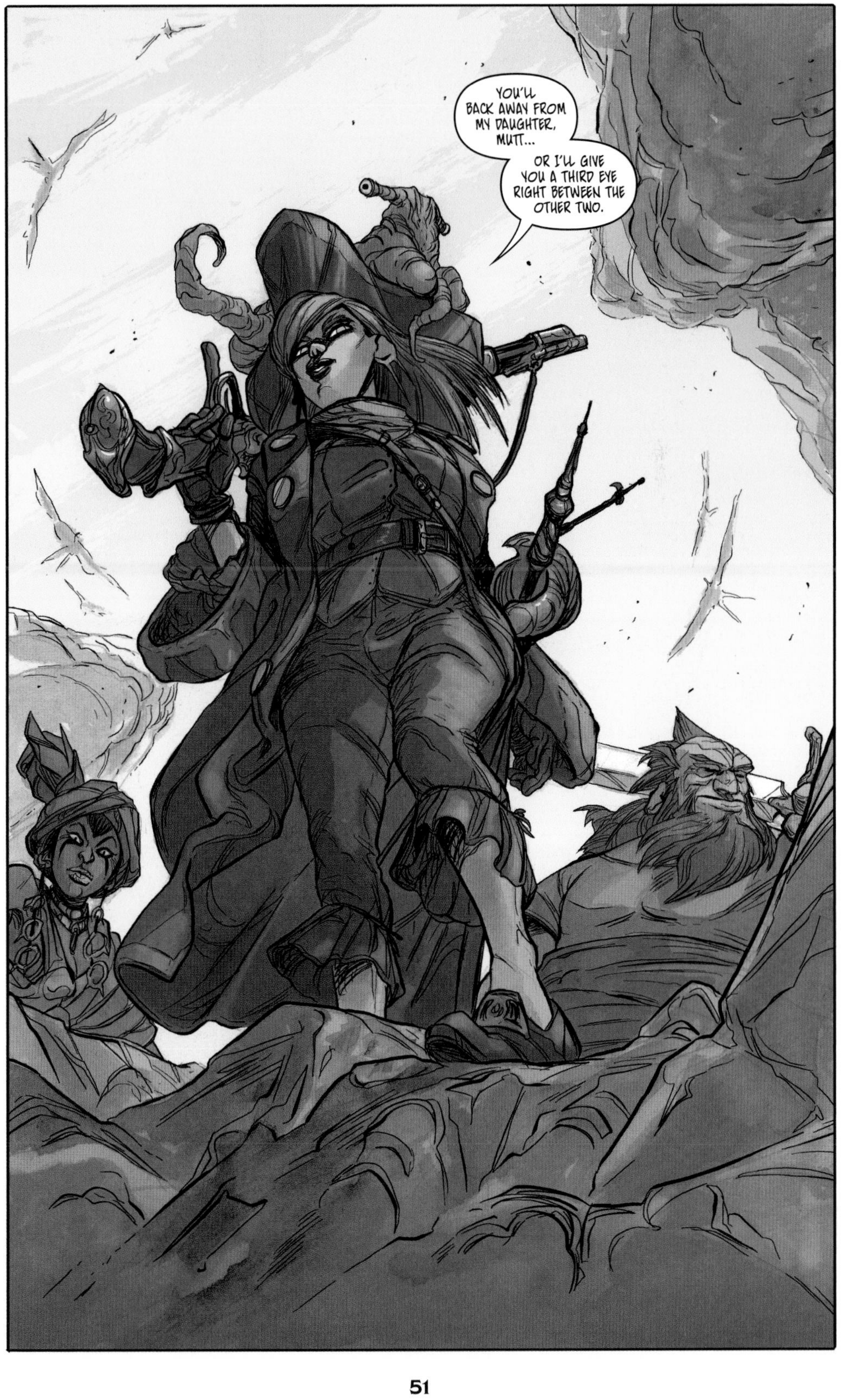
YOU'LL BACK AWAY FROM MY DAUGHTER, MUTT...
OR I'LL GIVE YOU A THIRD EYE RIGHT BETWEEN THE OTHER TWO.

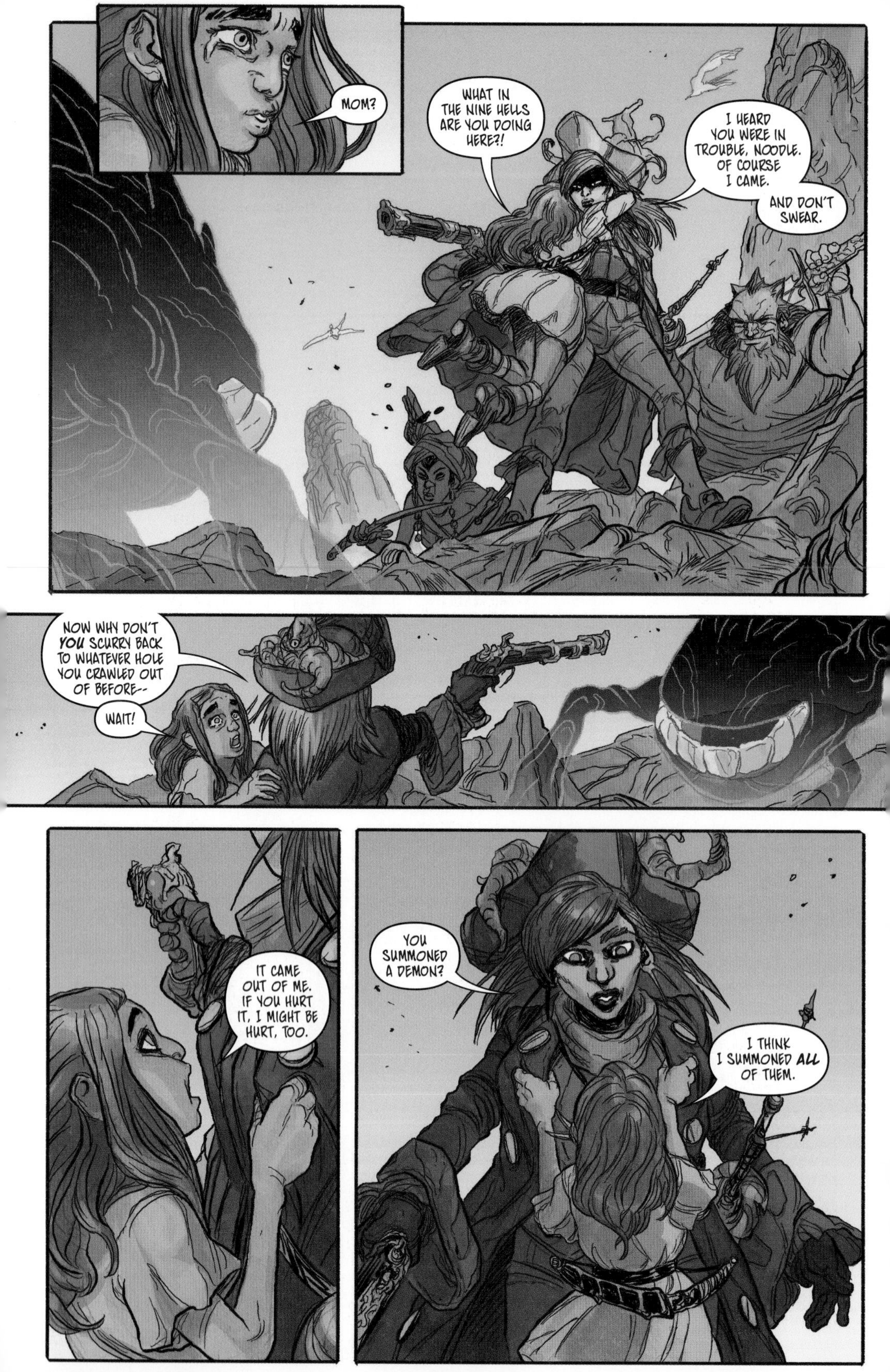
MOM?
WHAT IN THE NINE HELLS ARE YOU DOING HERE?!
I HEARD YOU WERE IN TROUBLE, NOODLE. OF COURSE I CAME.
AND DON'T SWEAR.
NOW WHY DON'T **YOU** SCURRY BACK TO WHATEVER HOLE YOU CRAWLED OUT OF BEFORE--
WAIT!
IT CAME OUT OF ME. IF YOU HURT IT, I MIGHT BE HURT, TOO.
YOU SUMMONED A DEMON?
I THINK I SUMMONED **ALL** OF THEM.

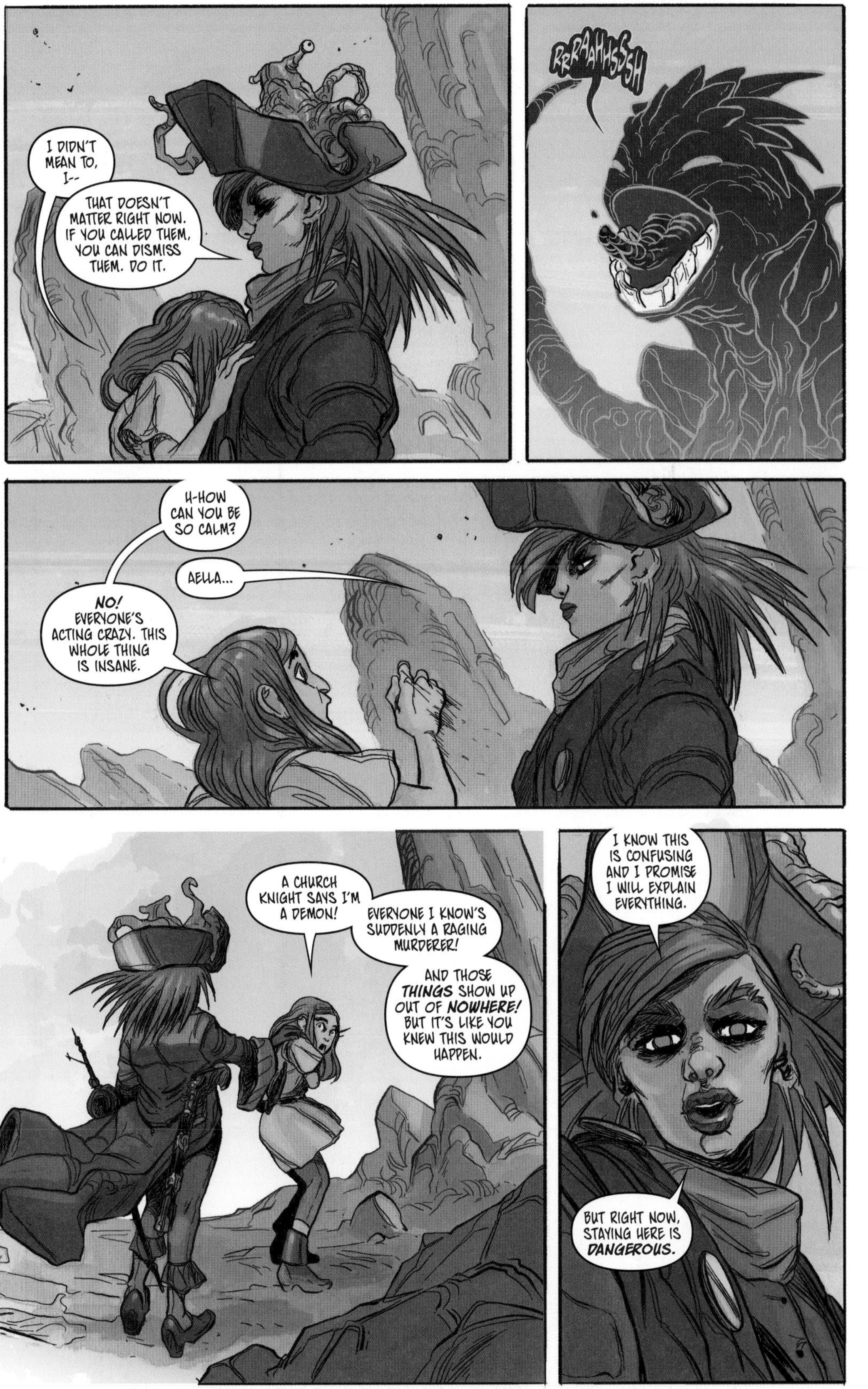
I DIDN'T MEAN TO, I--
THAT DOESN'T MATTER RIGHT NOW. IF YOU CALLED THEM, YOU CAN DISMISS THEM. DO IT.
RRRAAHHSSSH
H-HOW CAN YOU BE SO CALM?
AELLA...
NO! EVERYONE'S ACTING CRAZY. THIS WHOLE THING IS INSANE.
A CHURCH KNIGHT SAYS I'M A DEMON!
EVERYONE I KNOW'S SUDDENLY A RAGING MURDERER!
AND THOSE THINGS SHOW UP OUT OF NOWHERE! BUT IT'S LIKE YOU KNEW THIS WOULD HAPPEN.
I KNOW THIS IS CONFUSING AND I PROMISE I WILL EXPLAIN EVERYTHING.
BUT RIGHT NOW, STAYING HERE IS DANGEROUS.

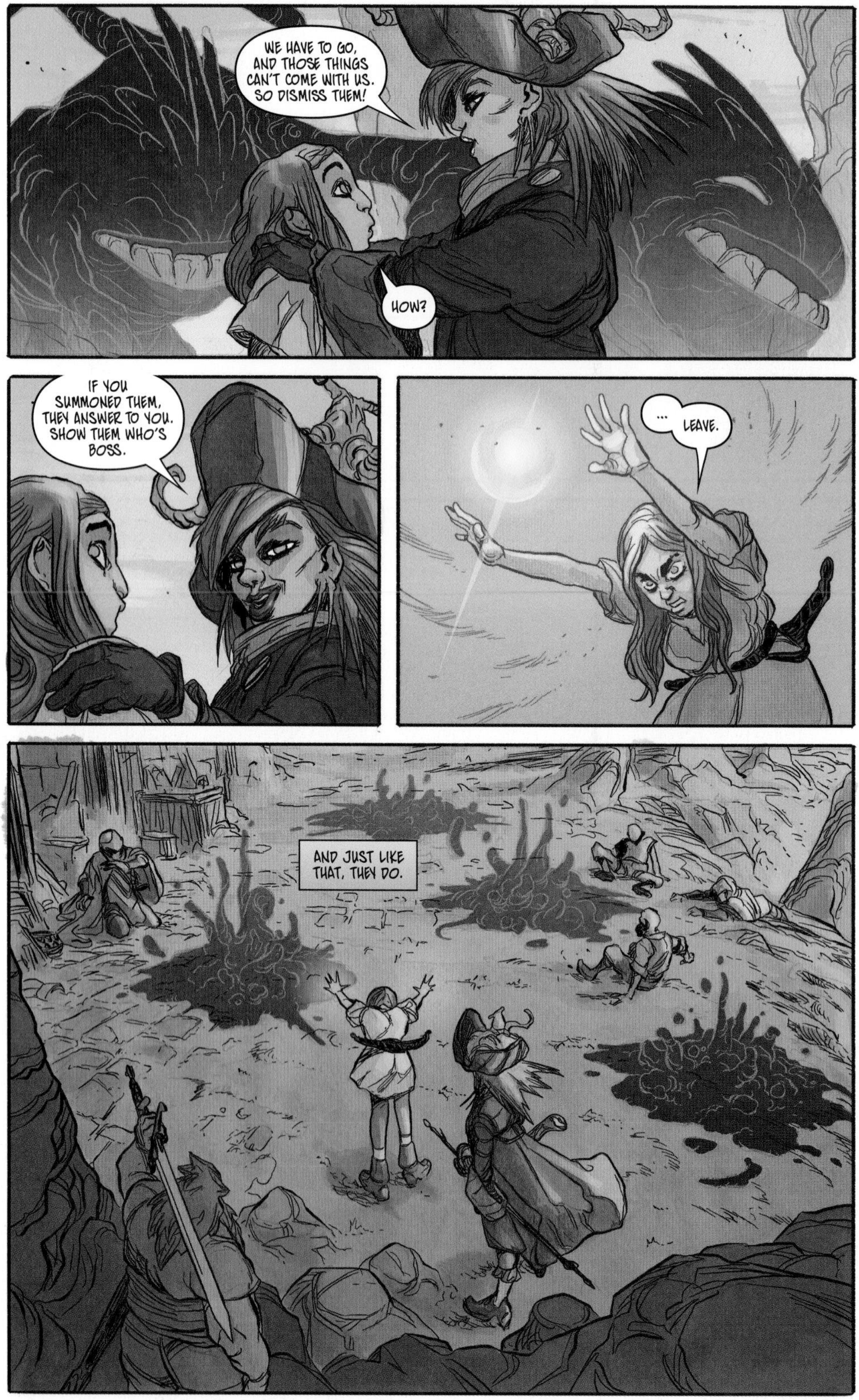
WE HAVE TO GO, AND THOSE THINGS CAN'T COME WITH US. SO DISMISS THEM!
HOW?
IF YOU SUMMONED THEM, THEY ANSWER TO YOU. SHOW THEM WHO'S BOSS.
... LEAVE.
AND JUST LIKE THAT, THEY DO.

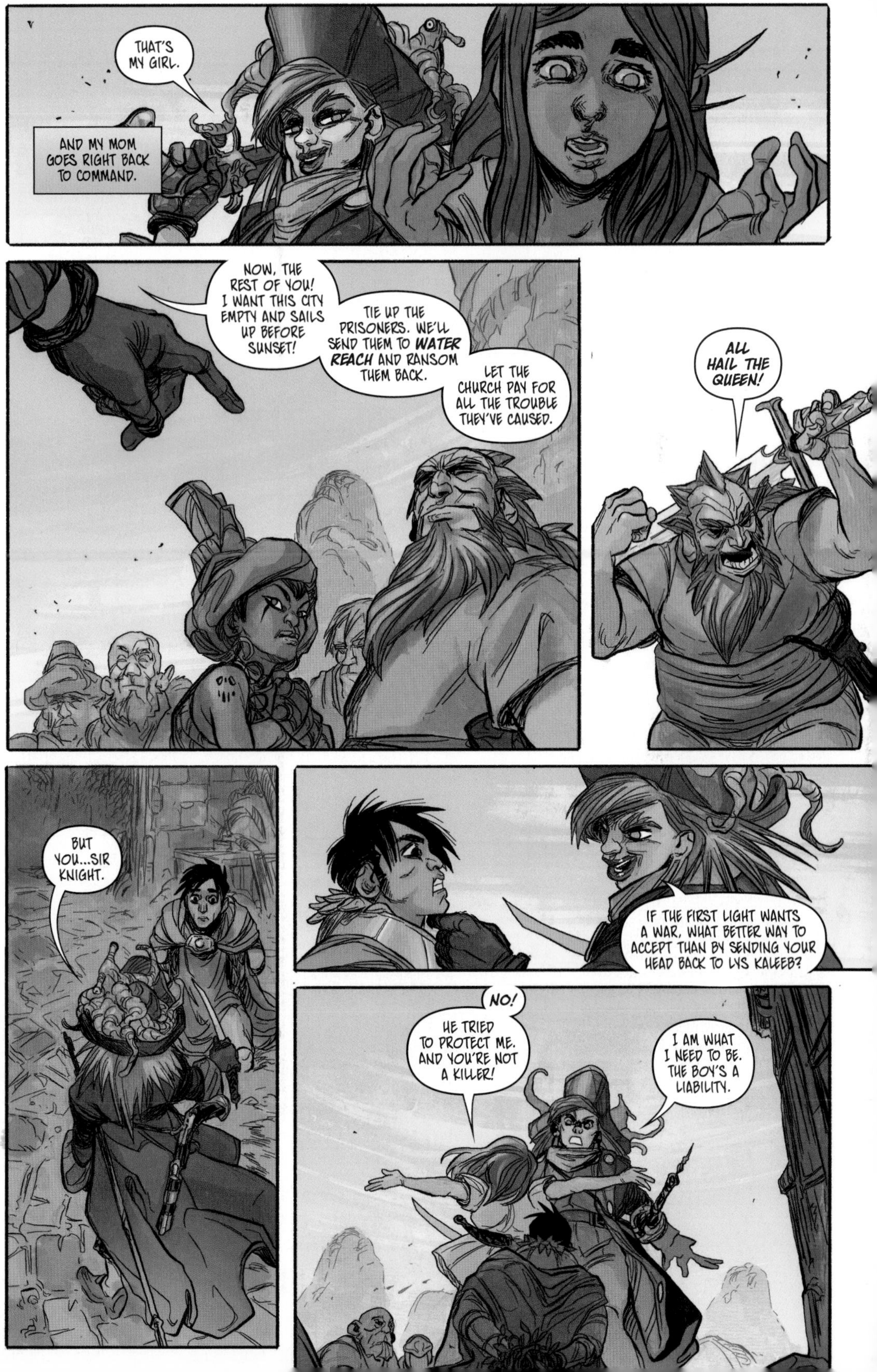
THAT'S MY GIRL.
AND MY MOM GOES RIGHT BACK TO COMMAND.
NOW, THE REST OF YOU! I WANT THIS CITY EMPTY AND SAILS UP BEFORE SUNSET!
TIE UP THE PRISONERS. WE'LL SEND THEM TO WATER REACH AND RANSOM THEM BACK.
LET THE CHURCH PAY FOR ALL THE TROUBLE THEY'VE CAUSED.
ALL HAIL THE QUEEN!
BUT YOU...SIR KNIGHT.
IF THE FIRST LIGHT WANTS A WAR, WHAT BETTER WAY TO ACCEPT THAN BY SENDING YOUR HEAD BACK TO LYS KALEEB?
NO!
HE TRIED TO PROTECT ME. AND YOU'RE NOT A KILLER!
I AM WHAT I NEED TO BE. THE BOY'S A LIABILITY.

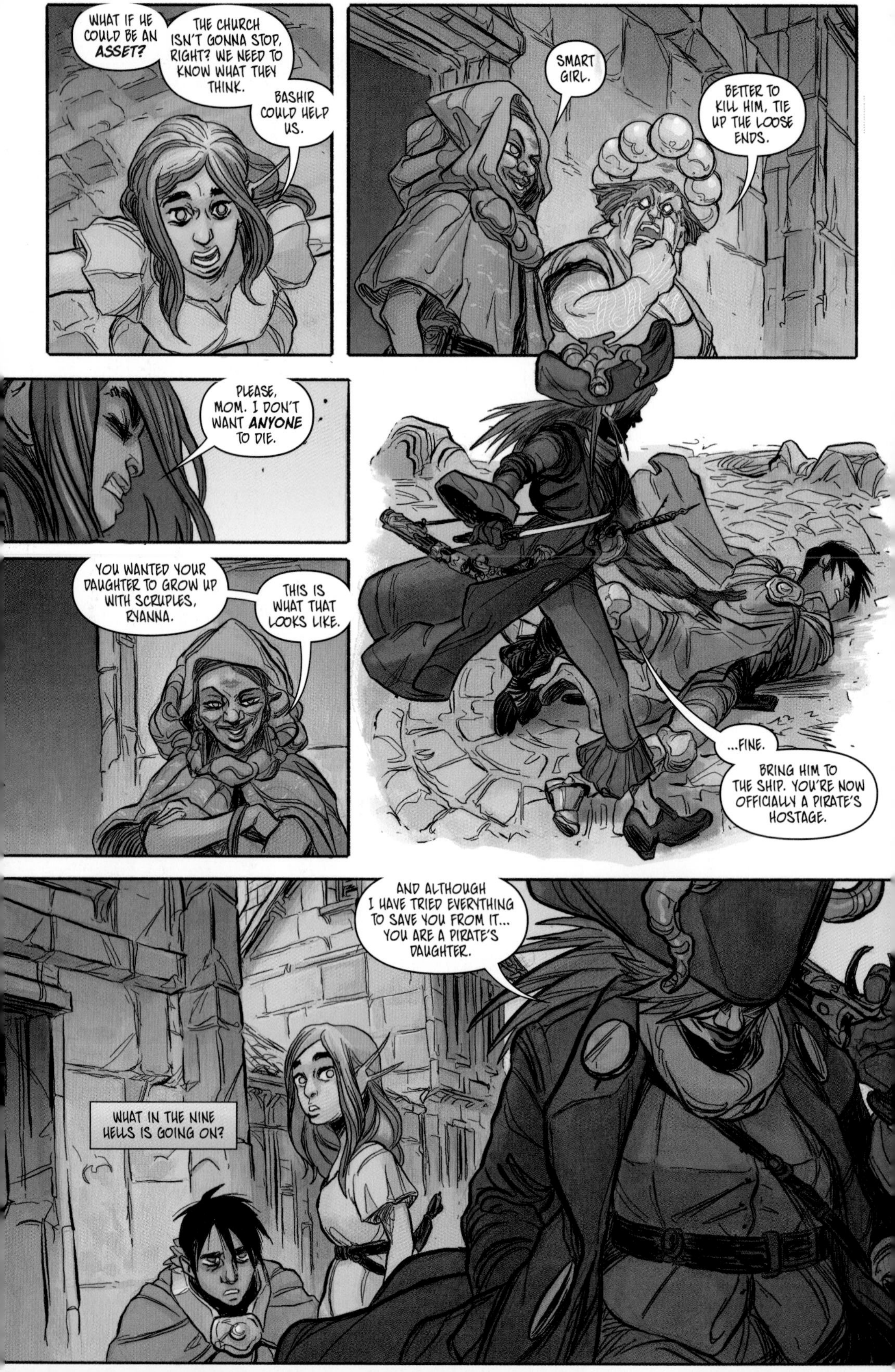
WHAT IF HE COULD BE AN ASSET?
THE CHURCH ISN'T GONNA STOP, RIGHT? WE NEED TO KNOW WHAT THEY THINK.
BASHIR COULD HELP US.
SMART GIRL.
BETTER TO KILL HIM, TIE UP THE LOOSE ENDS.
PLEASE, MOM. I DON'T WANT ANYONE TO DIE.
YOU WANTED YOUR DAUGHTER TO GROW UP WITH SCRUPLES, RYANNA.
THIS IS WHAT THAT LOOKS LIKE.
...FINE.
BRING HIM TO THE SHIP. YOU'RE NOW OFFICIALLY A PIRATE'S HOSTAGE.
AND ALTHOUGH I HAVE TRIED EVERYTHING TO SAVE YOU FROM IT... YOU ARE A PIRATE'S DAUGHTER.
WHAT IN THE NINE HELLS IS GOING ON?

Chapter Three

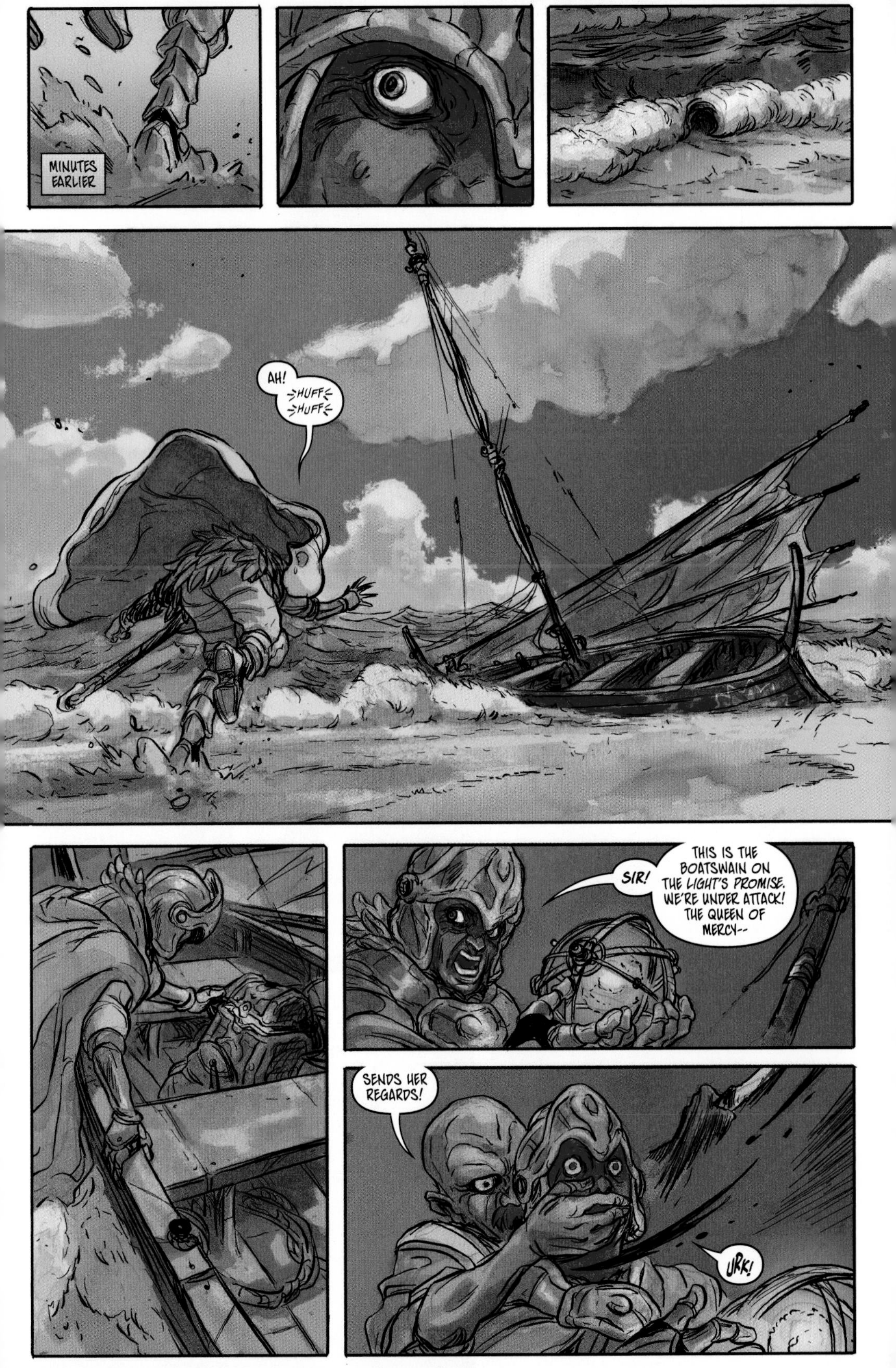
MINUTES EARLIER
AH! HUFF HUFF
SIR!
THIS IS THE BOATSWAIN ON THE LIGHT'S PROMISE. WE'RE UNDER ATTACK! THE QUEEN OF MERCY--
SENDS HER REGARDS!
URK!

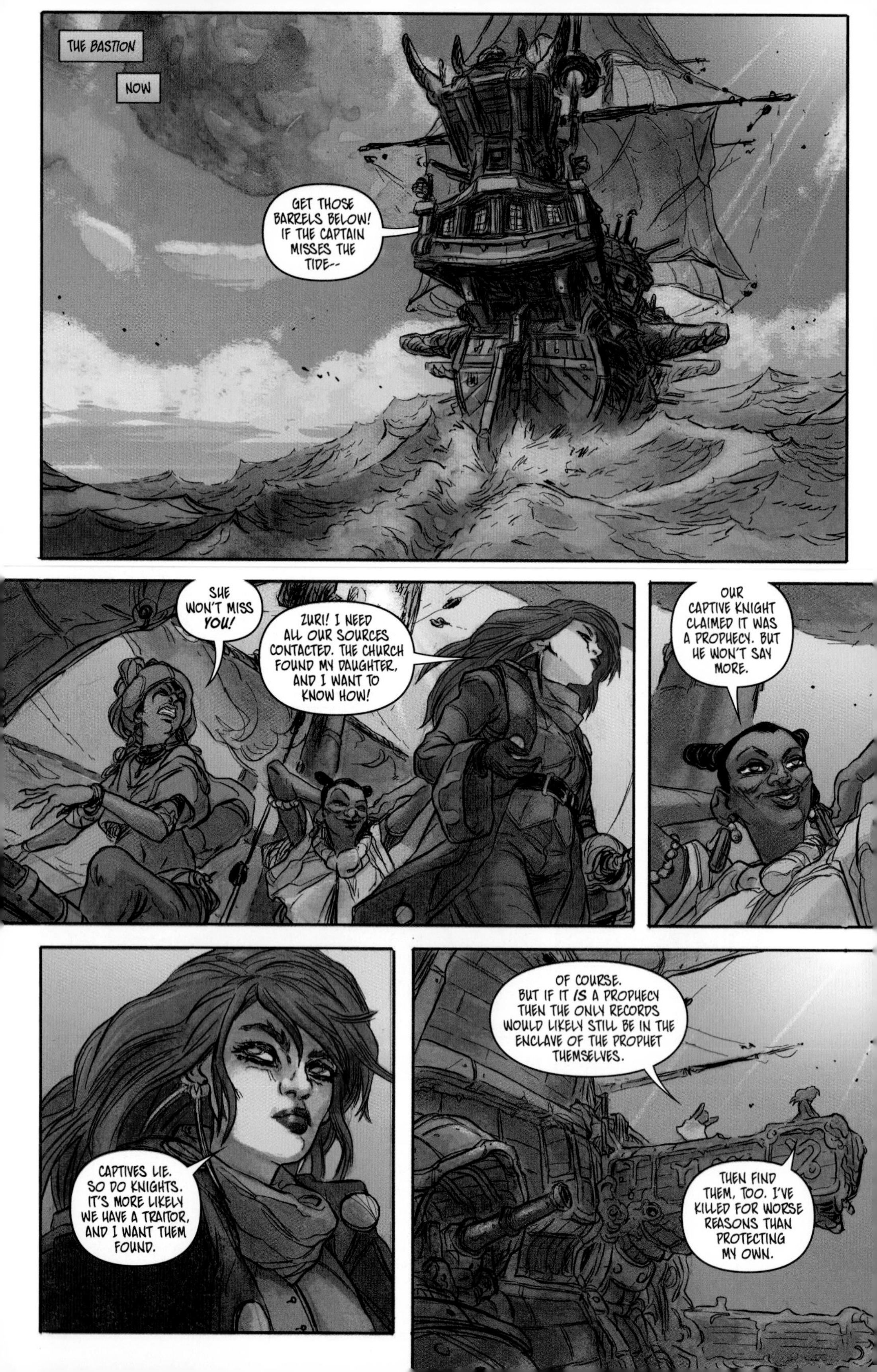
THE BASTION
NOW
GET THOSE BARRELS BELOW! IF THE CAPTAIN MISSES THE TIDE--
SHE WON'T MISS YOU!
ZURI! I NEED ALL OUR SOURCES CONTACTED. THE CHURCH FOUND MY DAUGHTER, AND I WANT TO KNOW HOW!
OUR CAPTIVE KNIGHT CLAIMED IT WAS A PROPHECY. BUT HE WON'T SAY MORE.
CAPTIVES LIE. SO DO KNIGHTS. IT'S MORE LIKELY WE HAVE A TRAITOR, AND I WANT THEM FOUND.
OF COURSE. BUT IF IT IS A PROPHECY THEN THE ONLY RECORDS WOULD LIKELY STILL BE IN THE ENCLAVE OF THE PROPHET THEMSELVES.
THEN FIND THEM, TOO. I'VE KILLED FOR WORSE REASONS THAN PROTECTING MY OWN.

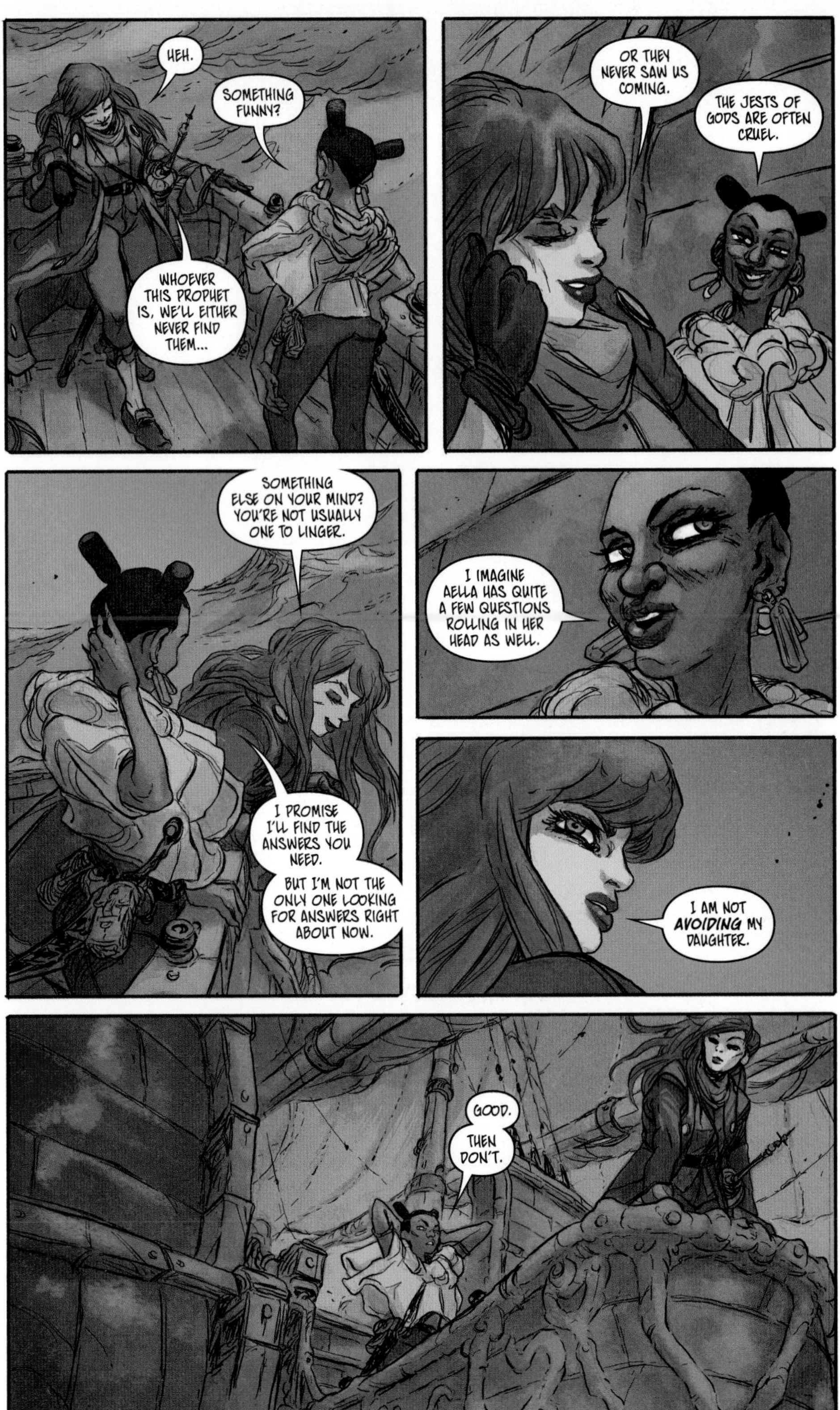
HEH.
SOMETHING FUNNY?
WHOEVER THIS PROPHET IS, WE'LL EITHER NEVER FIND THEM...
OR THEY NEVER SAW US COMING.
THE JESTS OF GODS ARE OFTEN CRUEL.
SOMETHING ELSE ON YOUR MIND? YOU'RE NOT USUALLY ONE TO LINGER.
I PROMISE I'LL FIND THE ANSWERS YOU NEED.
BUT I'M NOT THE ONLY ONE LOOKING FOR ANSWERS RIGHT ABOUT NOW.
I IMAGINE AELLA HAS QUITE A FEW QUESTIONS ROLLING IN HER HEAD AS WELL.
I AM NOT AVOIDING MY DAUGHTER.
GOOD.
THEN DON'T.

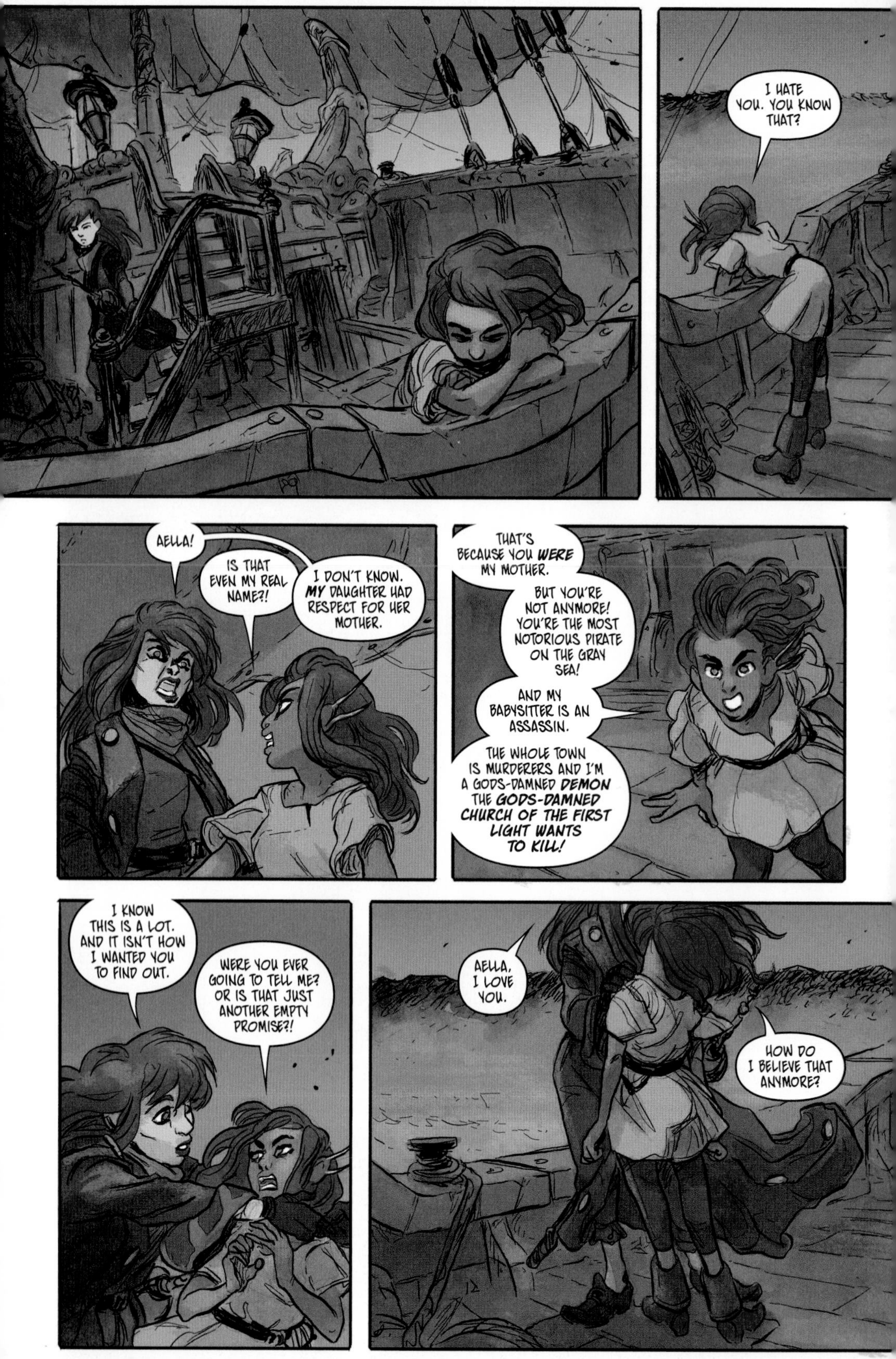
I HATE YOU. YOU KNOW THAT?
AELLA!
IS THAT EVEN MY REAL NAME?!
I DON'T KNOW. MY DAUGHTER HAD RESPECT FOR HER MOTHER.
THAT'S BECAUSE YOU WERE MY MOTHER.
BUT YOU'RE NOT ANYMORE! YOU'RE THE MOST NOTORIOUS PIRATE ON THE GRAY SEA!
AND MY BABYSITTER IS AN ASSASSIN.
THE WHOLE TOWN IS MURDERERS AND I'M A GODS-DAMNED DEMON THE GODS-DAMNED CHURCH OF THE FIRST LIGHT WANTS TO KILL!
I KNOW THIS IS A LOT. AND IT ISN'T HOW I WANTED YOU TO FIND OUT.
WERE YOU EVER GOING TO TELL ME? OR IS THAT JUST ANOTHER EMPTY PROMISE?!
AELLA, I LOVE YOU.
HOW DO I BELIEVE THAT ANYMORE?

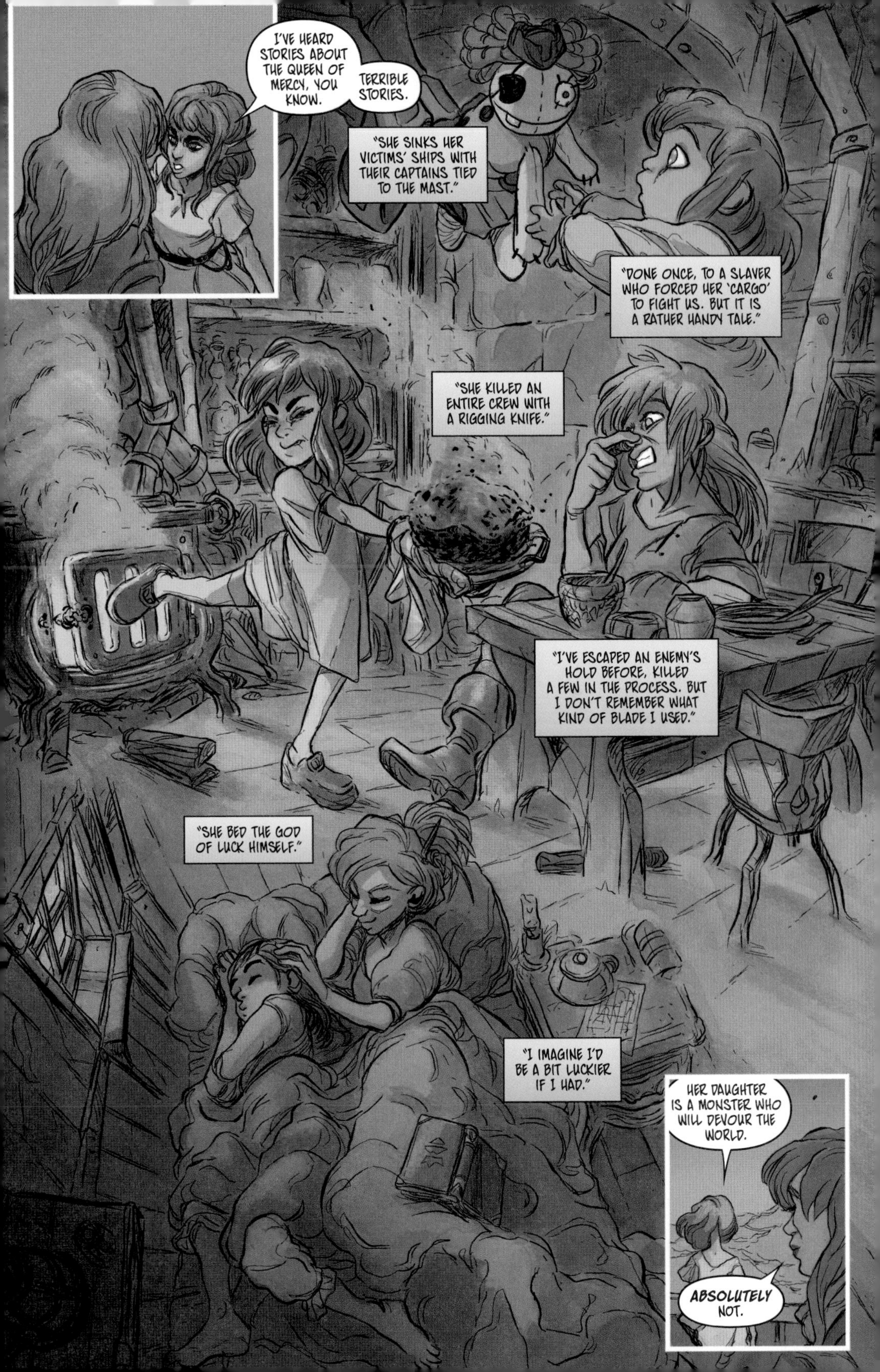
I'VE HEARD STORIES ABOUT THE QUEEN OF MERCY, YOU KNOW.
TERRIBLE STORIES.
"SHE SINKS HER VICTIMS' SHIPS WITH THEIR CAPTAINS TIED TO THE MAST."
"DONE ONCE, TO A SLAVER WHO FORCED HER 'CARGO' TO FIGHT US. BUT IT IS A RATHER HANDY TALE."
"SHE KILLED AN ENTIRE CREW WITH A RIGGING KNIFE."
"I'VE ESCAPED AN ENEMY'S HOLD BEFORE, KILLED A FEW IN THE PROCESS. BUT I DON'T REMEMBER WHAT KIND OF BLADE I USED."
"SHE BED THE GOD OF LUCK HIMSELF."
"I IMAGINE I'D BE A BIT LUCKIER IF I HAD."
HER DAUGHTER IS A MONSTER WHO WILL DEVOUR THE WORLD.
ABSOLUTELY NOT.

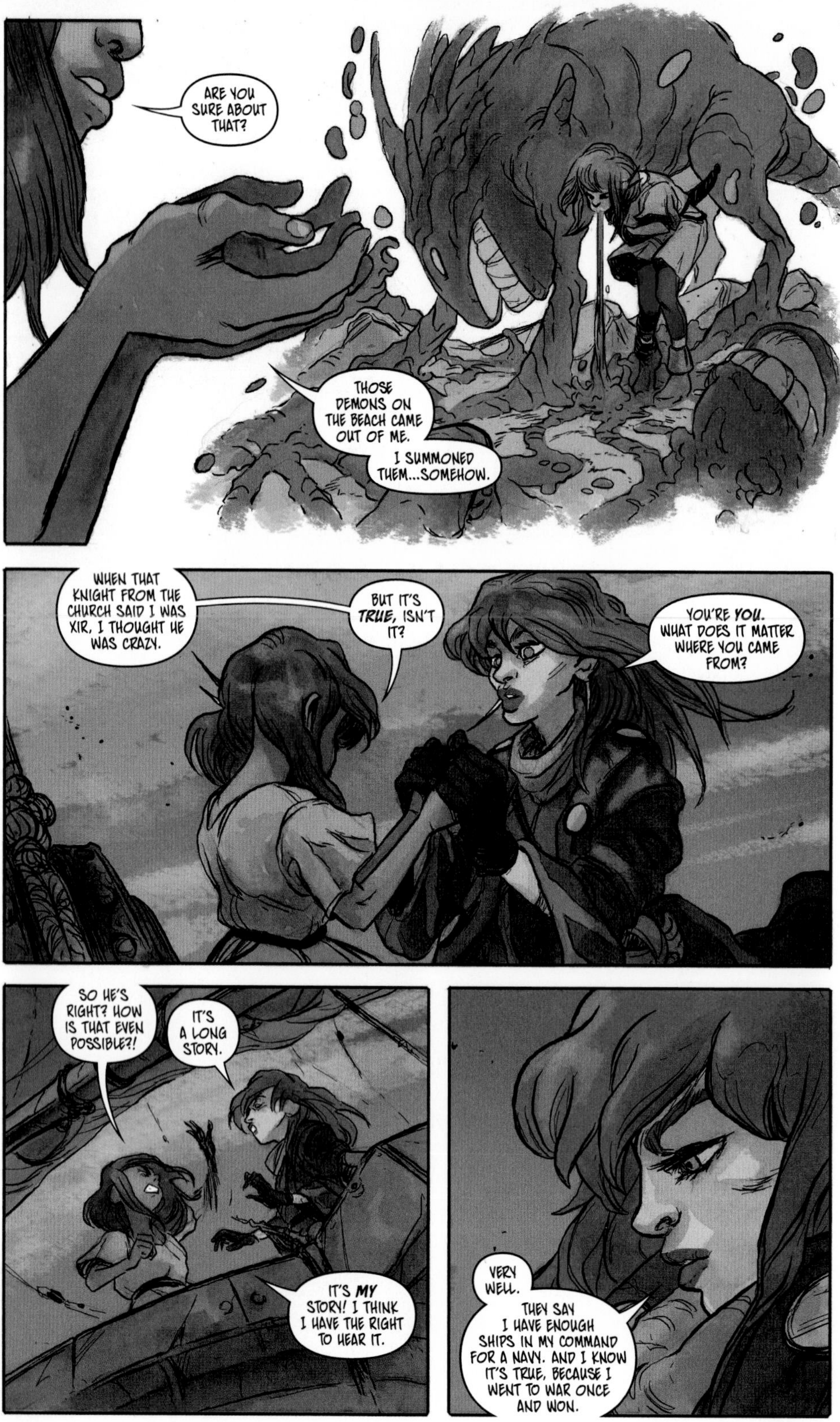
ARE YOU SURE ABOUT THAT?
THOSE DEMONS ON THE BEACH CAME OUT OF ME.
I SUMMONED THEM...SOMEHOW.
WHEN THAT KNIGHT FROM THE CHURCH SAID I WAS XIR, I THOUGHT HE WAS CRAZY.
BUT IT'S TRUE, ISN'T IT?
YOU'RE YOU. WHAT DOES IT MATTER WHERE YOU CAME FROM?
SO HE'S RIGHT? HOW IS THAT EVEN POSSIBLE?!
IT'S A LONG STORY.
IT'S MY STORY! I THINK I HAVE THE RIGHT TO HEAR IT.
VERY WELL.
THEY SAY I HAVE ENOUGH SHIPS IN MY COMMAND FOR A NAVY. AND I KNOW IT'S TRUE, BECAUSE I WENT TO WAR ONCE AND WON.

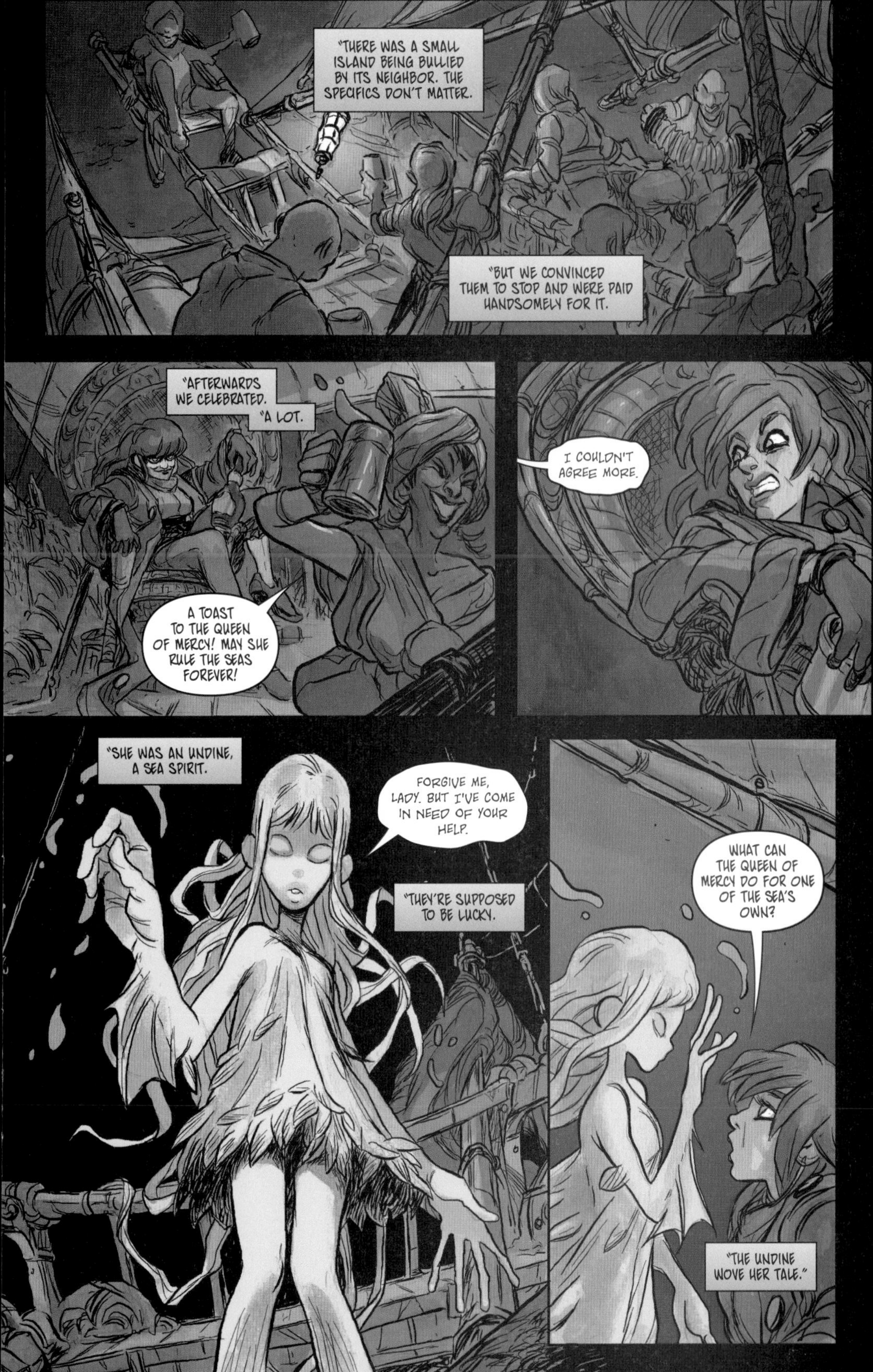
"THERE WAS A SMALL ISLAND BEING BULLIED BY ITS NEIGHBOR. THE SPECIFICS DON'T MATTER.
"BUT WE CONVINCED THEM TO STOP AND WERE PAID HANDSOMELY FOR IT.
"AFTERWARDS WE CELEBRATED.
"A LOT.
A TOAST TO THE QUEEN OF MERCY! MAY SHE RULE THE SEAS FOREVER!
I COULDN'T AGREE MORE.
"SHE WAS AN UNDINE, A SEA SPIRIT.
FORGIVE ME, LADY. BUT I'VE COME IN NEED OF YOUR HELP.
"THEY'RE SUPPOSED TO BE LUCKY.
WHAT CAN THE QUEEN OF MERCY DO FOR ONE OF THE SEA'S OWN?
"THE UNDINE WOVE HER TALE."

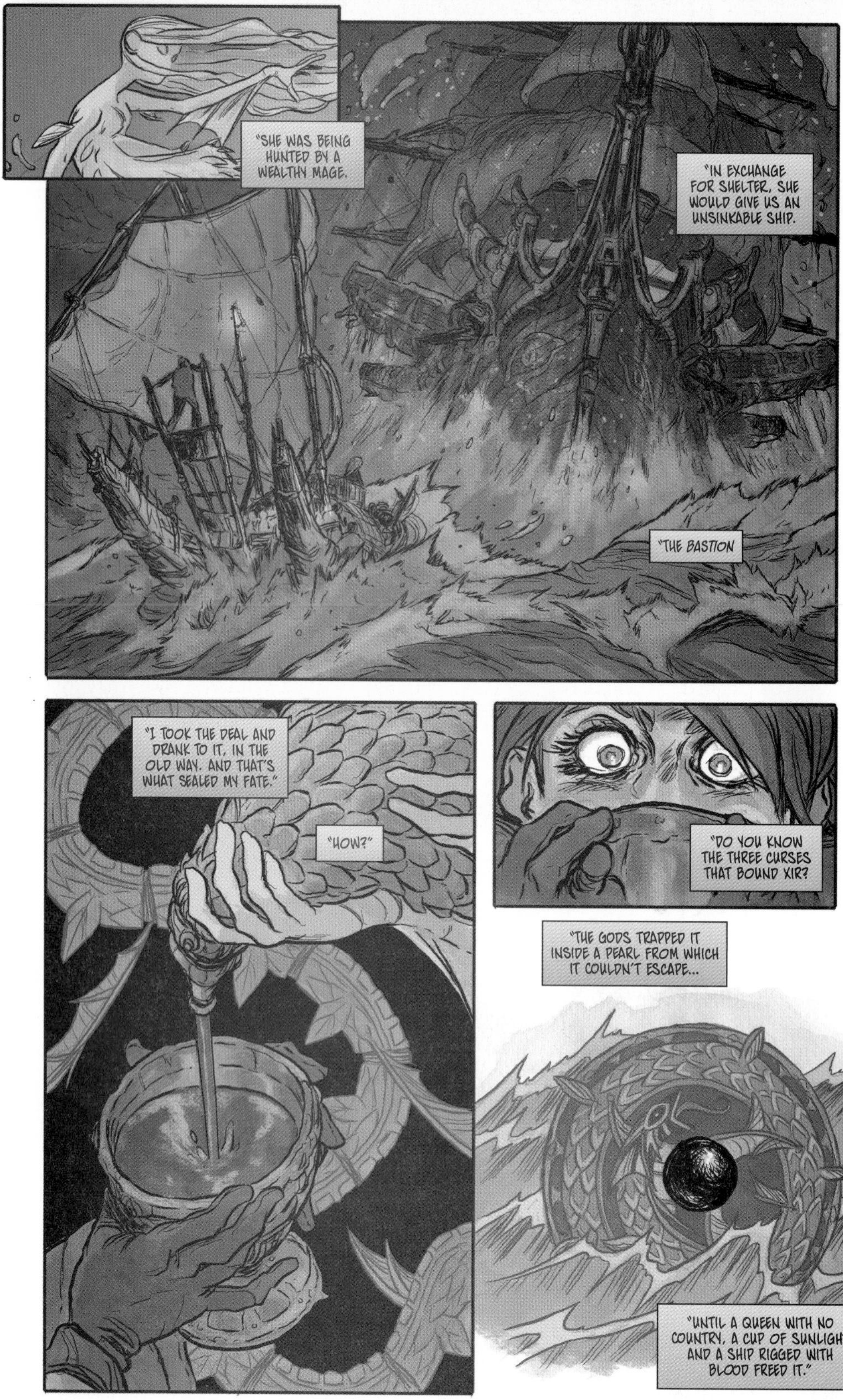
"SHE WAS BEING HUNTED BY A WEALTHY MAGE.
"IN EXCHANGE FOR SHELTER, SHE WOULD GIVE US AN UNSINKABLE SHIP.
"THE BASTION
"I TOOK THE DEAL AND DRANK TO IT, IN THE OLD WAY. AND THAT'S WHAT SEALED MY FATE."
"HOW?"
"DO YOU KNOW THE THREE CURSES THAT BOUND XIR?
"THE GODS TRAPPED IT INSIDE A PEARL FROM WHICH IT COULDN'T ESCAPE...
"UNTIL A QUEEN WITH NO COUNTRY, A CUP OF SUNLIGHT AND A SHIP RIGGED WITH BLOOD FREED IT."

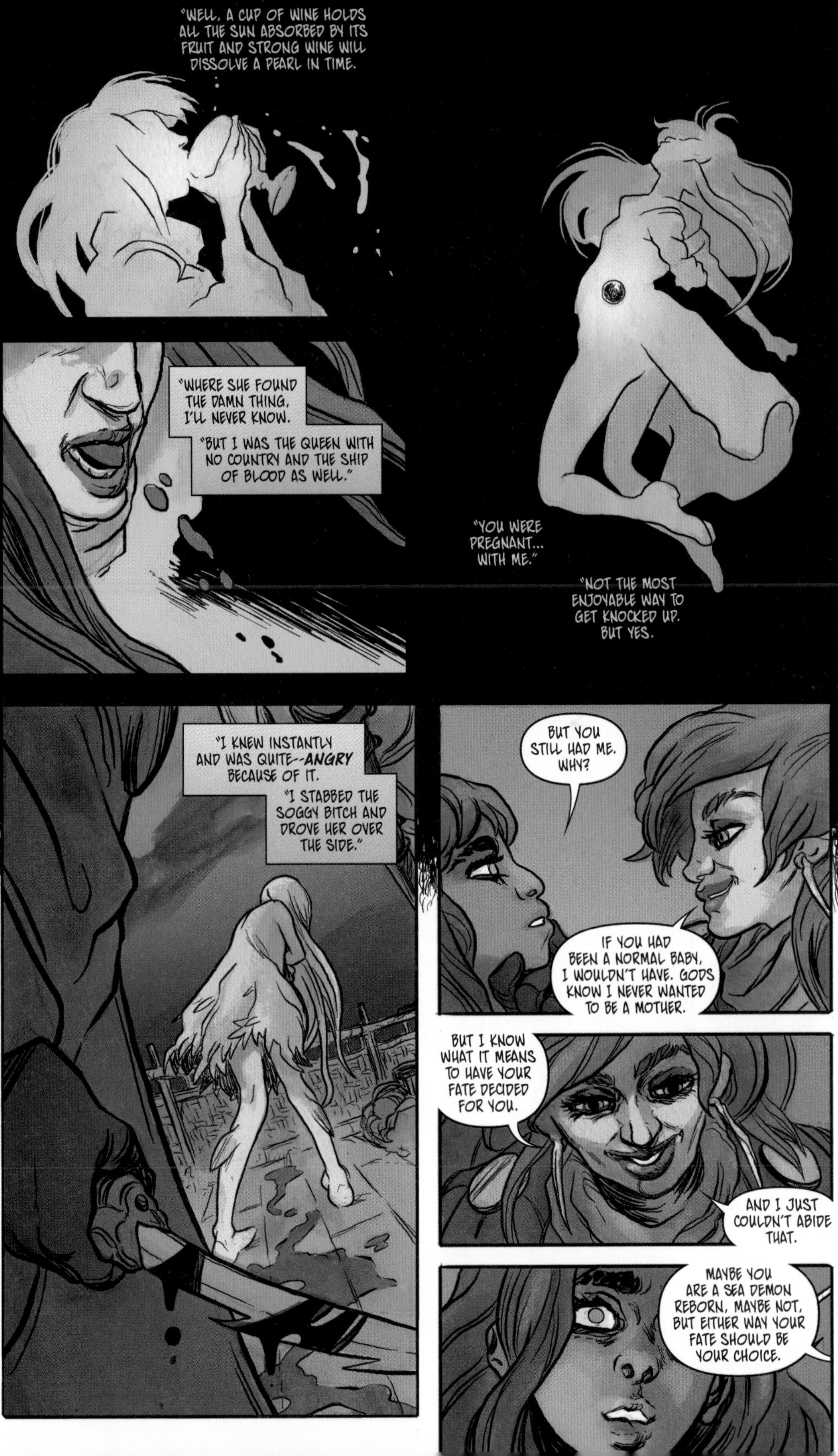
"WELL, A CUP OF WINE HOLDS ALL THE SUN ABSORBED BY ITS FRUIT AND STRONG WINE WILL DISSOLVE A PEARL IN TIME.
"WHERE SHE FOUND THE DAMN THING, I'LL NEVER KNOW.
"BUT I WAS THE QUEEN WITH NO COUNTRY AND THE SHIP OF BLOOD AS WELL."
"YOU WERE PREGNANT... WITH ME."
"NOT THE MOST ENJOYABLE WAY TO GET KNOCKED UP. BUT YES.
"I KNEW INSTANTLY AND WAS QUITE--ANGRY BECAUSE OF IT.
"I STABBED THE SOGGY BITCH AND DROVE HER OVER THE SIDE."
BUT YOU STILL HAD ME. WHY?
IF YOU HAD BEEN A NORMAL BABY, I WOULDN'T HAVE. GODS KNOW I NEVER WANTED TO BE A MOTHER.
BUT I KNOW WHAT IT MEANS TO HAVE YOUR FATE DECIDED FOR YOU.
AND I JUST COULDN'T ABIDE THAT.
MAYBE YOU ARE A SEA DEMON REBORN, MAYBE NOT, BUT EITHER WAY YOUR FATE SHOULD BE YOUR CHOICE.

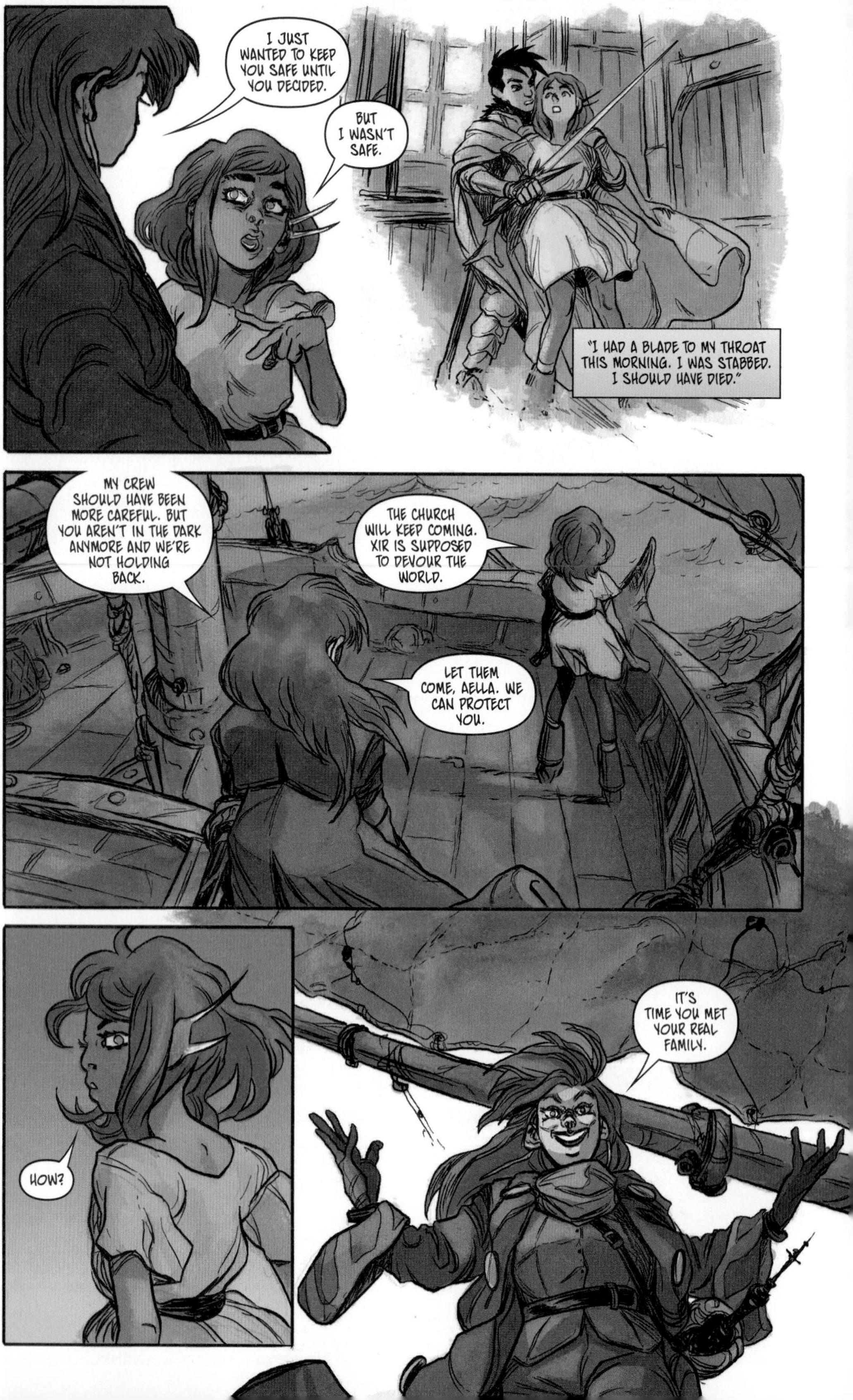
I JUST WANTED TO KEEP YOU SAFE UNTIL YOU DECIDED.
BUT I WASN'T SAFE.
"I HAD A BLADE TO MY THROAT THIS MORNING. I WAS STABBED. I SHOULD HAVE DIED."
MY CREW SHOULD HAVE BEEN MORE CAREFUL. BUT YOU AREN'T IN THE DARK ANYMORE AND WE'RE NOT HOLDING BACK.
THE CHURCH WILL KEEP COMING. XIR IS SUPPOSED TO DEVOUR THE WORLD.
LET THEM COME, AELLA. WE CAN PROTECT YOU.
HOW?
IT'S TIME YOU MET YOUR REAL FAMILY.

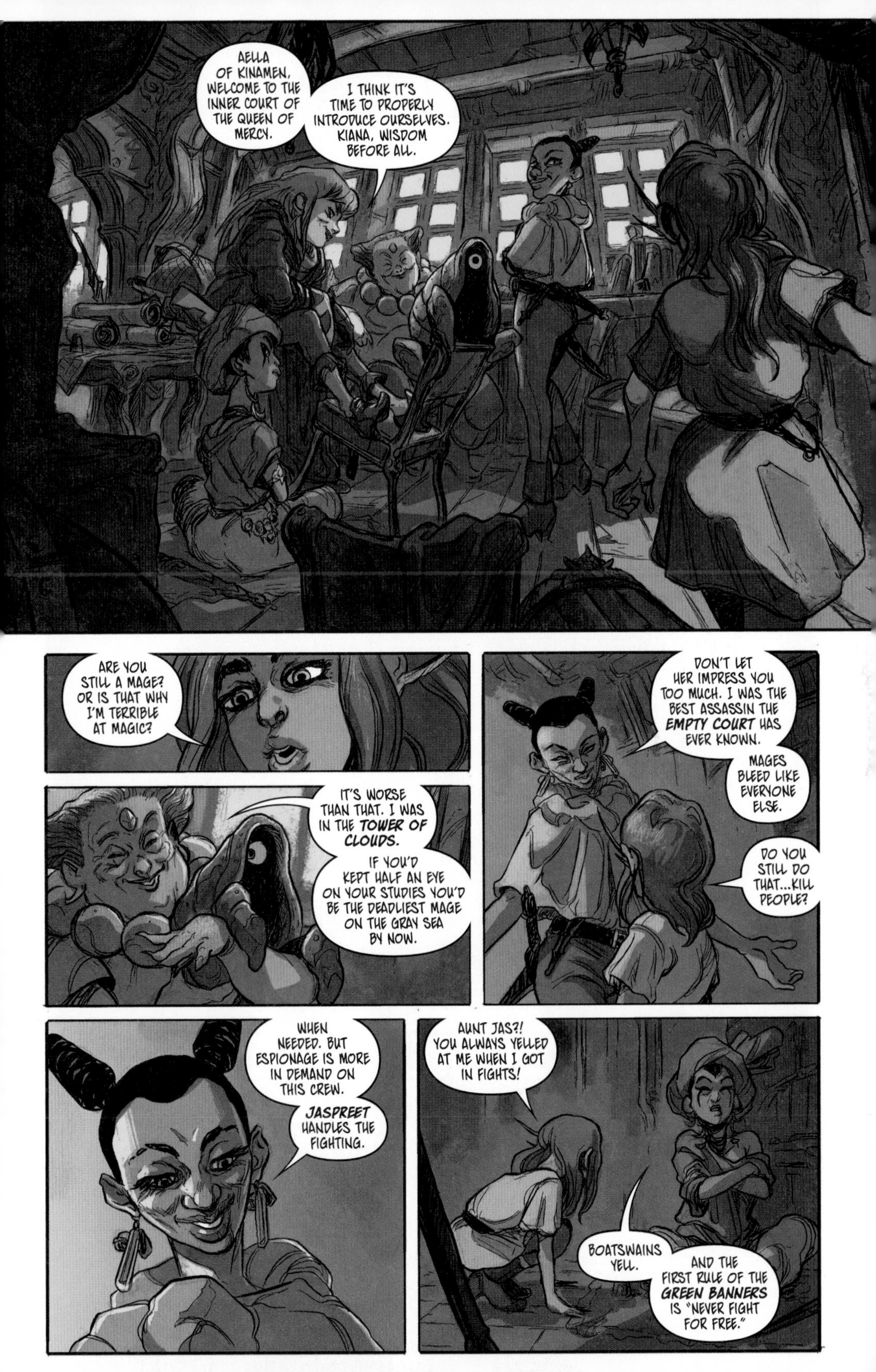
AELLA OF KINAMEN, WELCOME TO THE INNER COURT OF THE QUEEN OF MERCY.
I THINK IT'S TIME TO PROPERLY INTRODUCE OURSELVES. KIANA, WISDOM BEFORE ALL.
ARE YOU STILL A MAGE? OR IS THAT WHY I'M TERRIBLE AT MAGIC?
IT'S WORSE THAN THAT. I WAS IN THE **TOWER OF CLOUDS.**
IF YOU'D KEPT HALF AN EYE ON YOUR STUDIES YOU'D BE THE DEADLIEST MAGE ON THE GRAY SEA BY NOW.
DON'T LET HER IMPRESS YOU TOO MUCH. I WAS THE BEST ASSASSIN THE **EMPTY COURT** HAS EVER KNOWN.
MAGES BLEED LIKE EVERYONE ELSE.
DO YOU STILL DO THAT...KILL PEOPLE?
WHEN NEEDED. BUT ESPIONAGE IS MORE IN DEMAND ON THIS CREW.
JASPREET HANDLES THE FIGHTING.
AUNT JAS?! YOU ALWAYS YELLED AT ME WHEN I GOT IN FIGHTS!
BOATSWAINS YELL.
AND THE FIRST RULE OF THE **GREEN BANNERS** IS "NEVER FIGHT FOR FREE."

THE QUEEN OF MERCY.

THE TOWER OF CLOUDS.

THE EMPTY COURT.

THE GREEN BANNERS.

IT'S LIKE FINDING OUT YOU GREW UP WITH A NEST OF RAZOR SNAKES BENEATH YOUR BED.

THE SHIPS THAT SAIL WITH A TOWER MAGE CAN DECIDE FOR THEMSELVES WHAT THE WEATHER WILL BE

WELL, THAT'S THE POINT. NO ONE KNOWS HOW MANY SPIES THE EMPTY COURT HAS. NO ONE'S EVER EVEN SEEN ANYONE ENTER THE BUILDING.

YOU DON'T NEED AN ARMY WHEN THE EMPTY IS THERE. IT'S HARD TO LEAD MEN WHEN THEIR LEADERS GET THEIR THROATS SLIT IN THEIR BEDS.

...ONLY PAID FOR THREE DAYS SO THE GREENS WALKED OFF RIGHT AT SUNSET, IN THE MIDDLE OF BATTLE.

I FOUGHT A TOWER MAGE ONCE, JUST ONCE. HE RINGED THE ENTIRE DECK WITH FLAME. WE COULDN'T EVEN ABANDON SHIP.

ANY LAW-ABIDING SAILOR PAYS THE KING'S TAX ON LAND AND THE QUEEN'S ON THE SEA.

THE EMPTY COURT HAS EYES WATCHING, EARS LISTENING, AND KNIVES AT THE READY.

THE GREENS FIGHT LIKE DEVILS, DRINK LIKE DEVILS, AND COST YOU MORE THAN ESCAPING HELL ITSELF.

THE SAFEST PLACE IN THE WORLD IS IN THE MIDST OF THE GREEN BANNERS. ASSUMING YOU'RE WANTED THERE.

UNCLE GARRET. ARE YOU A DRAGON OR SOMETHING?

NOPE. JUST THE BEST CARPENTER NONE OF THIS LOT WANTED TO FIGHT OVER.

OH, HUSBAND.

ONLY BECAUSE I SAW YOU FIRST.

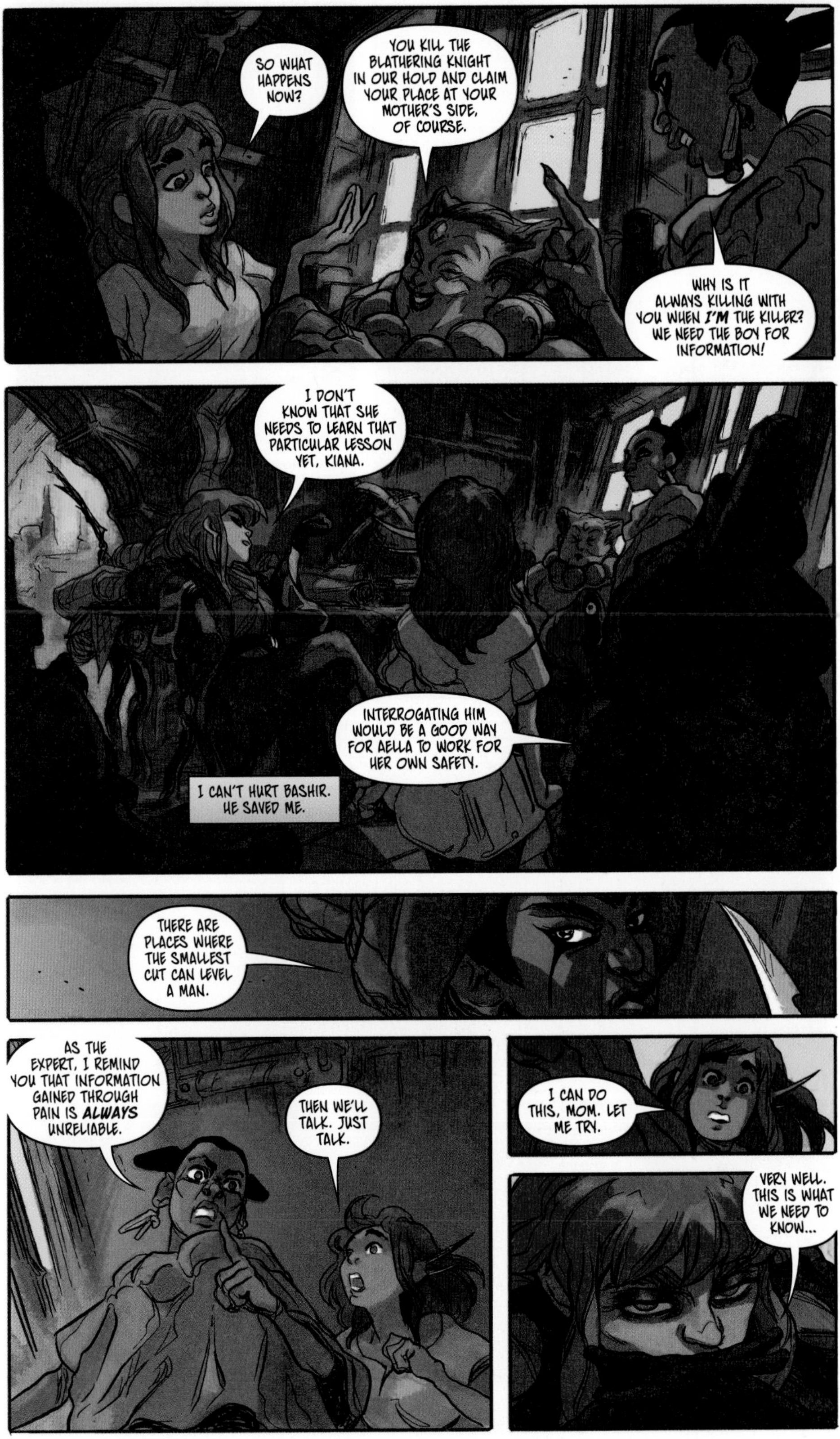
SO WHAT HAPPENS NOW?
YOU KILL THE BLATHERING KNIGHT IN OUR HOLD AND CLAIM YOUR PLACE AT YOUR MOTHER'S SIDE, OF COURSE.
WHY IS IT ALWAYS KILLING WITH YOU WHEN *I'M* THE KILLER? WE NEED THE BOY FOR INFORMATION!
I DON'T KNOW THAT SHE NEEDS TO LEARN THAT PARTICULAR LESSON YET, KIANA.
INTERROGATING HIM WOULD BE A GOOD WAY FOR AELLA TO WORK FOR HER OWN SAFETY.
I CAN'T HURT BASHIR. HE SAVED ME.
THERE ARE PLACES WHERE THE SMALLEST CUT CAN LEVEL A MAN.
AS THE EXPERT, I REMIND YOU THAT INFORMATION GAINED THROUGH PAIN IS **ALWAYS** UNRELIABLE.
THEN WE'LL TALK. JUST TALK.
I CAN DO THIS, MOM. LET ME TRY.
VERY WELL. THIS IS WHAT WE NEED TO KNOW...

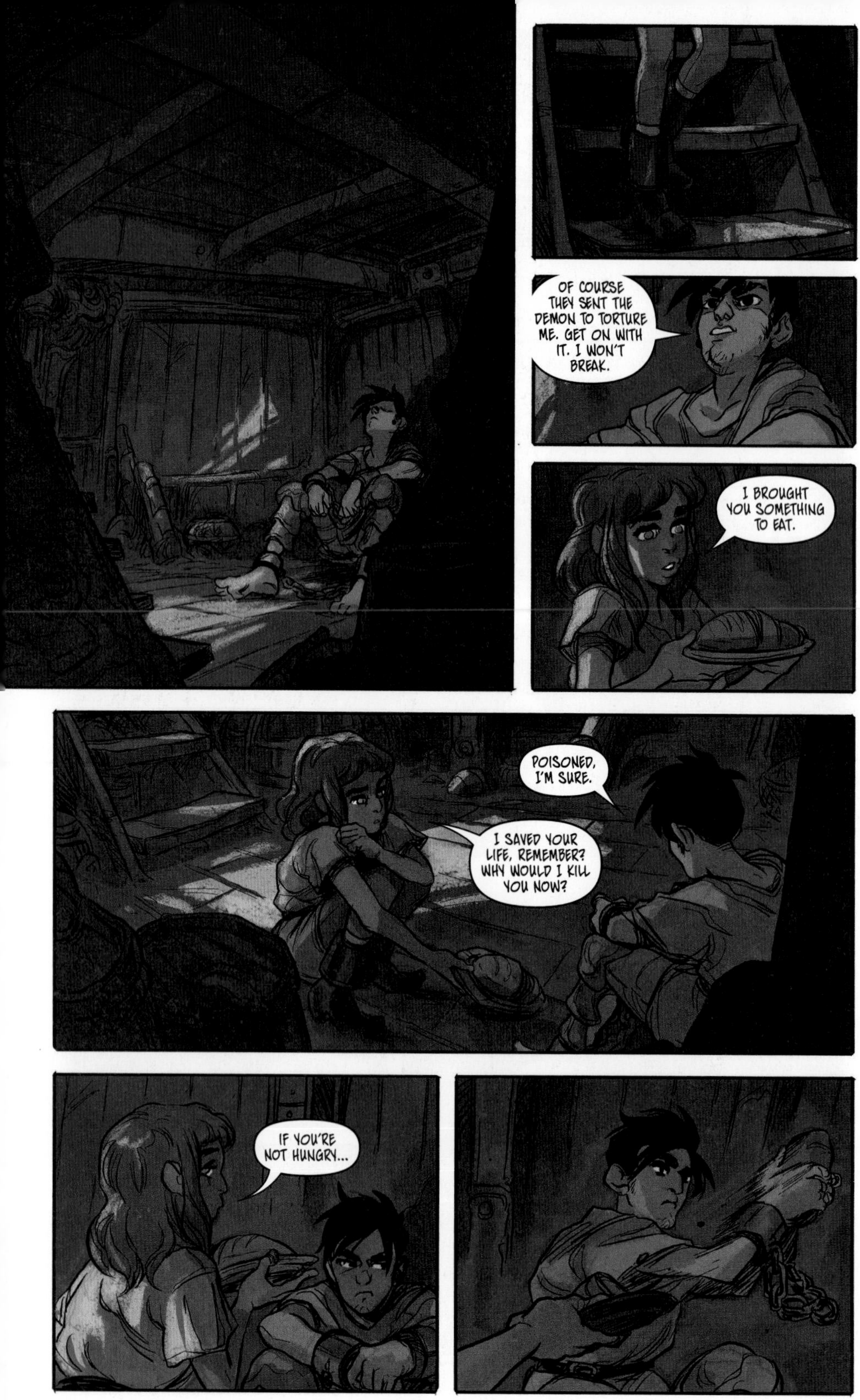
OF COURSE THEY SENT THE DEMON TO TORTURE ME. GET ON WITH IT. I WON'T BREAK.
I BROUGHT YOU SOMETHING TO EAT.
POISONED, I'M SURE.
I SAVED YOUR LIFE, REMEMBER? WHY WOULD I KILL YOU NOW?
IF YOU'RE NOT HUNGRY...

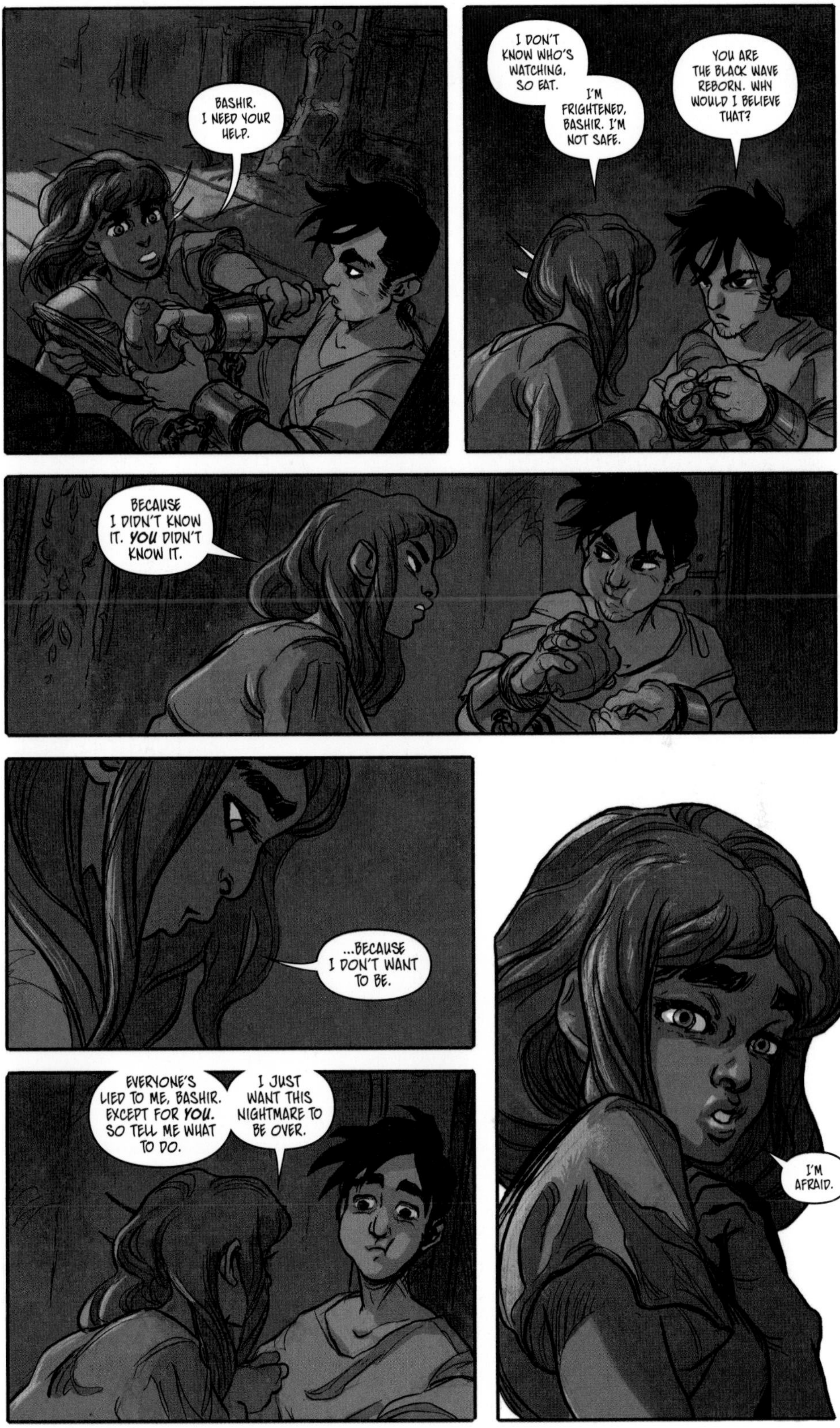
BASHIR. I NEED YOUR HELP.
I DON'T KNOW WHO'S WATCHING, SO EAT.
I'M FRIGHTENED, BASHIR. I'M NOT SAFE.
YOU ARE THE BLACK WAVE REBORN. WHY WOULD I BELIEVE THAT?
BECAUSE I DIDN'T KNOW IT. ***YOU*** DIDN'T KNOW IT.
...BECAUSE I DON'T WANT TO BE.
EVERYONE'S LIED TO ME, BASHIR. EXCEPT FOR ***YOU***. SO TELL ME WHAT TO DO.
I JUST WANT THIS NIGHTMARE TO BE OVER.
I'M AFRAID.

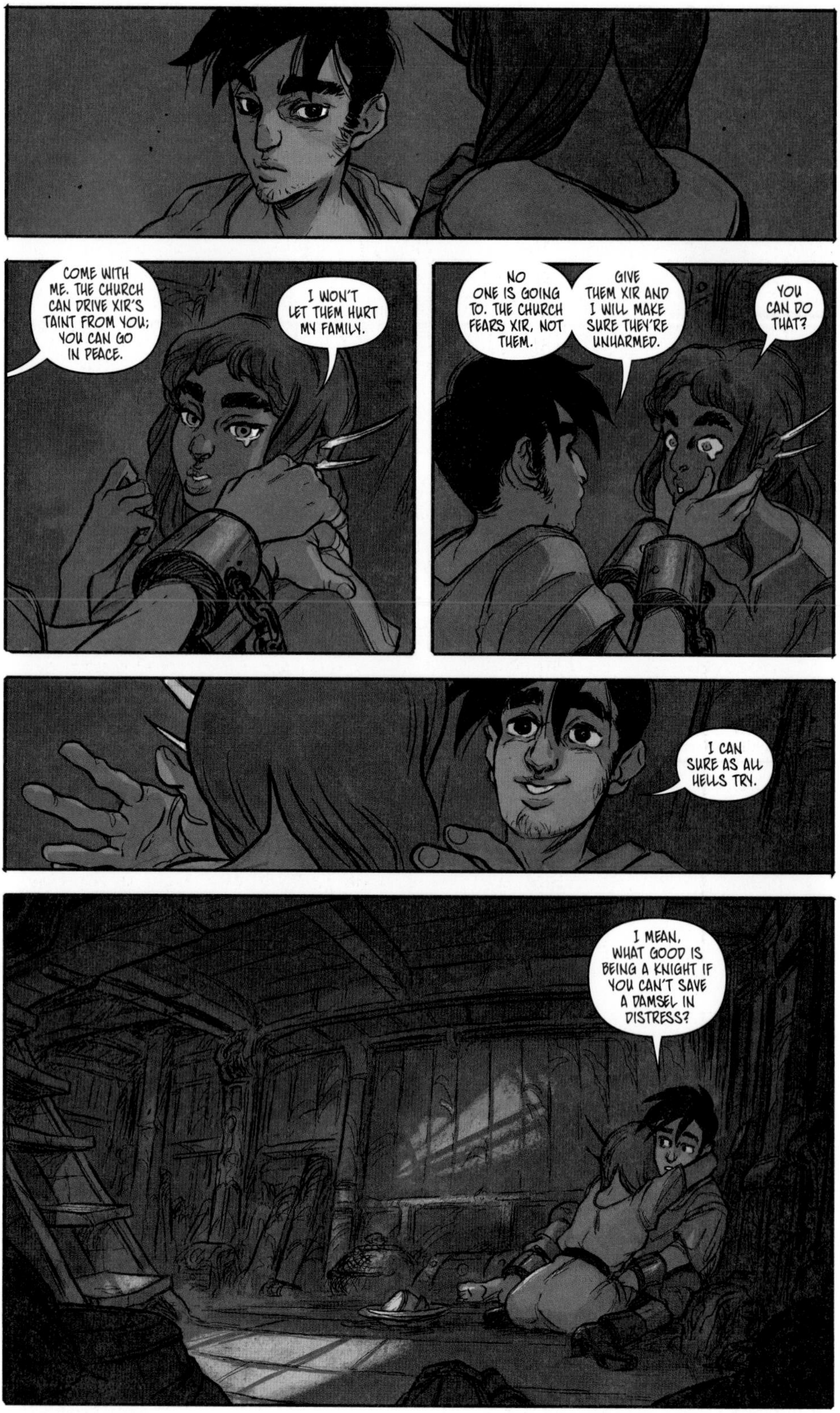
COME WITH ME. THE CHURCH CAN DRIVE XIR'S TAINT FROM YOU; YOU CAN GO IN PEACE.
I WON'T LET THEM HURT MY FAMILY.
NO ONE IS GOING TO. THE CHURCH FEARS XIR, NOT THEM.
GIVE THEM XIR AND I WILL MAKE SURE THEY'RE UNHARMED.
YOU CAN DO THAT?
I CAN SURE AS ALL HELLS TRY.
I MEAN, WHAT GOOD IS BEING A KNIGHT IF YOU CAN'T SAVE A DAMSEL IN DISTRESS?

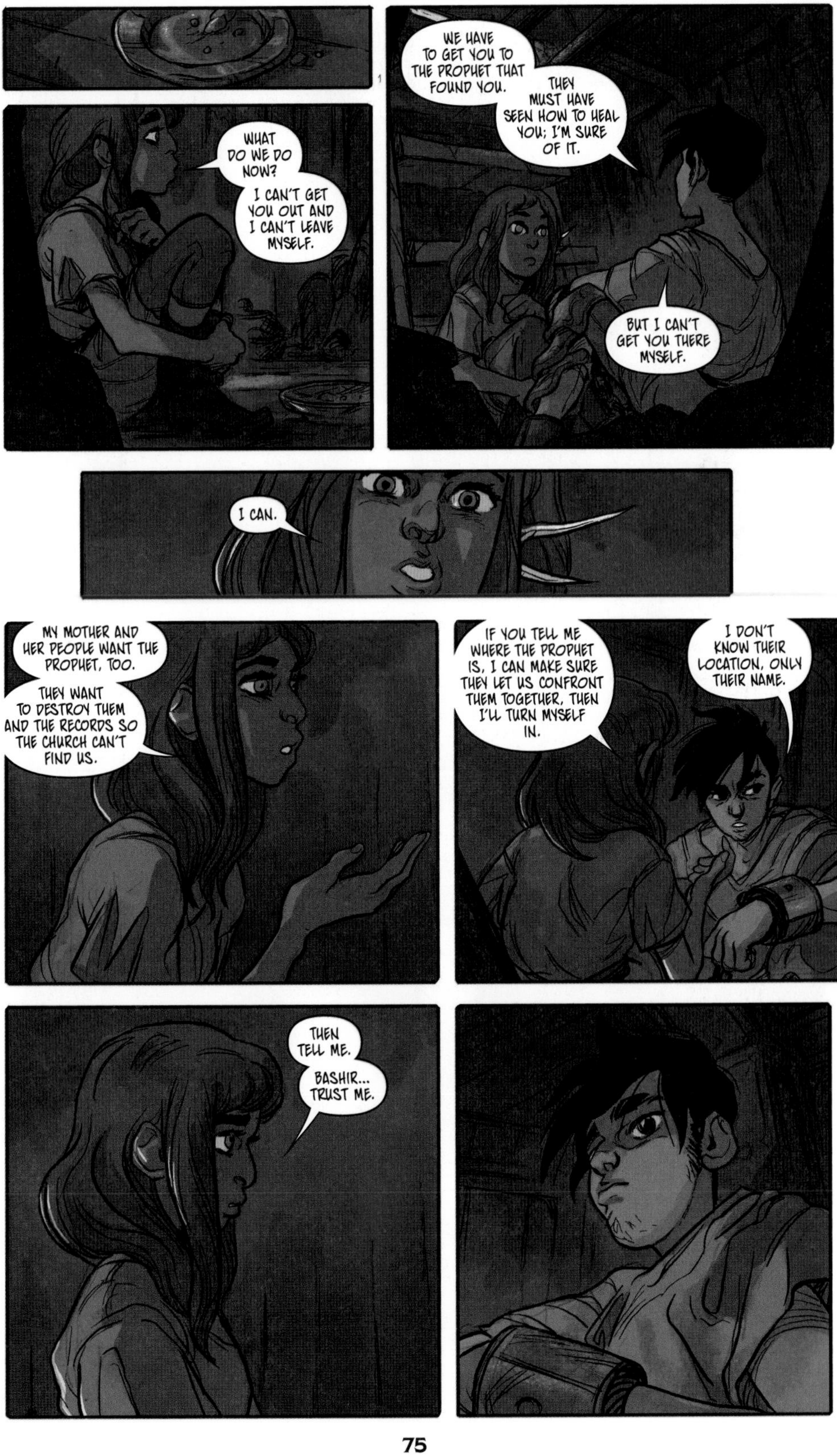
WHAT DO WE DO NOW?
I CAN'T GET YOU OUT AND I CAN'T LEAVE MYSELF.
WE HAVE TO GET YOU TO THE PROPHET THAT FOUND YOU.
THEY MUST HAVE SEEN HOW TO HEAL YOU; I'M SURE OF IT.
BUT I CAN'T GET YOU THERE MYSELF.
I CAN.
MY MOTHER AND HER PEOPLE WANT THE PROPHET, TOO.
THEY WANT TO DESTROY THEM AND THE RECORDS SO THE CHURCH CAN'T FIND US.
IF YOU TELL ME WHERE THE PROPHET IS, I CAN MAKE SURE THEY LET US CONFRONT THEM TOGETHER, THEN I'LL TURN MYSELF IN.
I DON'T KNOW THEIR LOCATION, ONLY THEIR NAME.
THEN TELL ME.
BASHIR... TRUST ME.

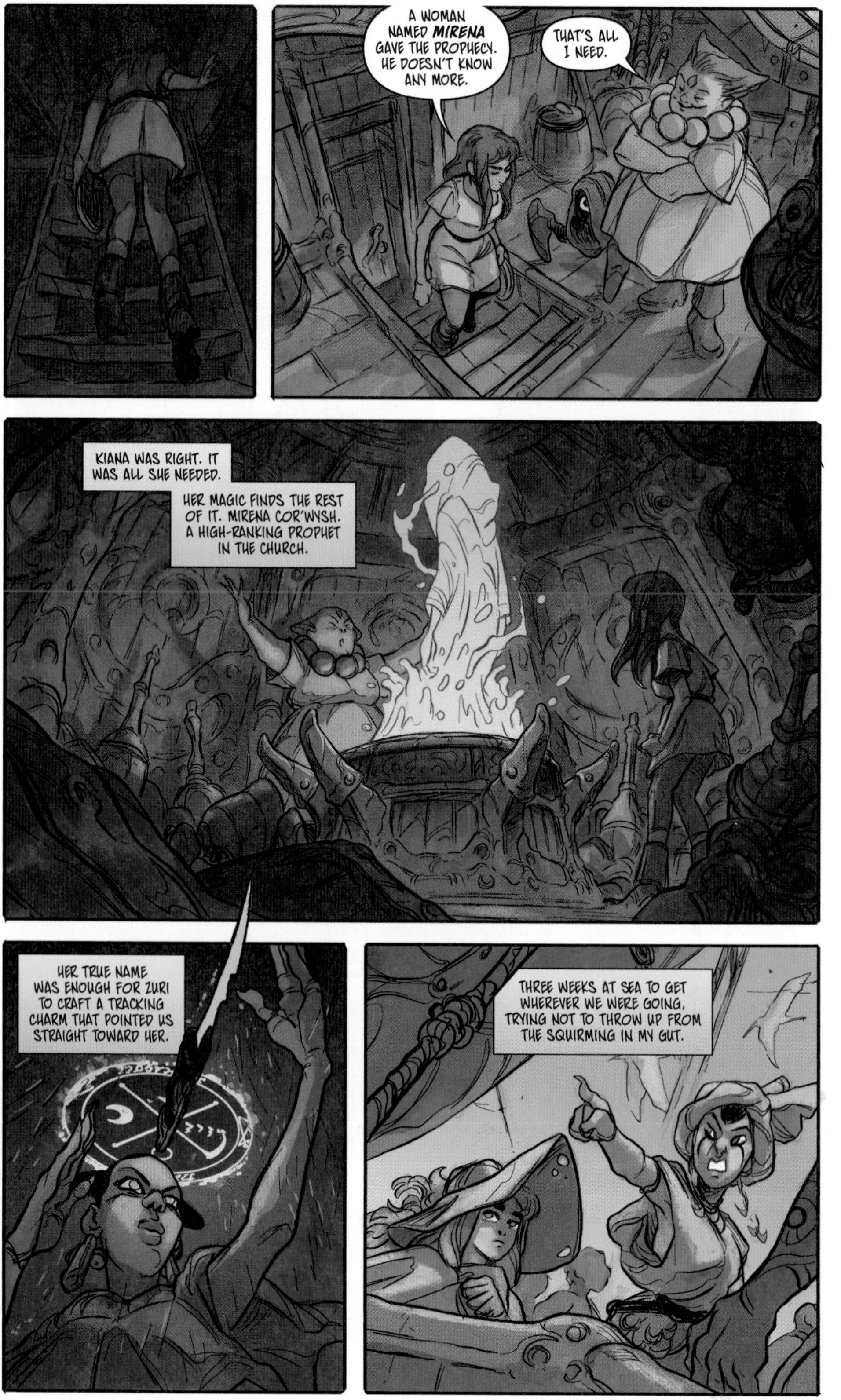
A WOMAN NAMED MIRENA GAVE THE PROPHECY. HE DOESN'T KNOW ANY MORE.
THAT'S ALL I NEED.
KIANA WAS RIGHT. IT WAS ALL SHE NEEDED.
HER MAGIC FINDS THE REST OF IT. MIRENA COR'WYSH. A HIGH-RANKING PROPHET IN THE CHURCH.
HER TRUE NAME WAS ENOUGH FOR ZURI TO CRAFT A TRACKING CHARM THAT POINTED US STRAIGHT TOWARD HER.
THREE WEEKS AT SEA TO GET WHEREVER WE WERE GOING, TRYING NOT TO THROW UP FROM THE SQUIRMING IN MY GUT.

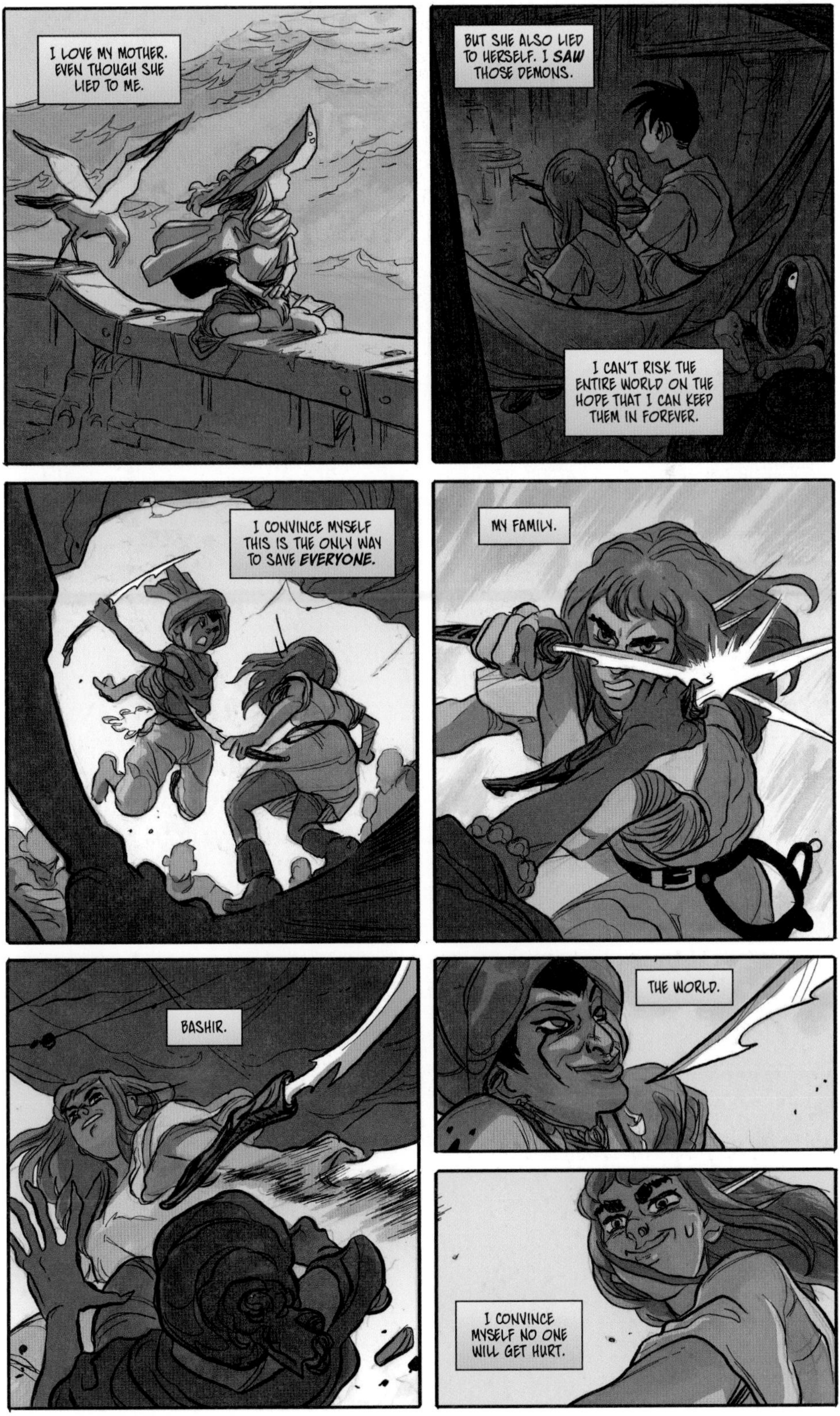
I LOVE MY MOTHER. EVEN THOUGH SHE LIED TO ME.
BUT SHE ALSO LIED TO HERSELF. I SAW THOSE DEMONS.
I CAN'T RISK THE ENTIRE WORLD ON THE HOPE THAT I CAN KEEP THEM IN FOREVER.
I CONVINCE MYSELF THIS IS THE ONLY WAY TO SAVE EVERYONE.
MY FAMILY.
BASHIR.
THE WORLD.
I CONVINCE MYSELF NO ONE WILL GET HURT.

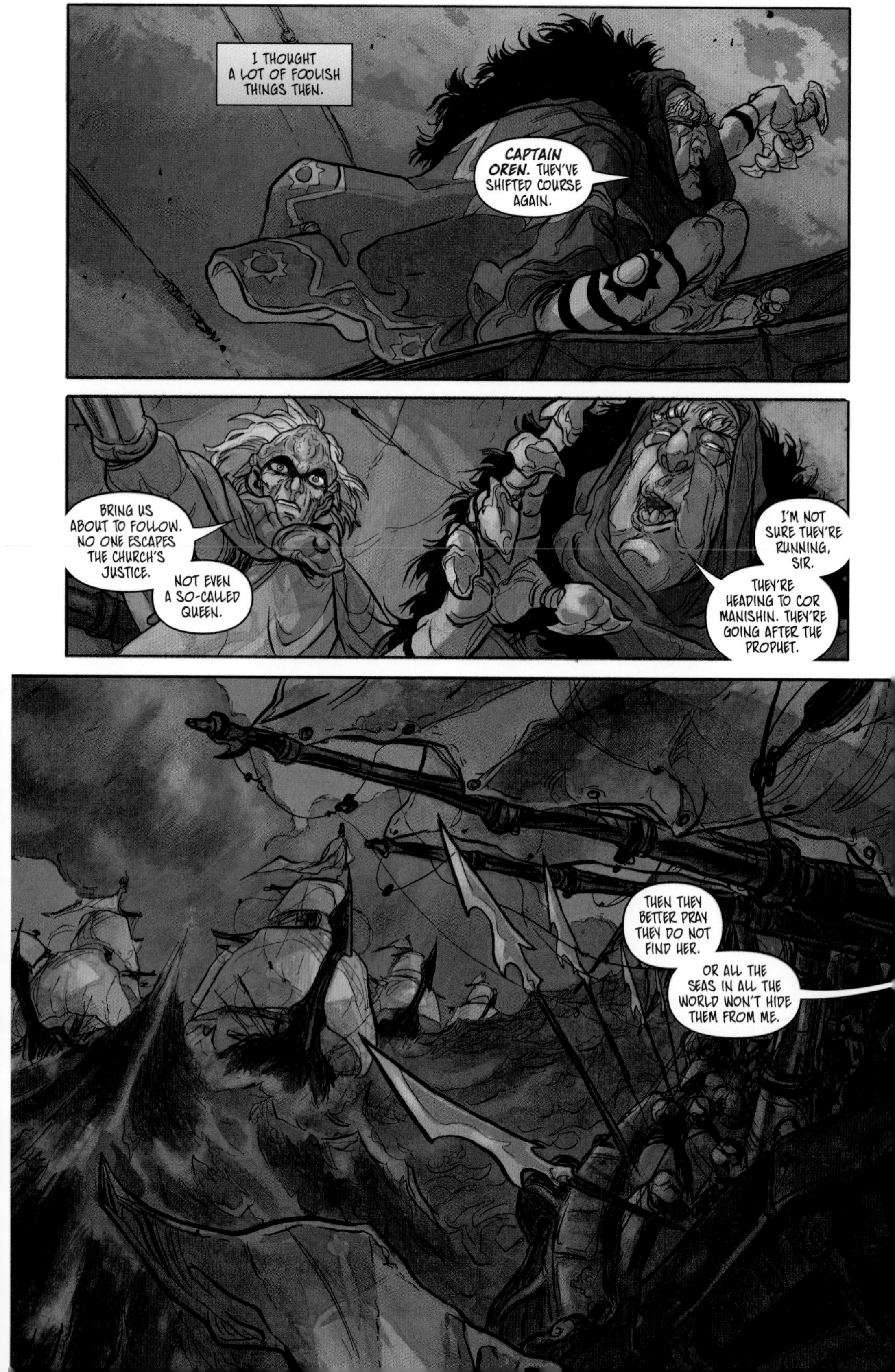
I THOUGHT A LOT OF FOOLISH THINGS THEN.
CAPTAIN OREN. THEY'VE SHIFTED COURSE AGAIN.
BRING US ABOUT TO FOLLOW. NO ONE ESCAPES THE CHURCH'S JUSTICE.
NOT EVEN A SO-CALLED QUEEN.
I'M NOT SURE THEY'RE RUNNING, SIR.
THEY'RE HEADING TO COR MANISHIN. THEY'RE GOING AFTER THE PROPHET.
THEN THEY BETTER PRAY THEY DO NOT FIND HER.
OR ALL THE SEAS IN ALL THE WORLD WON'T HIDE THEM FROM ME.

Chapter Four

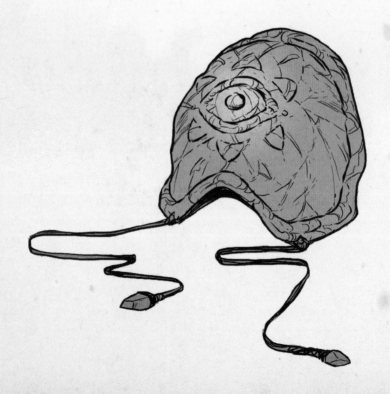

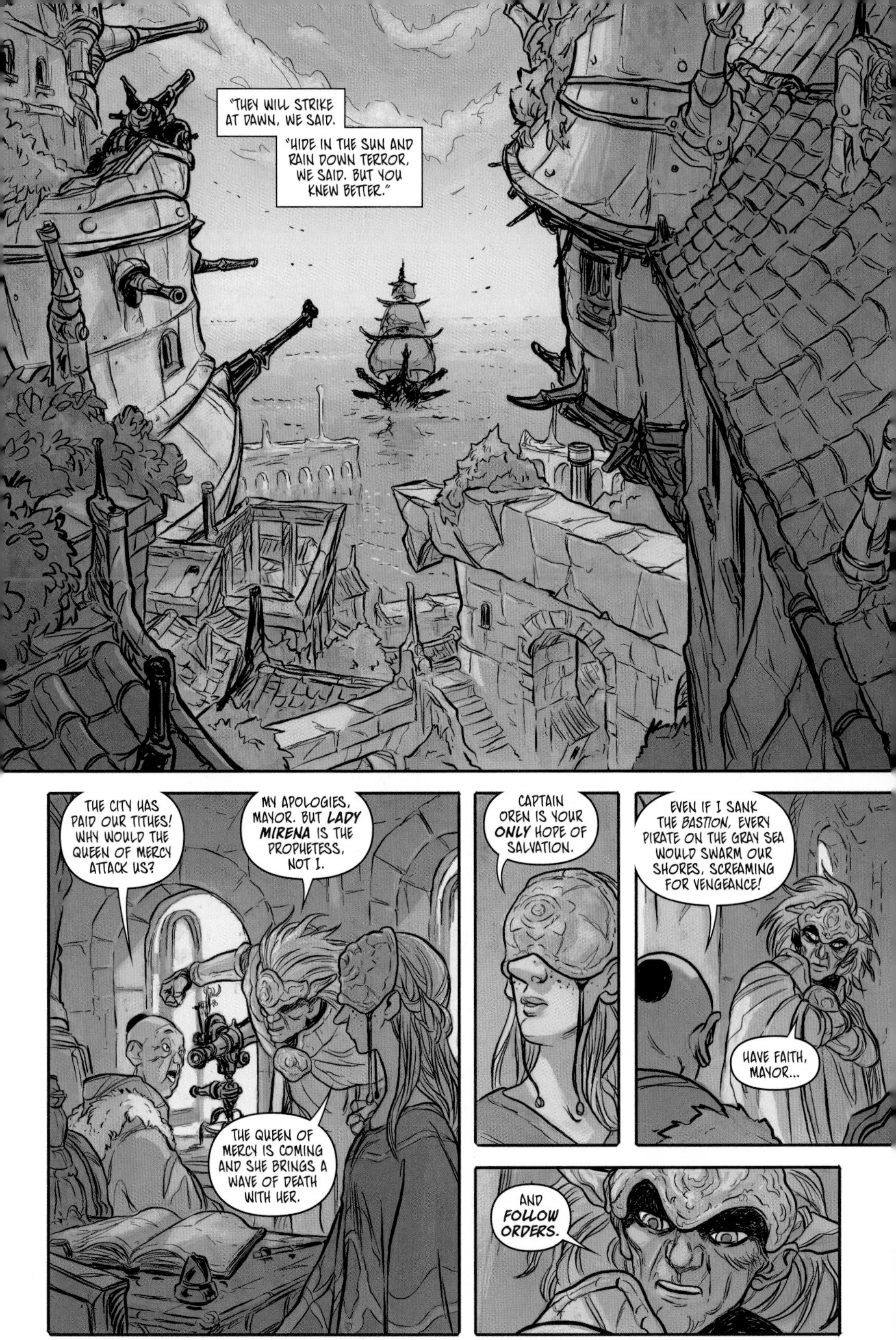
"THEY WILL STRIKE AT DAWN, WE SAID.
"HIDE IN THE SUN AND RAIN DOWN TERROR, WE SAID. BUT YOU KNEW BETTER."
THE CITY HAS PAID OUR TITHES! WHY WOULD THE QUEEN OF MERCY ATTACK US?
MY APOLOGIES, MAYOR. BUT **LADY MIRENA** IS THE PROPHETESS, NOT I.
THE QUEEN OF MERCY IS COMING AND SHE BRINGS A WAVE OF DEATH WITH HER.
CAPTAIN OREN IS YOUR **ONLY** HOPE OF SALVATION.
EVEN IF I SANK THE *BASTION*, EVERY PIRATE ON THE GRAY SEA WOULD SWARM OUR SHORES, SCREAMING FOR VENGEANCE!
HAVE FAITH, MAYOR...
AND **FOLLOW ORDERS.**

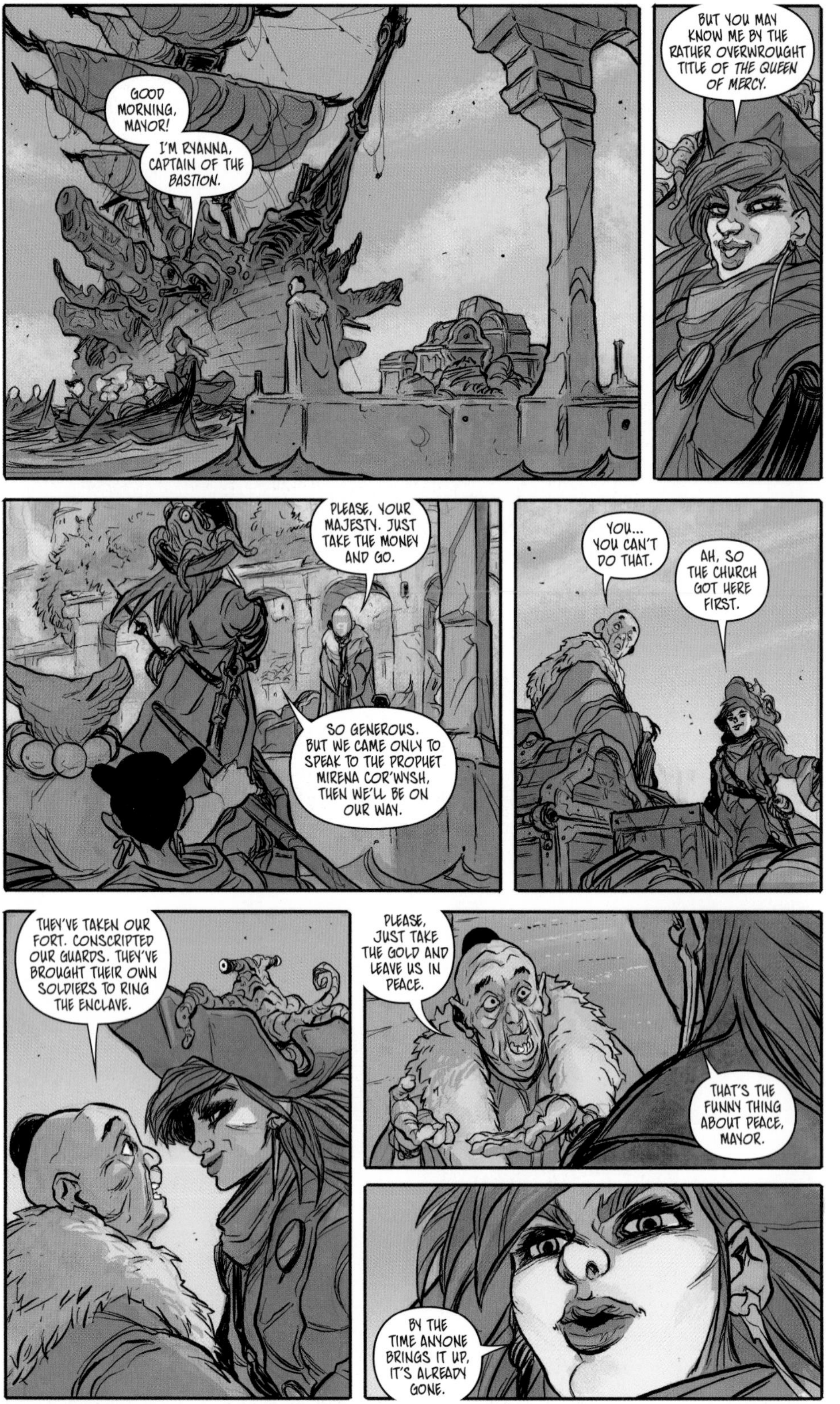
GOOD MORNING, MAYOR!
I'M RYANNA, CAPTAIN OF THE BASTION.
BUT YOU MAY KNOW ME BY THE RATHER OVERWROUGHT TITLE OF THE QUEEN OF MERCY.
PLEASE, YOUR MAJESTY. JUST TAKE THE MONEY AND GO.
SO GENEROUS. BUT WE CAME ONLY TO SPEAK TO THE PROPHET MIRENA COR'WYSH, THEN WE'LL BE ON OUR WAY.
YOU... YOU CAN'T DO THAT.
AH, SO THE CHURCH GOT HERE FIRST.
THEY'VE TAKEN OUR FORT. CONSCRIPTED OUR GUARDS. THEY'VE BROUGHT THEIR OWN SOLDIERS TO RING THE ENCLAVE.
PLEASE, JUST TAKE THE GOLD AND LEAVE US IN PEACE.
THAT'S THE FUNNY THING ABOUT PEACE, MAYOR.
BY THE TIME ANYONE BRINGS IT UP, IT'S ALREADY GONE.

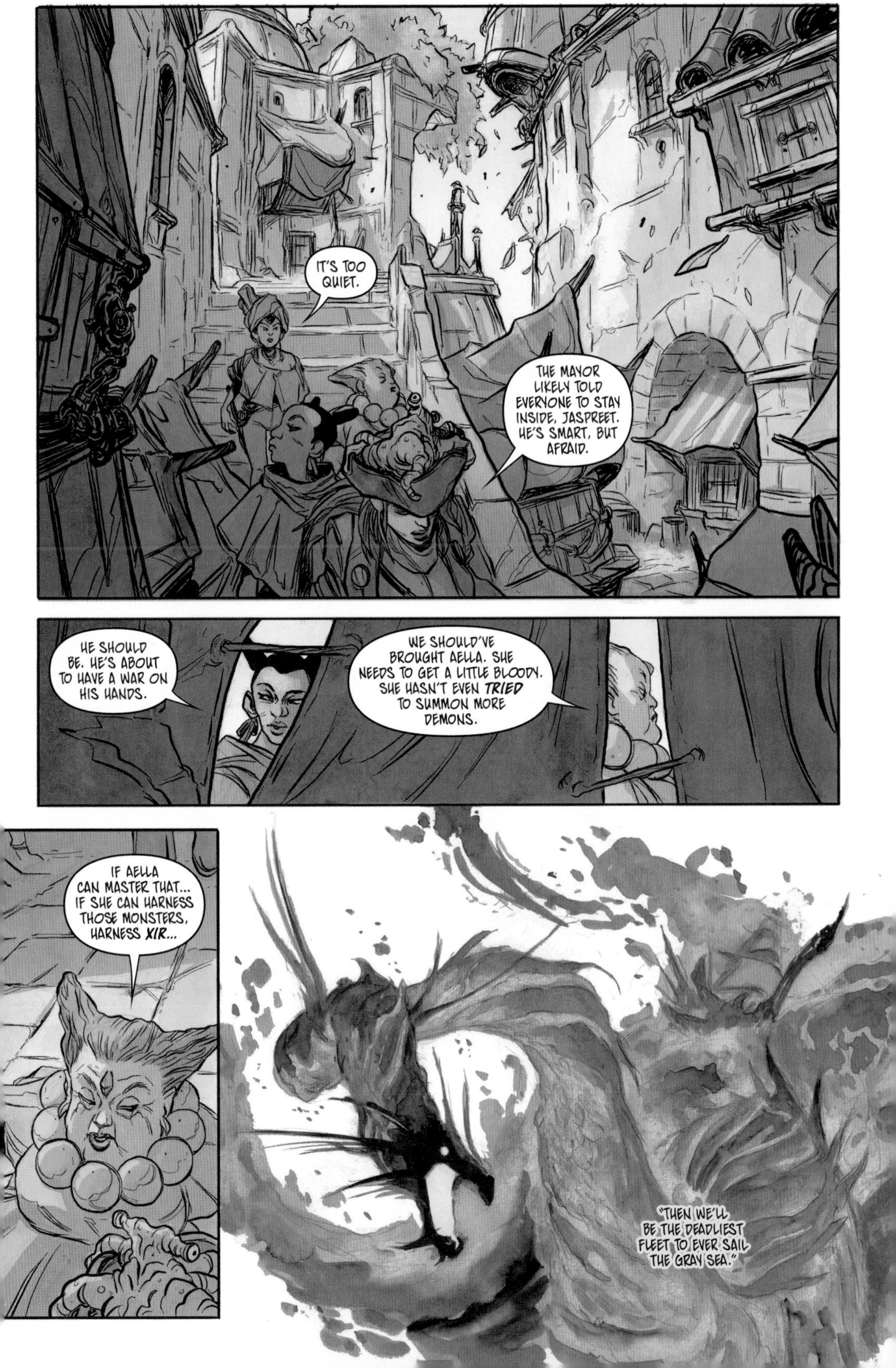
IT'S TOO QUIET.
THE MAYOR LIKELY TOLD EVERYONE TO STAY INSIDE, JASPREET. HE'S SMART, BUT AFRAID.
HE SHOULD BE. HE'S ABOUT TO HAVE A WAR ON HIS HANDS.
WE SHOULD'VE BROUGHT AELLA. SHE NEEDS TO GET A LITTLE BLOODY. SHE HASN'T EVEN TRIED TO SUMMON MORE DEMONS.
IF AELLA CAN MASTER THAT... IF SHE CAN HARNESS THOSE MONSTERS, HARNESS XIR...
"THEN WE'LL BE THE DEADLIEST FLEET TO EVER SAIL THE GRAY SEA."

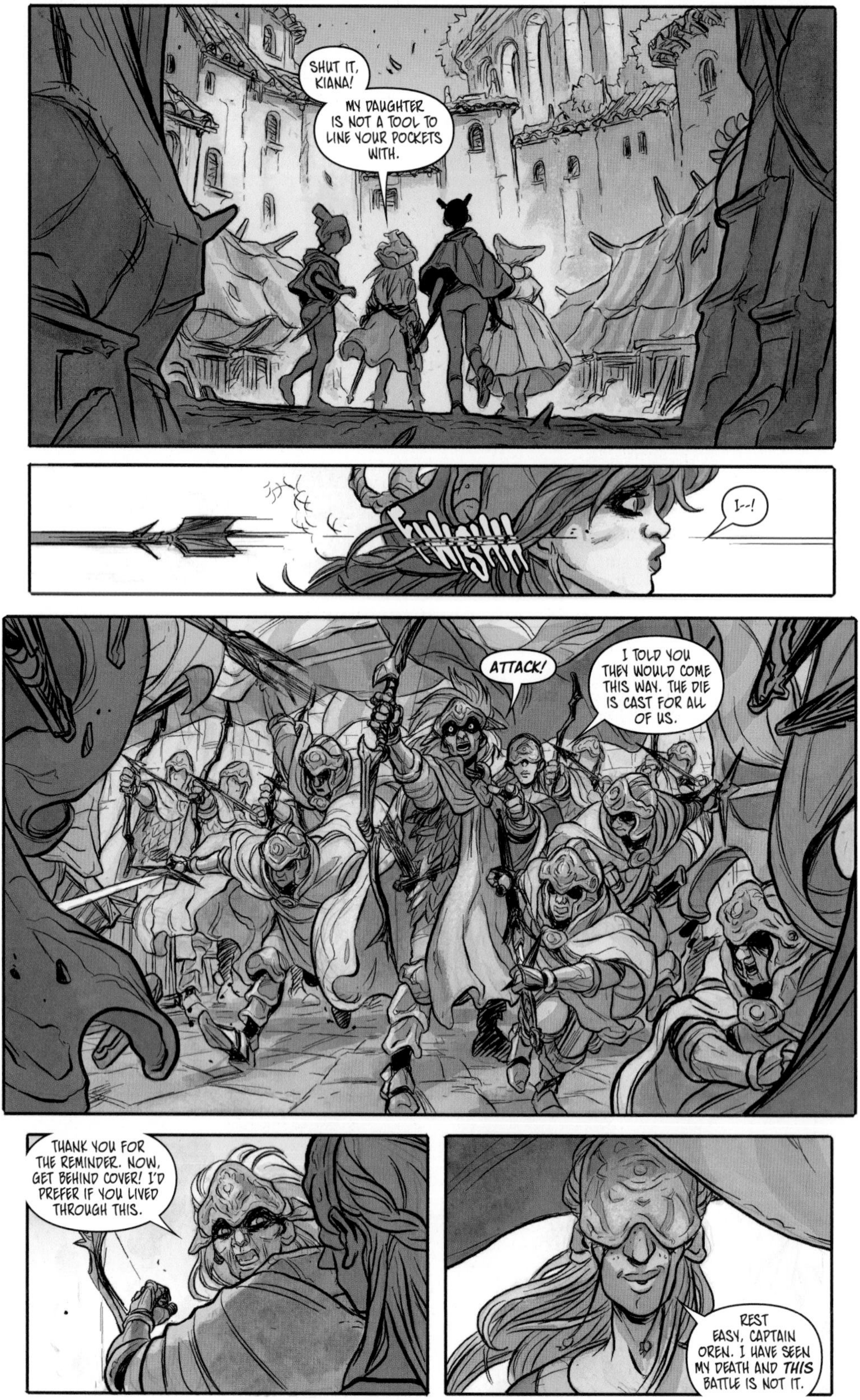
SHUT IT, KIANA!
MY DAUGHTER IS NOT A TOOL TO LINE YOUR POCKETS WITH.
I--!
ATTACK!
I TOLD YOU THEY WOULD COME THIS WAY. THE DIE IS CAST FOR ALL OF US.
THANK YOU FOR THE REMINDER. NOW, GET BEHIND COVER! I'D PREFER IF YOU LIVED THROUGH THIS.
REST EASY, CAPTAIN OREN. I HAVE SEEN MY DEATH AND *THIS* BATTLE IS NOT IT.

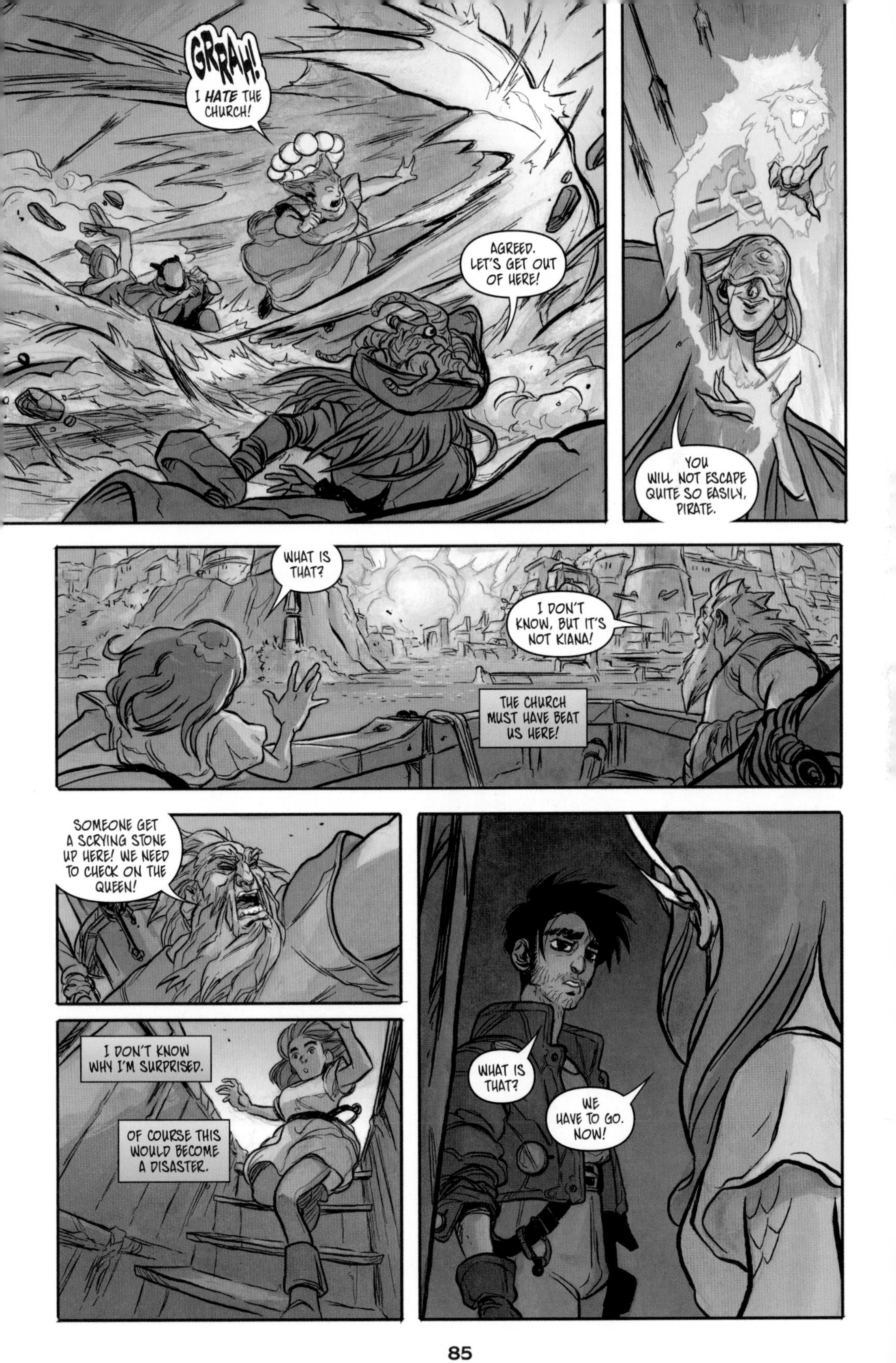
GRRAH!
I HATE THE CHURCH!
AGREED. LET'S GET OUT OF HERE!
YOU WILL NOT ESCAPE QUITE SO EASILY, PIRATE.
WHAT IS THAT?
I DON'T KNOW, BUT IT'S NOT KIANA!
THE CHURCH MUST HAVE BEAT US HERE!
SOMEONE GET A SCRYING STONE UP HERE! WE NEED TO CHECK ON THE QUEEN!
I DON'T KNOW WHY I'M SURPRISED.
OF COURSE THIS WOULD BECOME A DISASTER.
WHAT IS THAT?
WE HAVE TO GO. NOW!

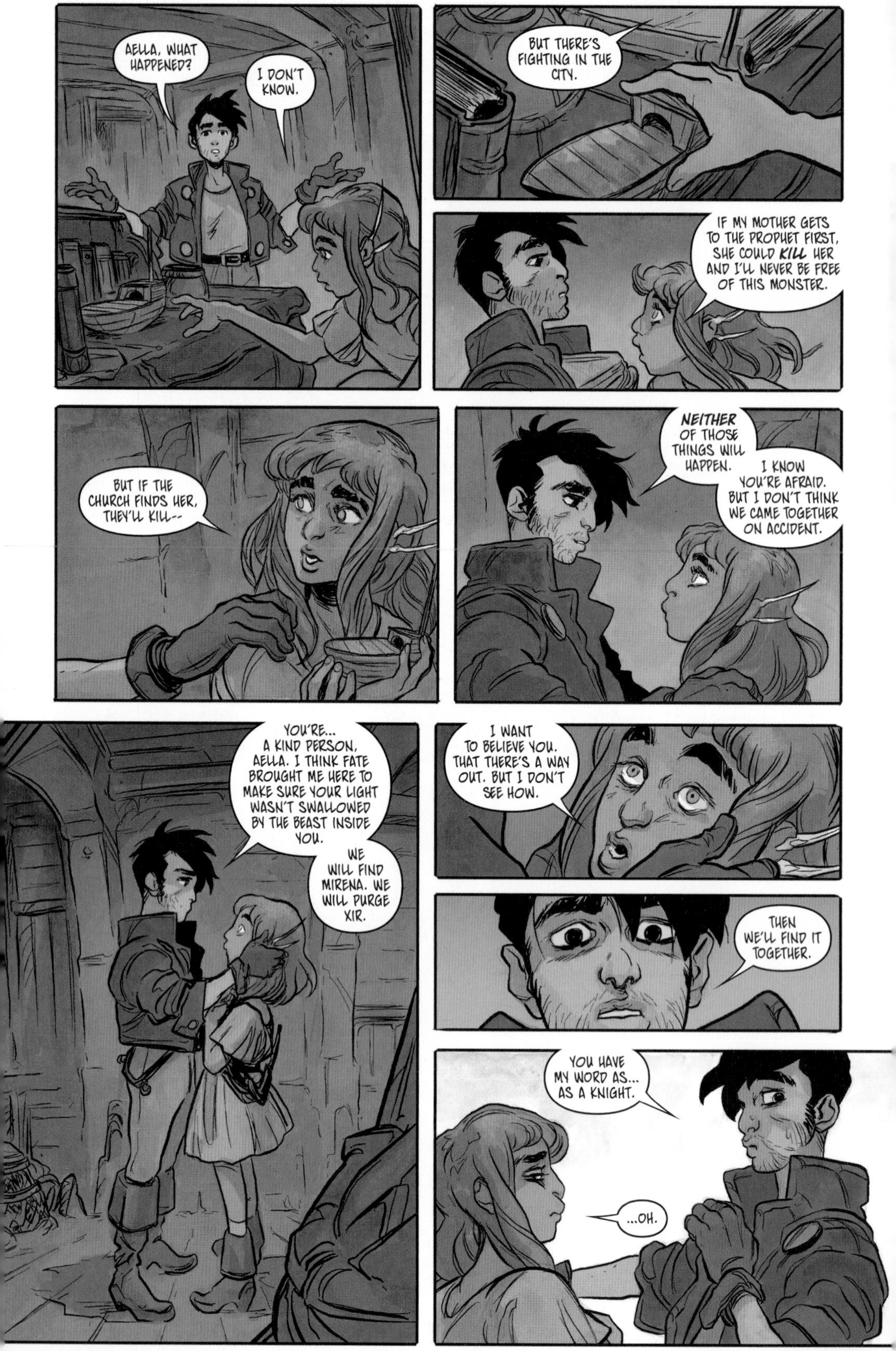
AELLA, WHAT HAPPENED?
I DON'T KNOW.
BUT THERE'S FIGHTING IN THE CITY.
IF MY MOTHER GETS TO THE PROPHET FIRST, SHE COULD KILL HER AND I'LL NEVER BE FREE OF THIS MONSTER.
BUT IF THE CHURCH FINDS HER, THEY'LL KILL--
NEITHER OF THOSE THINGS WILL HAPPEN.
I KNOW YOU'RE AFRAID. BUT I DON'T THINK WE CAME TOGETHER ON ACCIDENT.
YOU'RE... A KIND PERSON, AELLA. I THINK FATE BROUGHT ME HERE TO MAKE SURE YOUR LIGHT WASN'T SWALLOWED BY THE BEAST INSIDE YOU.
WE WILL FIND MIRENA. WE WILL PURGE XIR.
I WANT TO BELIEVE YOU. THAT THERE'S A WAY OUT. BUT I DON'T SEE HOW.
THEN WE'LL FIND IT TOGETHER.
YOU HAVE MY WORD AS... AS A KNIGHT.
...OH.

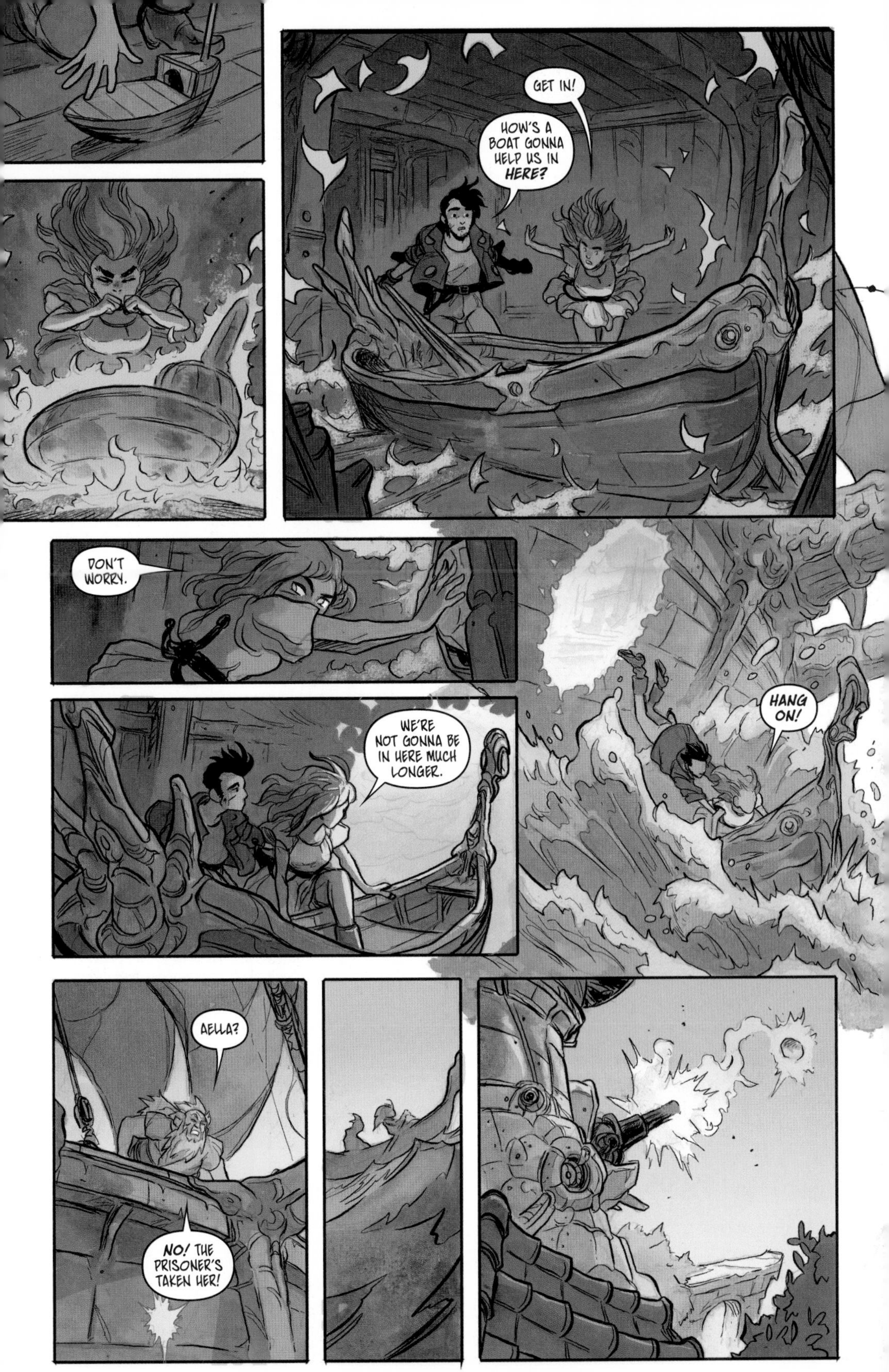
GET IN!
HOW'S A BOAT GONNA HELP US IN HERE?
DON'T WORRY.
WE'RE NOT GONNA BE IN HERE MUCH LONGER.
HANG ON!
AELLA?
NO! THE PRISONER'S TAKEN HER!

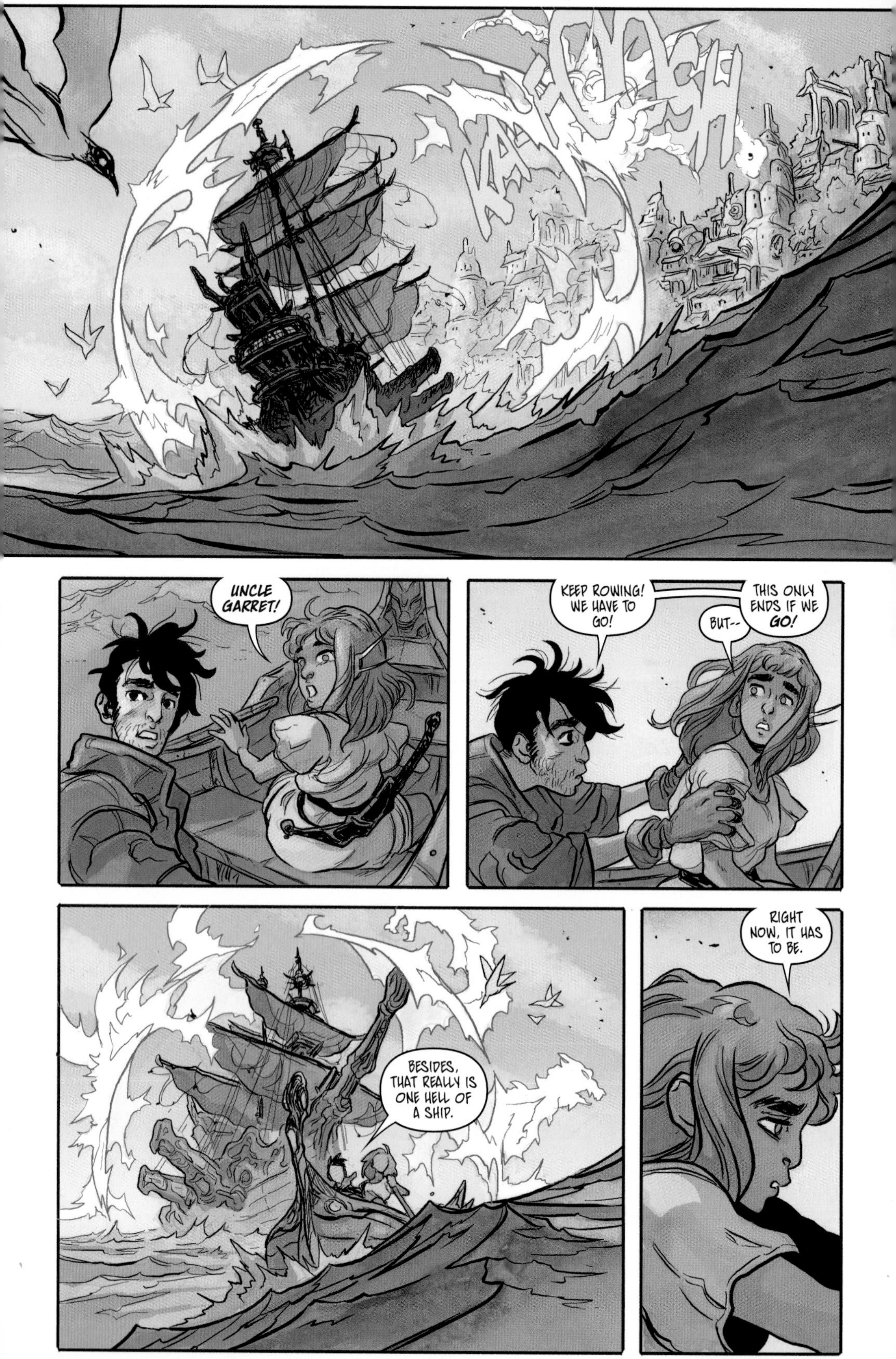
KA-CHOOSH
UNCLE GARRET!
KEEP ROWING! WE HAVE TO GO!
BUT--
THIS ONLY ENDS IF WE GO!
BESIDES, THAT REALLY IS ONE HELL OF A SHIP.
RIGHT NOW, IT HAS TO BE.

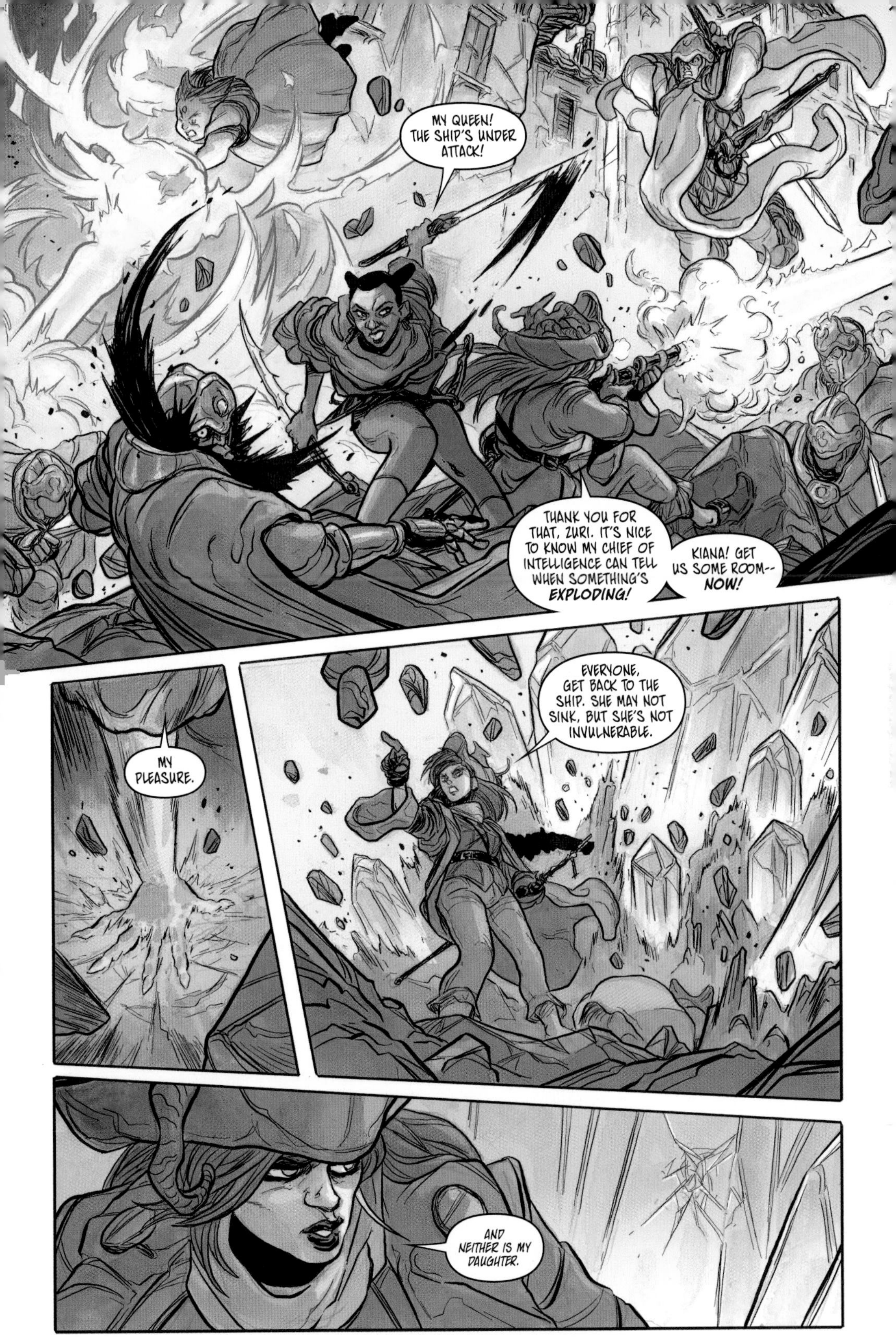
MY QUEEN! THE SHIP'S UNDER ATTACK!
THANK YOU FOR THAT, ZURI. IT'S NICE TO KNOW MY CHIEF OF INTELLIGENCE CAN TELL WHEN SOMETHING'S **EXPLODING!**
KIANA! GET US SOME ROOM-- **NOW!**
MY PLEASURE.
EVERYONE, GET BACK TO THE SHIP. SHE MAY NOT SINK, BUT SHE'S NOT INVULNERABLE.
AND NEITHER IS MY DAUGHTER.

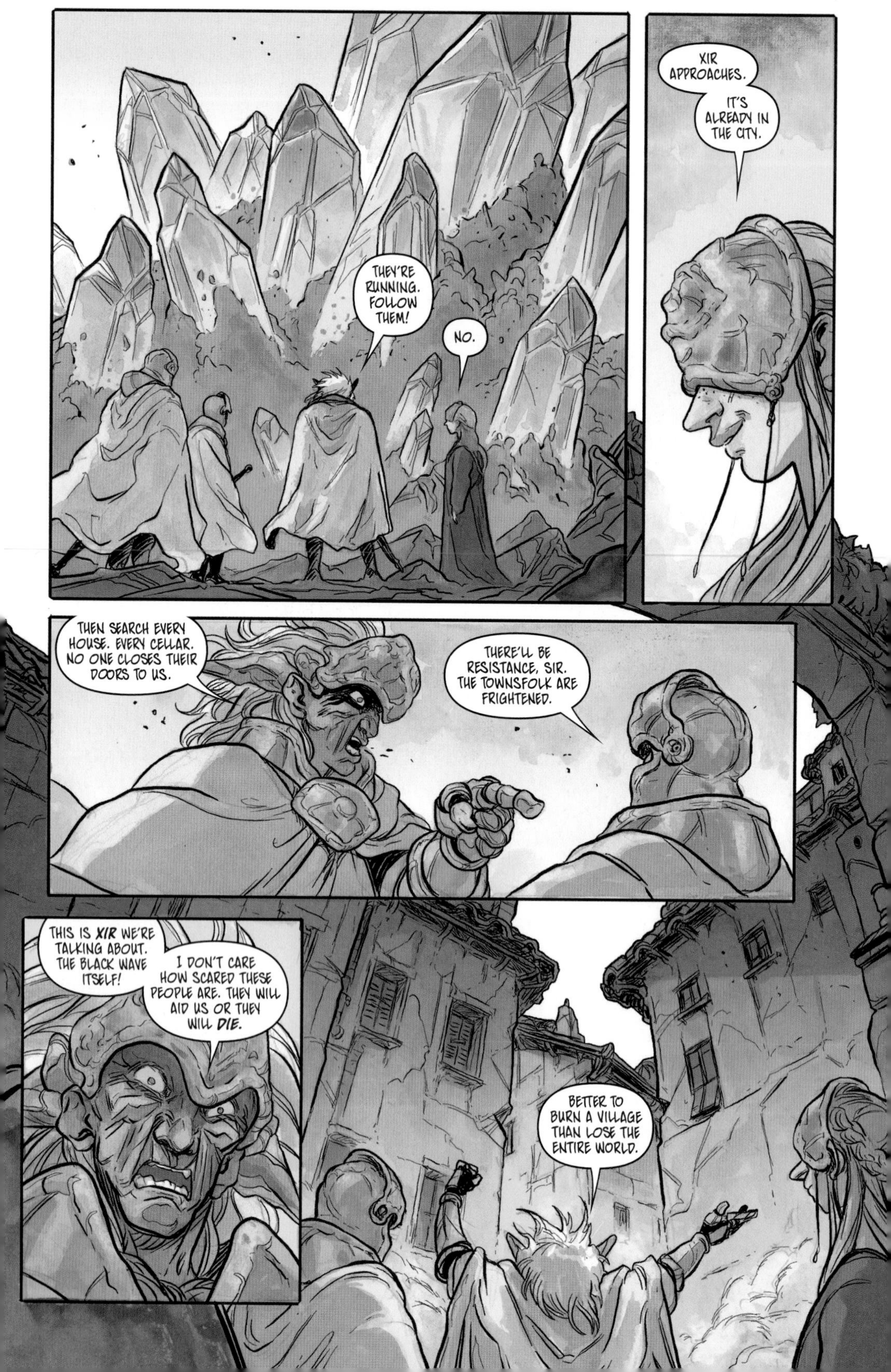
THEY'RE RUNNING. FOLLOW THEM!
NO.
XIR APPROACHES.
IT'S ALREADY IN THE CITY.
THEN SEARCH EVERY HOUSE. EVERY CELLAR. NO ONE CLOSES THEIR DOORS TO US.
THERE'LL BE RESISTANCE, SIR. THE TOWNSFOLK ARE FRIGHTENED.
THIS IS ***XIR*** WE'RE TALKING ABOUT. THE BLACK WAVE ITSELF!
I DON'T CARE HOW SCARED THESE PEOPLE ARE. THEY WILL AID US OR THEY WILL ***DIE***.
BETTER TO BURN A VILLAGE THAN LOSE THE ENTIRE WORLD.

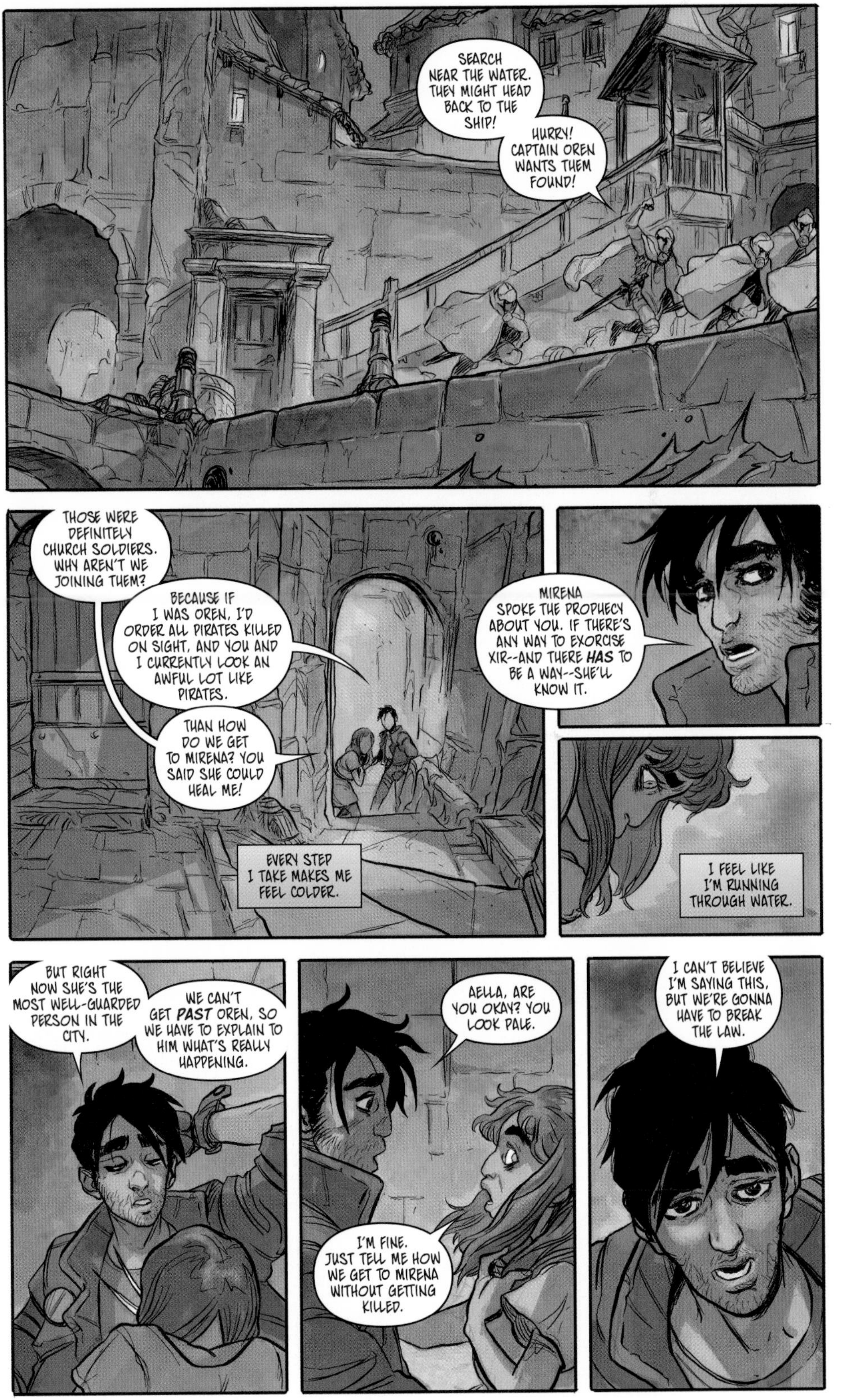
SEARCH NEAR THE WATER. THEY MIGHT HEAD BACK TO THE SHIP!
HURRY! CAPTAIN OREN WANTS THEM FOUND!
THOSE WERE DEFINITELY CHURCH SOLDIERS. WHY AREN'T WE JOINING THEM?
BECAUSE IF I WAS OREN, I'D ORDER ALL PIRATES KILLED ON SIGHT, AND YOU AND I CURRENTLY LOOK AN AWFUL LOT LIKE PIRATES.
THAN HOW DO WE GET TO MIRENA? YOU SAID SHE COULD HEAL ME!
EVERY STEP I TAKE MAKES ME FEEL COLDER.
MIRENA SPOKE THE PROPHECY ABOUT YOU. IF THERE'S ANY WAY TO EXORCISE XIR--AND THERE **HAS** TO BE A WAY--SHE'LL KNOW IT.
I FEEL LIKE I'M RUNNING THROUGH WATER.
BUT RIGHT NOW SHE'S THE MOST WELL-GUARDED PERSON IN THE CITY.
WE CAN'T GET **PAST** OREN, SO WE HAVE TO EXPLAIN TO HIM WHAT'S REALLY HAPPENING.
AELLA, ARE YOU OKAY? YOU LOOK PALE.
I'M FINE. JUST TELL ME HOW WE GET TO MIRENA WITHOUT GETTING KILLED.
I CAN'T BELIEVE I'M SAYING THIS, BUT WE'RE GONNA HAVE TO BREAK THE LAW.

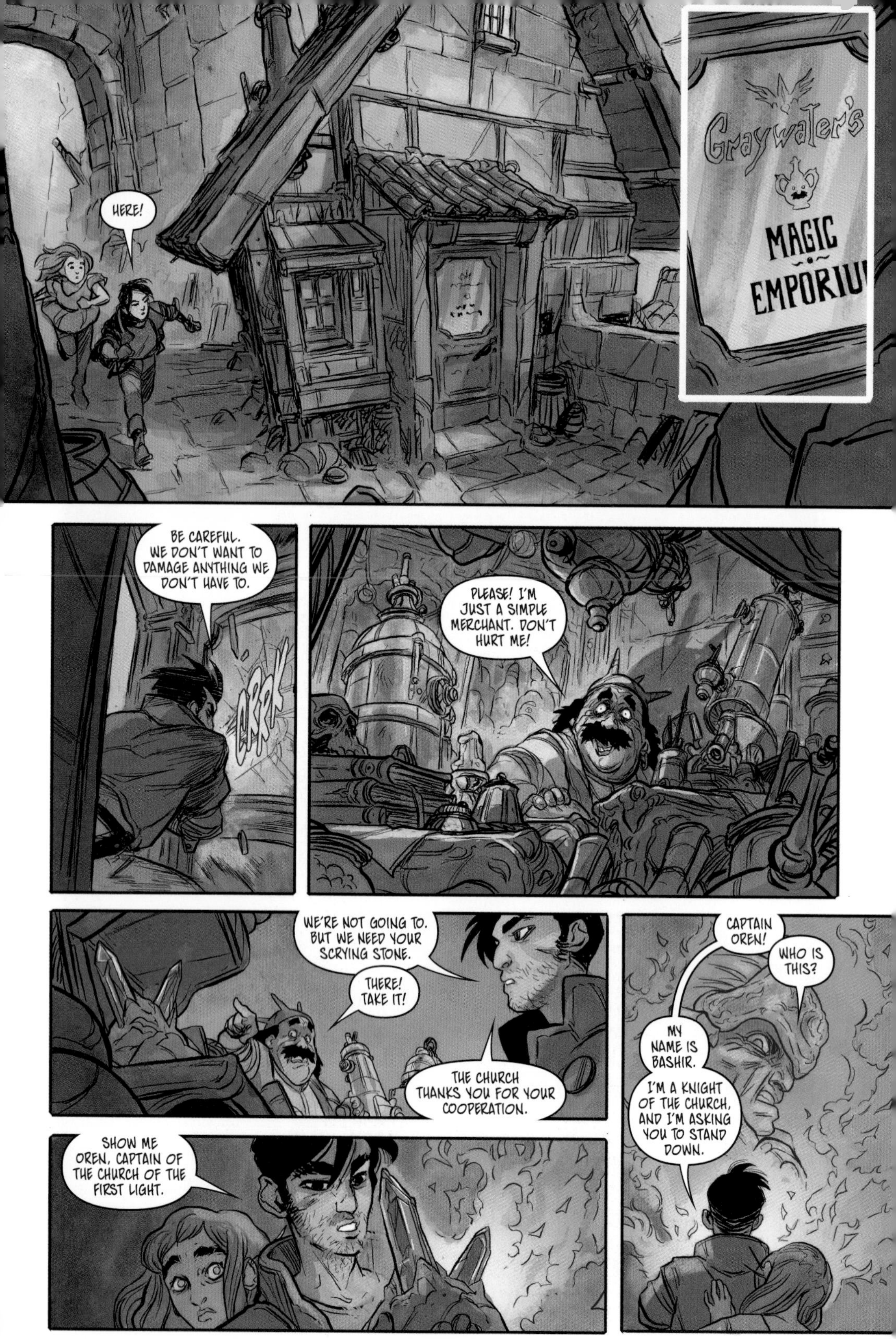
HERE!
Graywater's
MAGIC EMPORIU
BE CAREFUL. WE DON'T WANT TO DAMAGE ANYTHING WE DON'T HAVE TO.
CRRK
PLEASE! I'M JUST A SIMPLE MERCHANT. DON'T HURT ME!
WE'RE NOT GOING TO. BUT WE NEED YOUR SCRYING STONE.
THERE! TAKE IT!
THE CHURCH THANKS YOU FOR YOUR COOPERATION.
SHOW ME OREN, CAPTAIN OF THE CHURCH OF THE FIRST LIGHT.
CAPTAIN OREN!
WHO IS THIS?
MY NAME IS BASHIR.
I'M A KNIGHT OF THE CHURCH, AND I'M ASKING YOU TO STAND DOWN.

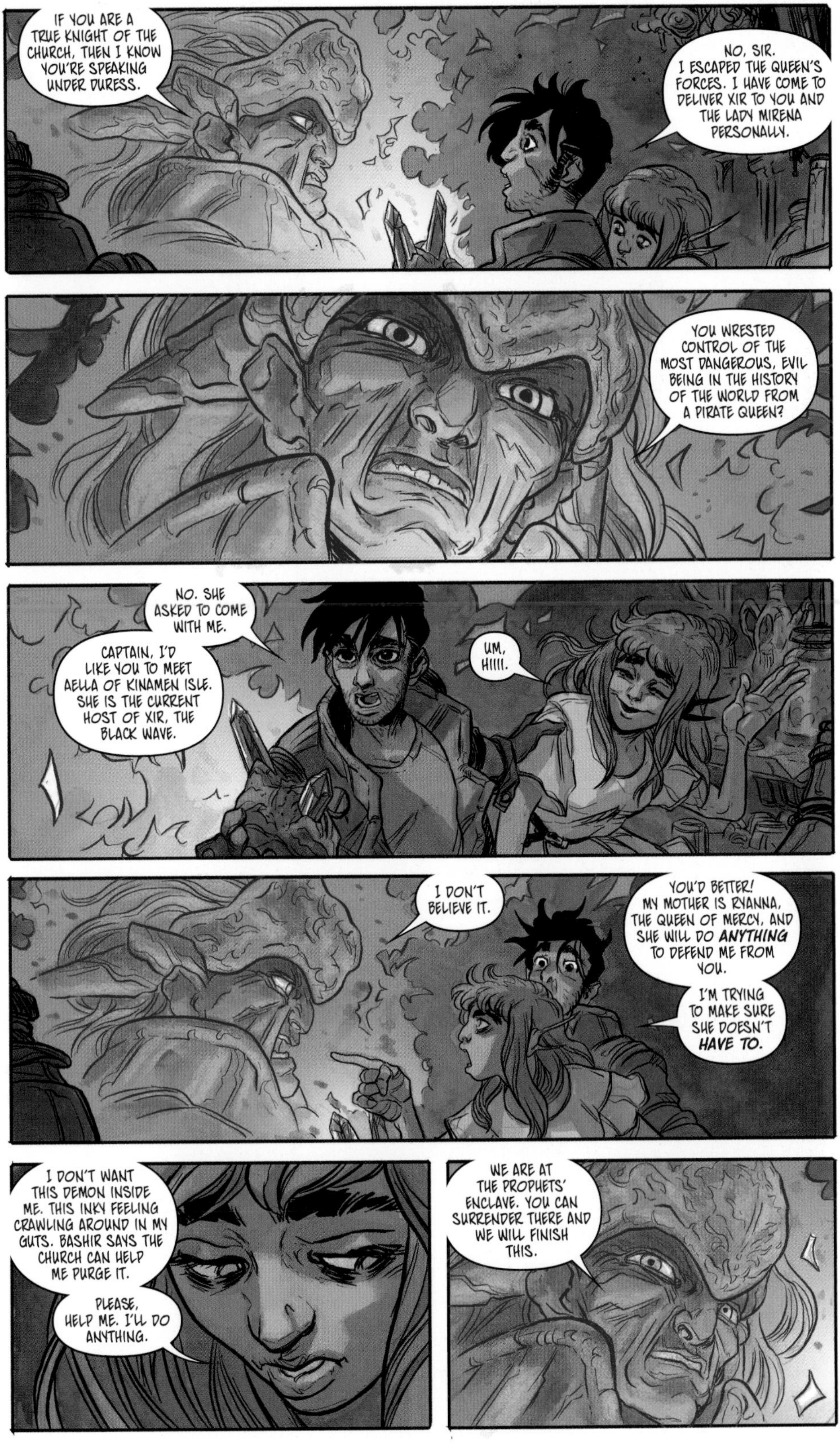
IF YOU ARE A TRUE KNIGHT OF THE CHURCH, THEN I KNOW YOU'RE SPEAKING UNDER DURESS.
NO, SIR. I ESCAPED THE QUEEN'S FORCES. I HAVE COME TO DELIVER XIR TO YOU AND THE LADY MIRENA PERSONALLY.
YOU WRESTED CONTROL OF THE MOST DANGEROUS, EVIL BEING IN THE HISTORY OF THE WORLD FROM A PIRATE QUEEN?
NO. SHE ASKED TO COME WITH ME.
CAPTAIN, I'D LIKE YOU TO MEET AELLA OF KINAMEN ISLE. SHE IS THE CURRENT HOST OF XIR, THE BLACK WAVE.
UM, HIIII.
I DON'T BELIEVE IT.
YOU'D BETTER! MY MOTHER IS RYANNA, THE QUEEN OF MERCY, AND SHE WILL DO ANYTHING TO DEFEND ME FROM YOU.
I'M TRYING TO MAKE SURE SHE DOESN'T HAVE TO.
I DON'T WANT THIS DEMON INSIDE ME. THIS INKY FEELING CRAWLING AROUND IN MY GUTS. BASHIR SAYS THE CHURCH CAN HELP ME PURGE IT.
PLEASE, HELP ME. I'LL DO ANYTHING.
WE ARE AT THE PROPHETS' ENCLAVE. YOU CAN SURRENDER THERE AND WE WILL FINISH THIS.

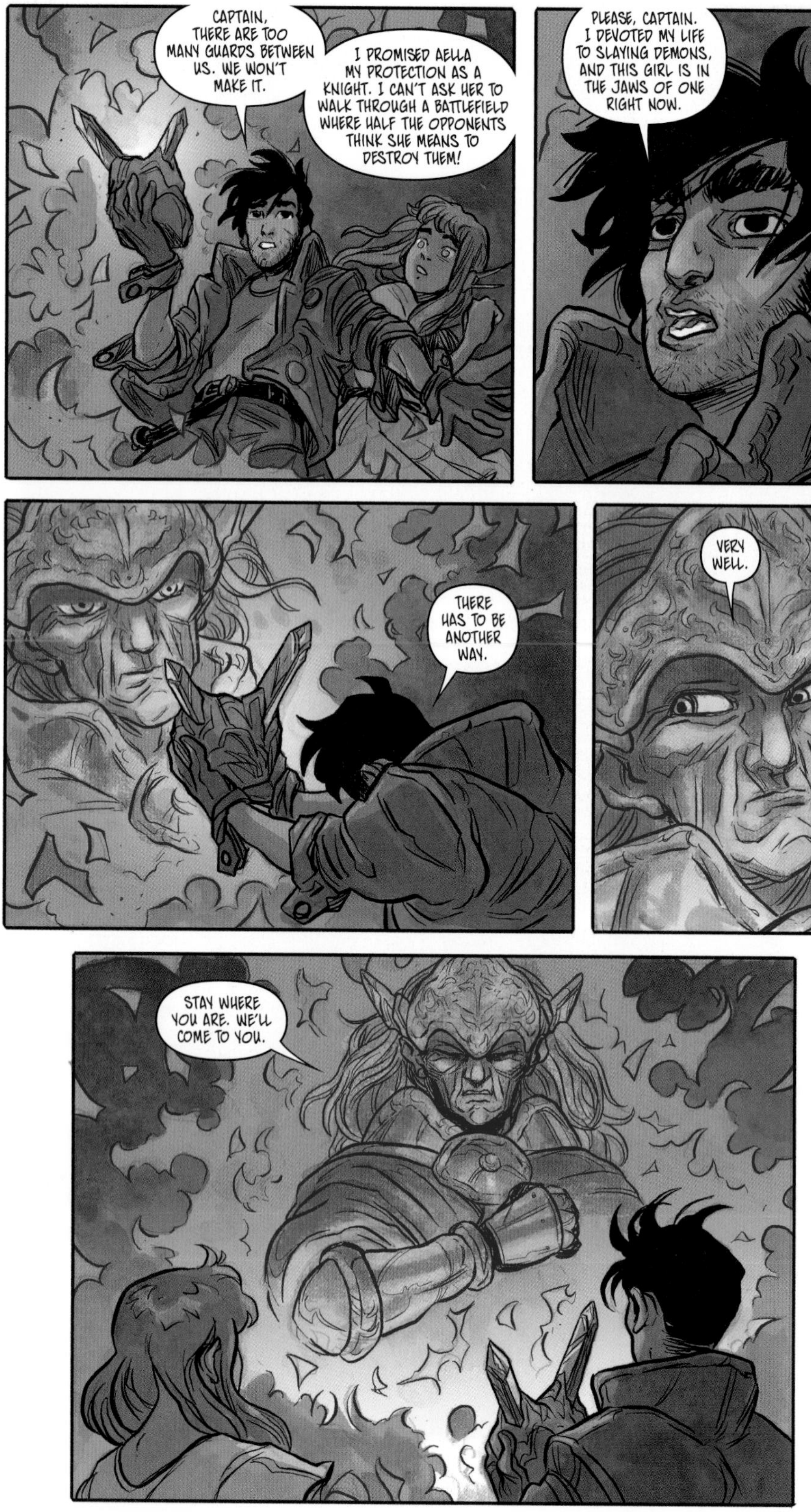
CAPTAIN, THERE ARE TOO MANY GUARDS BETWEEN US. WE WON'T MAKE IT.
I PROMISED AELLA MY PROTECTION AS A KNIGHT. I CAN'T ASK HER TO WALK THROUGH A BATTLEFIELD WHERE HALF THE OPPONENTS THINK SHE MEANS TO DESTROY THEM!
PLEASE, CAPTAIN. I DEVOTED MY LIFE TO SLAYING DEMONS, AND THIS GIRL IS IN THE JAWS OF ONE RIGHT NOW.
THERE HAS TO BE ANOTHER WAY.
VERY WELL.
STAY WHERE YOU ARE. WE'LL COME TO YOU.

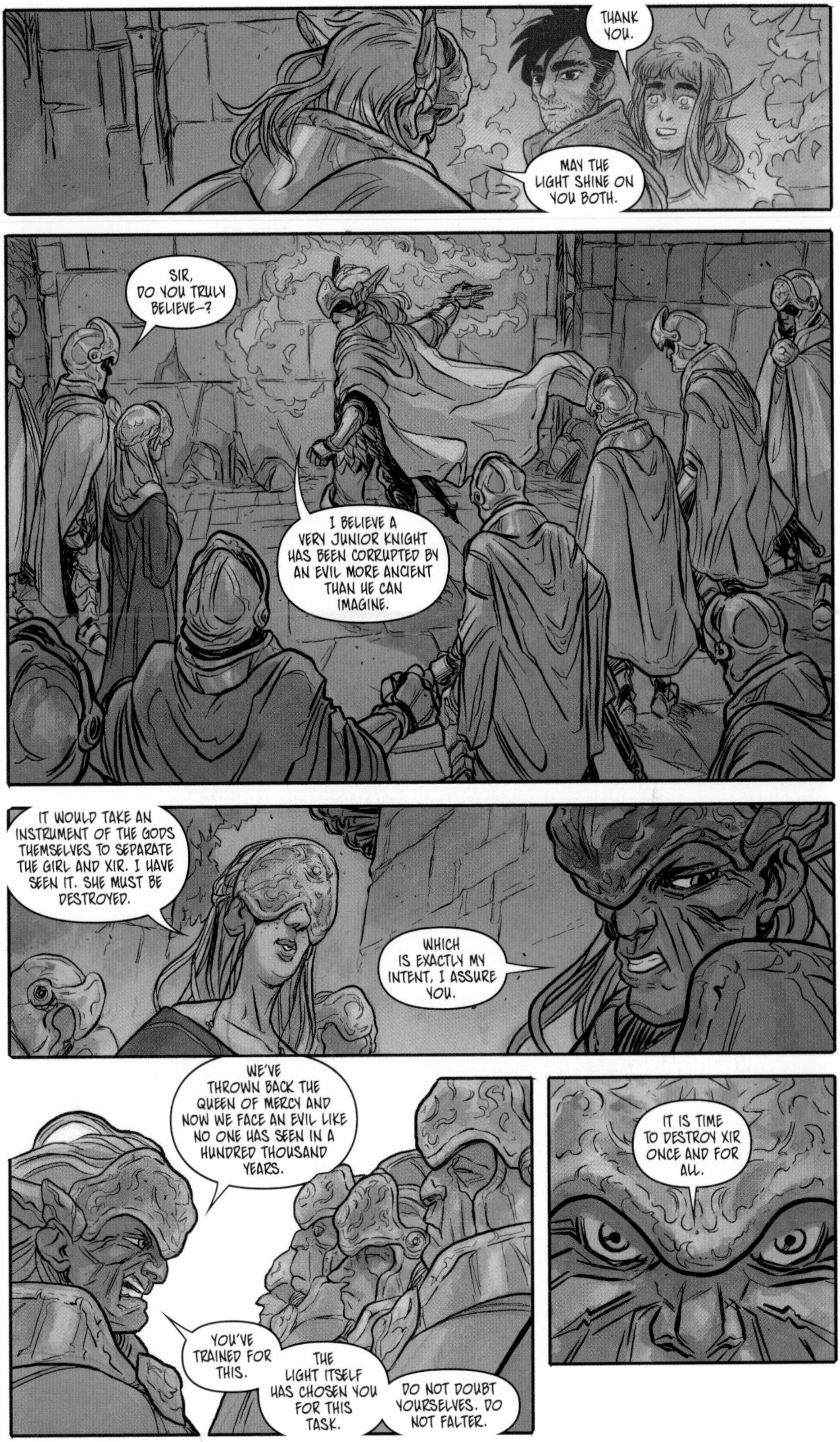
THANK YOU.
MAY THE LIGHT SHINE ON YOU BOTH.
SIR, DO YOU TRULY BELIEVE—?
I BELIEVE A VERY JUNIOR KNIGHT HAS BEEN CORRUPTED BY AN EVIL MORE ANCIENT THAN HE CAN IMAGINE.
IT WOULD TAKE AN INSTRUMENT OF THE GODS THEMSELVES TO SEPARATE THE GIRL AND XIR. I HAVE SEEN IT. SHE MUST BE DESTROYED.
WHICH IS EXACTLY MY INTENT, I ASSURE YOU.
WE'VE THROWN BACK THE QUEEN OF MERCY AND NOW WE FACE AN EVIL LIKE NO ONE HAS SEEN IN A HUNDRED THOUSAND YEARS.
YOU'VE TRAINED FOR THIS.
THE LIGHT ITSELF HAS CHOSEN YOU FOR THIS TASK.
DO NOT DOUBT YOURSELVES. DO NOT FALTER.
IT IS TIME TO DESTROY XIR ONCE AND FOR ALL.

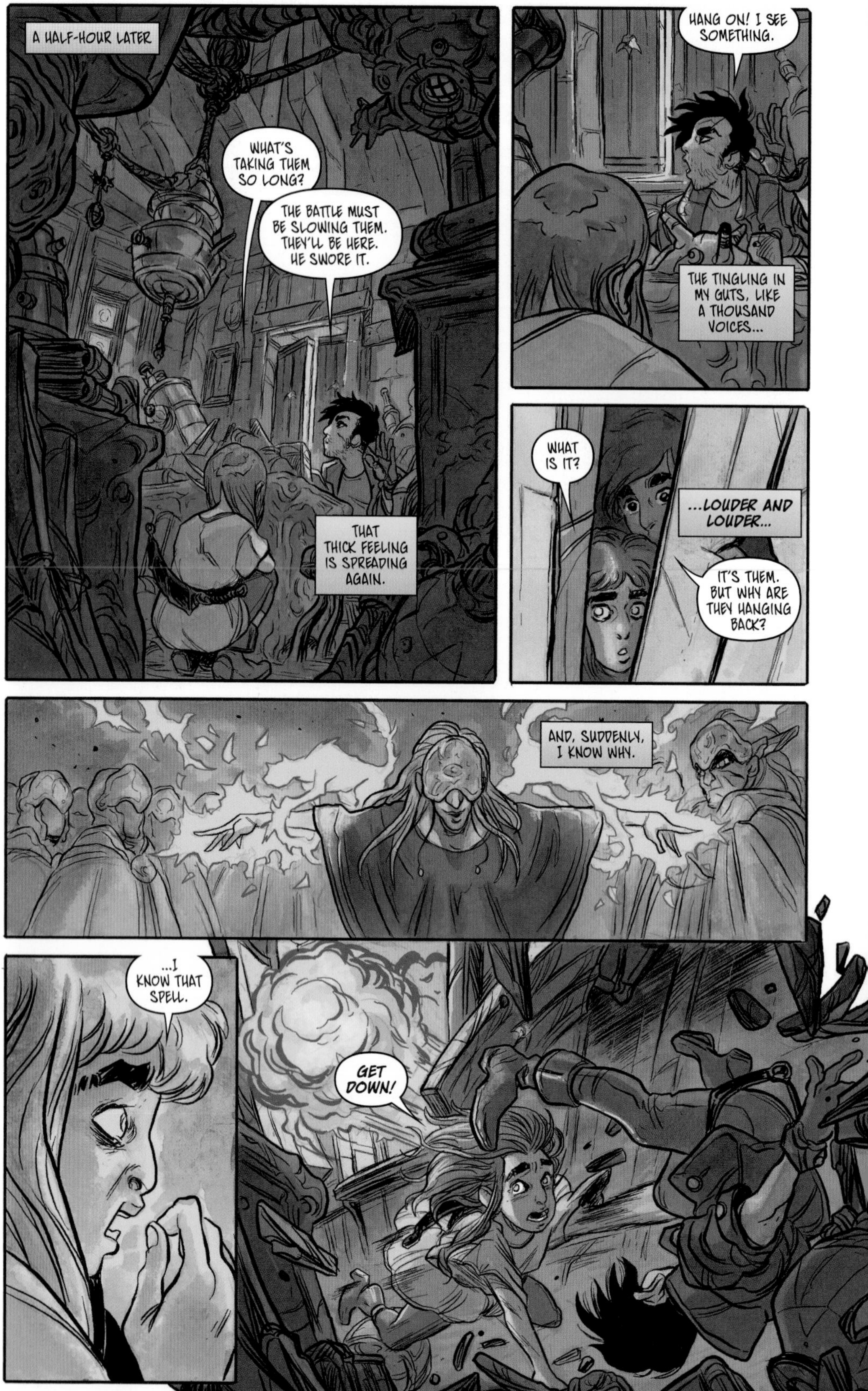
A HALF-HOUR LATER
WHAT'S TAKING THEM SO LONG?
THE BATTLE MUST BE SLOWING THEM. THEY'LL BE HERE. HE SWORE IT.
THAT THICK FEELING IS SPREADING AGAIN.
HANG ON! I SEE SOMETHING.
THE TINGLING IN MY GUTS, LIKE A THOUSAND VOICES...
WHAT IS IT?
...LOUDER AND LOUDER...
IT'S THEM. BUT WHY ARE THEY HANGING BACK?
AND, SUDDENLY, I KNOW WHY.
...I KNOW THAT SPELL.
GET DOWN!

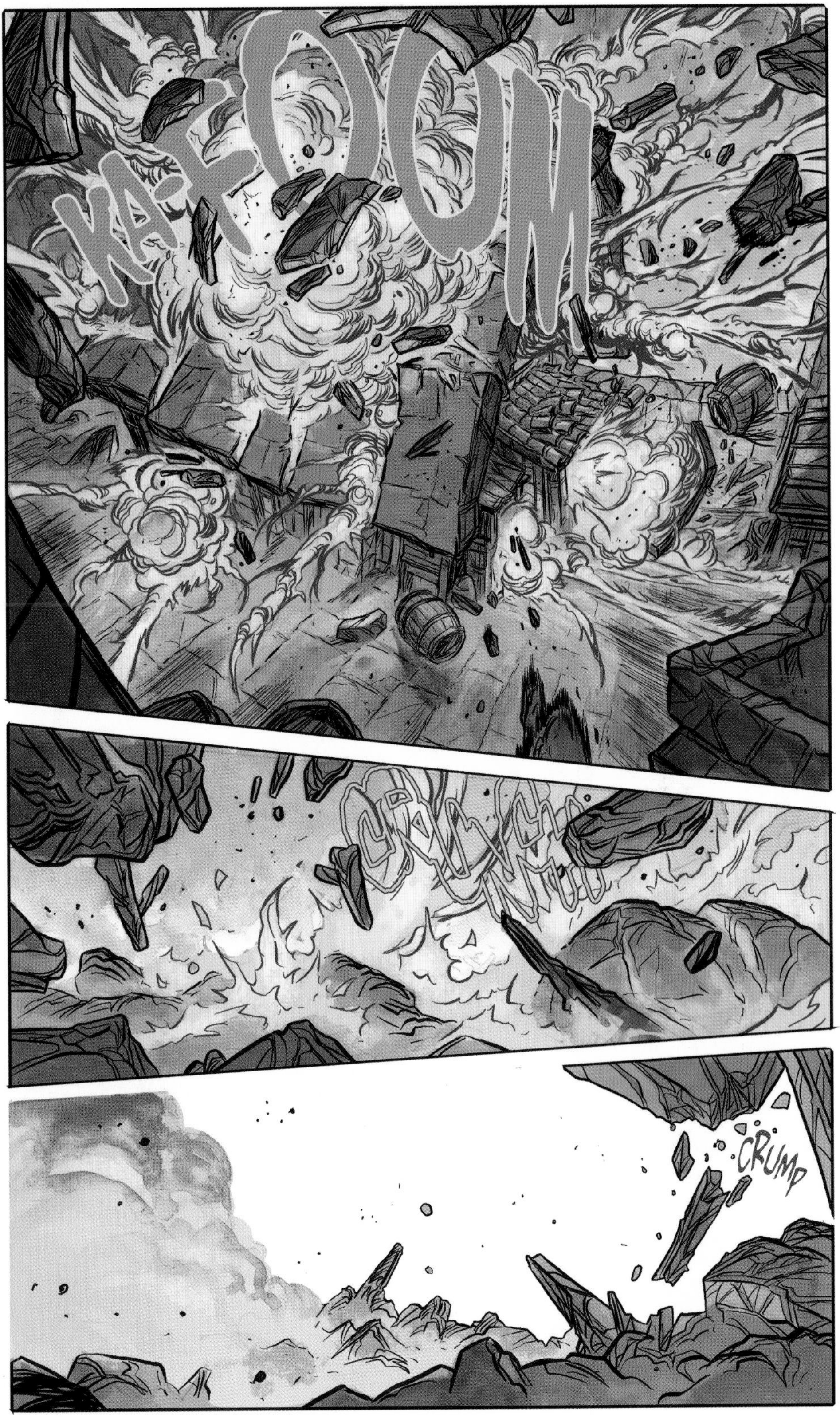
KA-FOOM
CRACKA
CRUMP

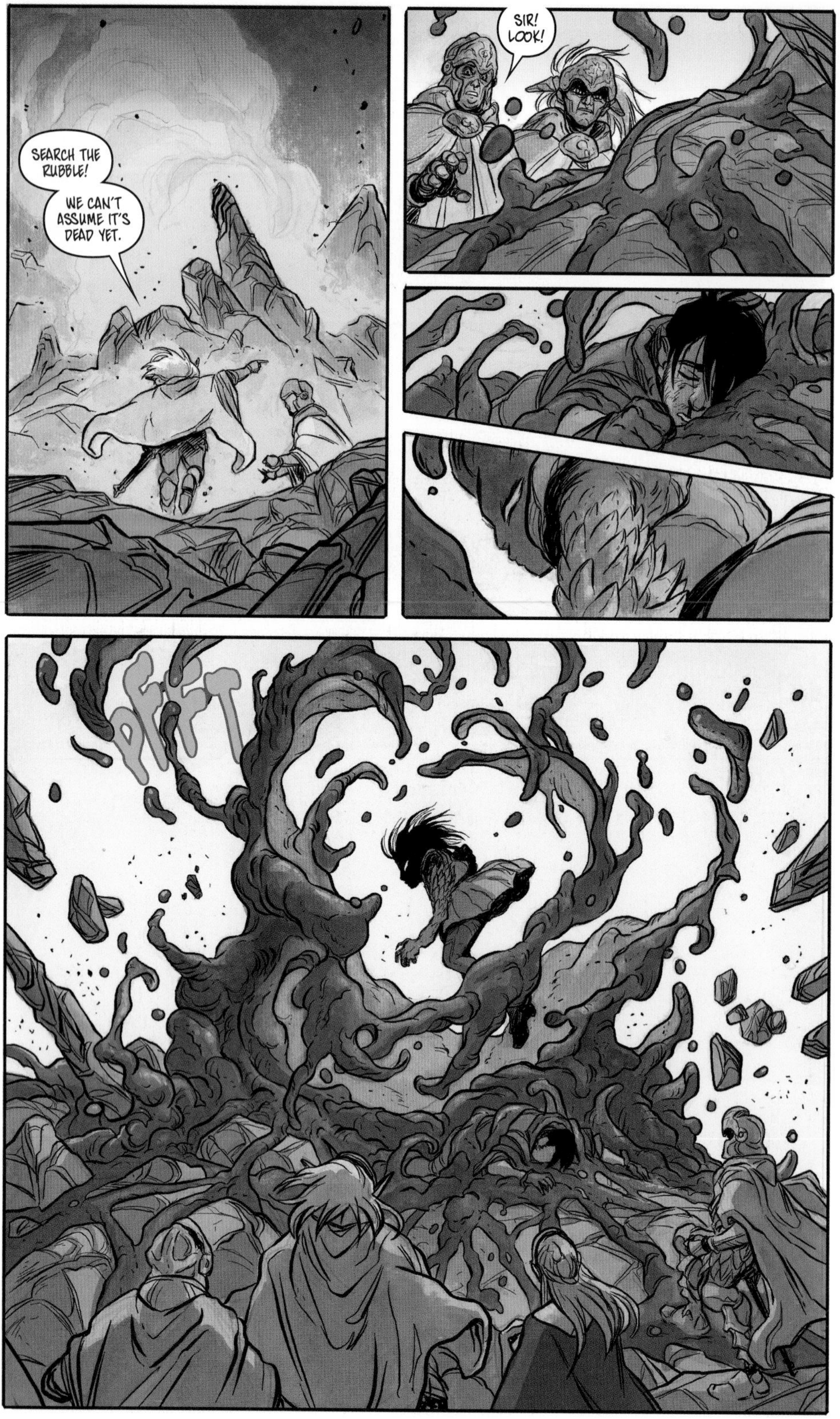
SEARCH THE RUBBLE!
WE CAN'T ASSUME IT'S DEAD YET.
SIR! LOOK!
PFFT

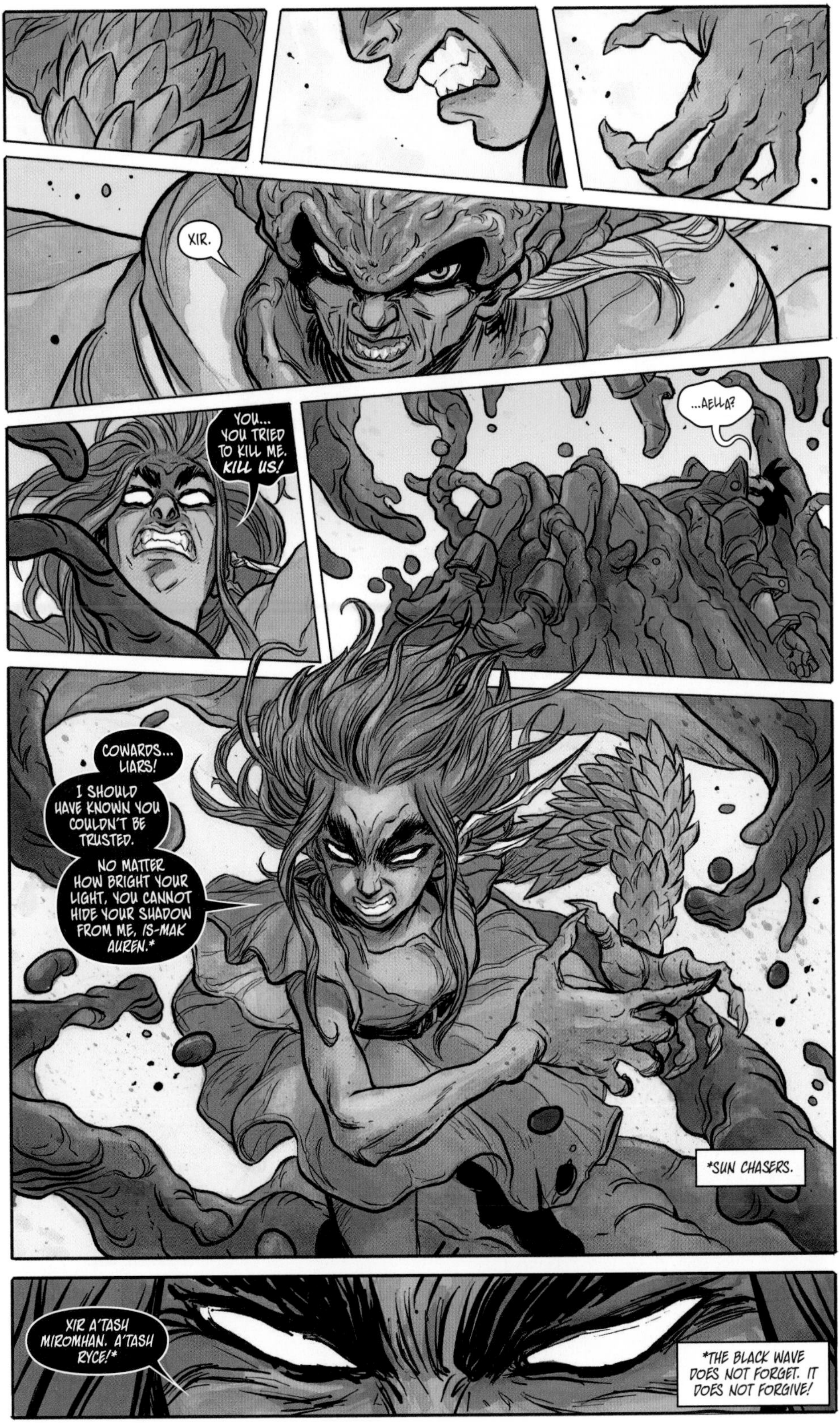
XIR.
YOU... YOU TRIED TO KILL ME. KILL US!
...AELLA?
COWARDS... LIARS!
I SHOULD HAVE KNOWN YOU COULDN'T BE TRUSTED.
NO MATTER HOW BRIGHT YOUR LIGHT, YOU CANNOT HIDE YOUR SHADOW FROM ME, IS-MAK AUREN.*
*SUN CHASERS.
XIR A'TASH MIROMHAN. A'TASH RYCE!*
*THE BLACK WAVE DOES NOT FORGET. IT DOES NOT FORGIVE!

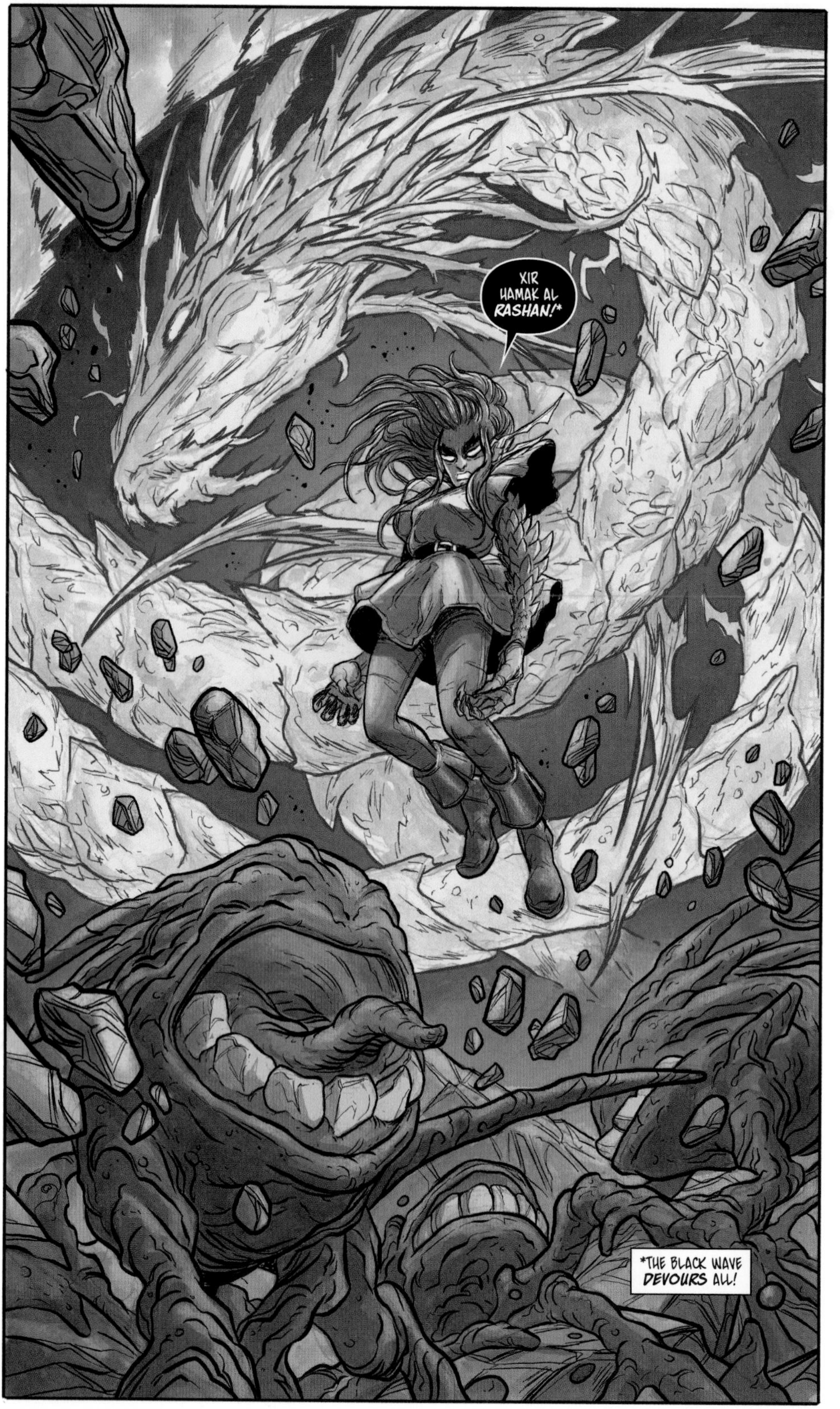
XIR HAMAK AL RASHAN!*
*THE BLACK WAVE DEVOURS ALL!

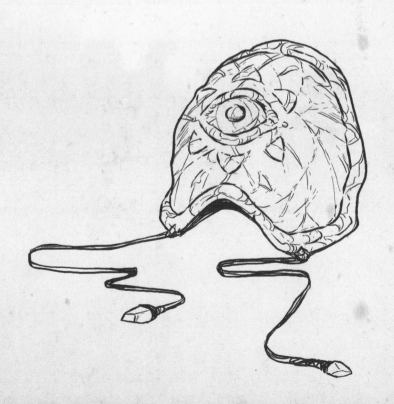

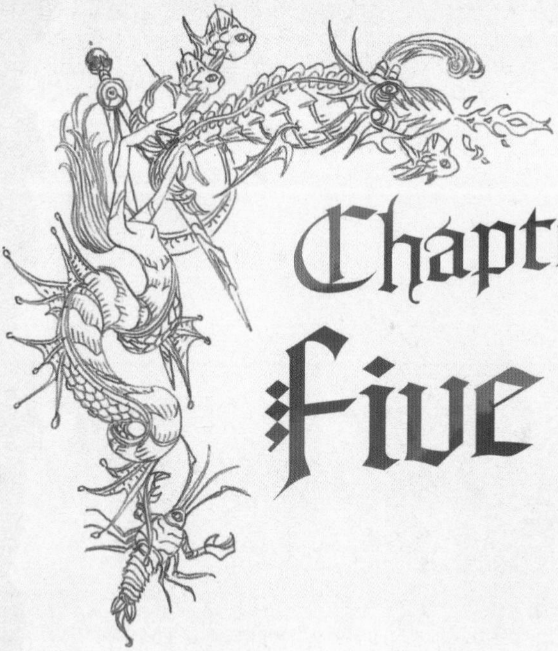

Chapter Five

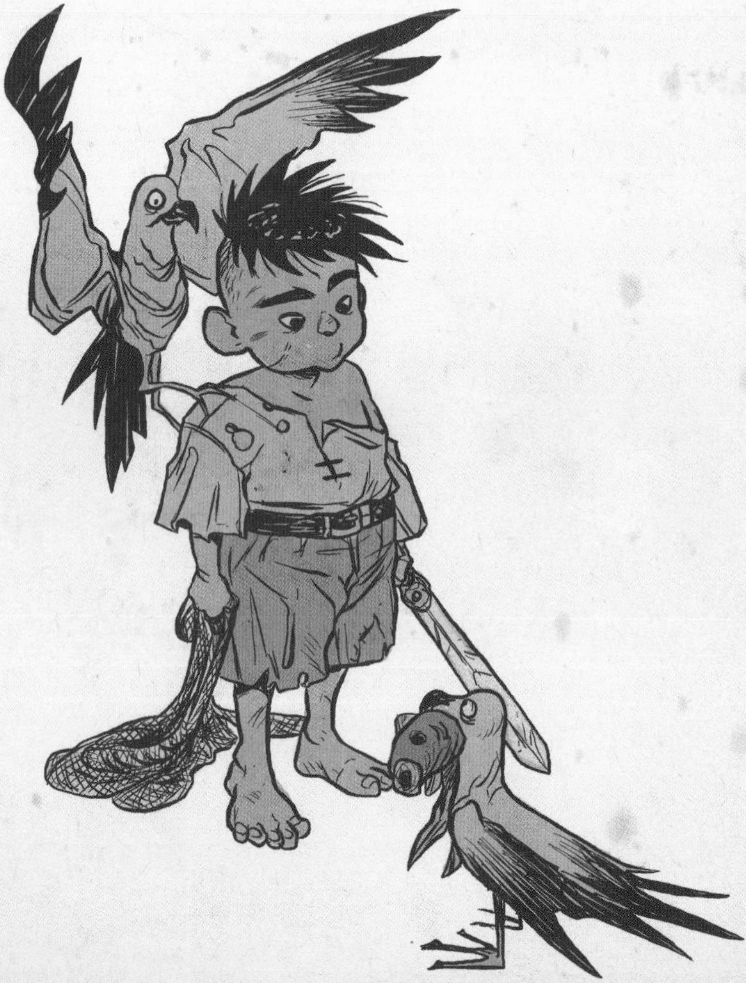

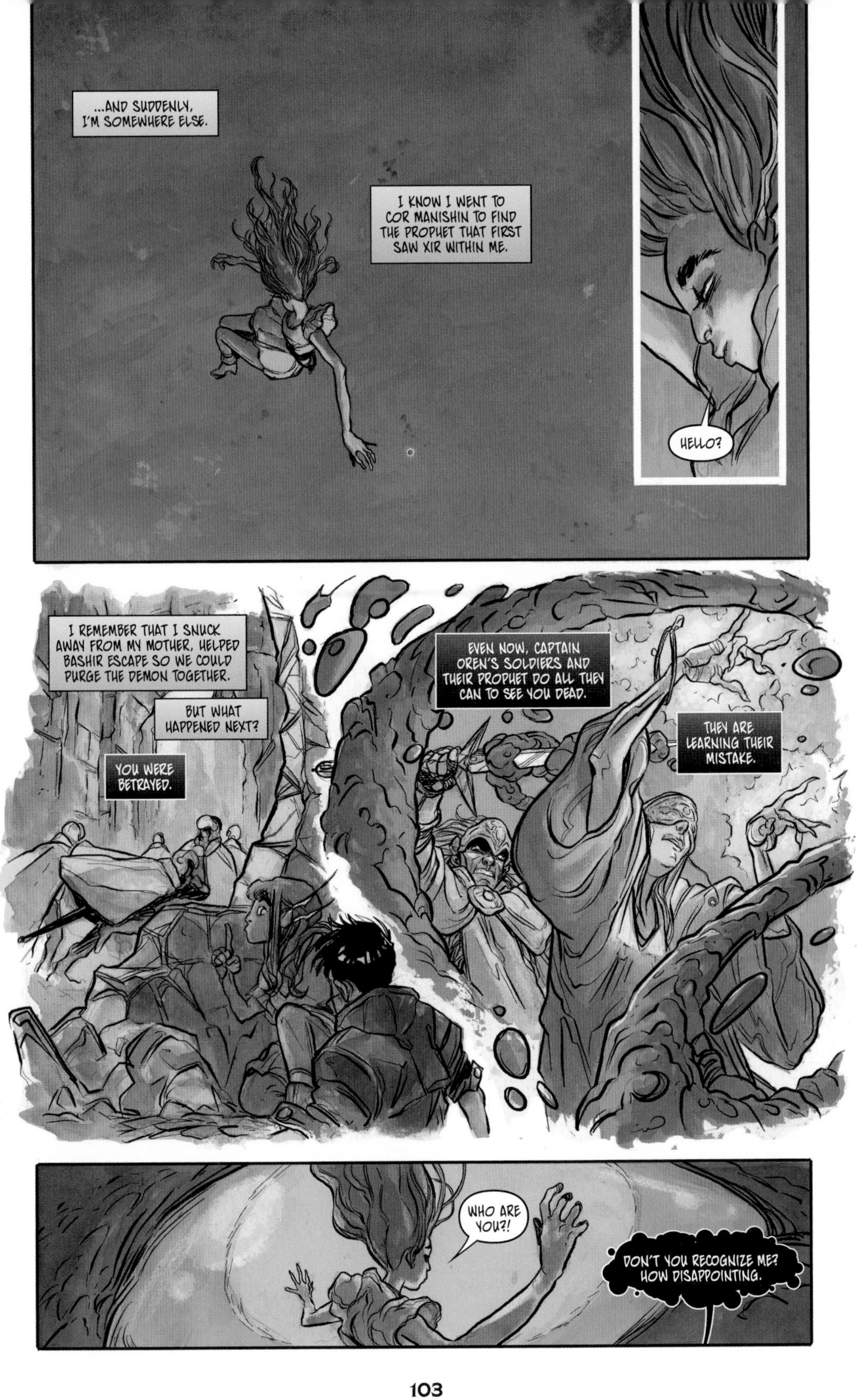
...AND SUDDENLY, I'M SOMEWHERE ELSE.
I KNOW I WENT TO COR MANISHIN TO FIND THE PROPHET THAT FIRST SAW XIR WITHIN ME.
HELLO?
I REMEMBER THAT I SNUCK AWAY FROM MY MOTHER, HELPED BASHIR ESCAPE SO WE COULD PURGE THE DEMON TOGETHER.
BUT WHAT HAPPENED NEXT?
YOU WERE BETRAYED.
EVEN NOW, CAPTAIN OREN'S SOLDIERS AND THEIR PROPHET DO ALL THEY CAN TO SEE YOU DEAD.
THEY ARE LEARNING THEIR MISTAKE.
WHO ARE YOU?!
DON'T YOU RECOGNIZE ME? HOW DISAPPOINTING.

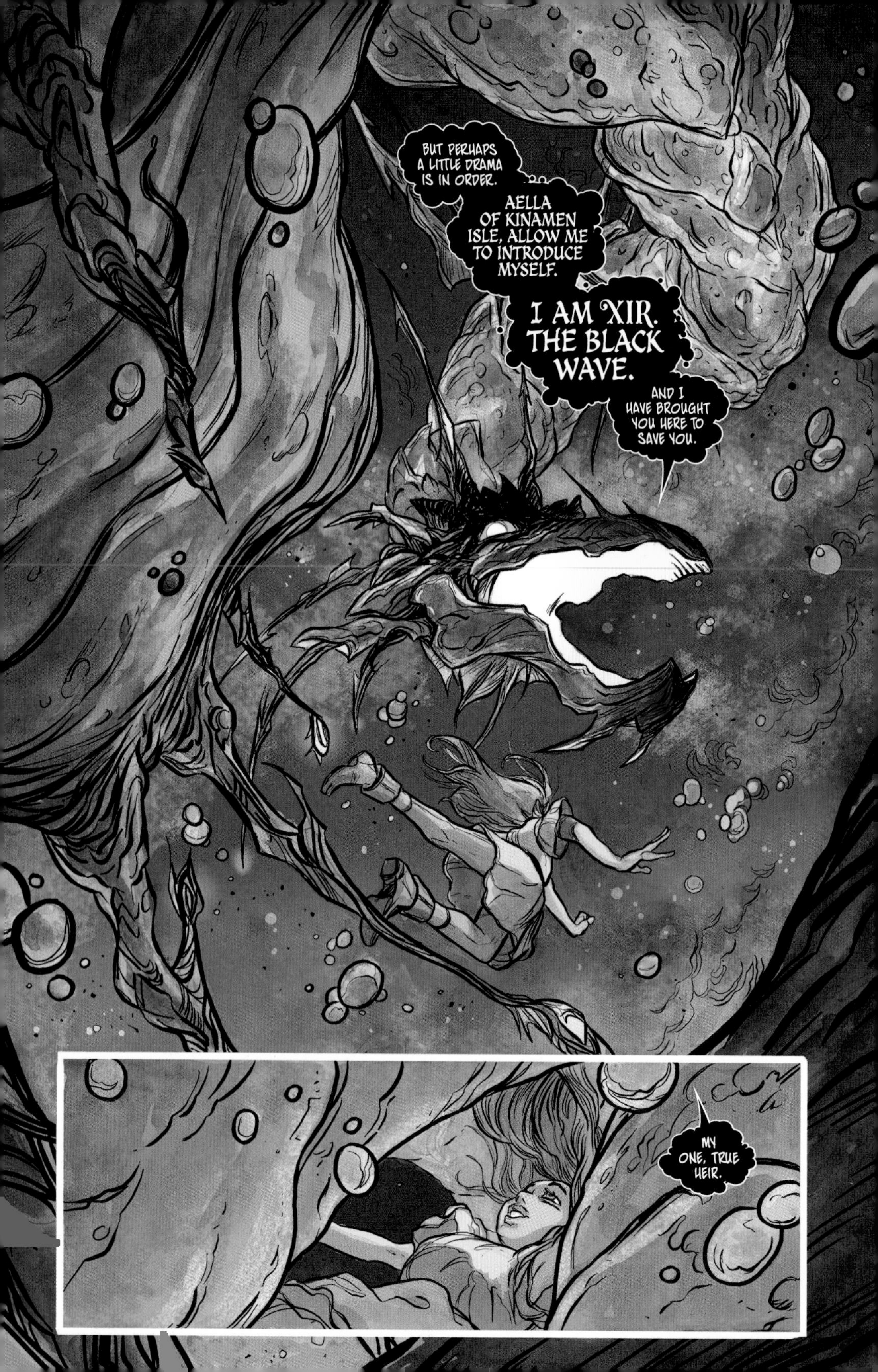
BUT PERHAPS A LITTLE DRAMA IS IN ORDER.
AELLA OF KINAMEN ISLE, ALLOW ME TO INTRODUCE MYSELF.
I AM XIR. THE BLACK WAVE.
AND I HAVE BROUGHT YOU HERE TO SAVE YOU.
MY ONE, TRUE HEIR.

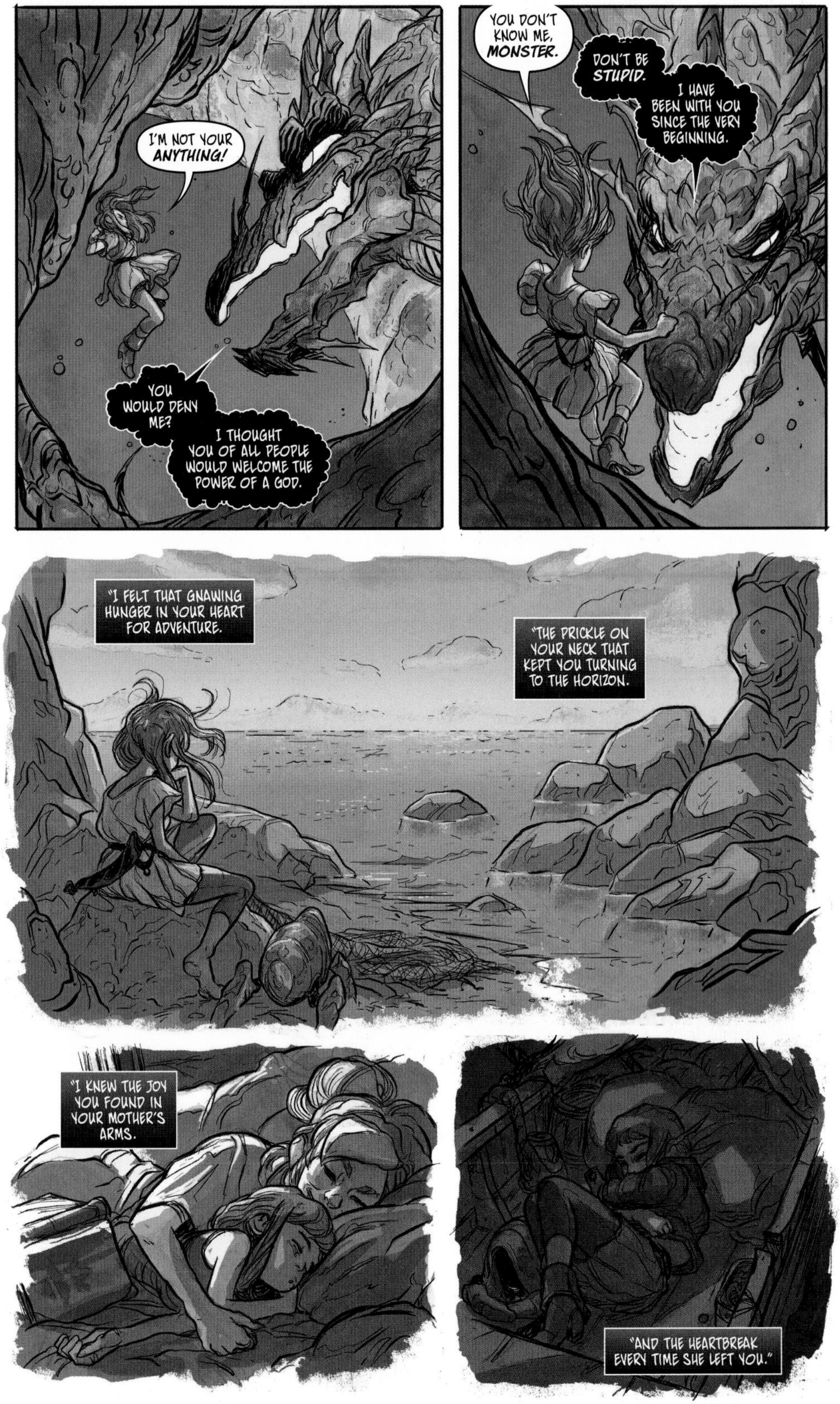
I'M NOT YOUR **ANYTHING!**
YOU WOULD DENY ME?
I THOUGHT YOU OF ALL PEOPLE WOULD WELCOME THE POWER OF A GOD.
YOU DON'T KNOW ME, **MONSTER.**
DON'T BE **STUPID.**
I HAVE BEEN WITH YOU SINCE THE VERY BEGINNING.
"I FELT THAT GNAWING HUNGER IN YOUR HEART FOR ADVENTURE.
"THE PRICKLE ON YOUR NECK THAT KEPT YOU TURNING TO THE HORIZON.
"I KNEW THE JOY YOU FOUND IN YOUR MOTHER'S ARMS.
"AND THE HEARTBREAK EVERY TIME SHE LEFT YOU."

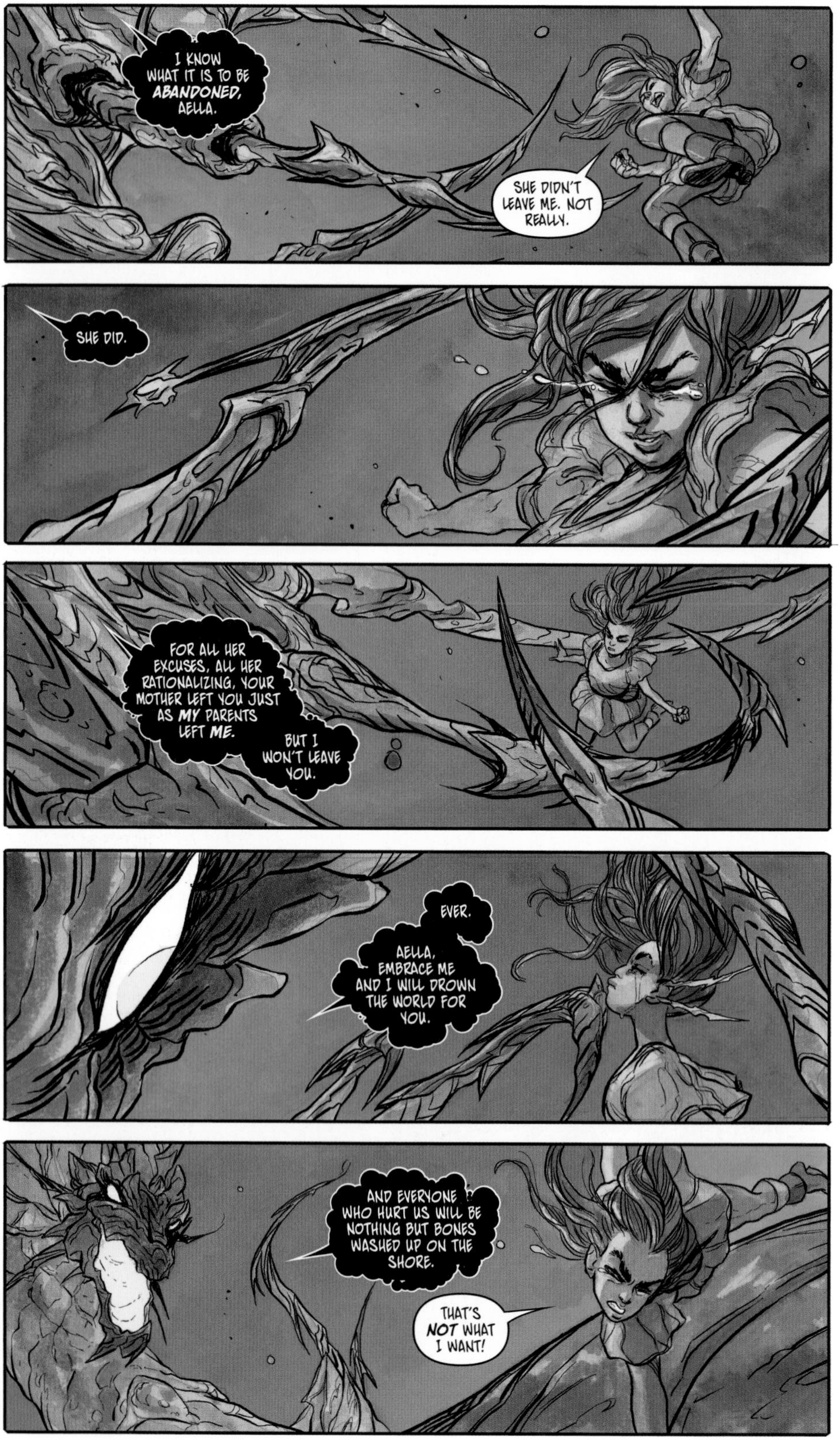
I KNOW WHAT IT IS TO BE ABANDONED, AELLA.
SHE DIDN'T LEAVE ME. NOT REALLY.
SHE DID.
FOR ALL HER EXCUSES, ALL HER RATIONALIZING, YOUR MOTHER LEFT YOU JUST AS MY PARENTS LEFT ME.
BUT I WON'T LEAVE YOU.
EVER.
AELLA, EMBRACE ME AND I WILL DROWN THE WORLD FOR YOU.
AND EVERYONE WHO HURT US WILL BE NOTHING BUT BONES WASHED UP ON THE SHORE.
THAT'S NOT WHAT I WANT!

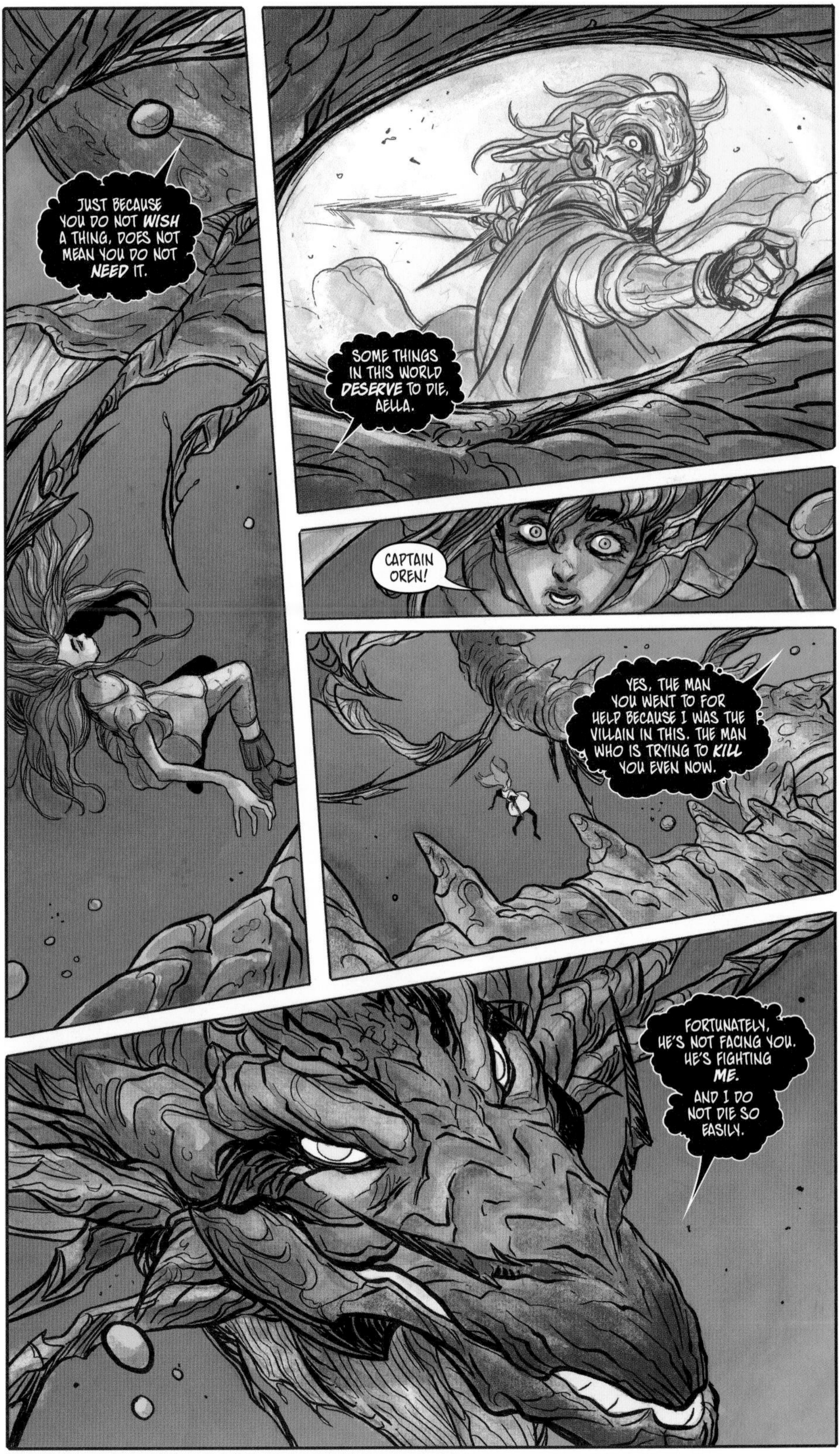
JUST BECAUSE YOU DO NOT WISH A THING, DOES NOT MEAN YOU DO NOT NEED IT.
SOME THINGS IN THIS WORLD DESERVE TO DIE, AELLA.
CAPTAIN OREN!
YES, THE MAN YOU WENT TO FOR HELP BECAUSE I WAS THE VILLAIN IN THIS. THE MAN WHO IS TRYING TO KILL YOU EVEN NOW.
FORTUNATELY, HE'S NOT FACING YOU. HE'S FIGHTING ME.
AND I DO NOT DIE SO EASILY.

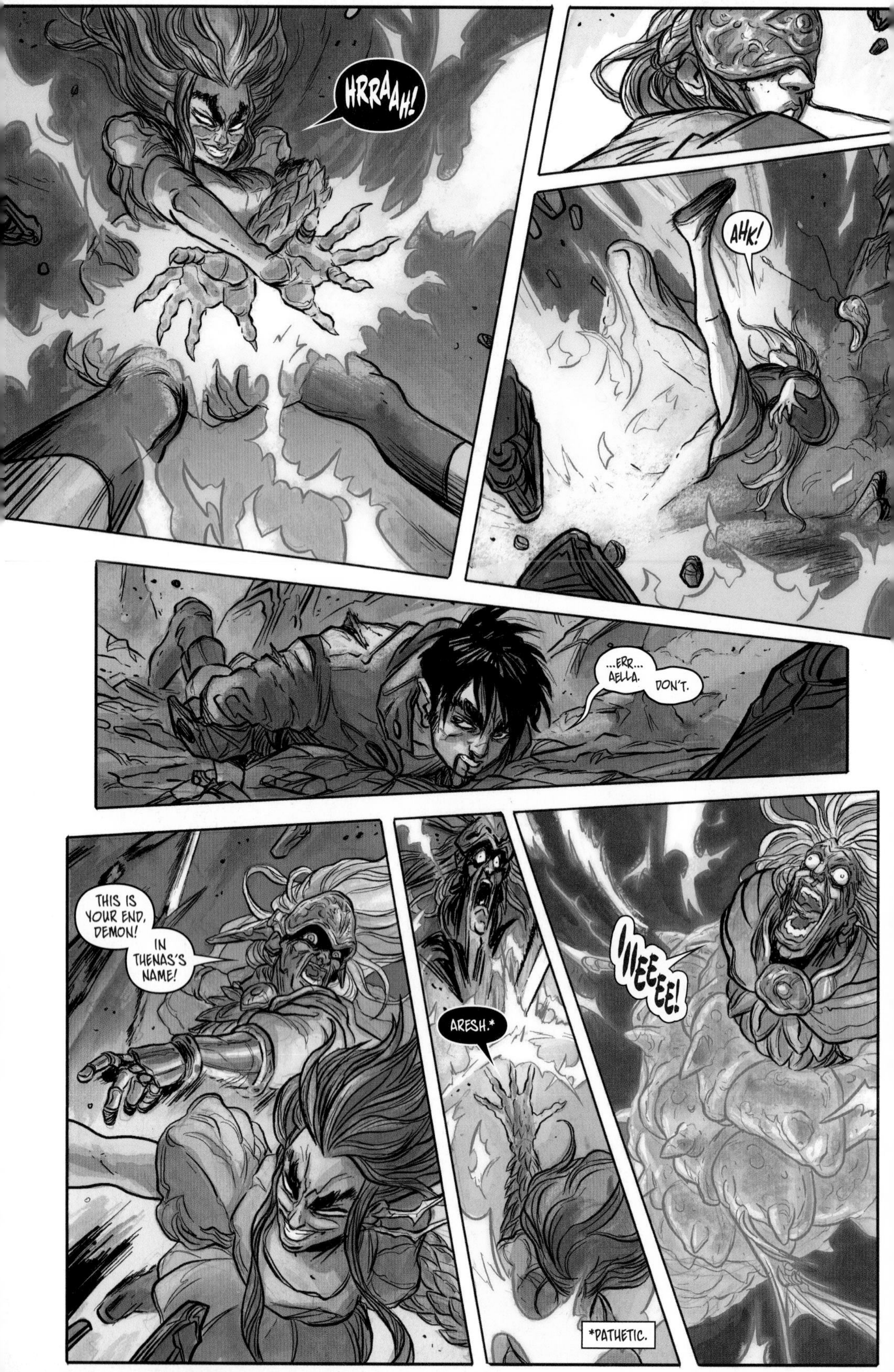
HRRAAH!
AHK!
...ERR... AELLA.
DON'T.
THIS IS YOUR END, DEMON!
IN THENAS'S NAME!
ARESH.*
IIIEEEEE!
*PATHETIC.

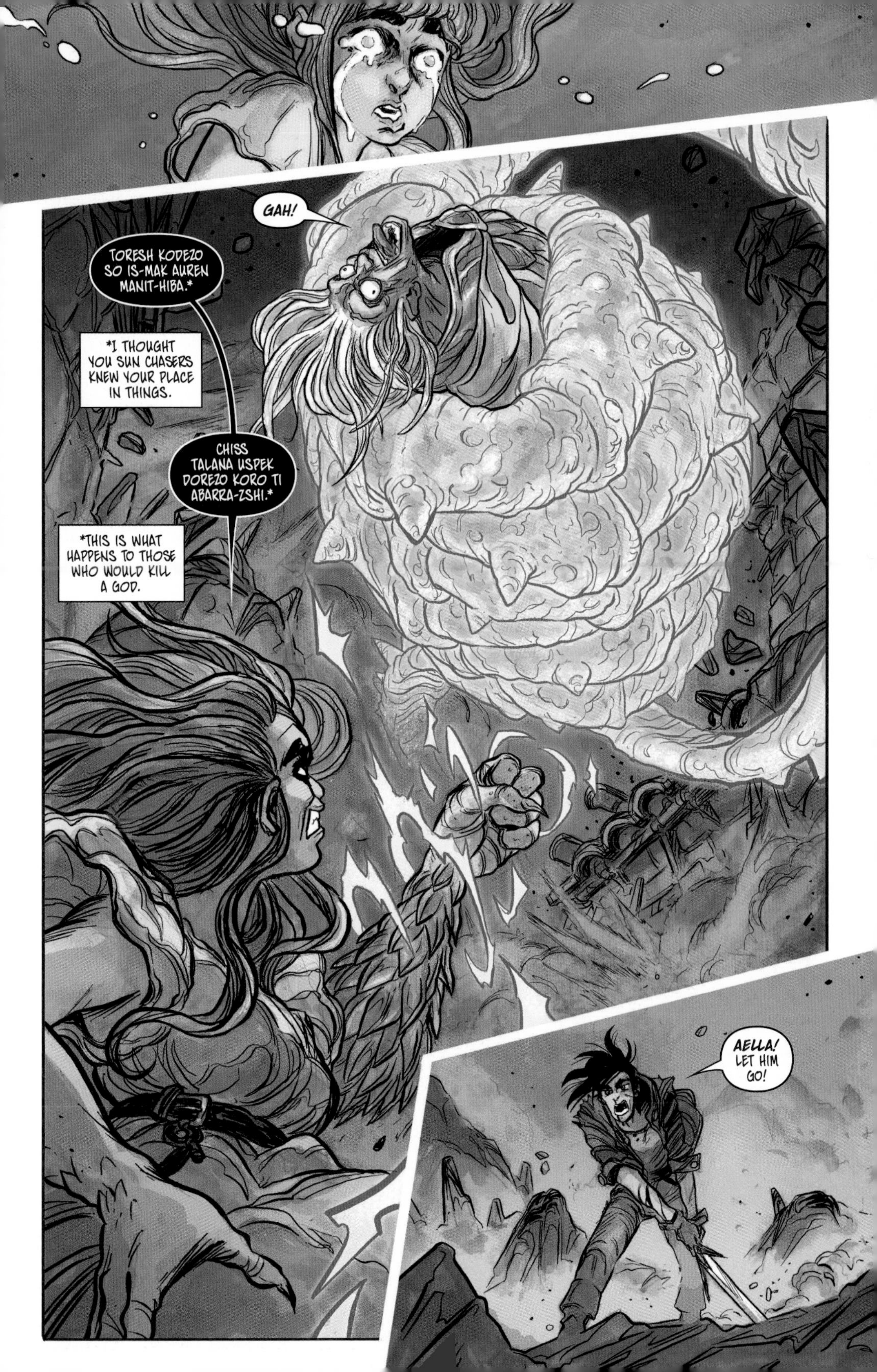
GAH!
TORESH KODEZO SO IS-MAK AUREN MANIT-HIBA.*
*I THOUGHT YOU SUN CHASERS KNEW YOUR PLACE IN THINGS.
CHISS TALANA USPEK DOREZO KORO TI ABARRA-ZSHI.*
*THIS IS WHAT HAPPENS TO THOSE WHO WOULD KILL A GOD.
AELLA! LET HIM GO!

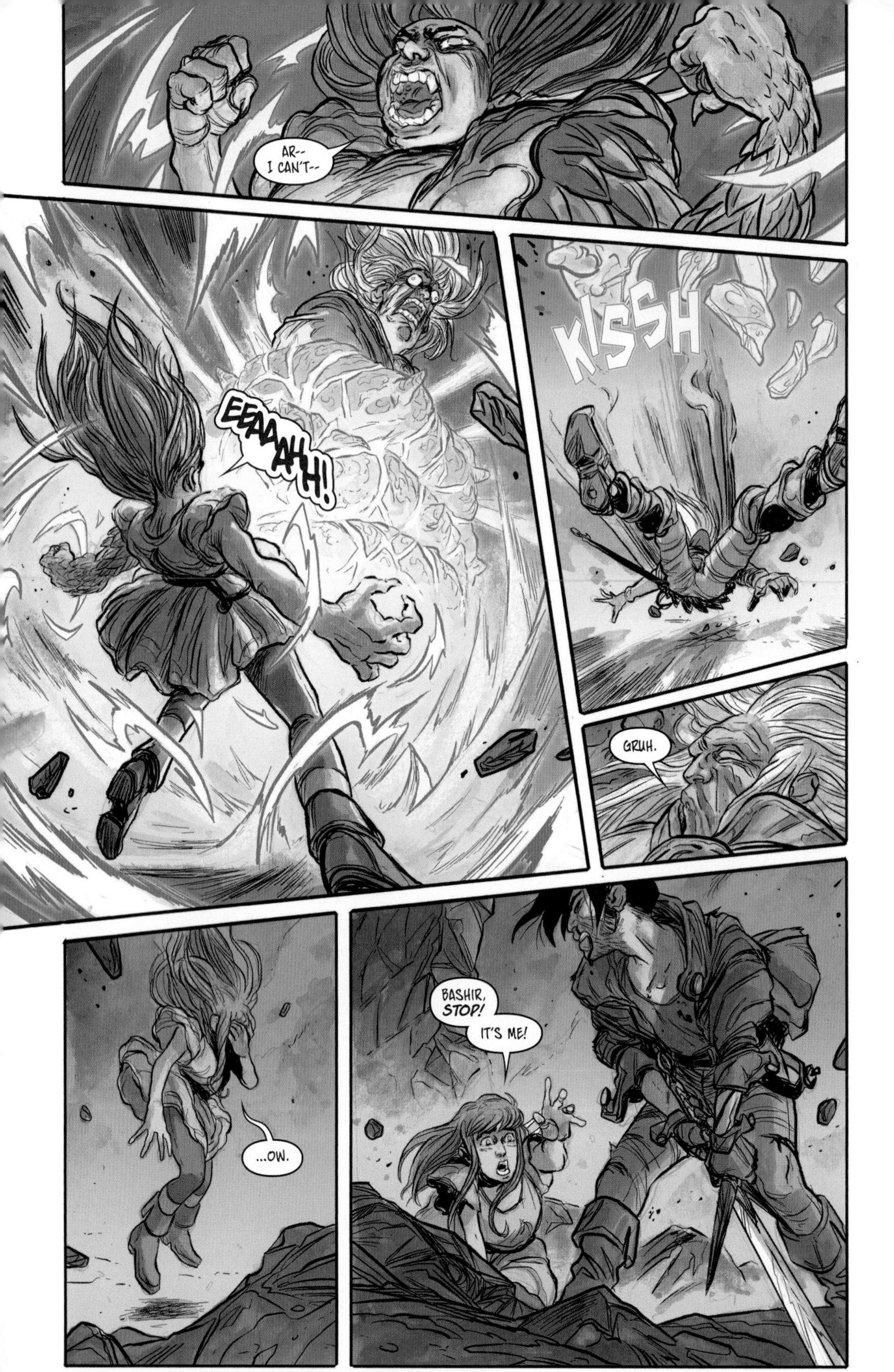
AR--
I CAN'T--
EEAAAAHH!
KISSH
GRUH.
...OW.
BASHIR, STOP!
IT'S ME!

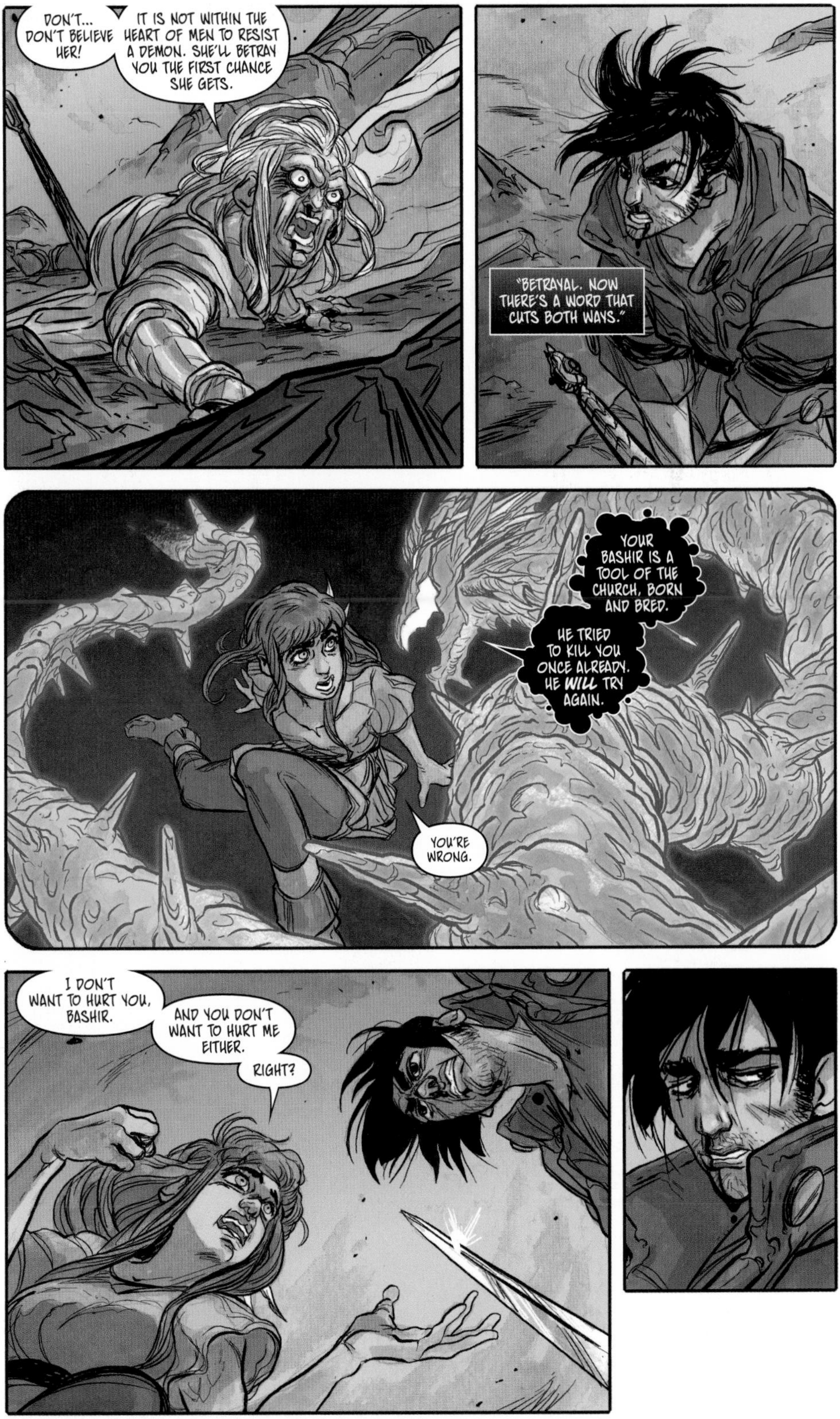

DON'T... DON'T BELIEVE HER!
IT IS NOT WITHIN THE HEART OF MEN TO RESIST A DEMON. SHE'LL BETRAY YOU THE FIRST CHANCE SHE GETS.
"BETRAYAL. NOW THERE'S A WORD THAT CUTS BOTH WAYS."
YOUR BASHIR IS A TOOL OF THE CHURCH, BORN AND BRED.
HE TRIED TO KILL YOU ONCE ALREADY. HE ***WILL*** TRY AGAIN.
YOU'RE WRONG.
I DON'T WANT TO HURT YOU, BASHIR.
AND YOU DON'T WANT TO HURT ME EITHER.
RIGHT?

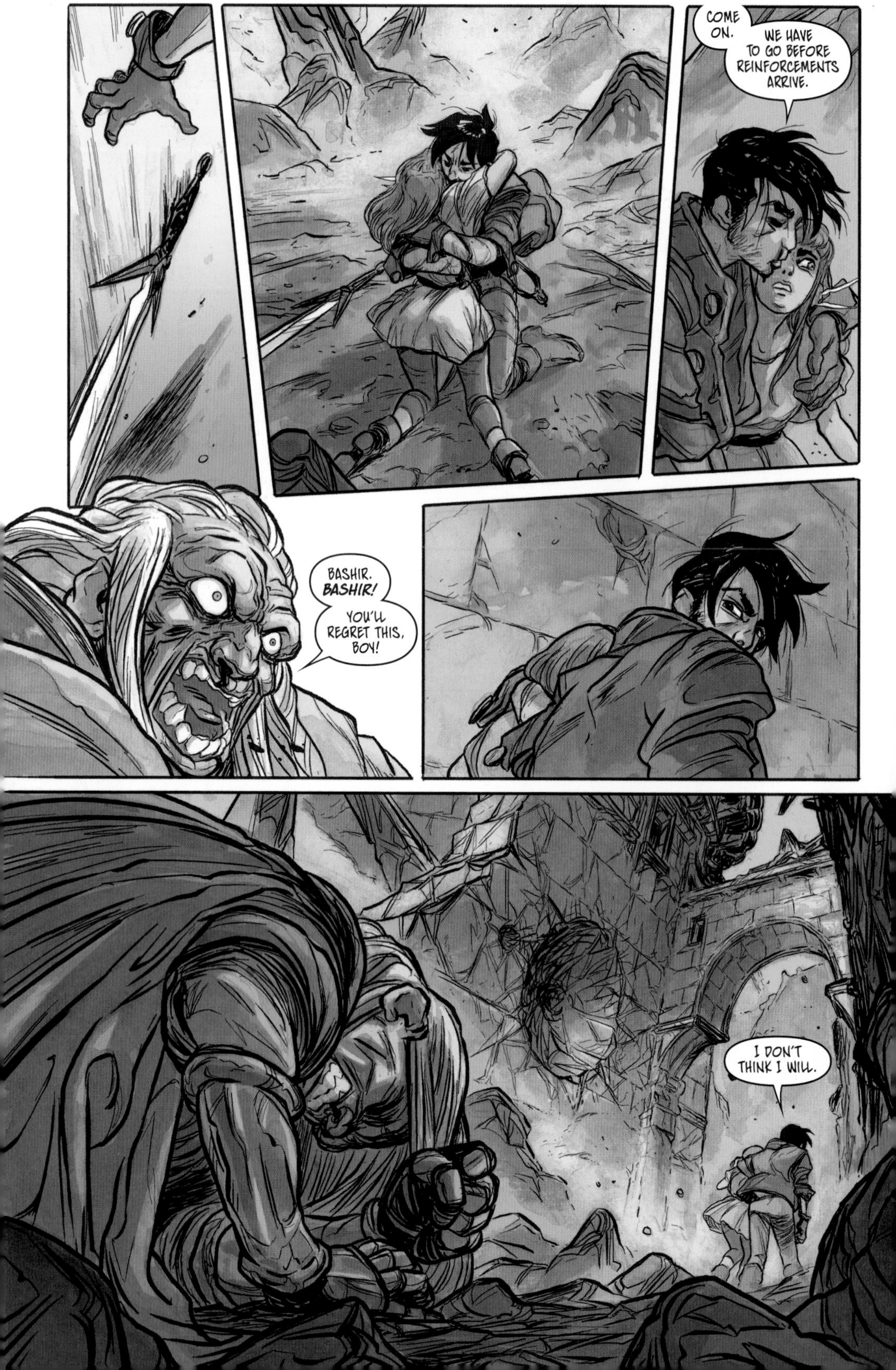
COME ON.
WE HAVE TO GO BEFORE REINFORCEMENTS ARRIVE.
BASHIR. BASHIR!
YOU'LL REGRET THIS, BOY!
I DON'T THINK I WILL.

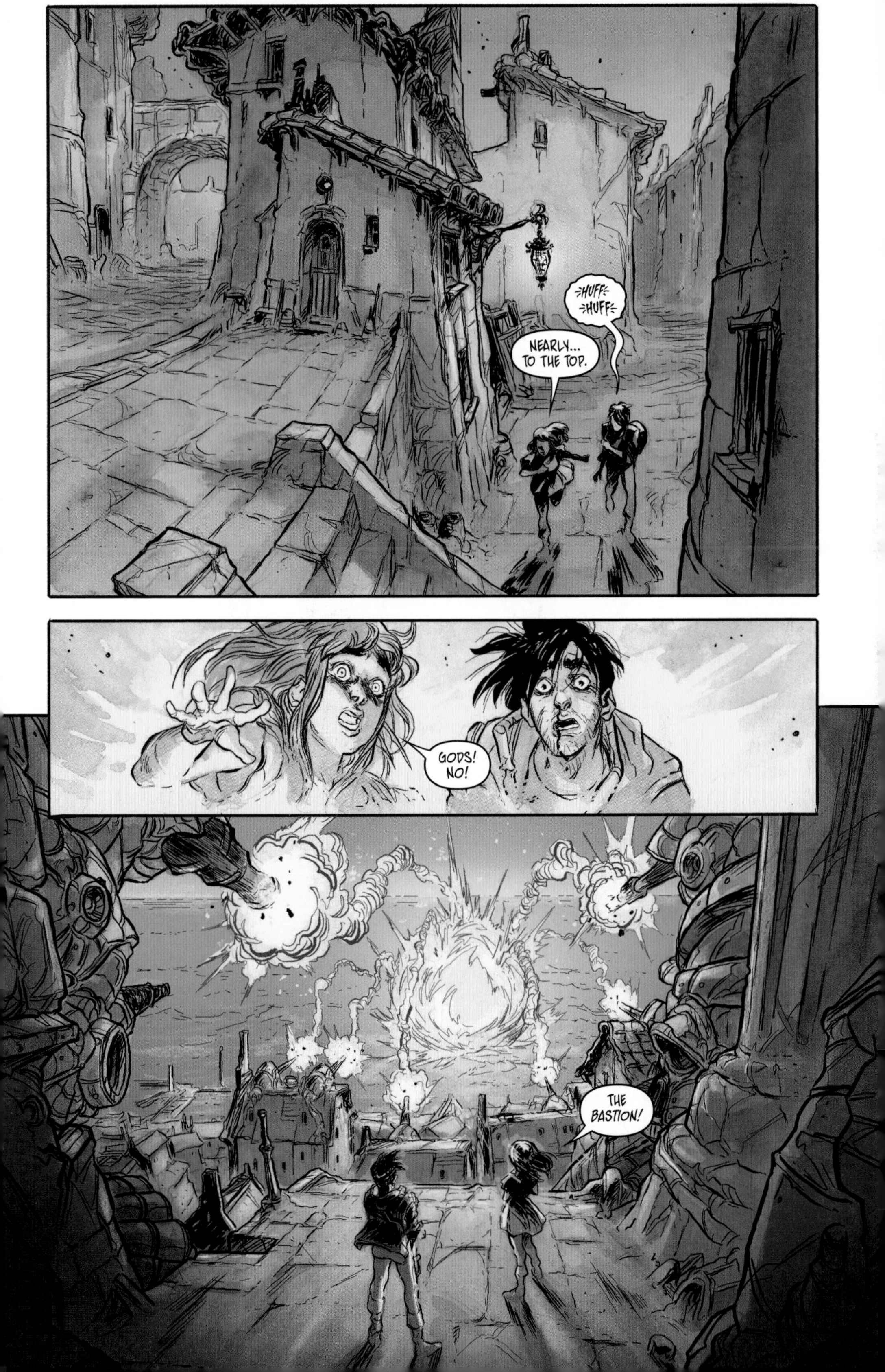
HUFF HUFF
NEARLY... TO THE TOP.
GODS! NO!
THE BASTION!

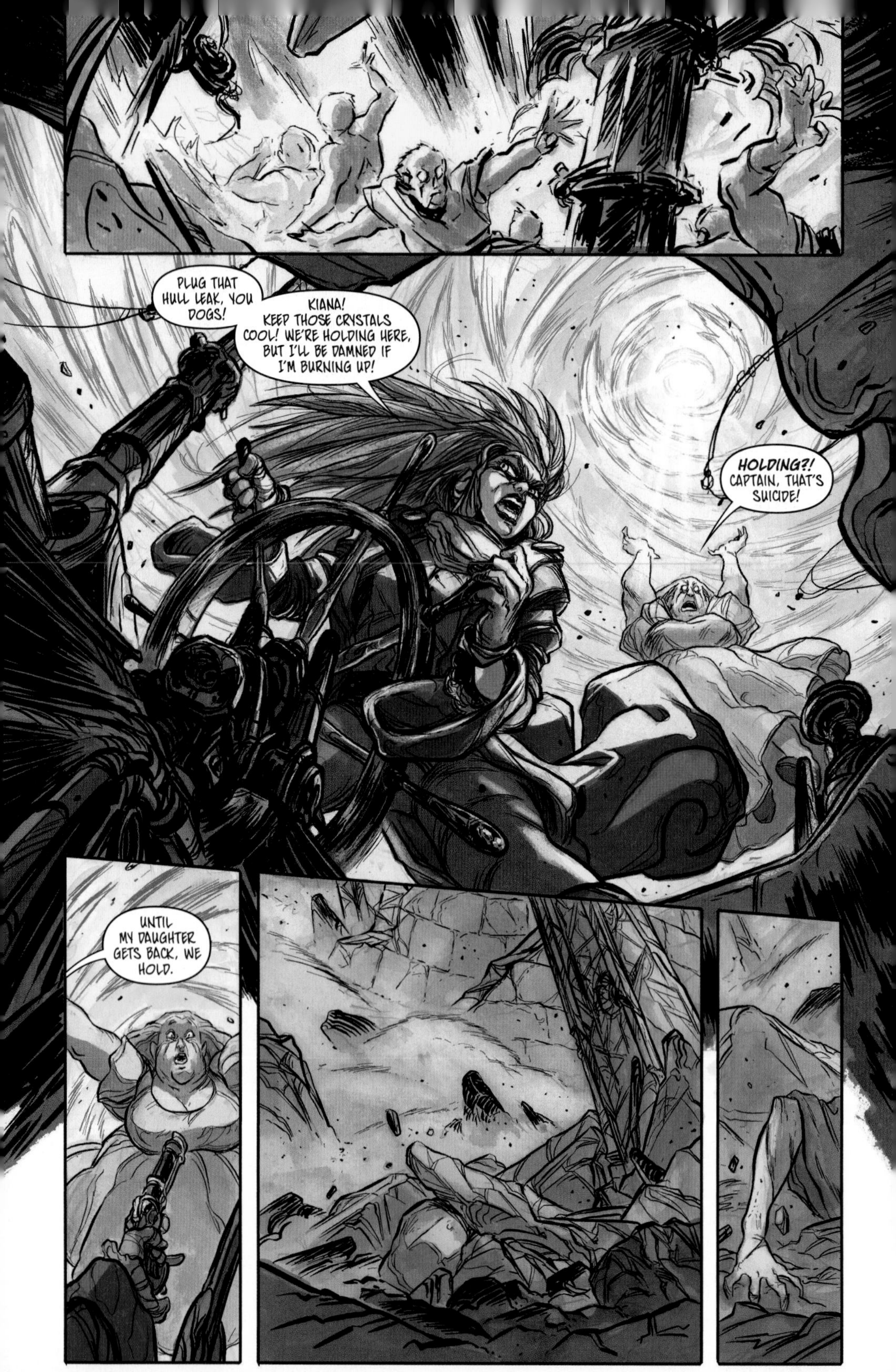
PLUG THAT HULL LEAK, YOU DOGS!
KIANA! KEEP THOSE CRYSTALS COOL! WE'RE HOLDING HERE, BUT I'LL BE DAMNED IF I'M BURNING UP!
HOLDING?! CAPTAIN, THAT'S SUICIDE!
UNTIL MY DAUGHTER GETS BACK, WE HOLD.

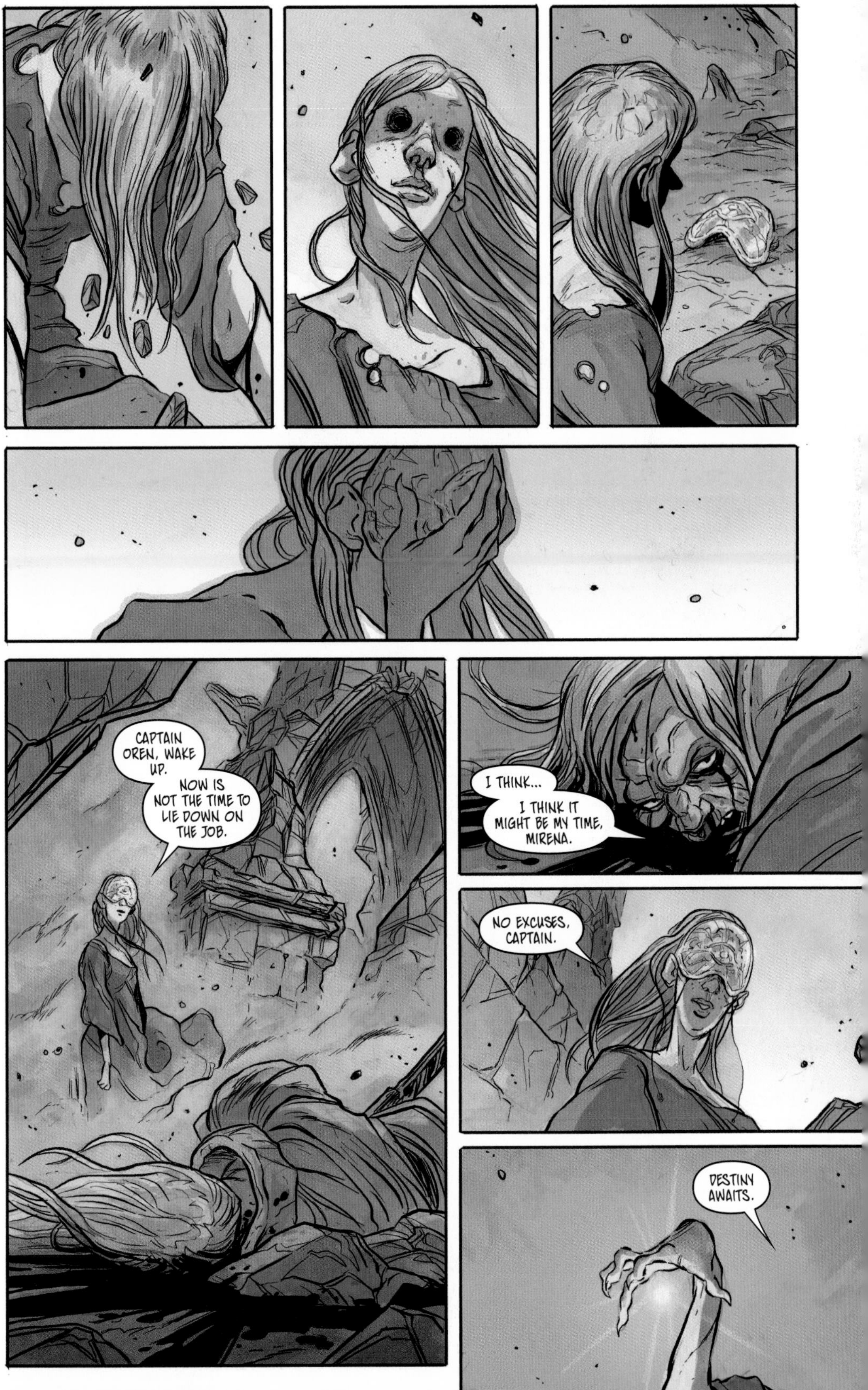
CAPTAIN OREN, WAKE UP.
NOW IS NOT THE TIME TO LIE DOWN ON THE JOB.
I THINK...
I THINK IT MIGHT BE MY TIME, MIRENA.
NO EXCUSES, CAPTAIN.
DESTINY AWAITS.

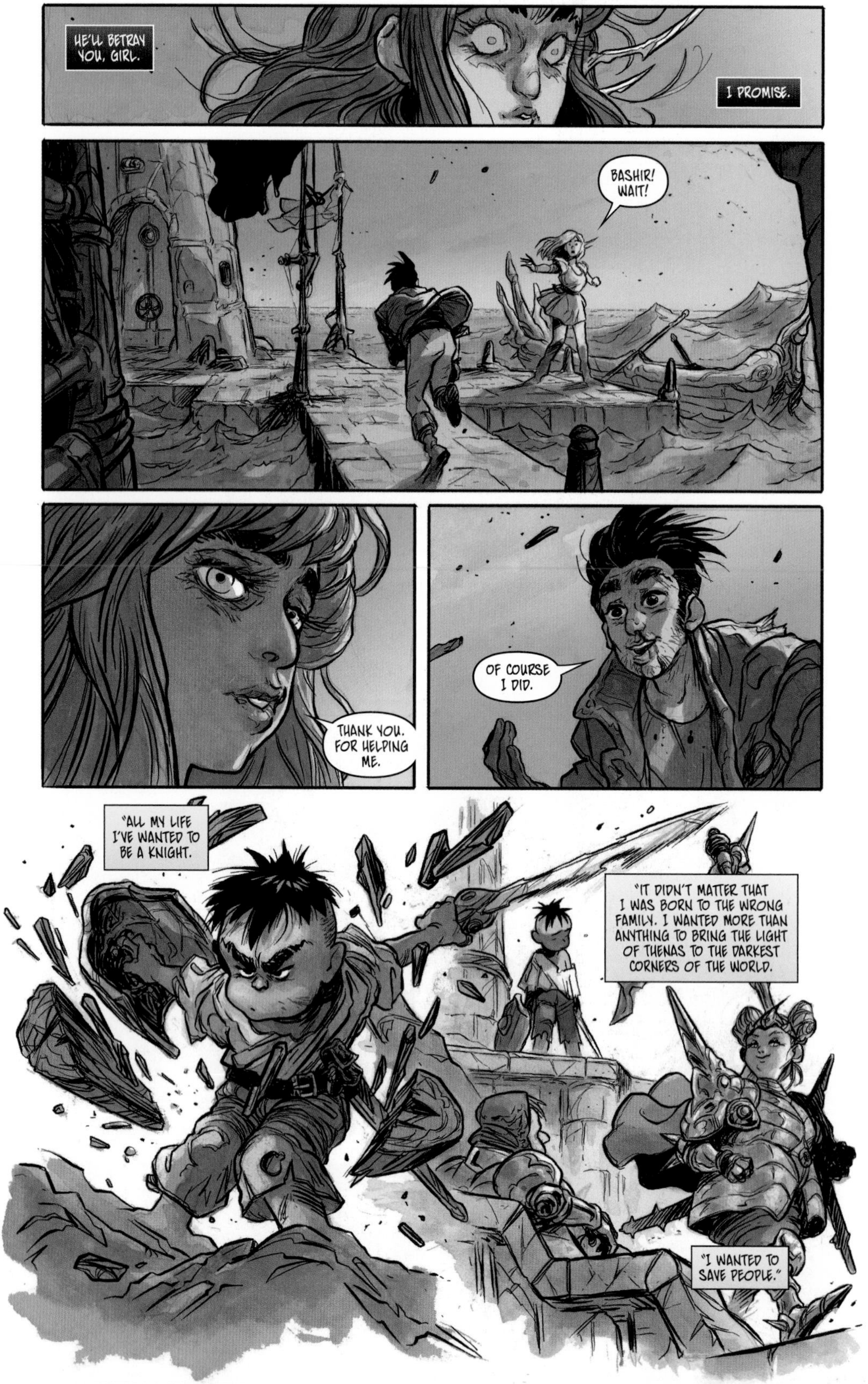
HE'LL BETRAY YOU, GIRL.
I PROMISE.
BASHIR! WAIT!
THANK YOU. FOR HELPING ME.
OF COURSE I DID.
"ALL MY LIFE I'VE WANTED TO BE A KNIGHT.
"IT DIDN'T MATTER THAT I WAS BORN TO THE WRONG FAMILY. I WANTED MORE THAN ANYTHING TO BRING THE LIGHT OF THENAS TO THE DARKEST CORNERS OF THE WORLD.
"I WANTED TO SAVE PEOPLE."

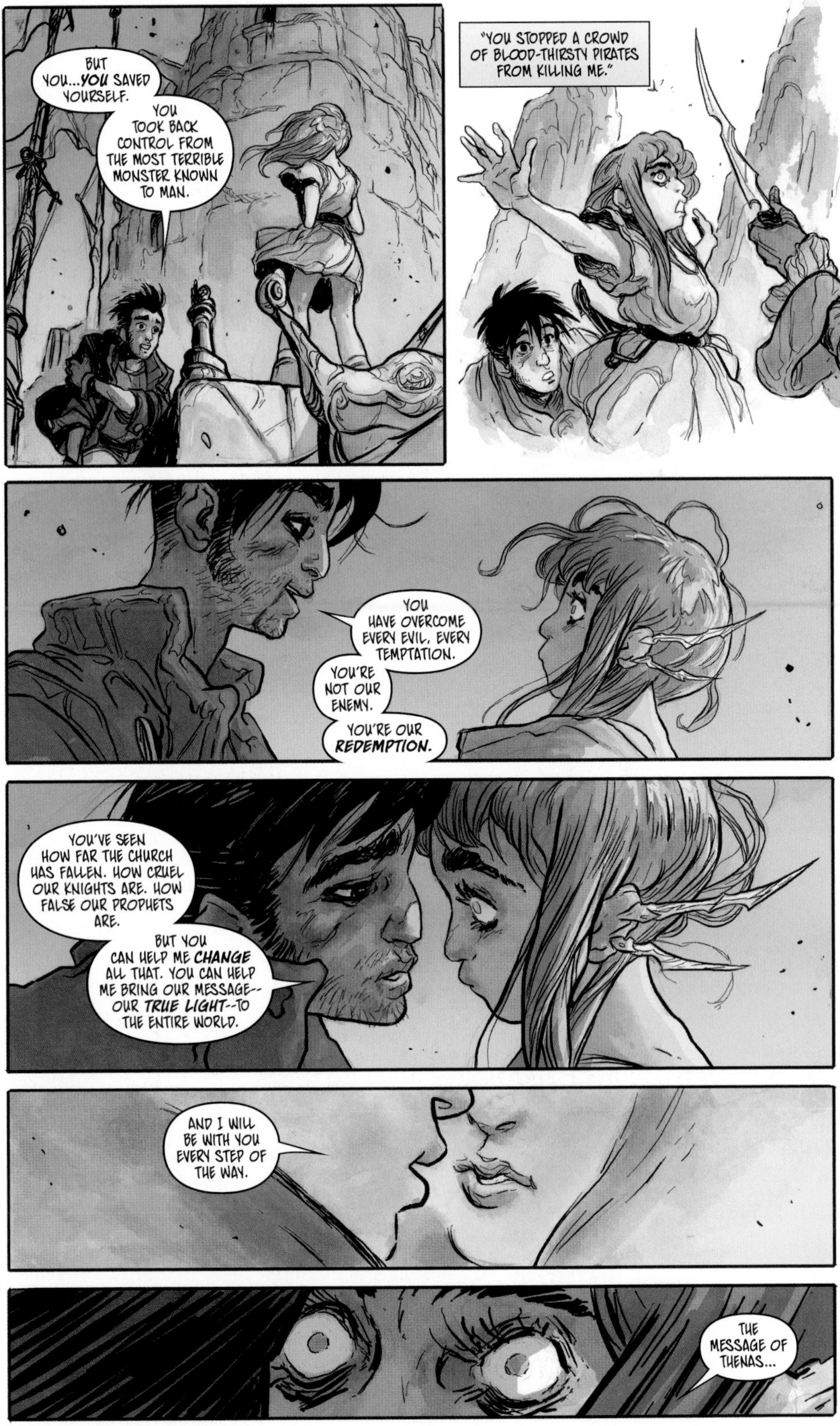
BUT YOU...YOU SAVED YOURSELF.
YOU TOOK BACK CONTROL FROM THE MOST TERRIBLE MONSTER KNOWN TO MAN.
"YOU STOPPED A CROWD OF BLOOD-THIRSTY PIRATES FROM KILLING ME."
YOU HAVE OVERCOME EVERY EVIL, EVERY TEMPTATION.
YOU'RE NOT OUR ENEMY.
YOU'RE OUR REDEMPTION.
YOU'VE SEEN HOW FAR THE CHURCH HAS FALLEN. HOW CRUEL OUR KNIGHTS ARE. HOW FALSE OUR PROPHETS ARE.
BUT YOU CAN HELP ME CHANGE ALL THAT. YOU CAN HELP ME BRING OUR MESSAGE--OUR TRUE LIGHT--TO THE ENTIRE WORLD.
AND I WILL BE WITH YOU EVERY STEP OF THE WAY.
THE MESSAGE OF THENAS...

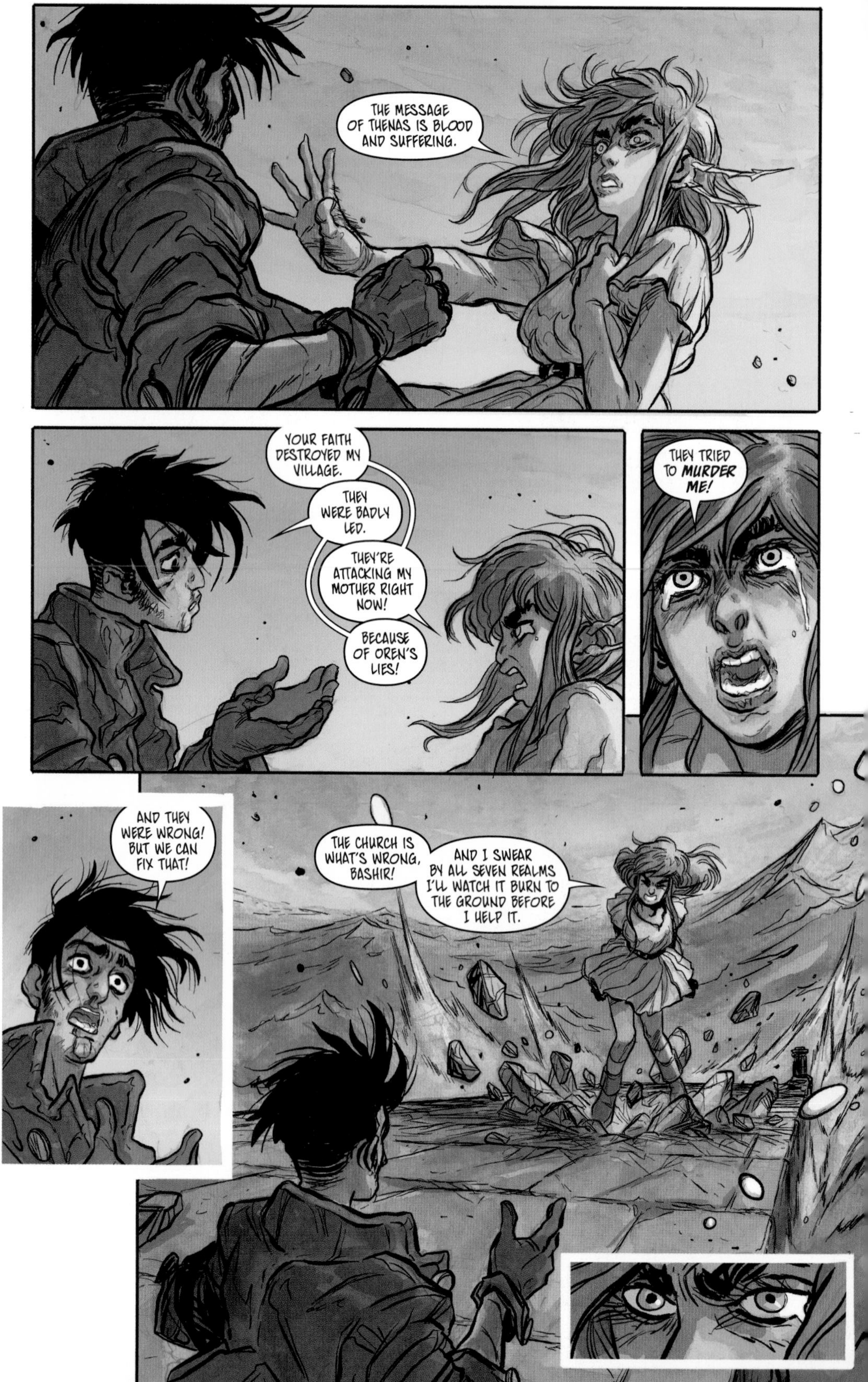
THE MESSAGE OF THENAS IS BLOOD AND SUFFERING.
YOUR FAITH DESTROYED MY VILLAGE.
THEY WERE BADLY LED.
THEY'RE ATTACKING MY MOTHER RIGHT NOW!
BECAUSE OF OREN'S LIES!
THEY TRIED TO MURDER ME!
AND THEY WERE WRONG! BUT WE CAN FIX THAT!
THE CHURCH IS WHAT'S WRONG, BASHIR!
AND I SWEAR BY ALL SEVEN REALMS I'LL WATCH IT BURN TO THE GROUND BEFORE I HELP IT.

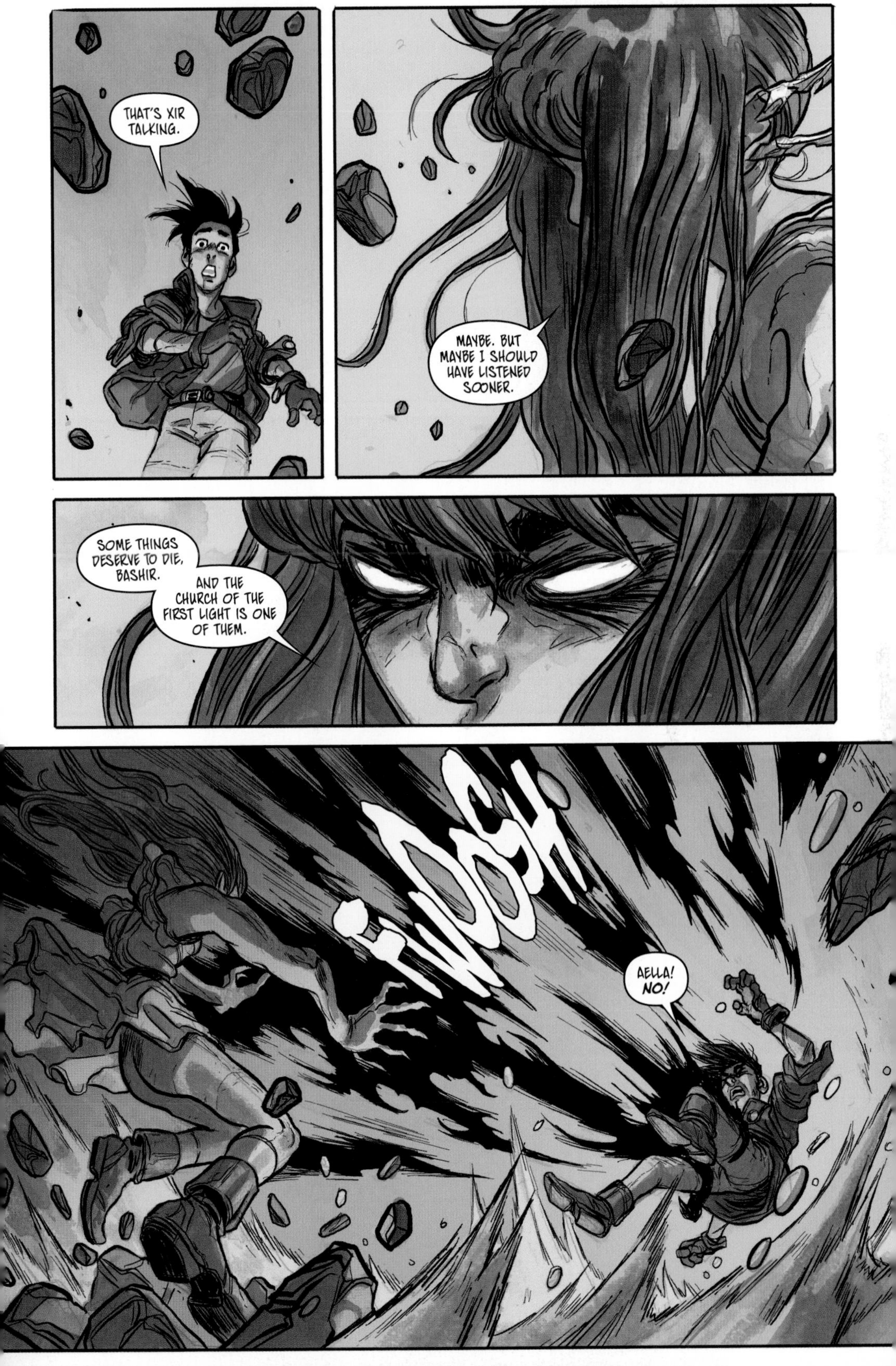
THAT'S XIR TALKING.
MAYBE. BUT MAYBE I SHOULD HAVE LISTENED SOONER.
SOME THINGS DESERVE TO DIE, BASHIR.
AND THE CHURCH OF THE FIRST LIGHT IS ONE OF THEM.
WOOSH
AELLA! NO!

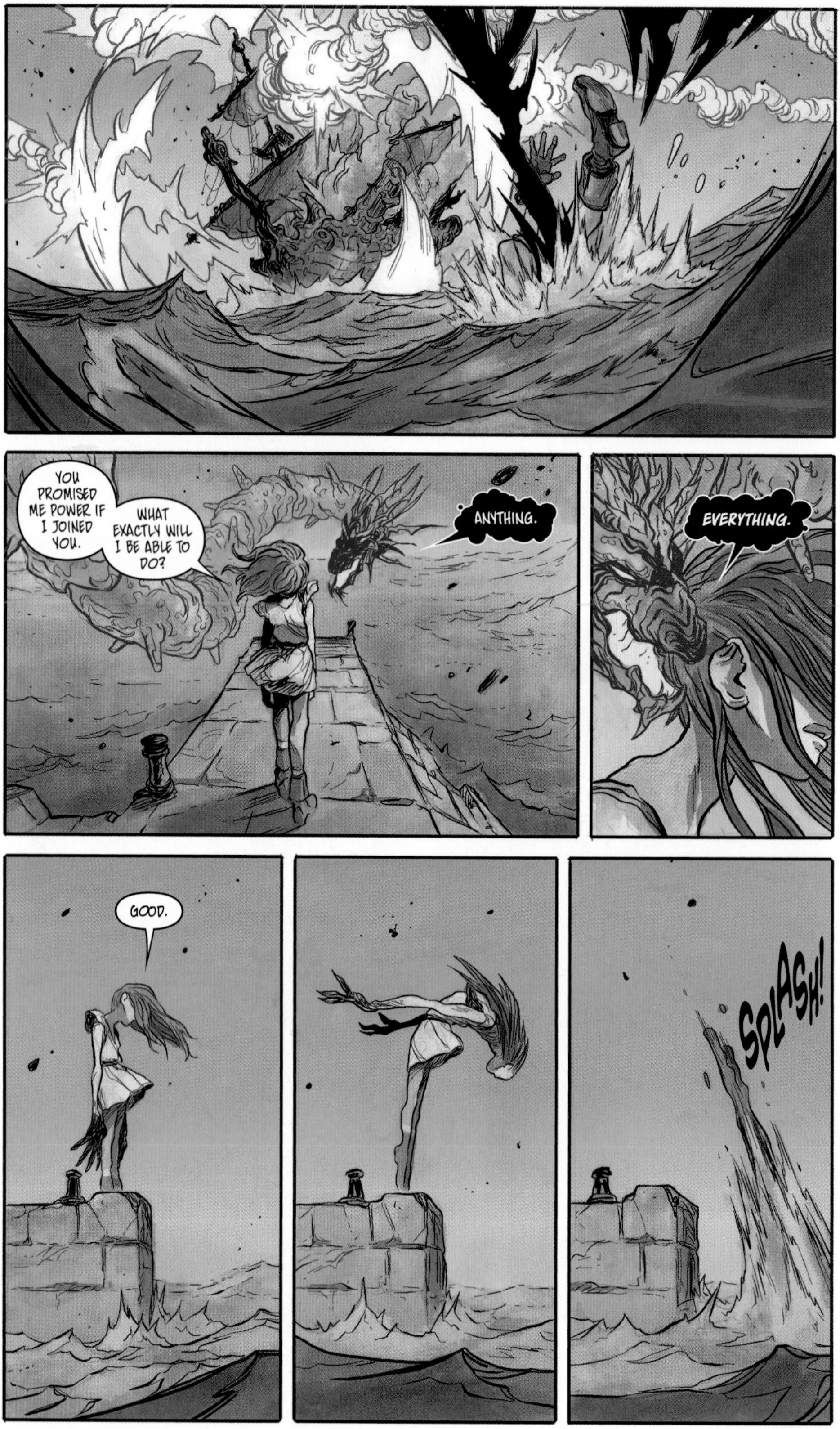
YOU PROMISED ME POWER IF I JOINED YOU.
WHAT EXACTLY WILL I BE ABLE TO DO?
ANYTHING.
EVERYTHING.
GOOD.
SPLASH!

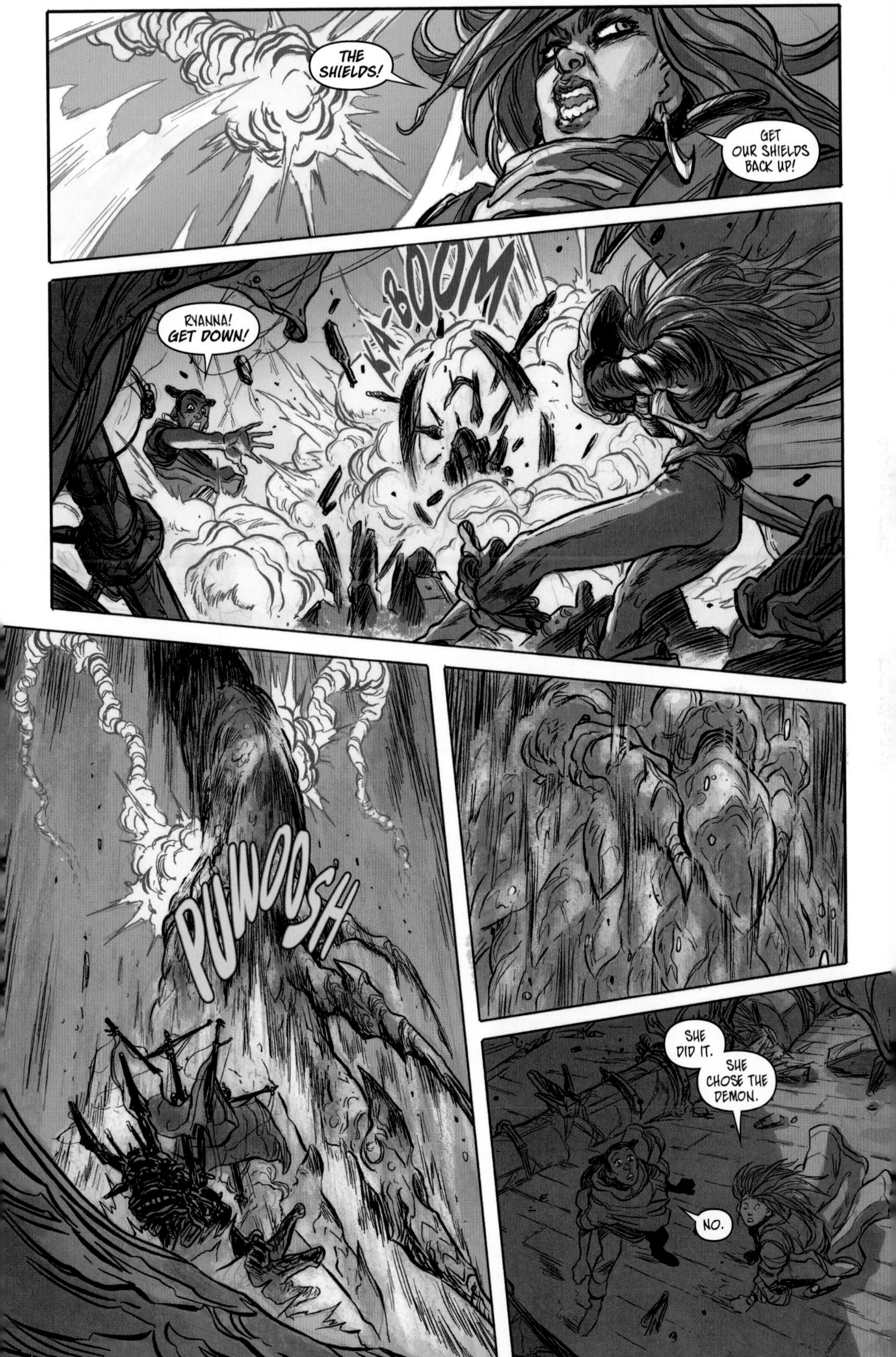
THE SHIELDS!
GET OUR SHIELDS BACK UP!
KA-BOOM
RYANNA! GET DOWN!
PUWOOSH
SHE DID IT.
SHE CHOSE THE DEMON.
NO.

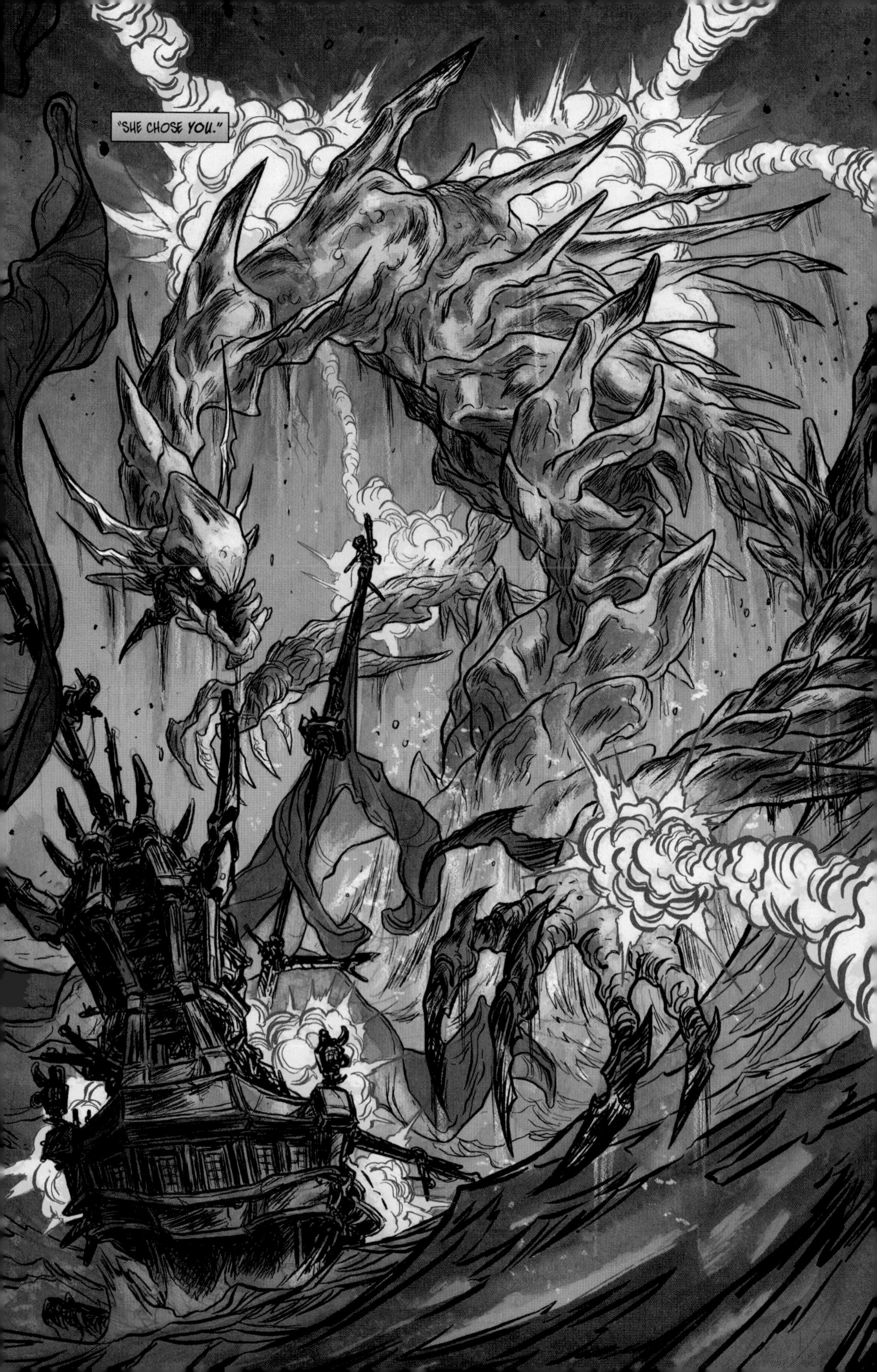
"SHE CHOSE YOU."

Chapter Six

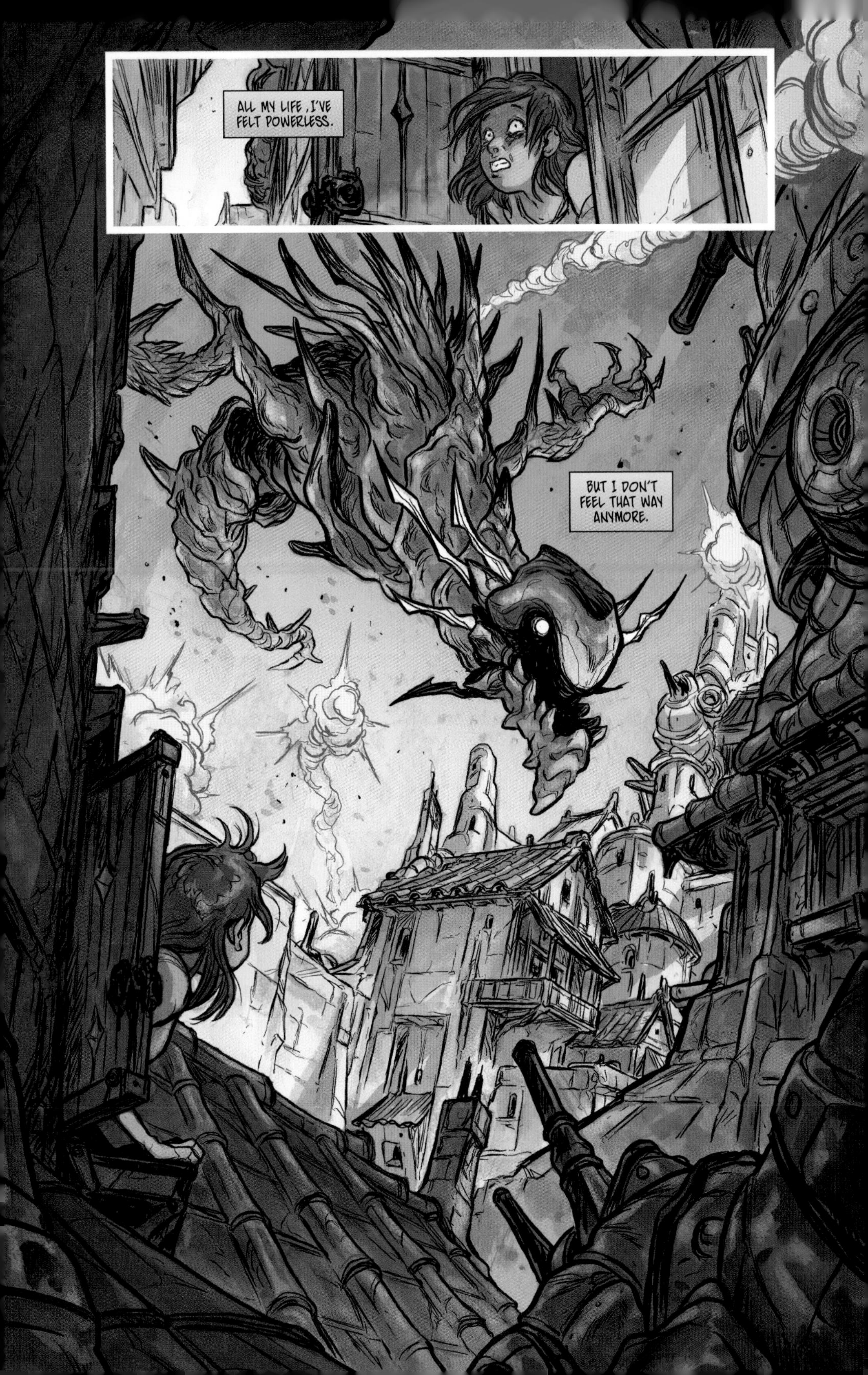
ALL MY LIFE, I'VE FELT POWERLESS.
BUT I DON'T FEEL THAT WAY ANYMORE.

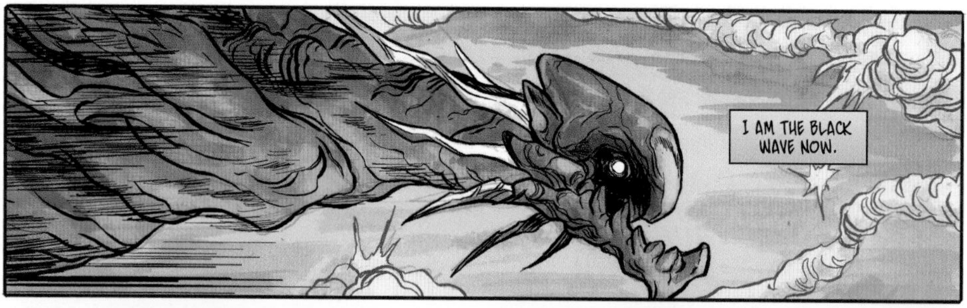
I AM THE BLACK WAVE NOW.

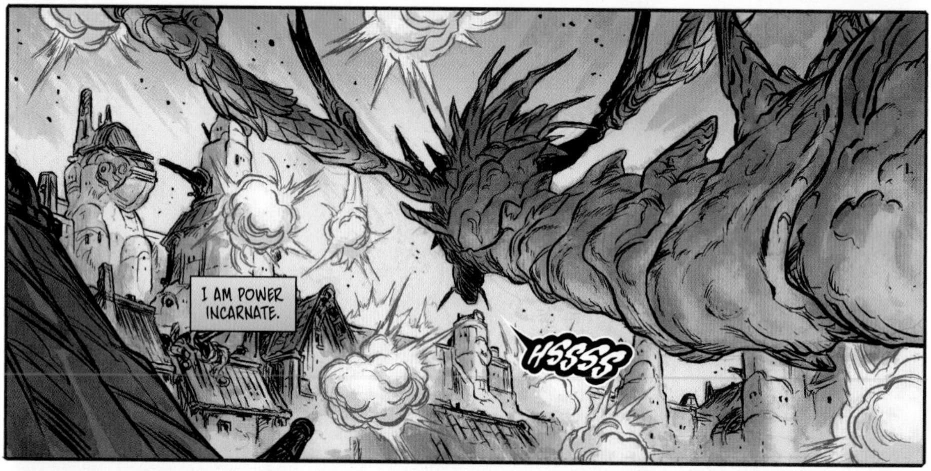
I AM POWER INCARNATE.
HSSSS

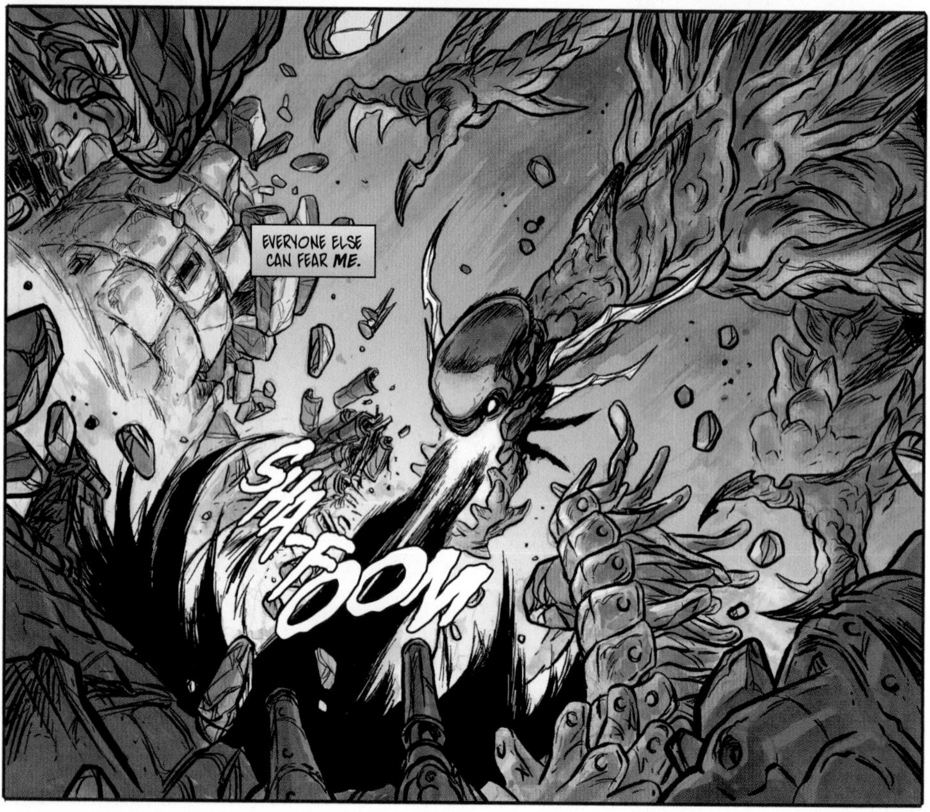
EVERYONE ELSE CAN FEAR **ME**.
SHA-BOOM

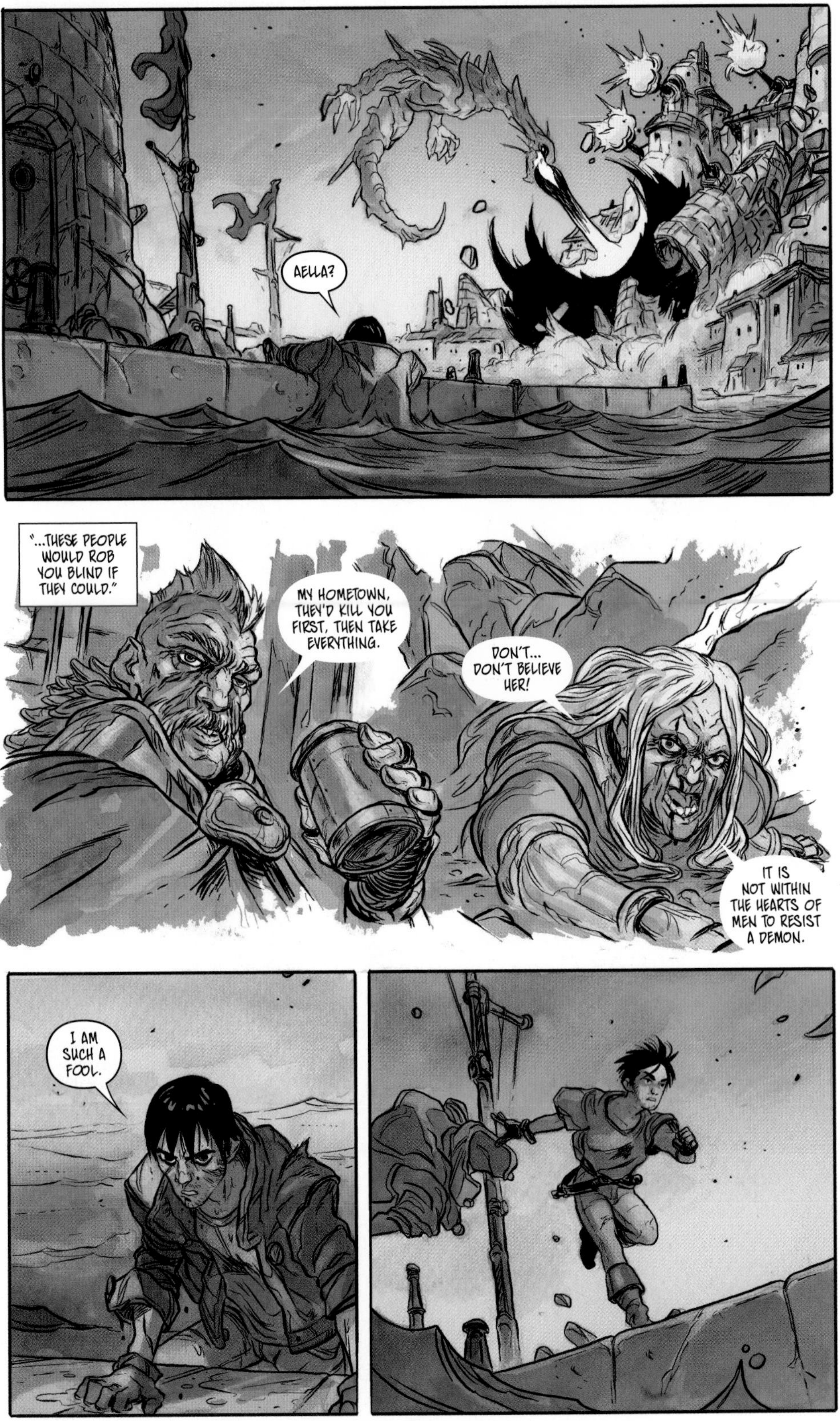
AELLA?
"...THESE PEOPLE WOULD ROB YOU BLIND IF THEY COULD."
MY HOMETOWN, THEY'D KILL YOU FIRST, THEN TAKE EVERYTHING.
DON'T... DON'T BELIEVE HER!
IT IS NOT WITHIN THE HEARTS OF MEN TO RESIST A DEMON.
I AM SUCH A FOOL.

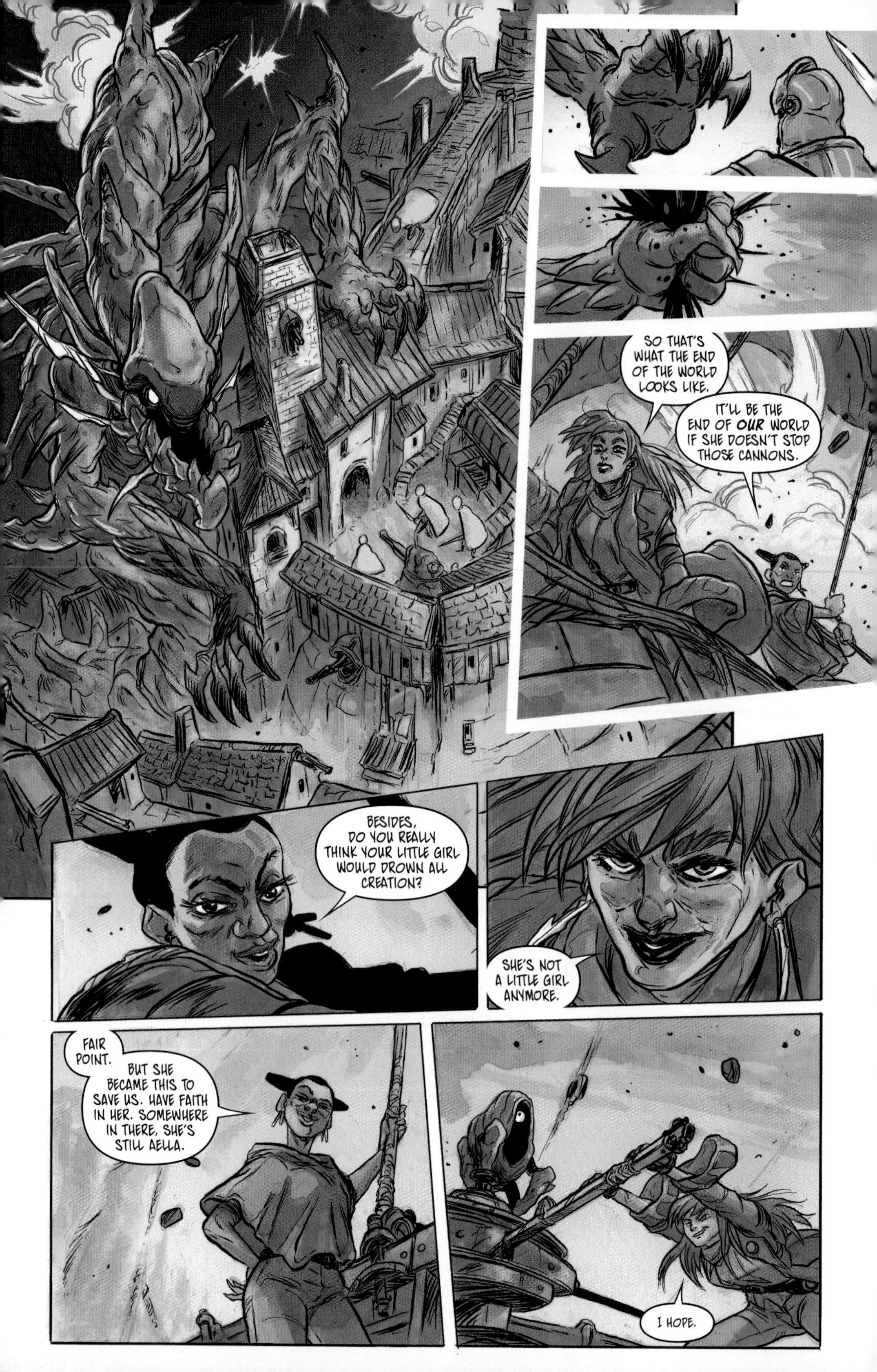
SO THAT'S WHAT THE END OF THE WORLD LOOKS LIKE.
IT'LL BE THE END OF **OUR** WORLD IF SHE DOESN'T STOP THOSE CANNONS.
BESIDES, DO YOU REALLY THINK YOUR LITTLE GIRL WOULD DROWN ALL CREATION?
SHE'S NOT A LITTLE GIRL ANYMORE.
FAIR POINT.
BUT SHE BECAME THIS TO SAVE US. HAVE FAITH IN HER. SOMEWHERE IN THERE, SHE'S STILL AELLA.
I HOPE.

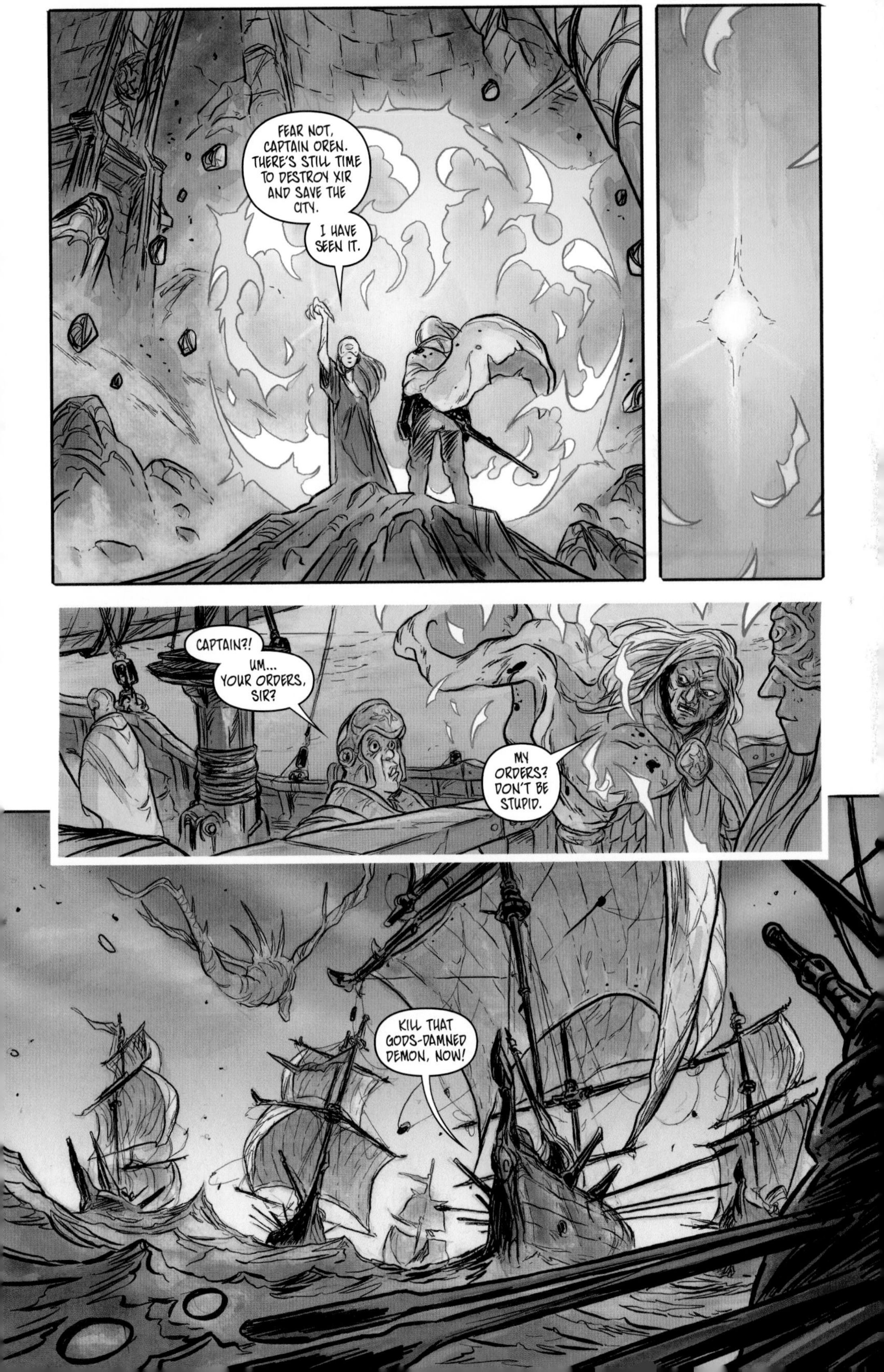
FEAR NOT, CAPTAIN OREN. THERE'S STILL TIME TO DESTROY XIR AND SAVE THE CITY.
I HAVE SEEN IT.
CAPTAIN?!
UM... YOUR ORDERS, SIR?
MY ORDERS? DON'T BE STUPID.
KILL THAT GODS-DAMNED DEMON, NOW!

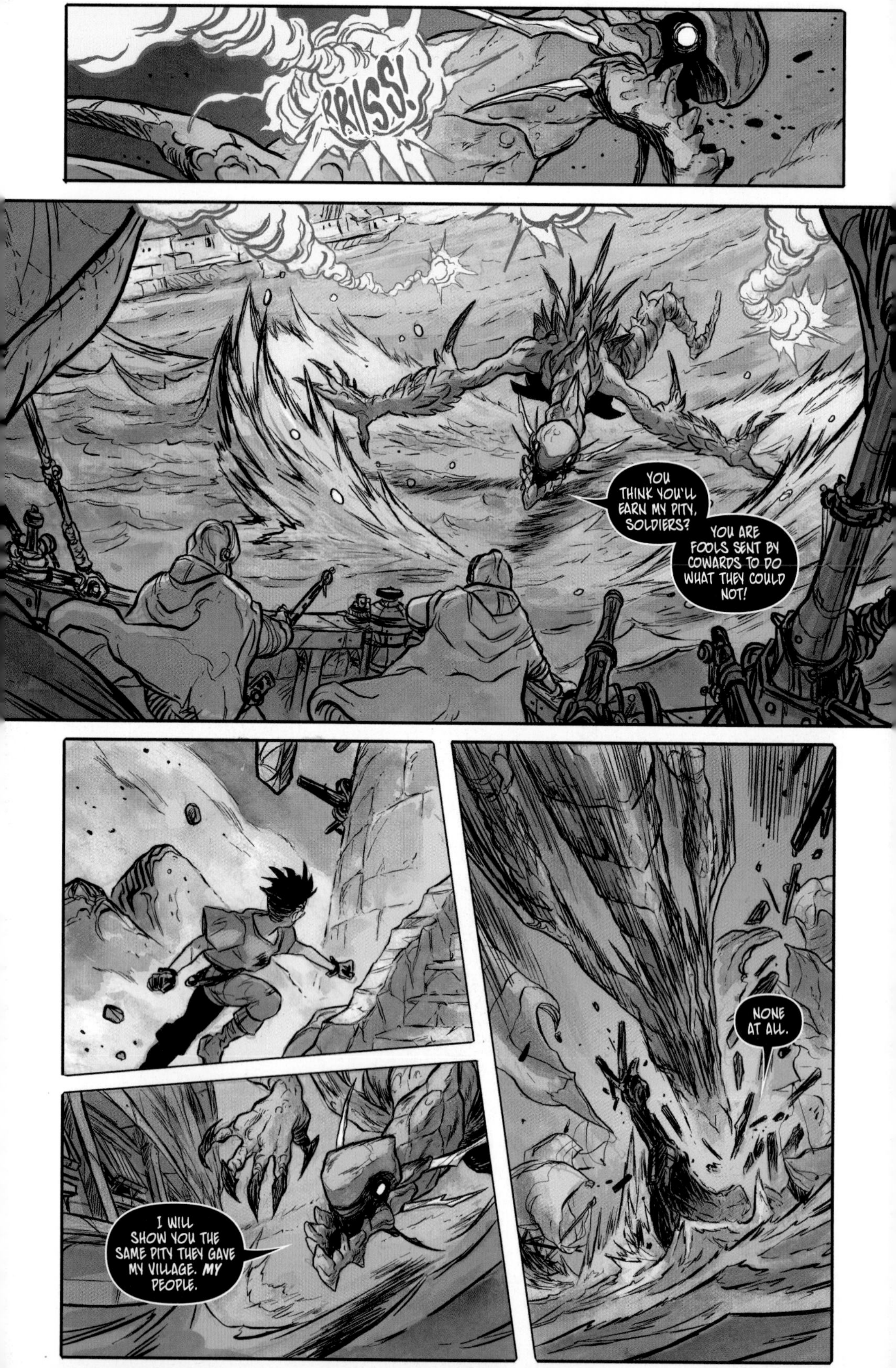
RBISS!
YOU THINK YOU'LL EARN MY PITY, SOLDIERS?
YOU ARE FOOLS SENT BY COWARDS TO DO WHAT THEY COULD NOT!
I WILL SHOW YOU THE SAME PITY THEY GAVE MY VILLAGE. MY PEOPLE.
NONE AT ALL.

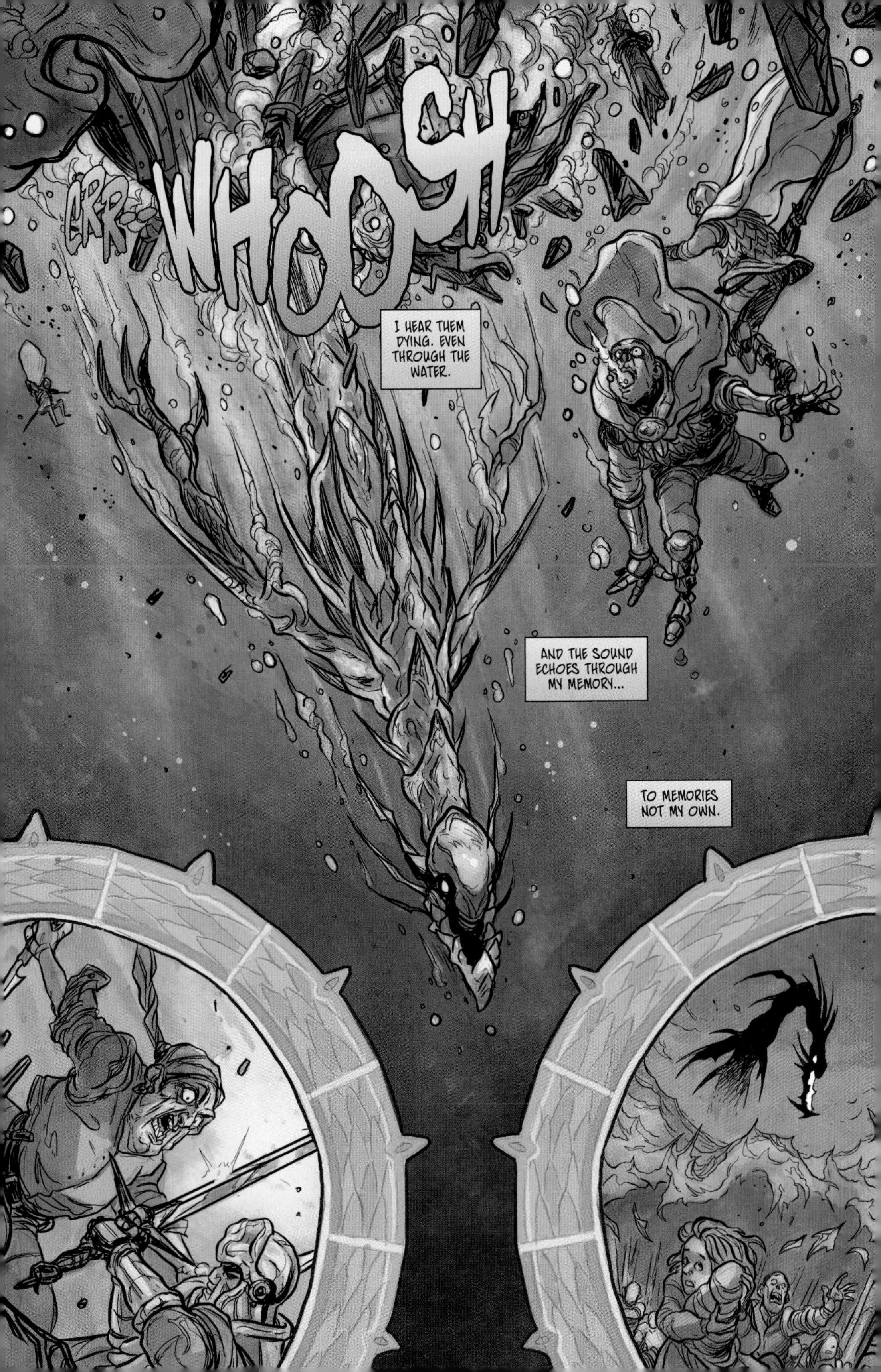
CRR
WHOOSH
I HEAR THEM DYING. EVEN THROUGH THE WATER.
AND THE SOUND ECHOES THROUGH MY MEMORY...
TO MEMORIES NOT MY OWN.

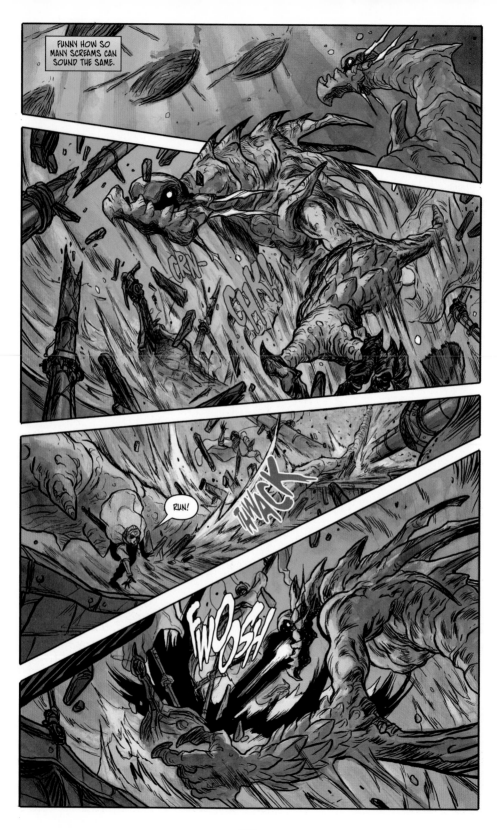

FUNNY HOW SO MANY SCREAMS CAN SOUND THE SAME.

RUN!

THWACK

FWOOSH

132

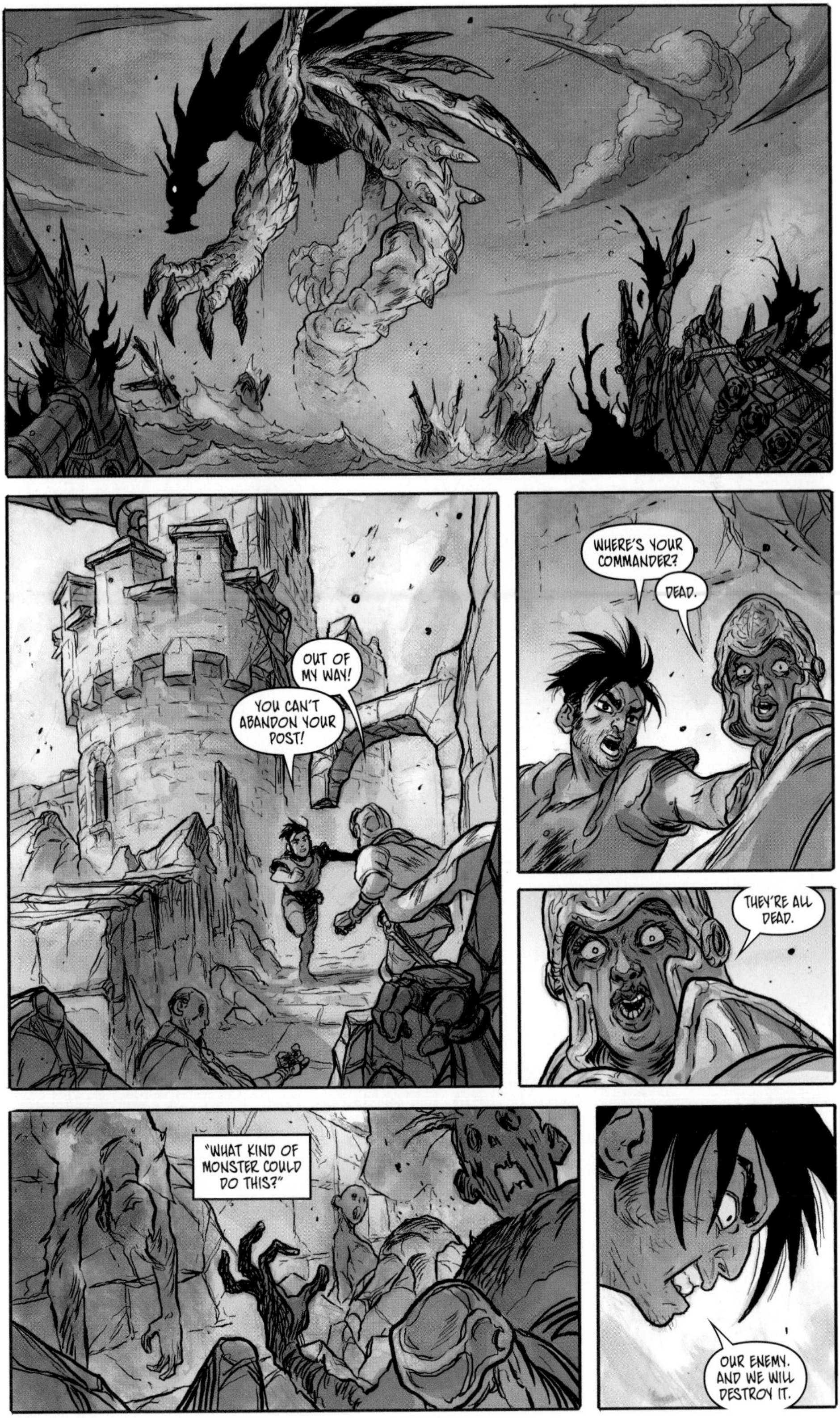
OUT OF MY WAY!
YOU CAN'T ABANDON YOUR POST!
WHERE'S YOUR COMMANDER?
DEAD.
THEY'RE ALL DEAD.
"WHAT KIND OF MONSTER COULD DO THIS?"
OUR ENEMY. AND WE WILL DESTROY IT.

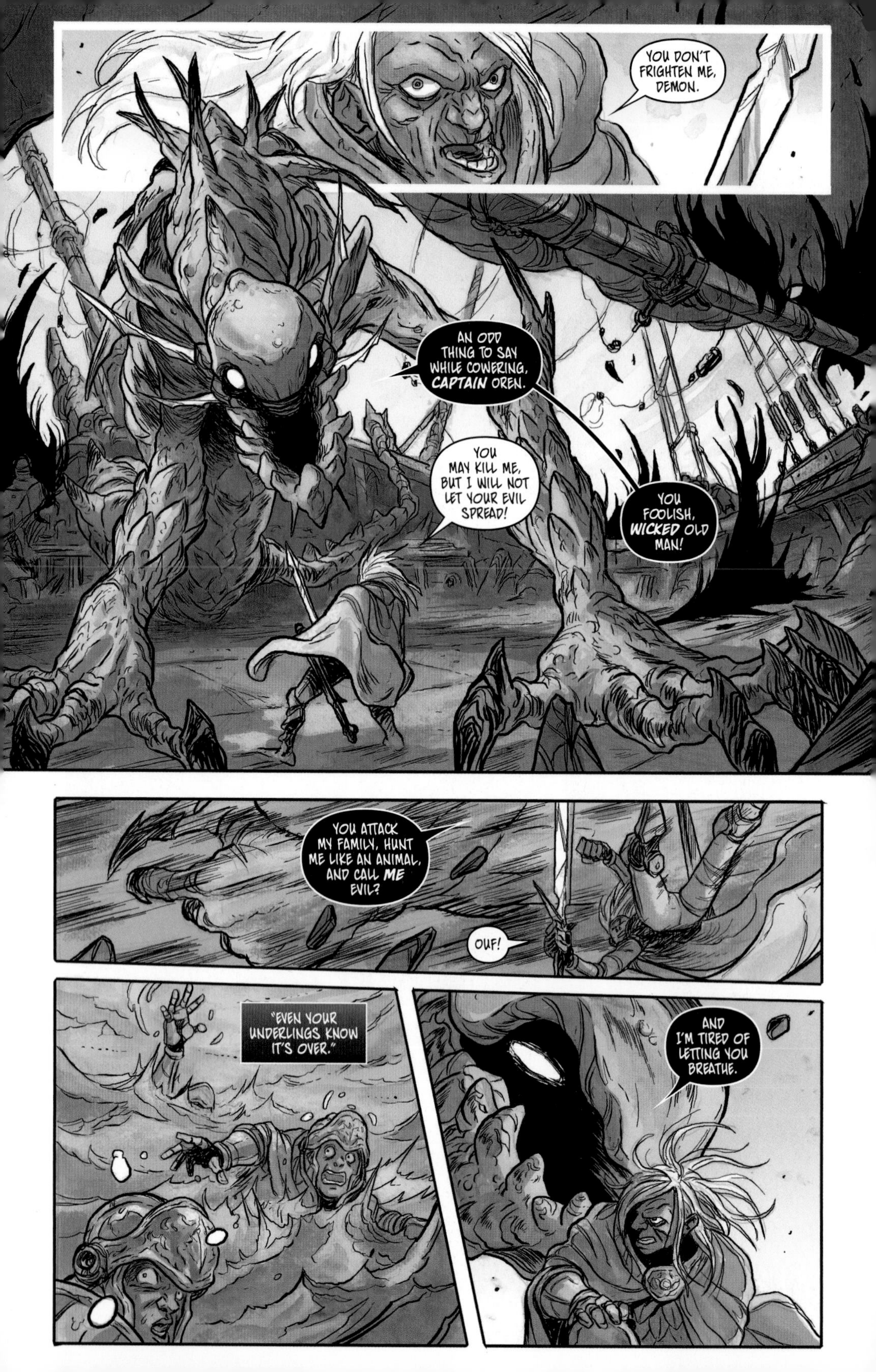

YOU DON'T FRIGHTEN ME, DEMON.
AN ODD THING TO SAY WHILE COWERING, CAPTAIN OREN.
YOU MAY KILL ME, BUT I WILL NOT LET YOUR EVIL SPREAD!
YOU FOOLISH, WICKED OLD MAN!
YOU ATTACK MY FAMILY, HUNT ME LIKE AN ANIMAL, AND CALL ME EVIL?
OUF!
"EVEN YOUR UNDERLINGS KNOW IT'S OVER."
AND I'M TIRED OF LETTING YOU BREATHE.

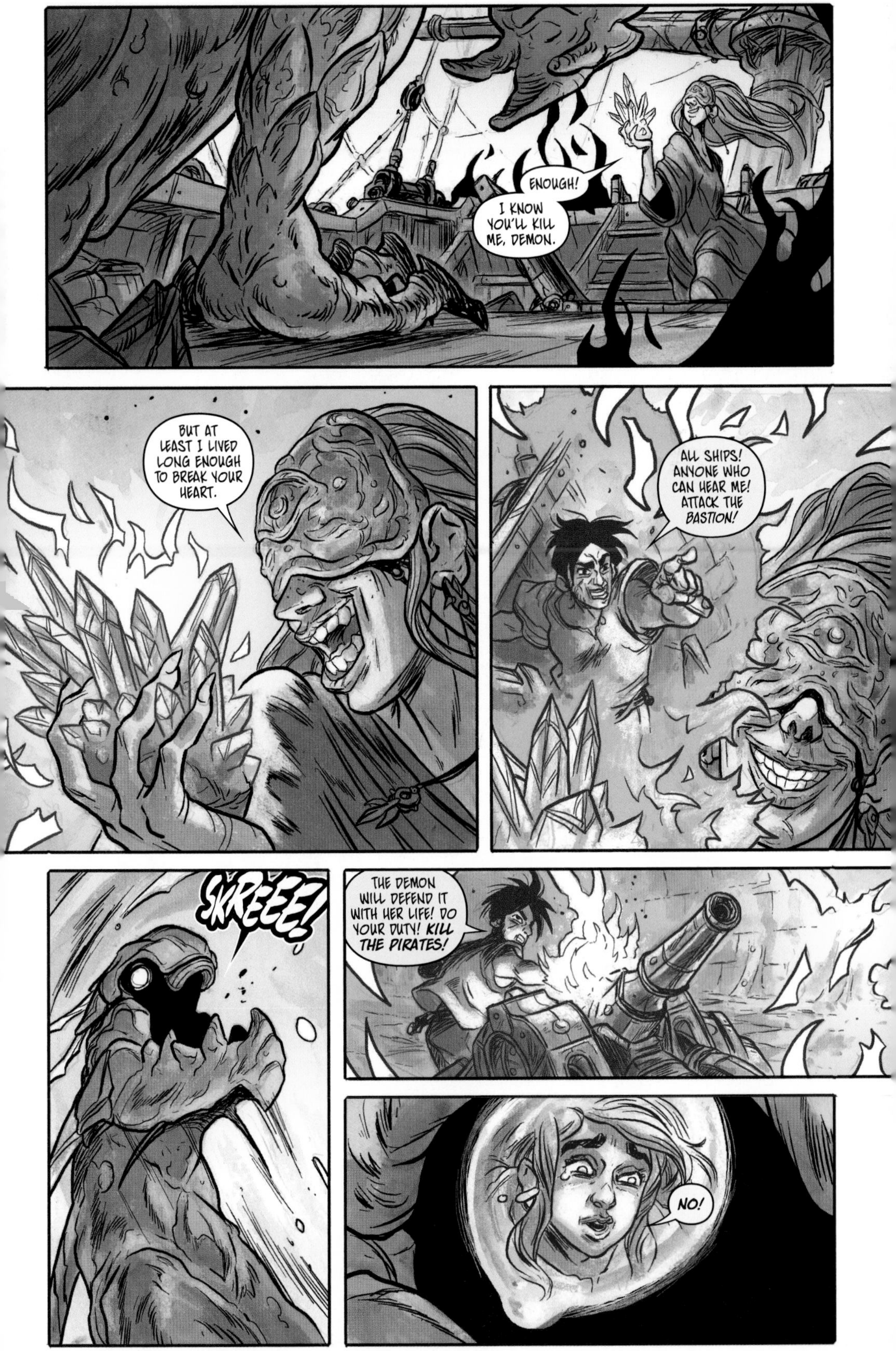
ENOUGH!
I KNOW YOU'LL KILL ME, DEMON.
BUT AT LEAST I LIVED LONG ENOUGH TO BREAK YOUR HEART.
ALL SHIPS! ANYONE WHO CAN HEAR ME! ATTACK THE BASTION!
SKREEE!
THE DEMON WILL DEFEND IT WITH HER LIFE! DO YOUR DUTY! KILL THE PIRATES!
NO!

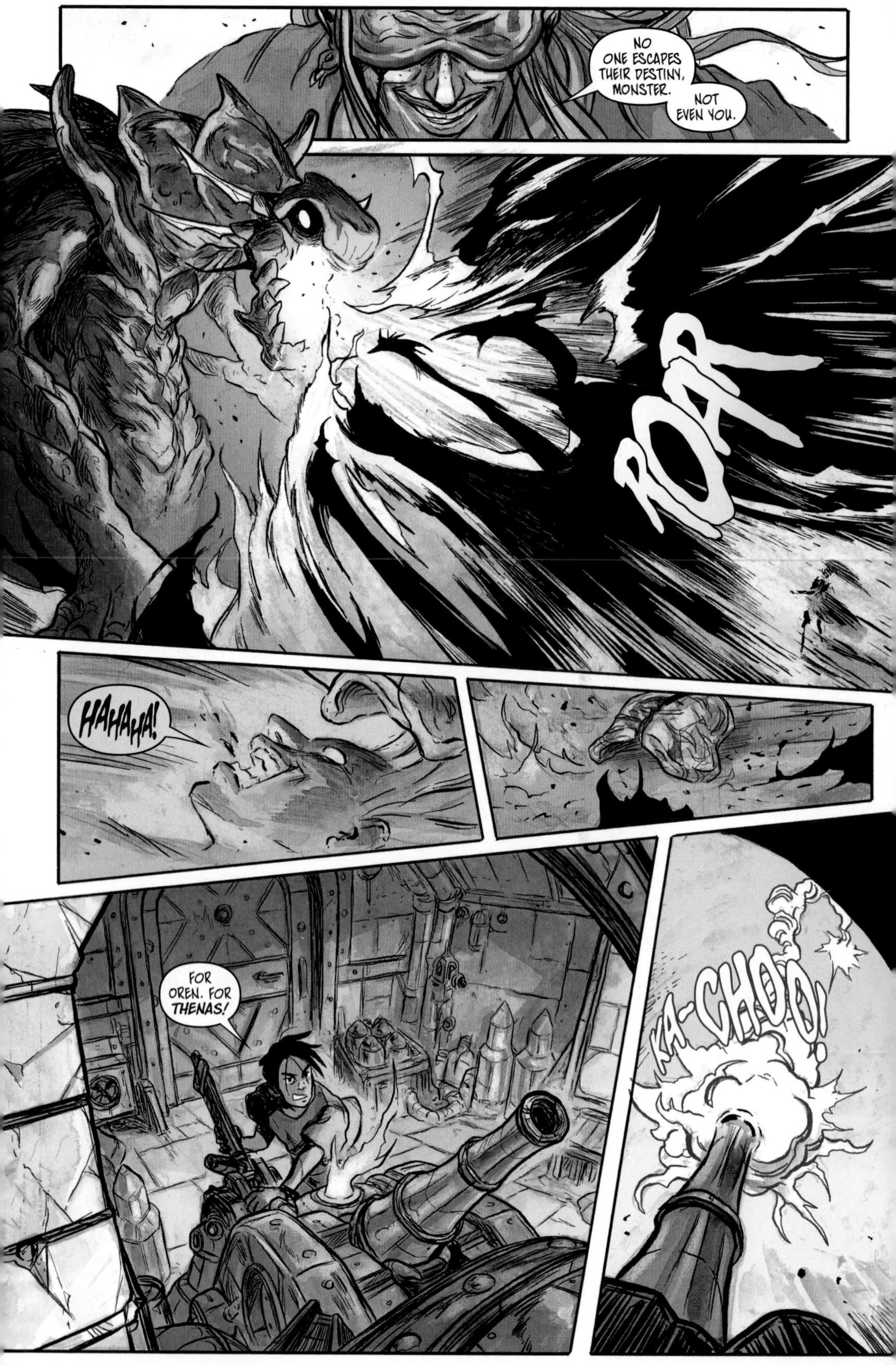
NO ONE ESCAPES THEIR DESTINY, MONSTER.
NOT EVEN YOU.
ROAR
HAHAHA!
FOR OREN. FOR THENAS!
KA-CHOO!

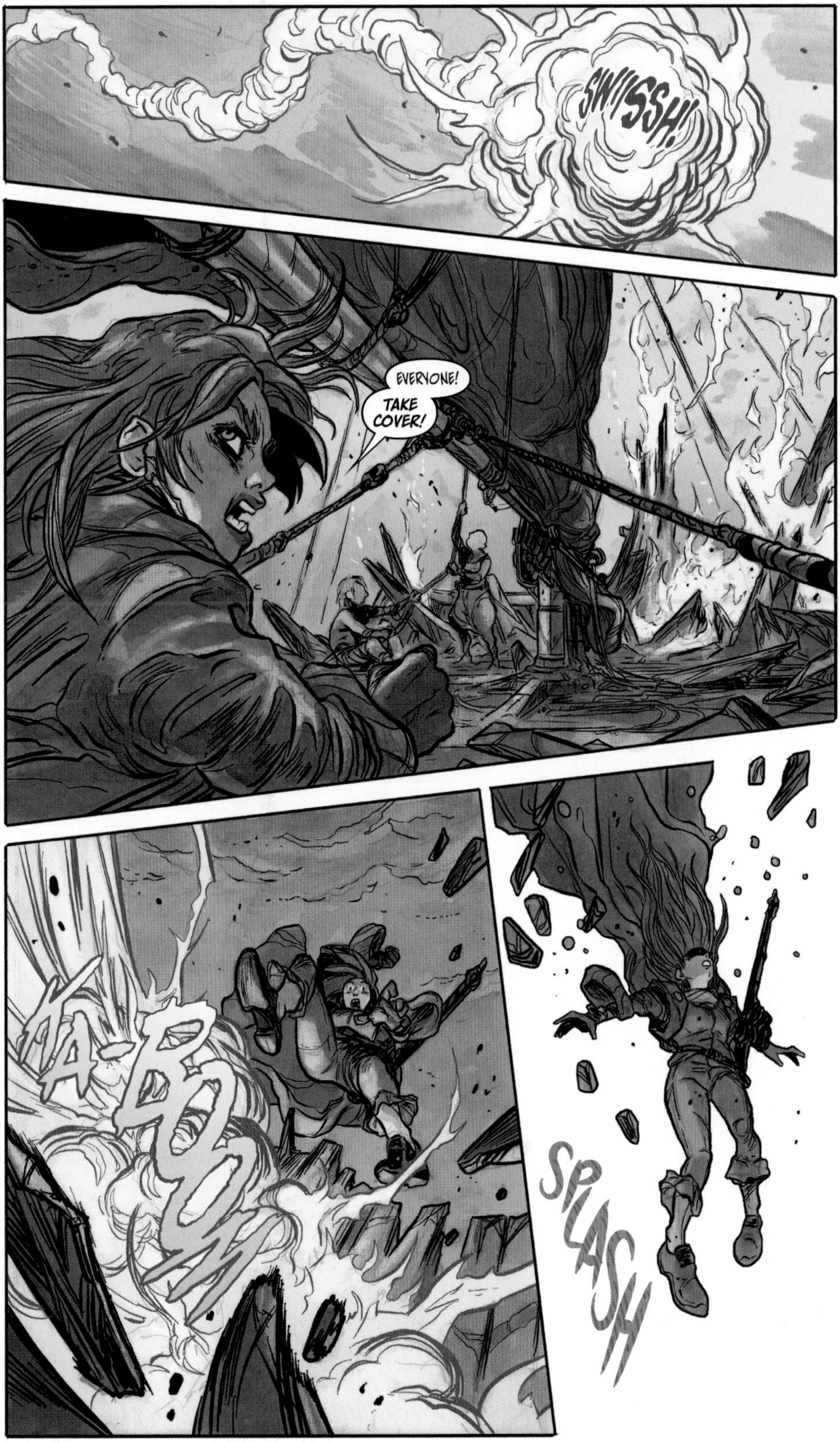
SWISSH!
EVERYONE!
TAKE COVER!
KA-BOOM
SPLASH

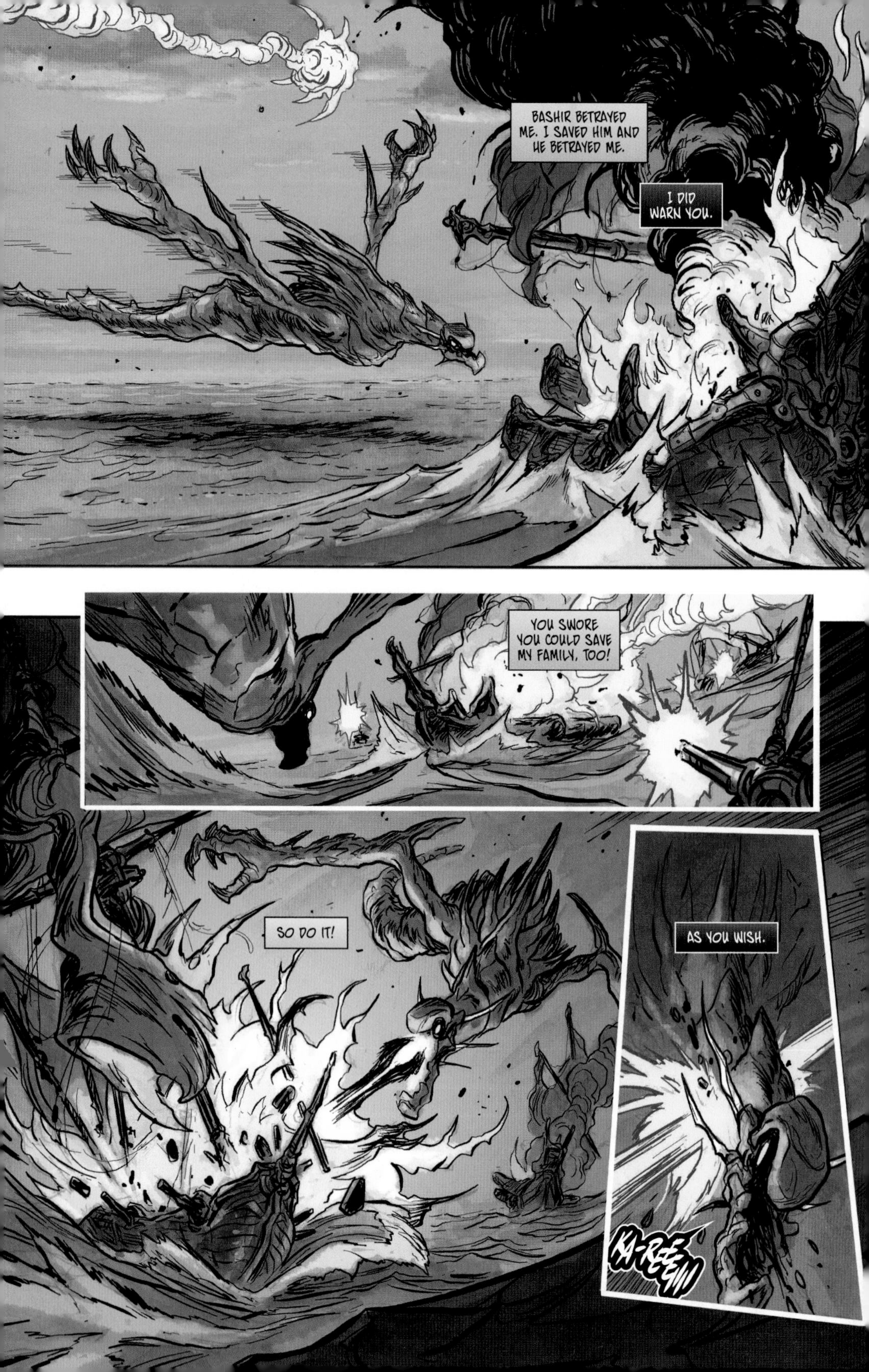
BASHIR BETRAYED ME. I SAVED HIM AND HE BETRAYED ME.
I DID WARN YOU.
YOU SWORE YOU COULD SAVE MY FAMILY, TOO!
SO DO IT!
AS YOU WISH.
KA-REEEM

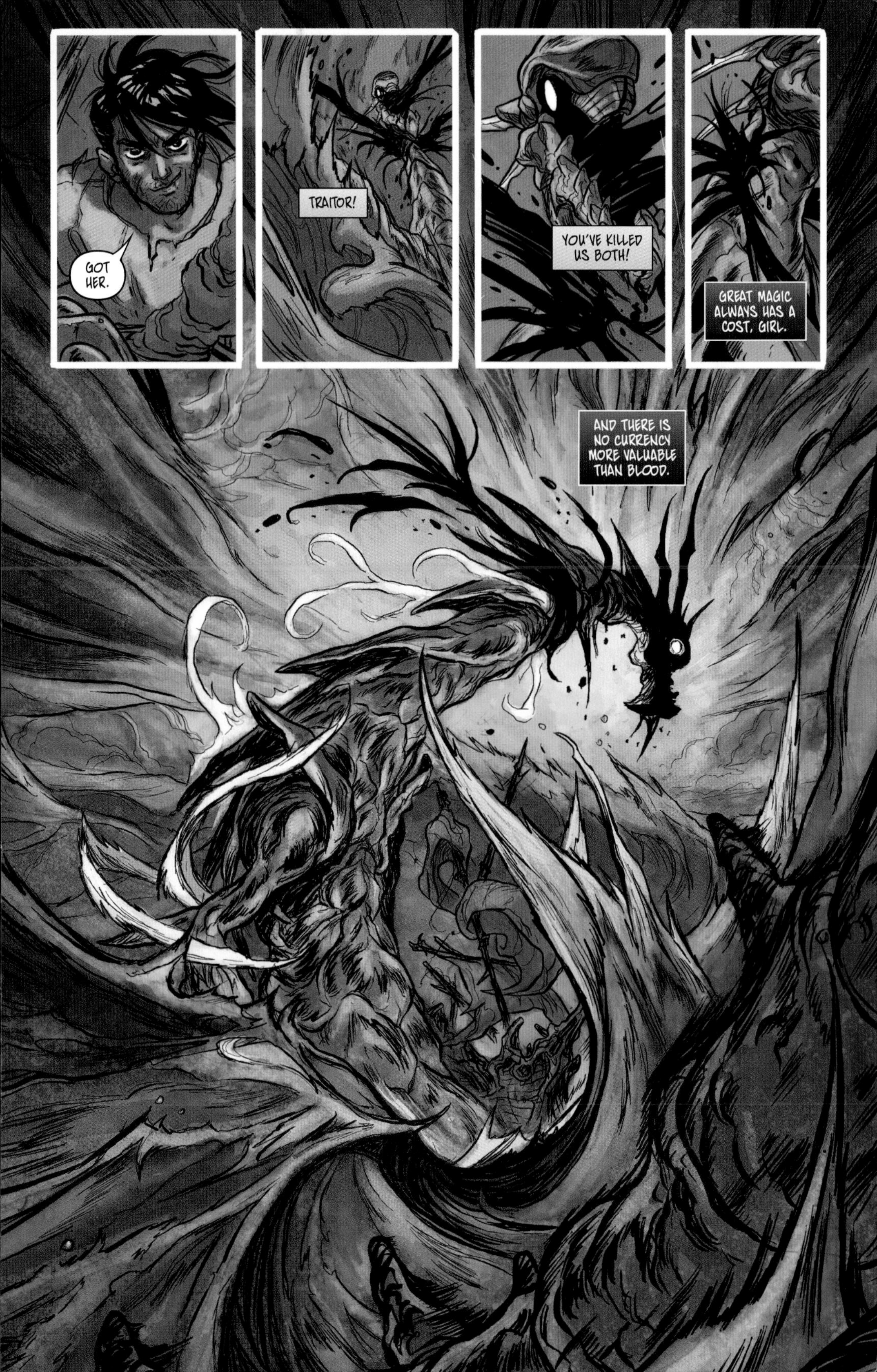
GOT HER.
TRAITOR!
YOU'VE KILLED US BOTH!
GREAT MAGIC ALWAYS HAS A COST, GIRL.
AND THERE IS NO CURRENCY MORE VALUABLE THAN BLOOD.

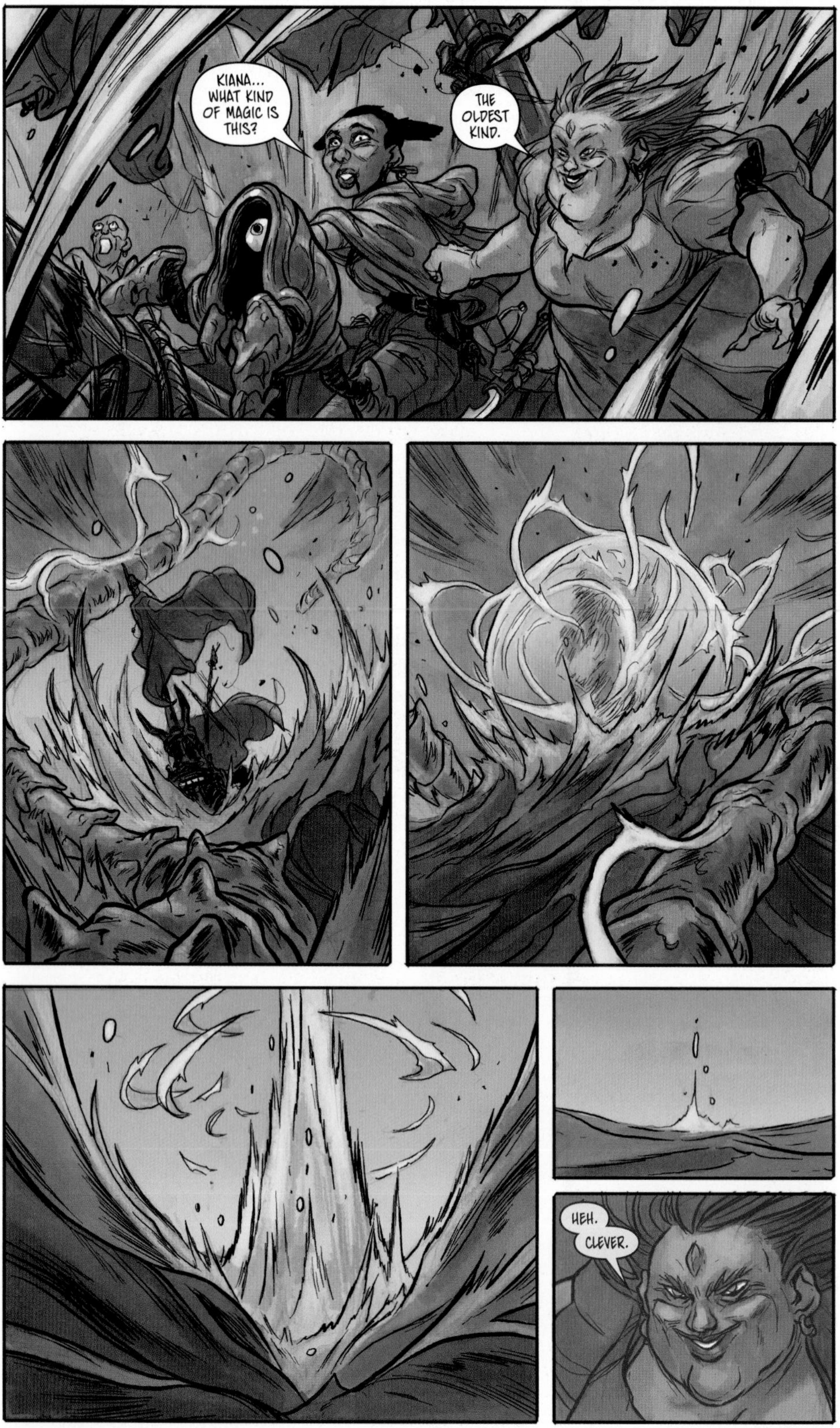
KIANA... WHAT KIND OF MAGIC IS THIS?
THE OLDEST KIND.
HEH.
CLEVER.

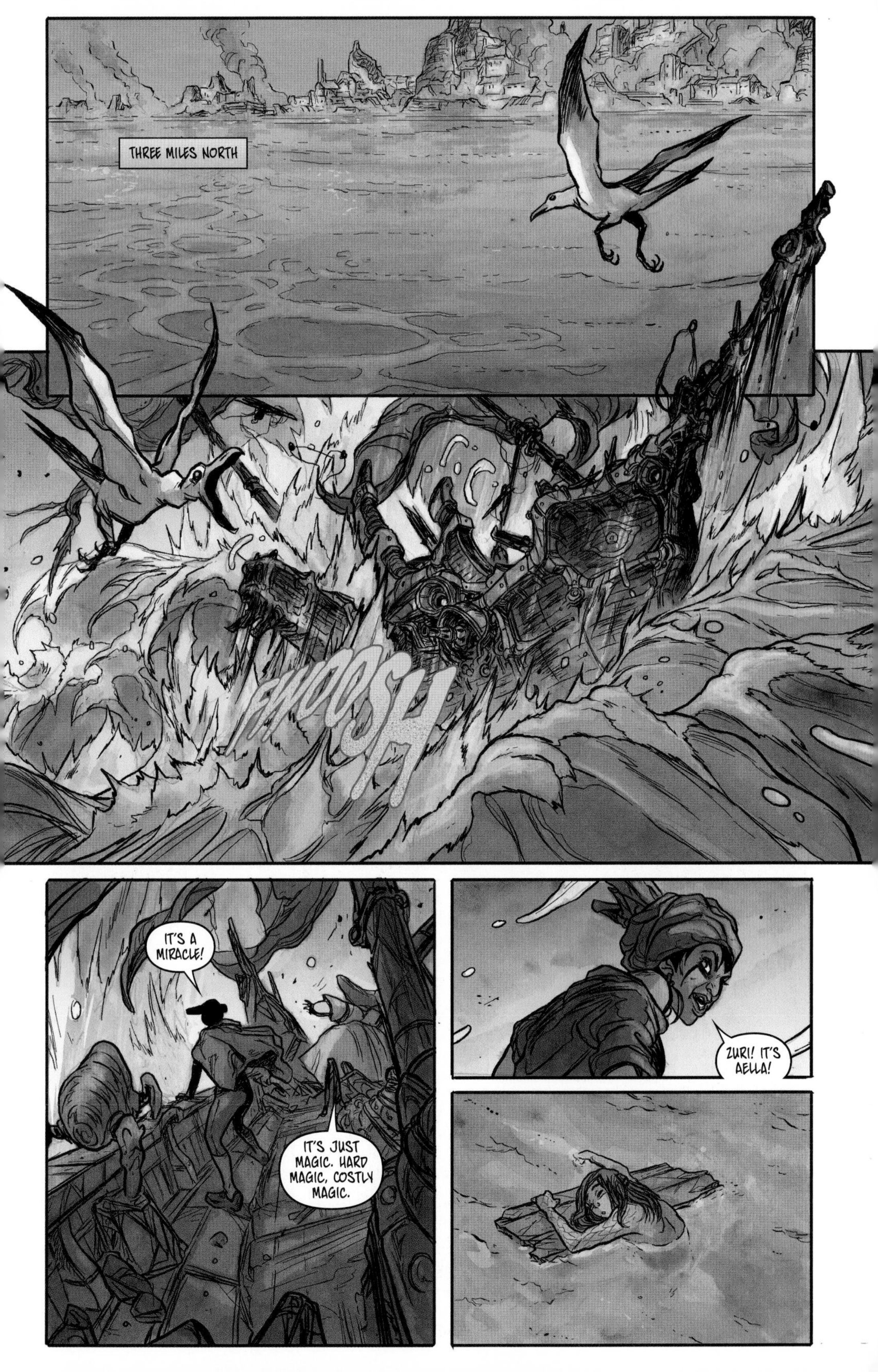
THREE MILES NORTH
FWOOSH
IT'S A MIRACLE!
IT'S JUST MAGIC. HARD MAGIC, COSTLY MAGIC.
ZURI! IT'S AELLA!

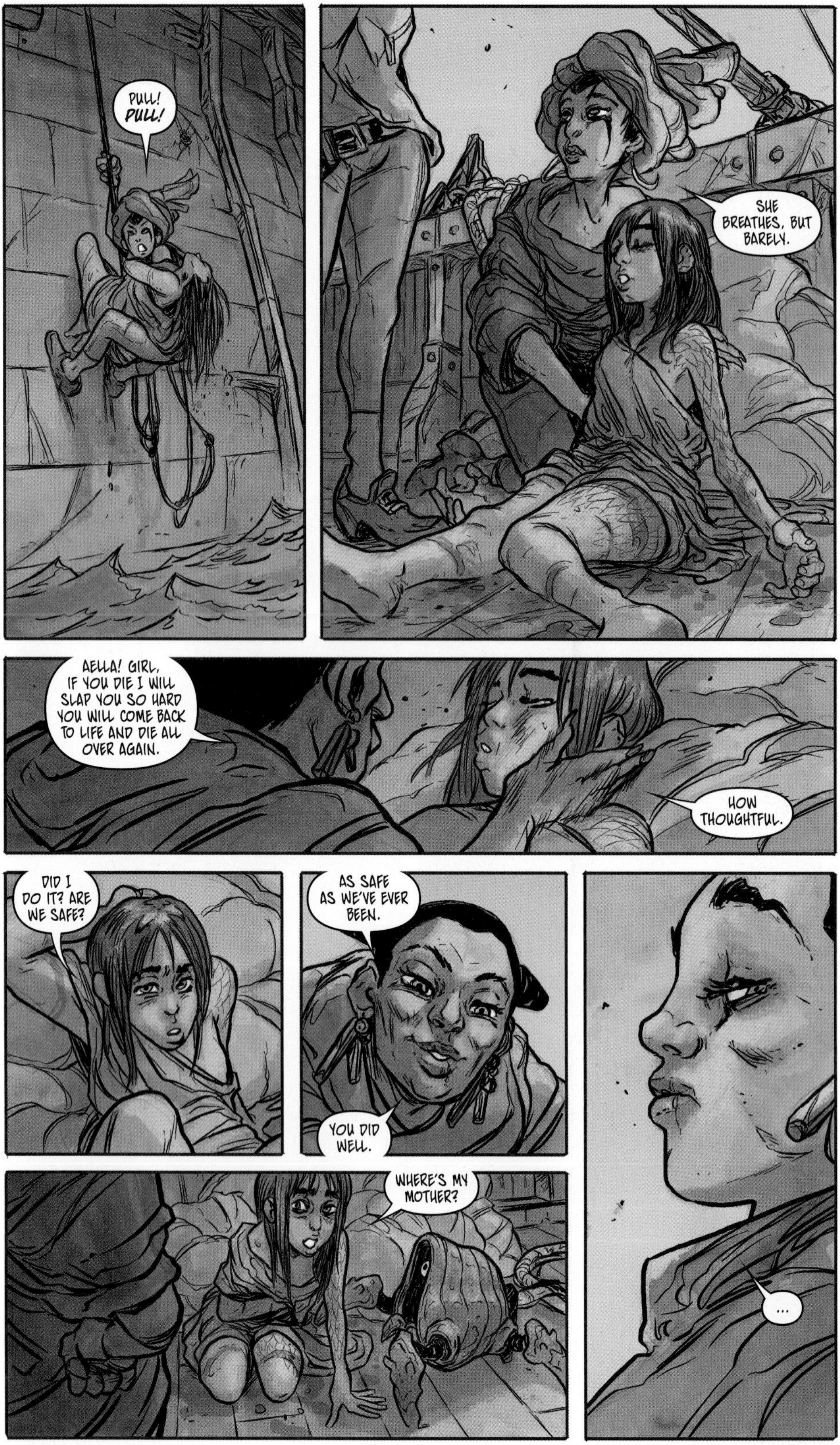
PULL! PULL!
SHE BREATHES, BUT BARELY.
AELLA! GIRL, IF YOU DIE I WILL SLAP YOU SO HARD YOU WILL COME BACK TO LIFE AND DIE ALL OVER AGAIN.
HOW THOUGHTFUL.
DID I DO IT? ARE WE SAFE?
AS SAFE AS WE'VE EVER BEEN.
YOU DID WELL.
...
WHERE'S MY MOTHER?

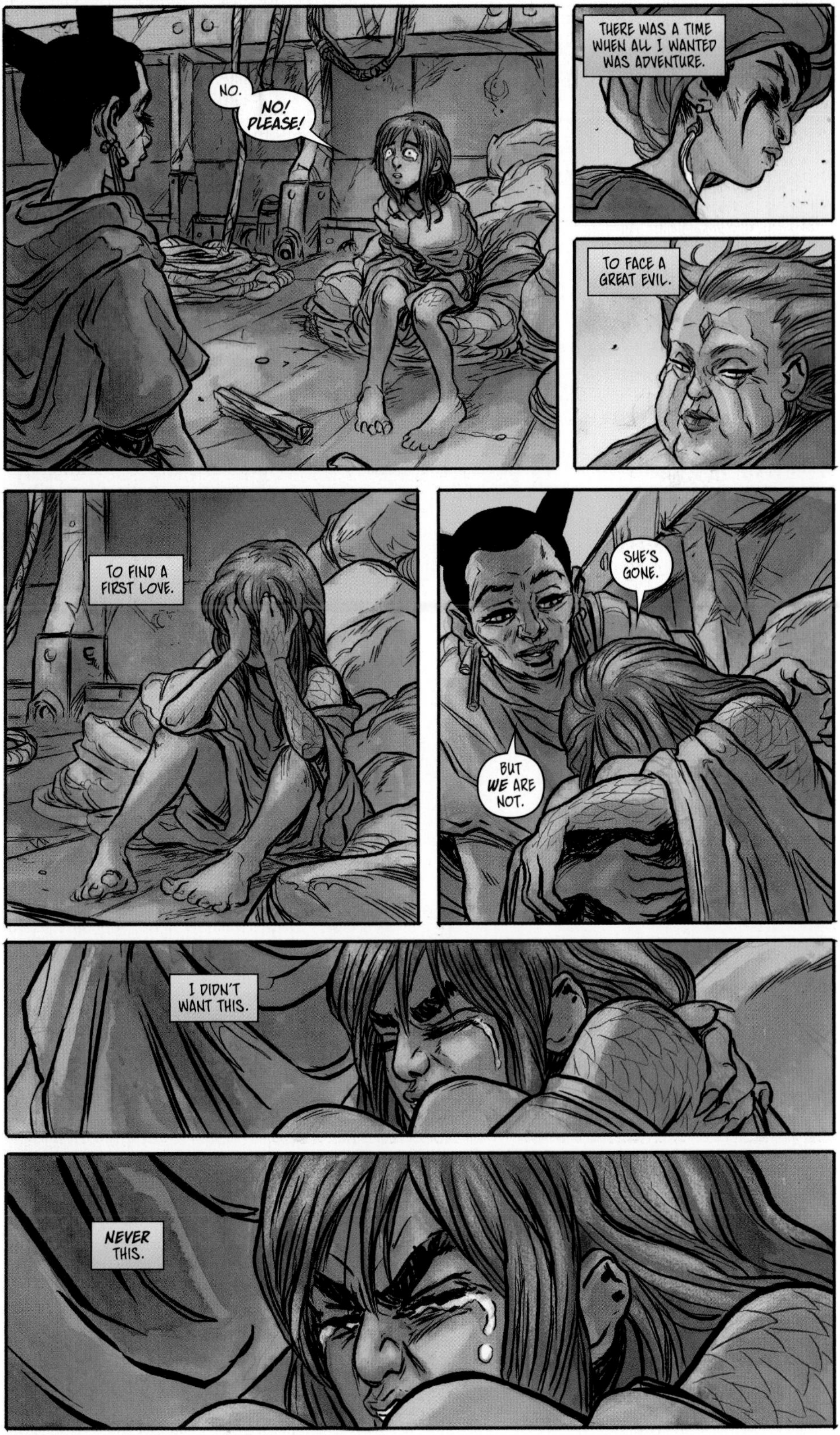
NO.
NO! PLEASE!
THERE WAS A TIME WHEN ALL I WANTED WAS ADVENTURE.
TO FACE A GREAT EVIL.
TO FIND A FIRST LOVE.
SHE'S GONE.
BUT WE ARE NOT.
I DIDN'T WANT THIS.
NEVER THIS.

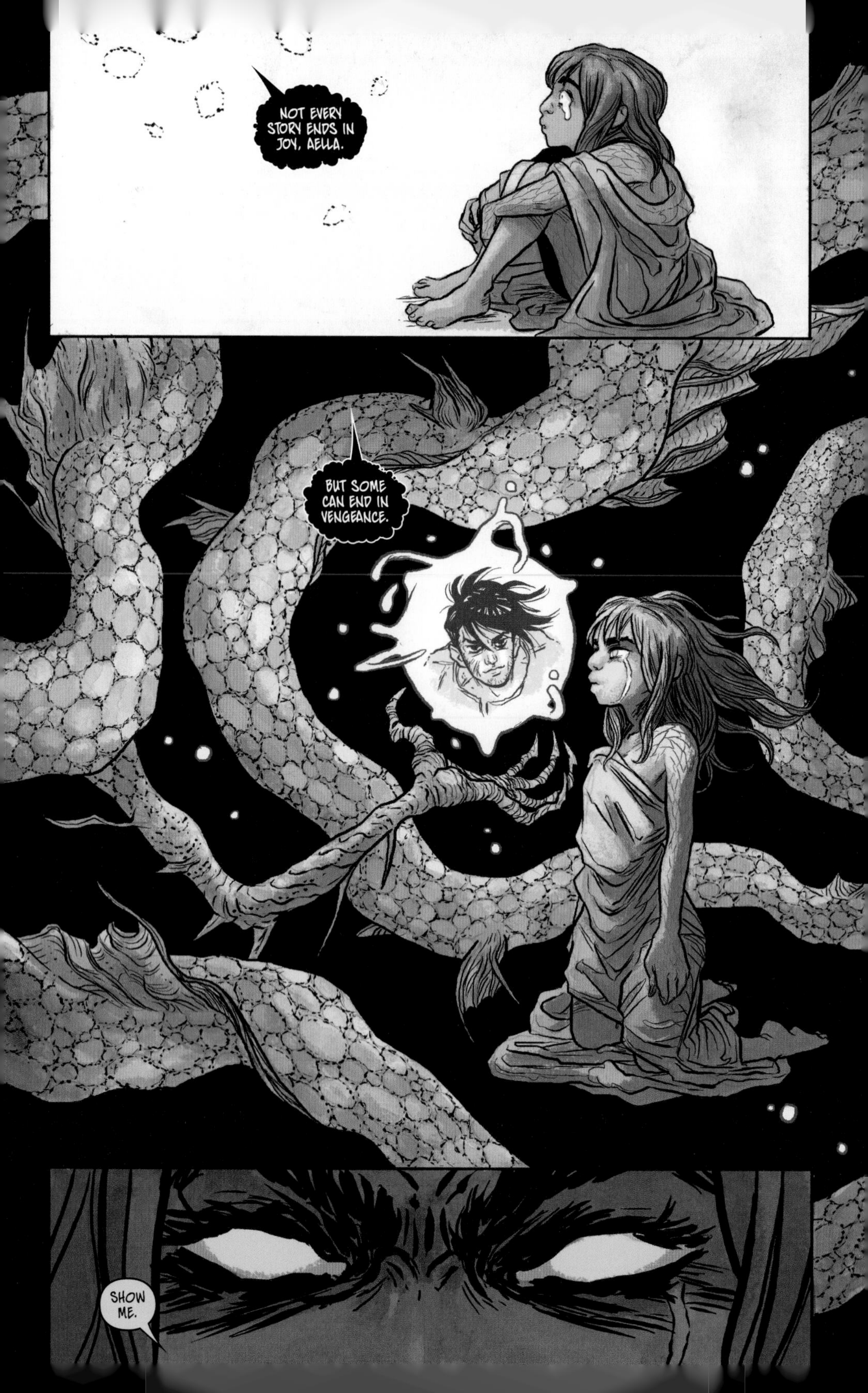
NOT EVERY STORY ENDS IN JOY, AELLA.
BUT SOME CAN END IN VENGEANCE.
SHOW ME.

Aella will return in

SEA SERPENT'S HEIR BOOK TWO: BLACK WAVE

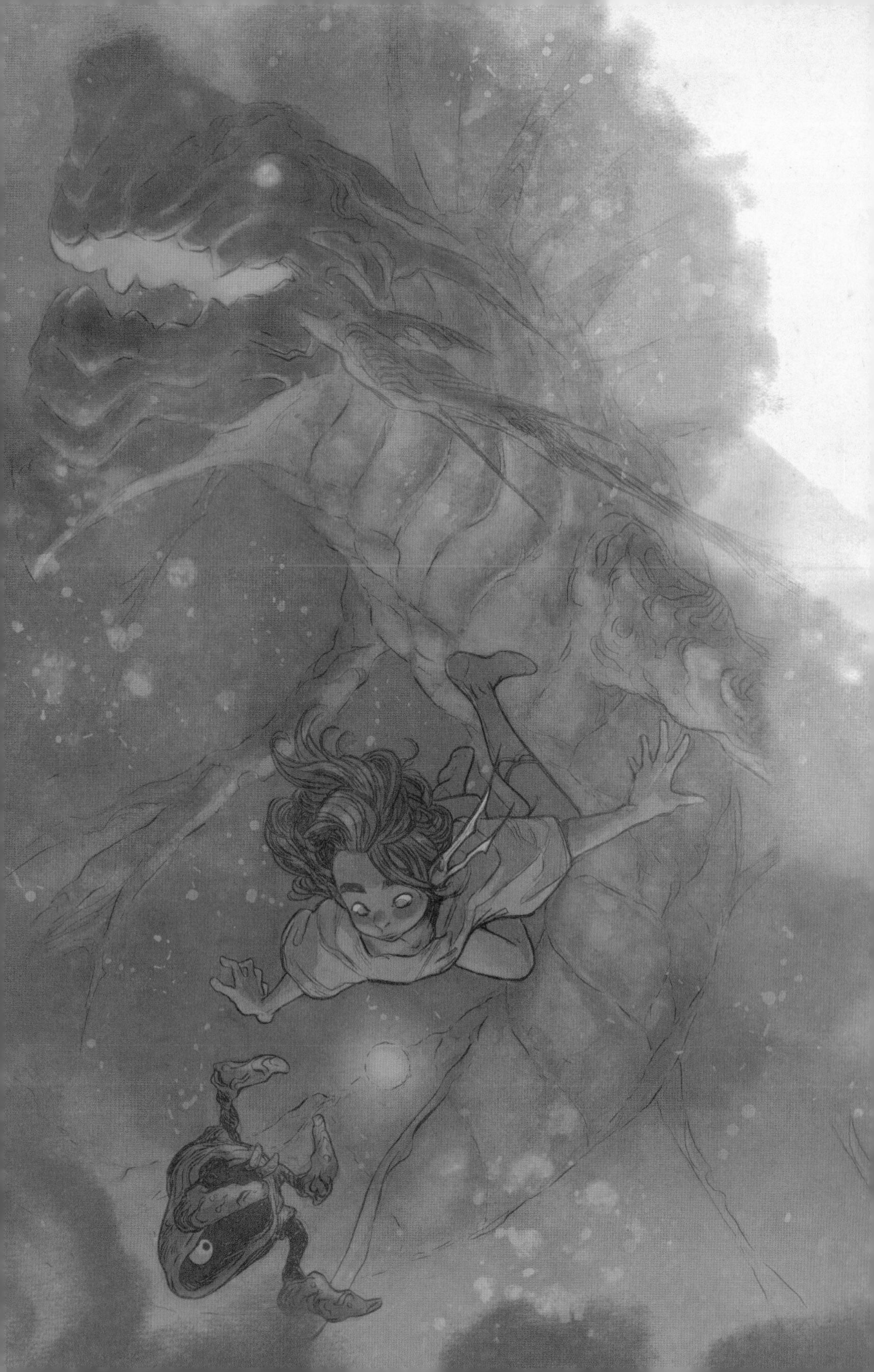

Acknowledgements

So much effort goes into a book of this size. First and foremost, I want to thank Pablo for truly making the world of SEA SERPENT'S HEIR shine. I also need to thank Ariana for actually getting these words on the page and making them look gorgeous. Thanks to my editor, Jon, for taking a chance on this book in the first place. Thanks to Alex for getting us over the finish line. And thanks to the entire team at Skybound for their tireless efforts. Lastly, thanks to all my family and friends (especially Jason), for all their love and support.

See you in Book Two!

MAIRGHREAD SCOTT

What an amazing journey we took with Aella. Thanks to Mairghread and Jon for trusting me to materialize this enigmatic and wonderful world. Thanks to all the Skybound Comet team for their patience and concern while making the books. There's a lot of care put into this collection! Last, thanks to my dear colleague and friend Lucas Varela for all his inevitable suggestions and help. But nothing ends here, we are just starting.

Farewell, till the next time.

PABLO TUNICA

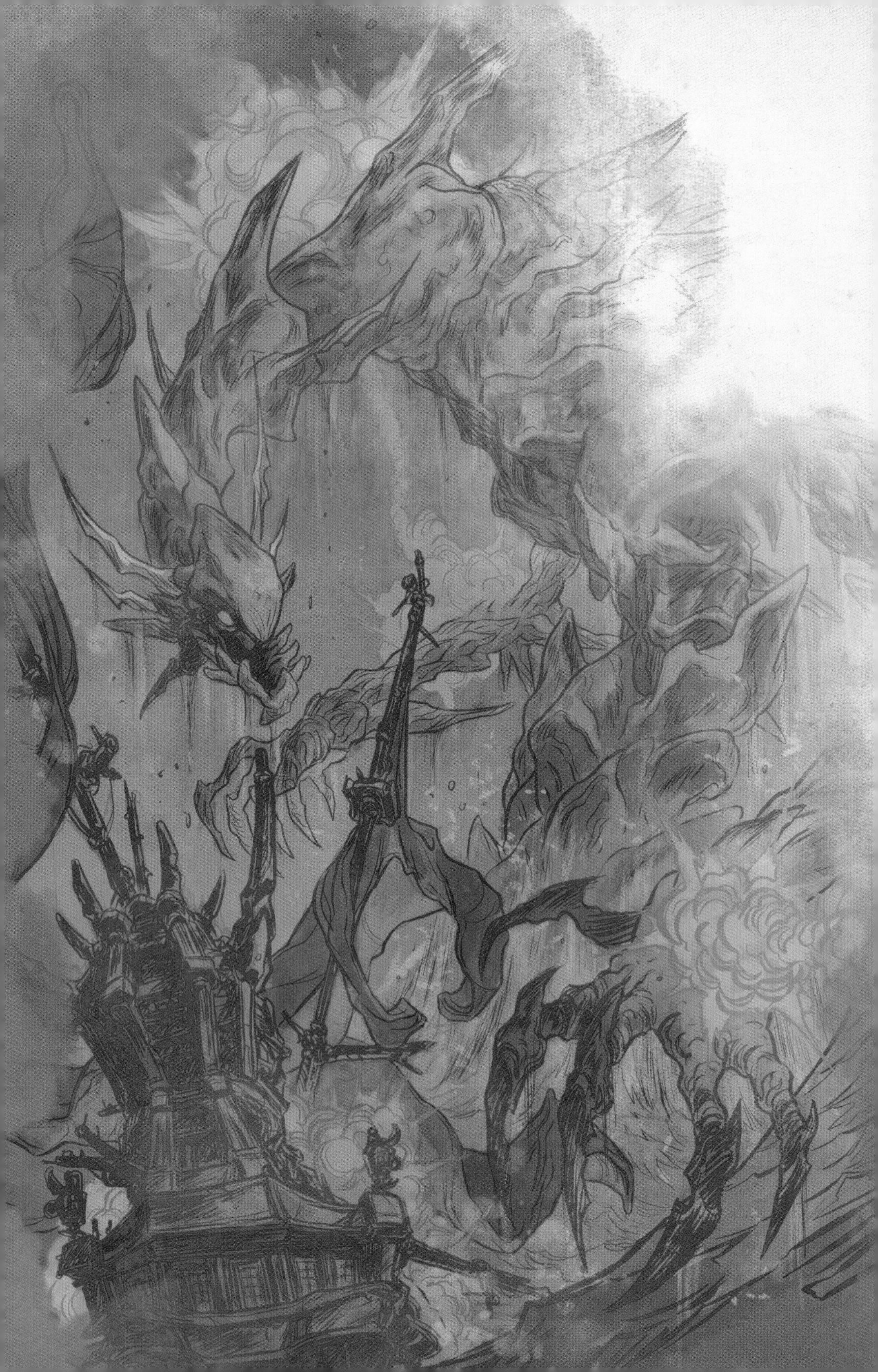

About the Creators

MAIRGHREAD SCOTT (she/her) is an animation and comic book writer. Her animated work includes *Justice League Dark: Apokolips War, Star Wars: Resistance,* and *Guardians of the Galaxy.* Her comics work ranges from *Batgirl* to *Transformers.* She's also released two original graphic novels, *The City on the Other Side* and *Toil and Trouble.* A native of Dearborn, Michigan, she now lives in sunny Los Angeles with her husband and son, even though she spends most of her days writing dragons and aliens in your favorite fictional universes.

PABLO TUNICA (he/him) is an Argentinian comic artist who has worked on several franchises including *Teenage Mutant Ninja Turtles* and *Godzilla.* His credits include *Godzilla: Rage Across Time, Bebop & Rocksteady Destroy Everything,* and *Teenage Mutant Ninja Turtles/ Ghostbusters 2.*

ARIANA MAHER (she/her) is a queer Brazilian-American comic book letterer based in the Pacific Northwest. A freelance letterer for Skybound, Marvel Comics, DC Comics, and more, her most recent work includes *S.W.O.R.D., Lupina, Crush & Lobo,* and, of course, SEA SERPENT'S HEIR.

Sketchbook

by Pablo Tunica

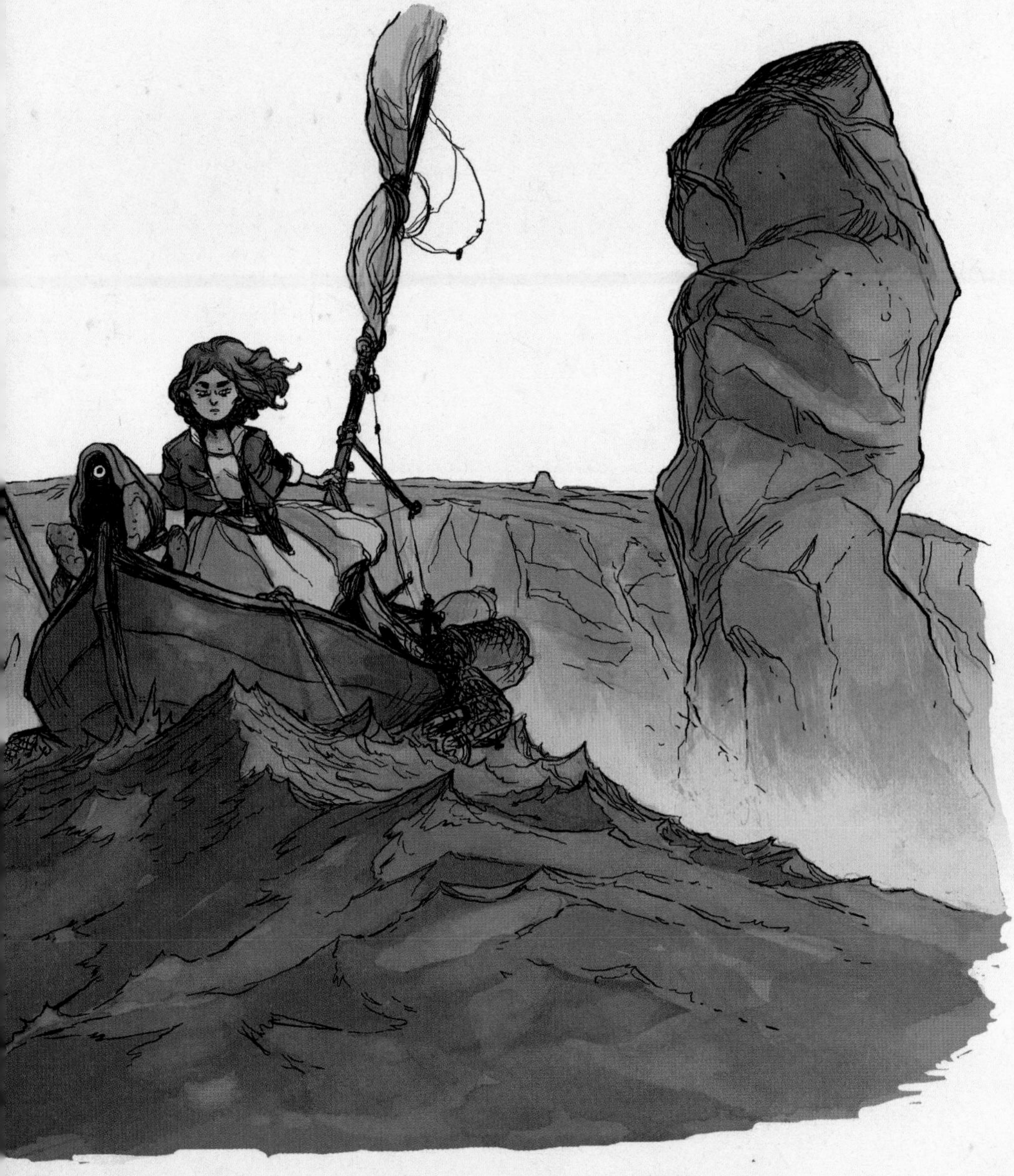

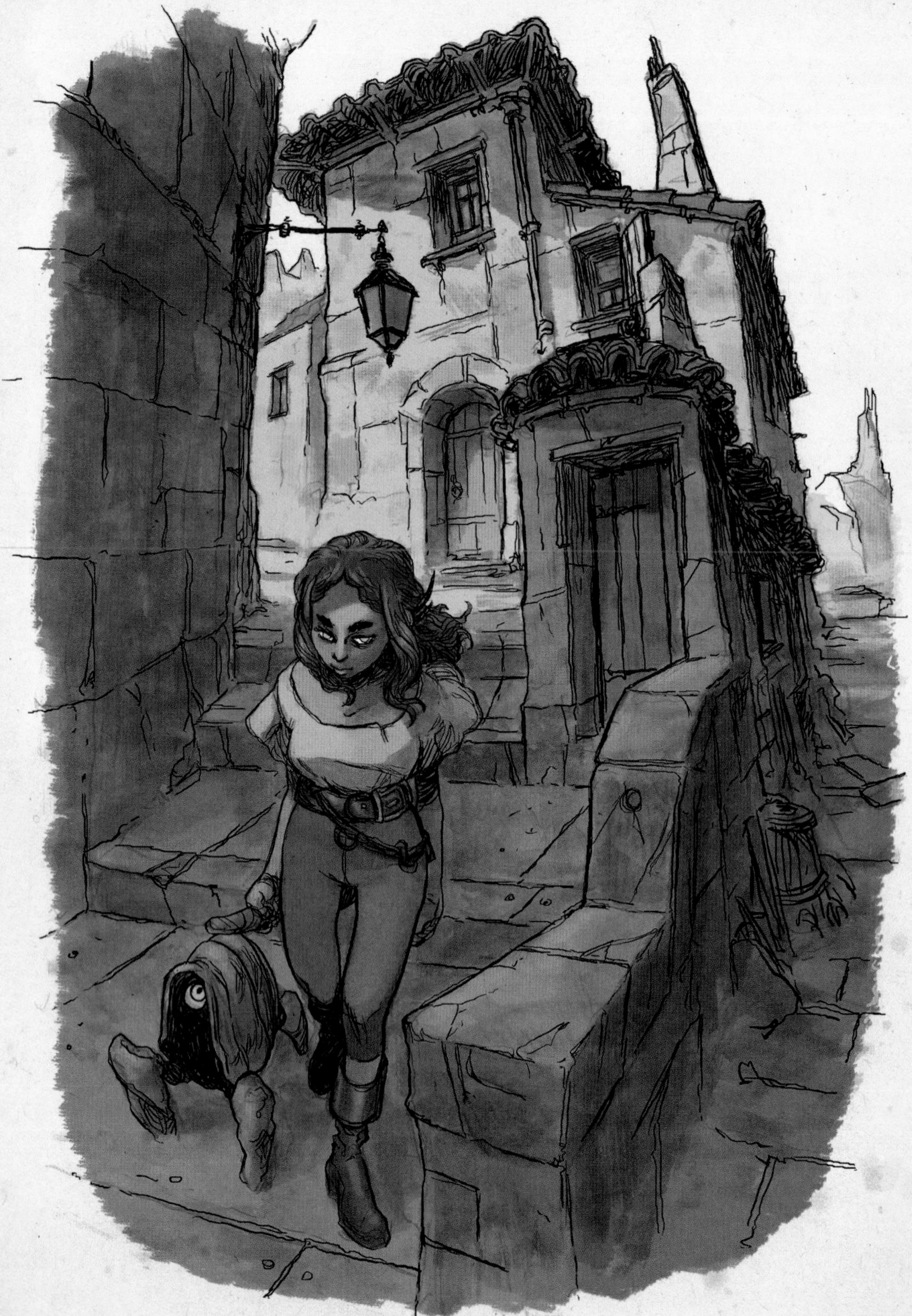

KINAMEN

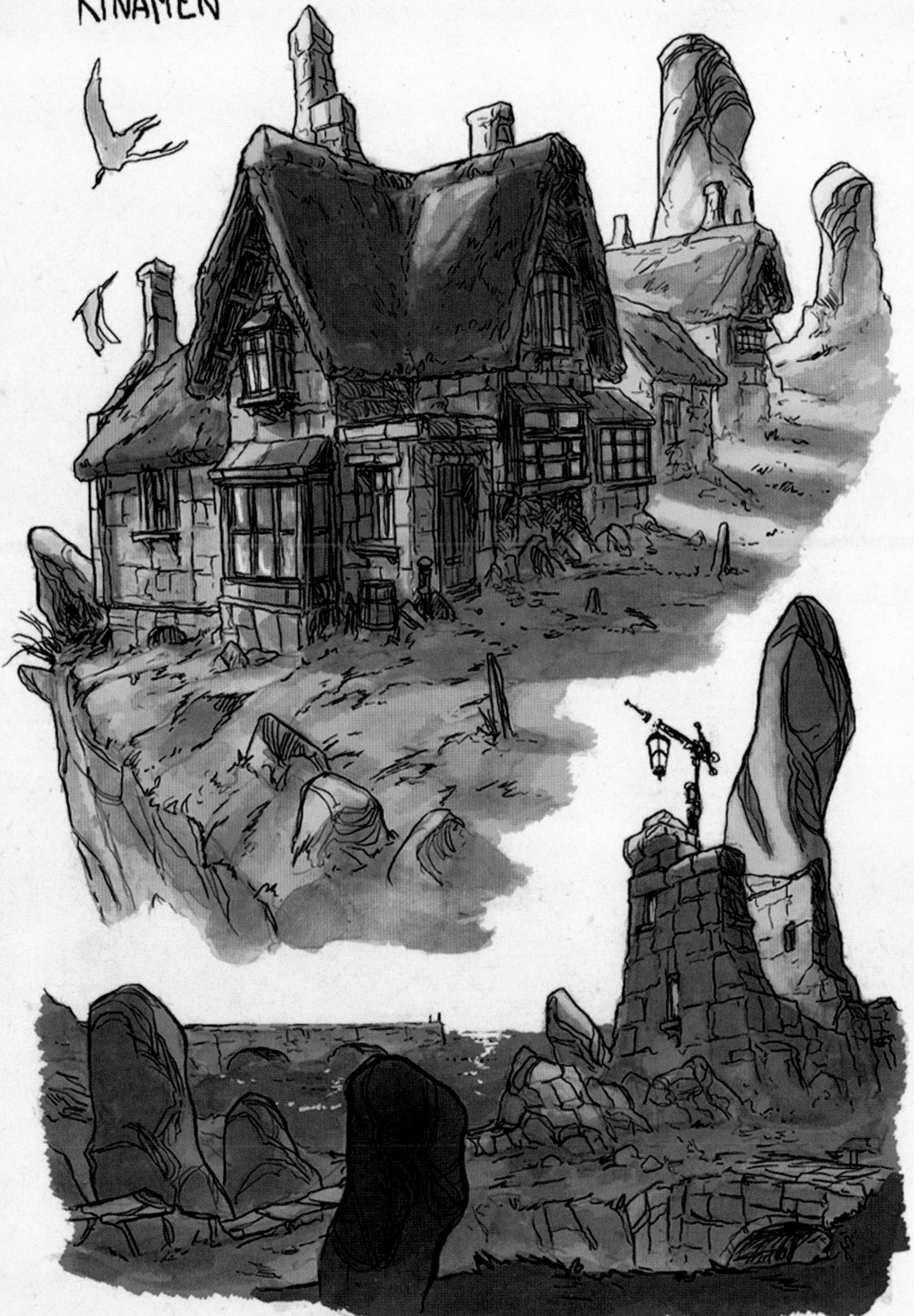

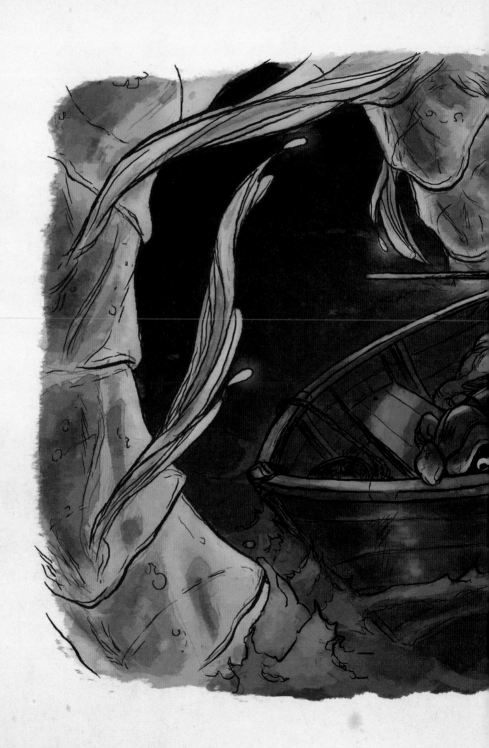

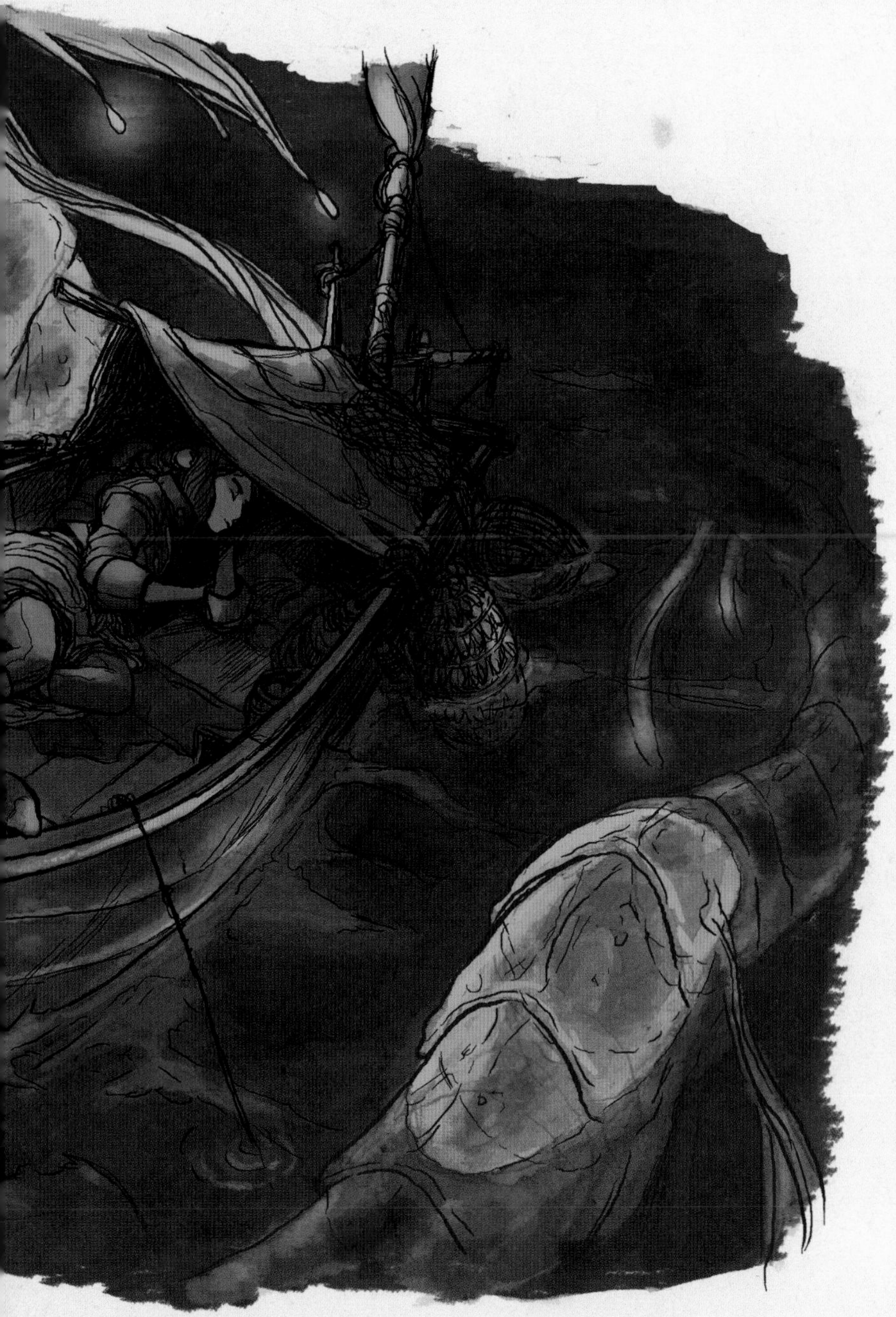

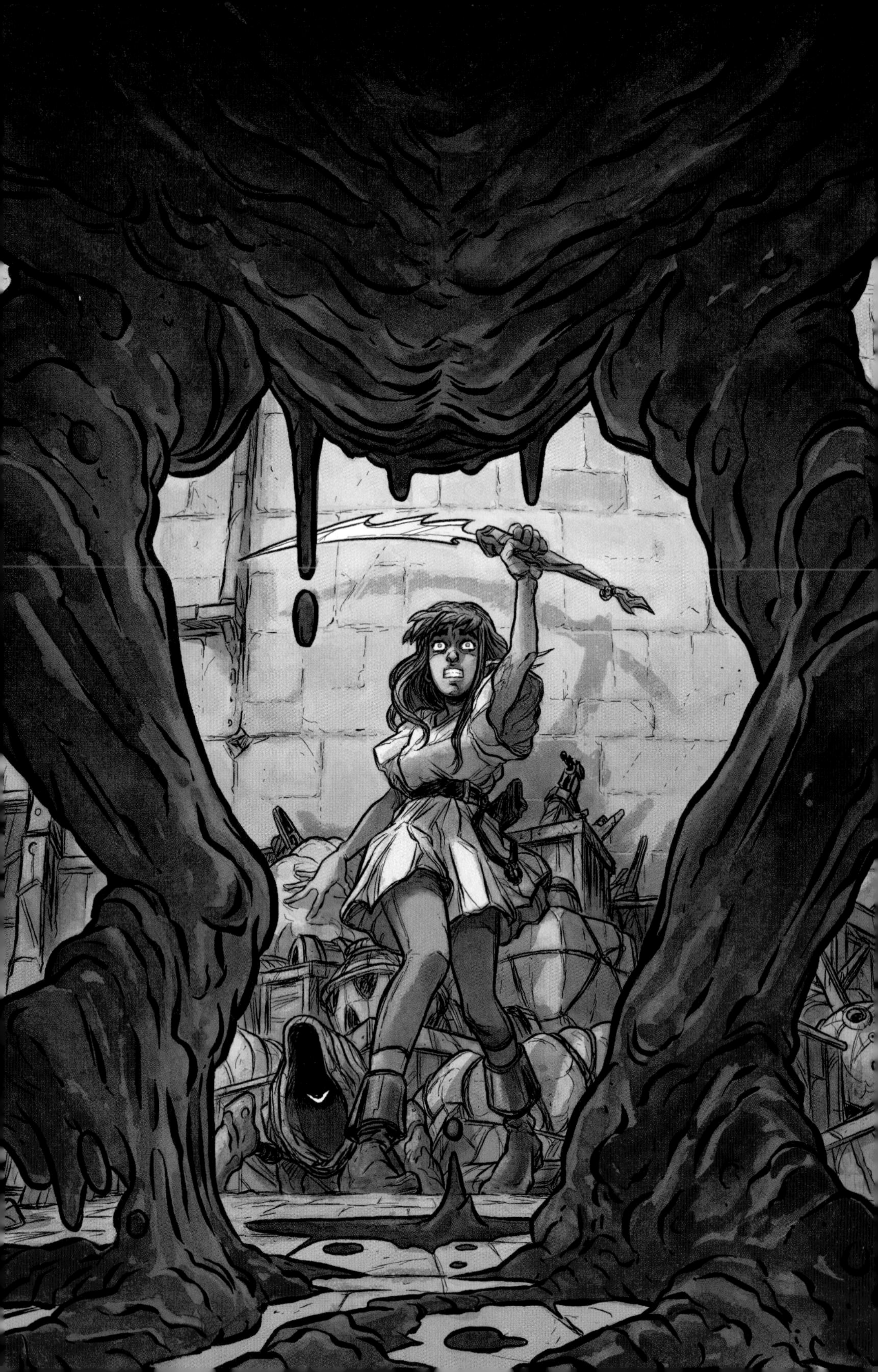

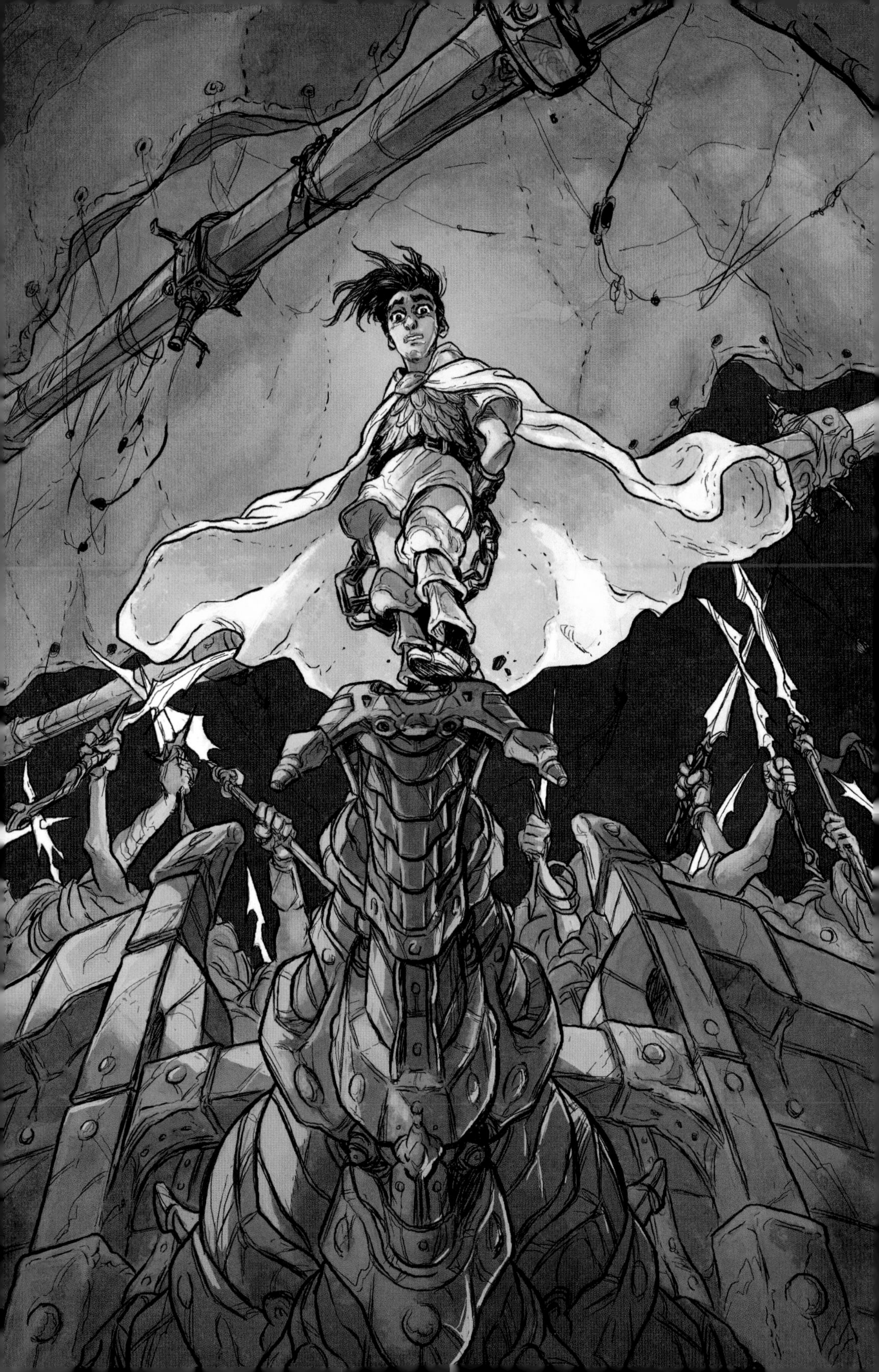

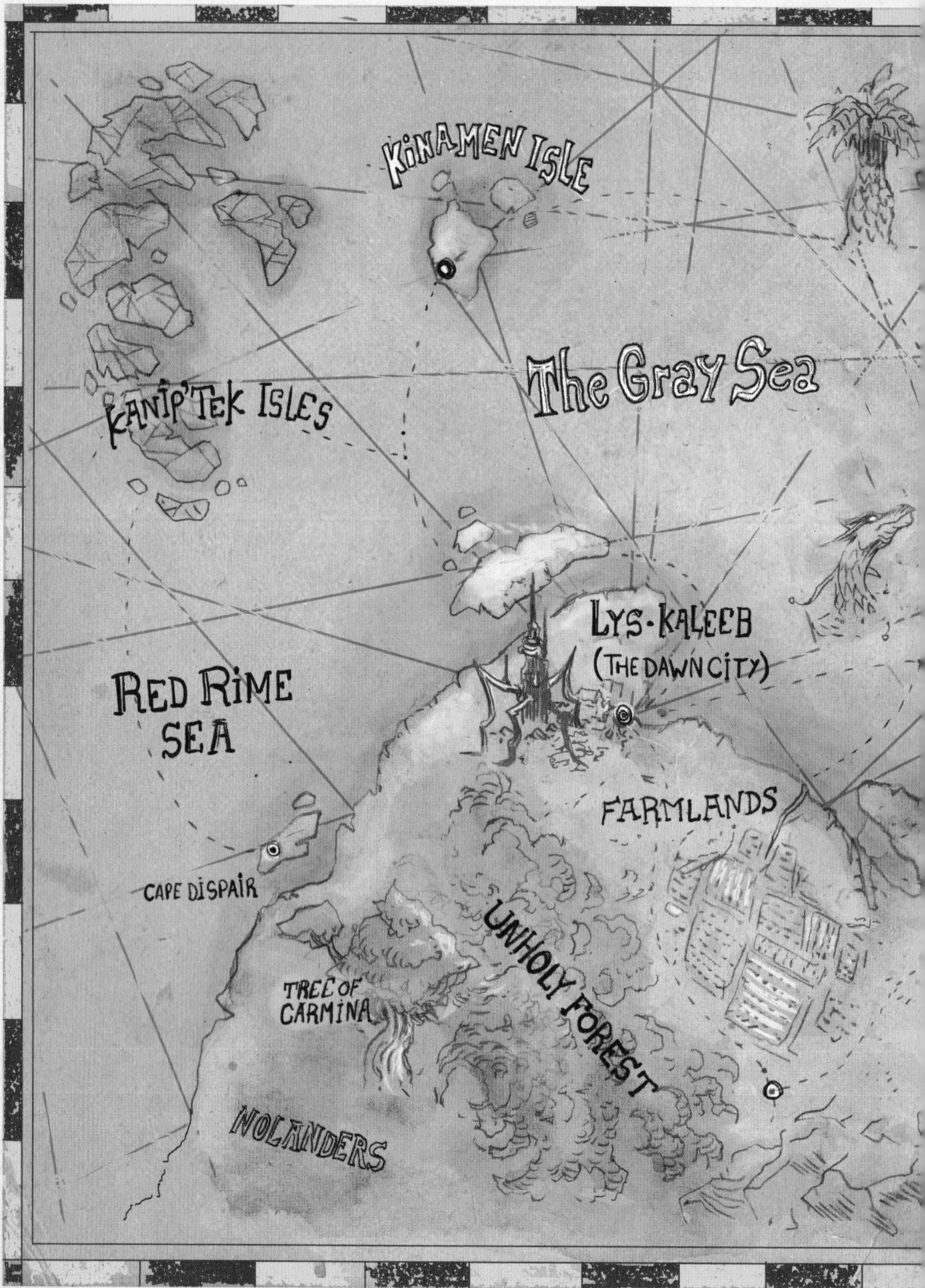

KINAMEN ISLE
The Gray Sea
KANIP'TEK ISLES
LYS-KALEEB
(THE DAWN CITY)
RED RIME
SEA
FARMLANDS
CAPE DISPAIR
UNHOLY FOREST
TREE OF
CARMINA
NOLANDERS

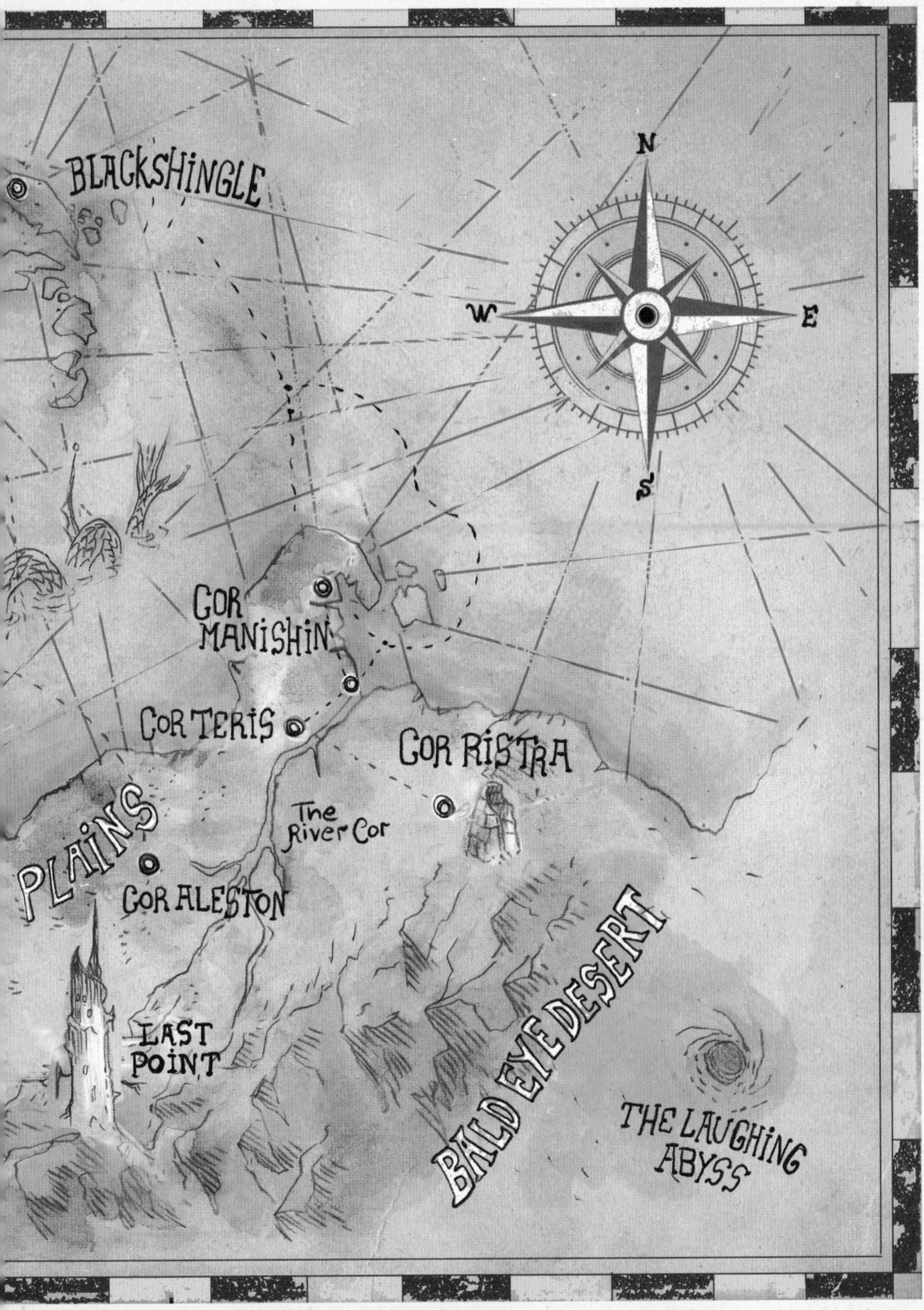
BLACKSHINGLE
N
W
E
S
COR MANISHIN
COR TERIS
COR RISTRA
PLAINS
The River Cor
COR ALESTON
LAST POINT
BALD EYE DESERT
THE LAUGHING ABYSS

SEA SERPENT'S HEIR BOOK ONE: PIRATE'S DAUGHTER
Mairghread Scott: Creator, Writer
Pablo Tunica: Creator, Artist
Ariana Maher: Letterer
Jon Moisan: Editor
Carina Taylor: Logo & Book Design
Jillian Crab: Book Design & Production
Teaching Guide by Creators, Assemble Inc.
Lexile Measure: HL350L

SKYBOUND ENTERTAINMENT
Robert Kirkman: *Chairman*
David Alpert: *CEO*
Sean Mackiewicz: *SVP, Publisher*
Shawn Kirkham: *SVP, Business Development*
Andres Juarez: *Art Director*
Arune Singh: *Director of Brand, Editorial*
Shannon Meehan: *Public Relations Manager*

Alex Antone: *Editorial Director*
Amanda LaFranco: *Editor*
Jillian Crab: *Graphic Designer*
Morgan Perry: *Brand Manager, Editorial*
Sarah Clements: *Brand Coordinator, Editorial*
Dan Petersen: *Sr. Director, Operations & Events*
Foreign Rights & Licensing Inquiries: contact@skybound.com
SKYBOUND.COM

IMAGE COMICS, INC.
Robert Kirkman: *Chief Operating Officer*
Erik Larsen: *Chief Financial Officer*
Todd McFarlane: *President*
Marc Silvestri: *Chief Executive Officer*
Jim Valentino: *Vice President*
Eric Stephenson: *Publisher / Chief Creative Officer*
Nicole Lapalme: *Vice President of Finance*
Leanna Caunter: *Accounting Analyst*
Sue Korpela: *Accounting & HR Manager*
Matt Parkinson: *Vice President of Sales & Publishing*
Lorelei Bunjes: *Vice President of Digital Strategy*
Dirk Wood: *Director of International Sales & Licensing*
Ryan Brewer: *International Sales & Licensing Manager*
Alex Cox: *Director of Direct Market Sales*

Chloe Ramos: *Book Market & Library Sales Manager*
Emilio Bautista: *Digital Sales Coordinator*
Jon Schlaffman: *Specialty Sales Coordinator*
Kat Salazar: *Vice President of PR & Marketing*
Deanna Phelps: *Marketing Design Manager*
Drew Fitzgerald: *Marketing Content Associate*
Heather Doornink: *Vice President of Production*
Drew Gill: *Art Director*
Hilary DiLoreto: *Print Manager*
Tricia Ramos: *Traffic Manager*
Melissa Gifford: *Content Manager*
Erika Schnatz: *Senior Production Artist*
Wesley Griffith: *Production Artist*
IMAGECOMICS.COM

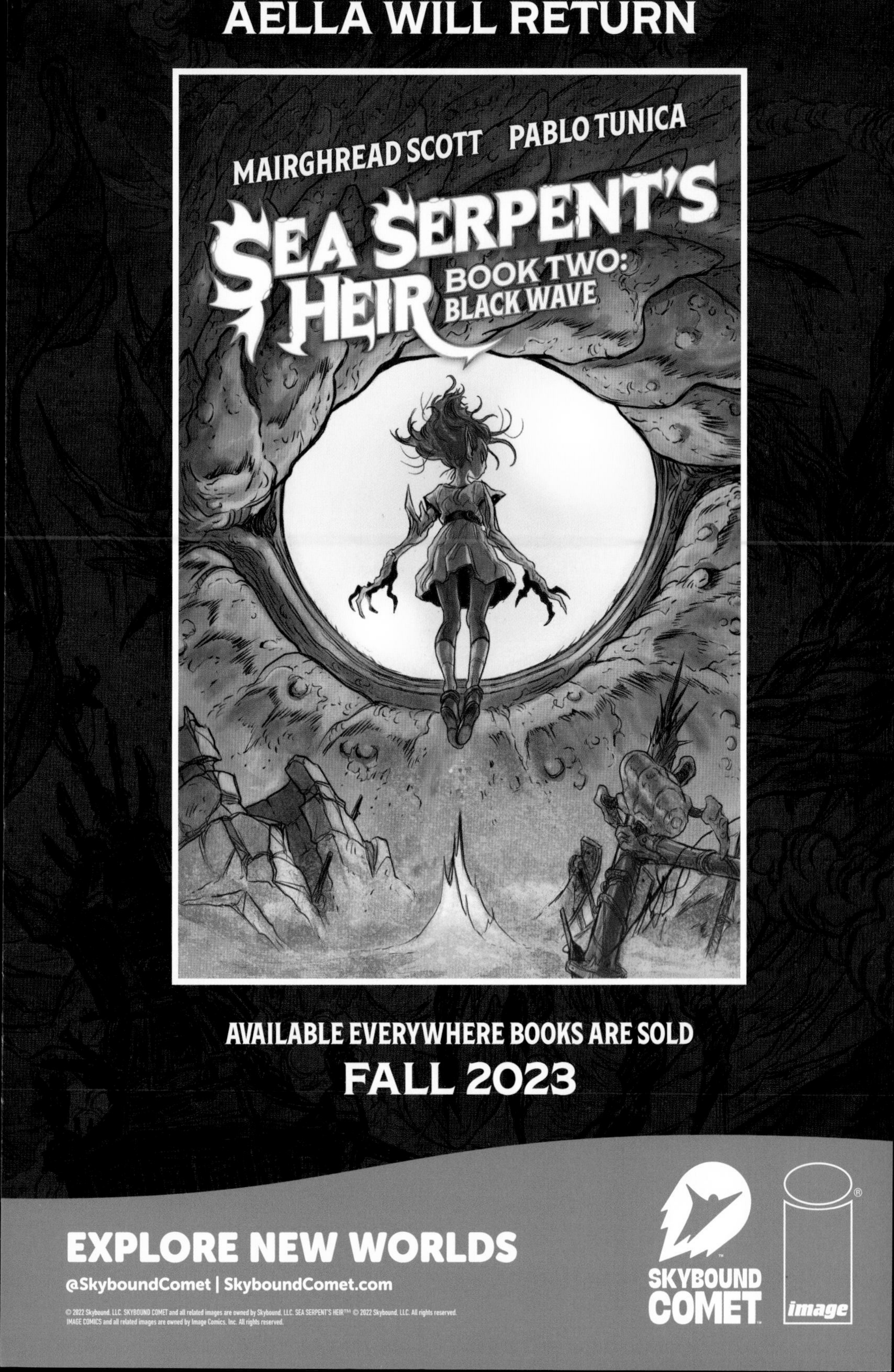
AELLA WILL RETURN
MAIRGHREAD SCOTT
PABLO TUNICA
SEA SERPENT'S HEIR
BOOK TWO: BLACK WAVE
AVAILABLE EVERYWHERE BOOKS ARE SOLD
FALL 2023
EXPLORE NEW WORLDS
@SkyboundComet | SkyboundComet.com
© 2022 Skybound, LLC. SKYBOUND COMET and all related images are owned by Skybound, LLC. SEA SERPENT'S HEIR™ © 2022 Skybound, LLC. All rights reserved.
IMAGE COMICS and all related images are owned by Image Comics, Inc. All rights reserved.
SKYBOUND COMET
image

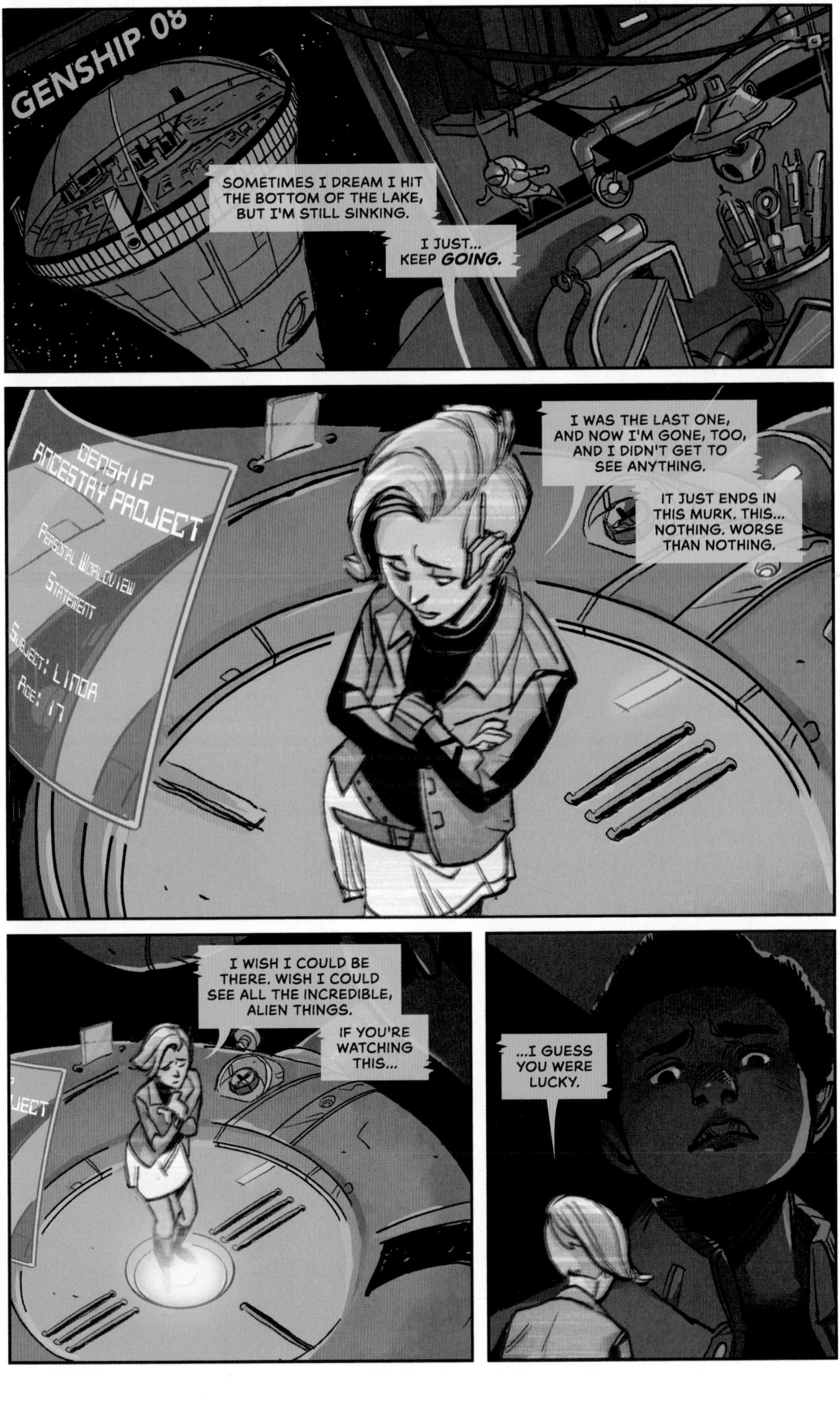
GENSHIP 08
SOMETIMES I DREAM I HIT THE BOTTOM OF THE LAKE, BUT I'M STILL SINKING.
I JUST... KEEP GOING.
GENSHIP ANCESTRY PROJECT
PERSONAL WORLDVIEW STATEMENT
SUBJECT: LINDA
AGE: 17
I WAS THE LAST ONE, AND NOW I'M GONE, TOO, AND I DIDN'T GET TO SEE ANYTHING.
IT JUST ENDS IN THIS MURK. THIS... NOTHING. WORSE THAN NOTHING.
I WISH I COULD BE THERE. WISH I COULD SEE ALL THE INCREDIBLE, ALIEN THINGS.
IF YOU'RE WATCHING THIS...
...I GUESS YOU WERE LUCKY.

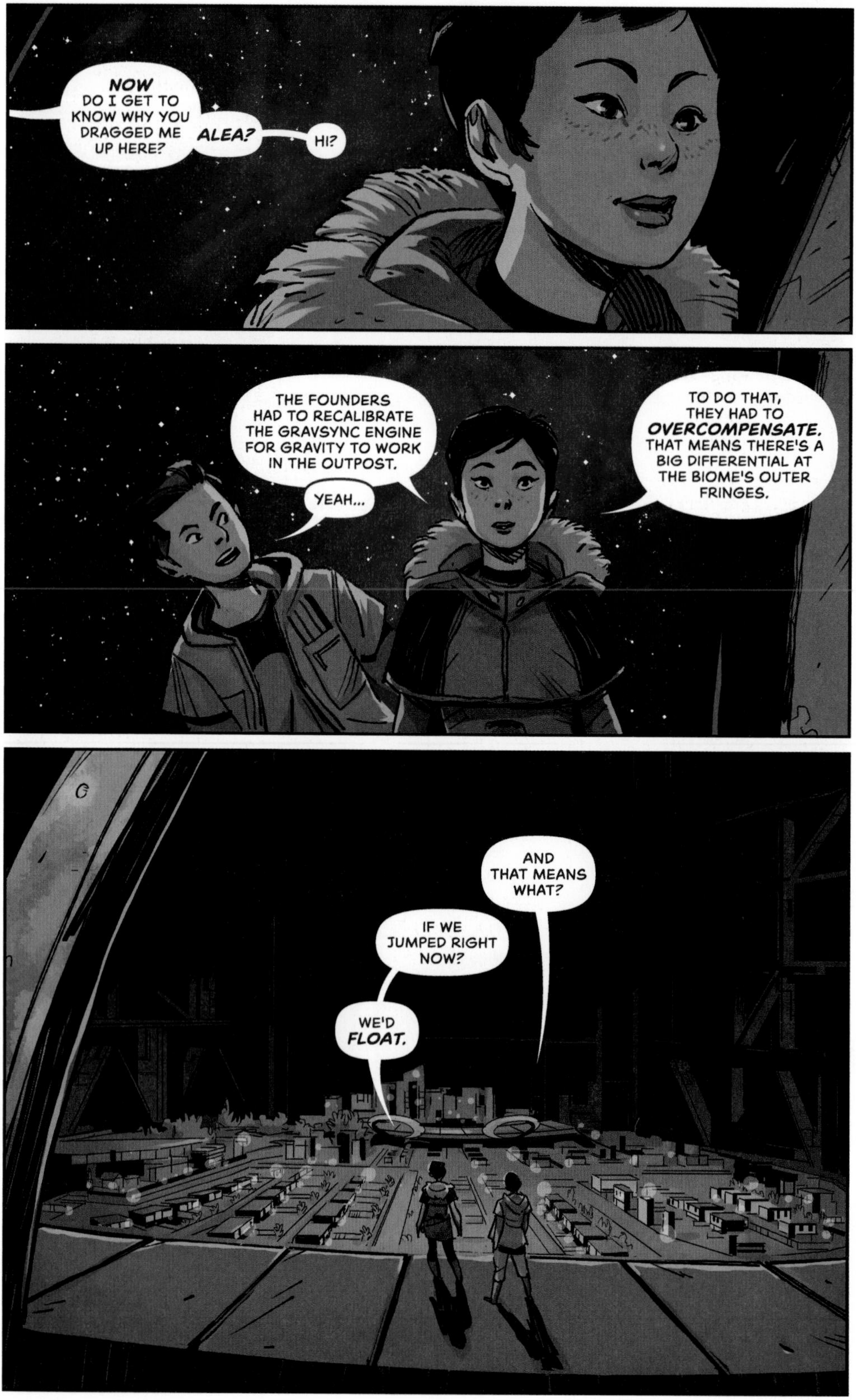
NOW DO I GET TO KNOW WHY YOU DRAGGED ME UP HERE?
ALEA?
HI?
THE FOUNDERS HAD TO RECALIBRATE THE GRAVSYNC ENGINE FOR GRAVITY TO WORK IN THE OUTPOST.
YEAH...
TO DO THAT, THEY HAD TO OVERCOMPENSATE. THAT MEANS THERE'S A BIG DIFFERENTIAL AT THE BIOME'S OUTER FRINGES.
AND THAT MEANS WHAT?
IF WE JUMPED RIGHT NOW?
WE'D FLOAT.

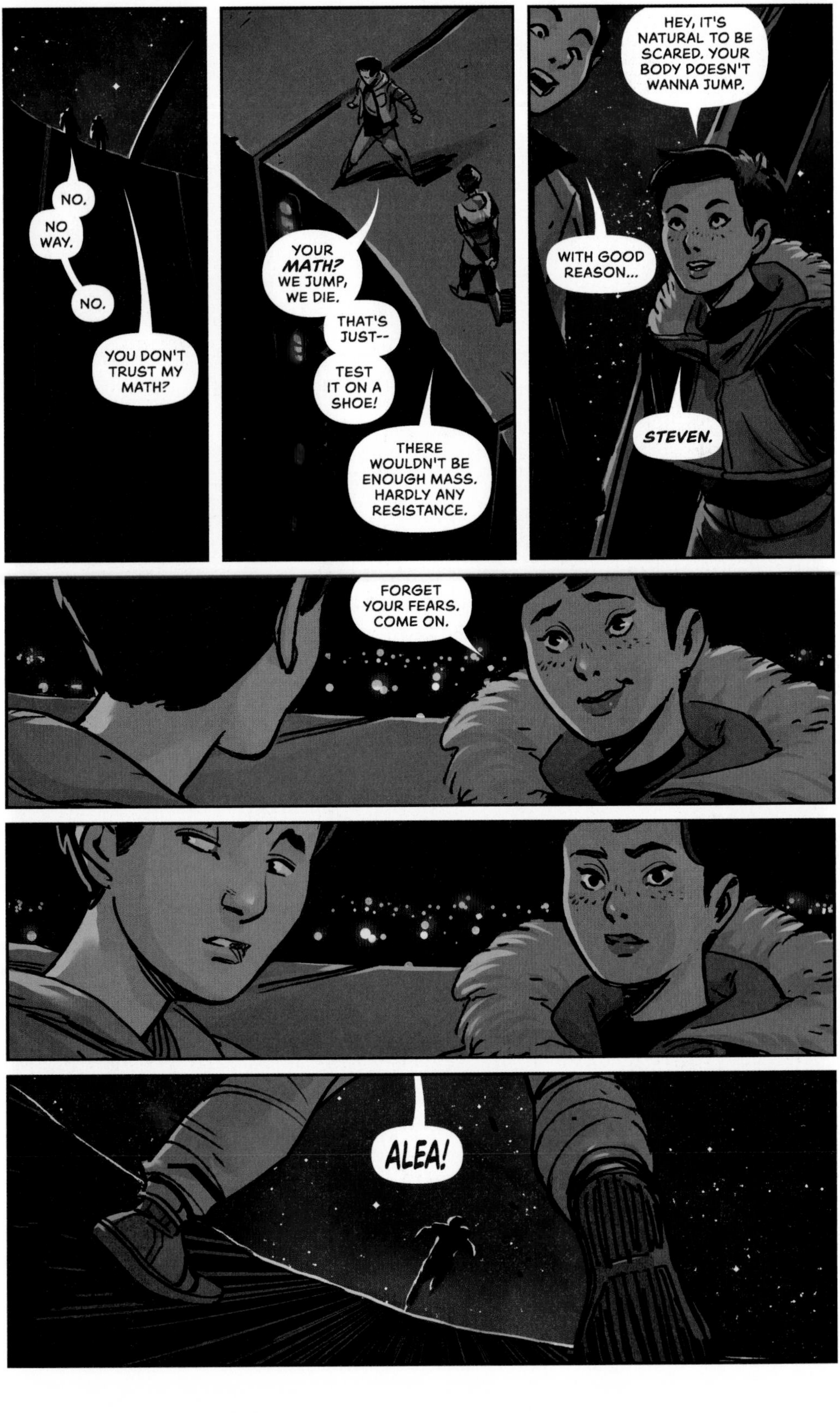
NO.
NO WAY.
NO.
YOU DON'T TRUST MY MATH?
YOUR *MATH?* WE JUMP, WE DIE.
THAT'S JUST--
TEST IT ON A SHOE!
THERE WOULDN'T BE ENOUGH MASS. HARDLY ANY RESISTANCE.
HEY, IT'S NATURAL TO BE SCARED. YOUR BODY DOESN'T WANNA JUMP.
WITH GOOD REASON...
STEVEN.
FORGET YOUR FEARS. COME ON.
ALEA!

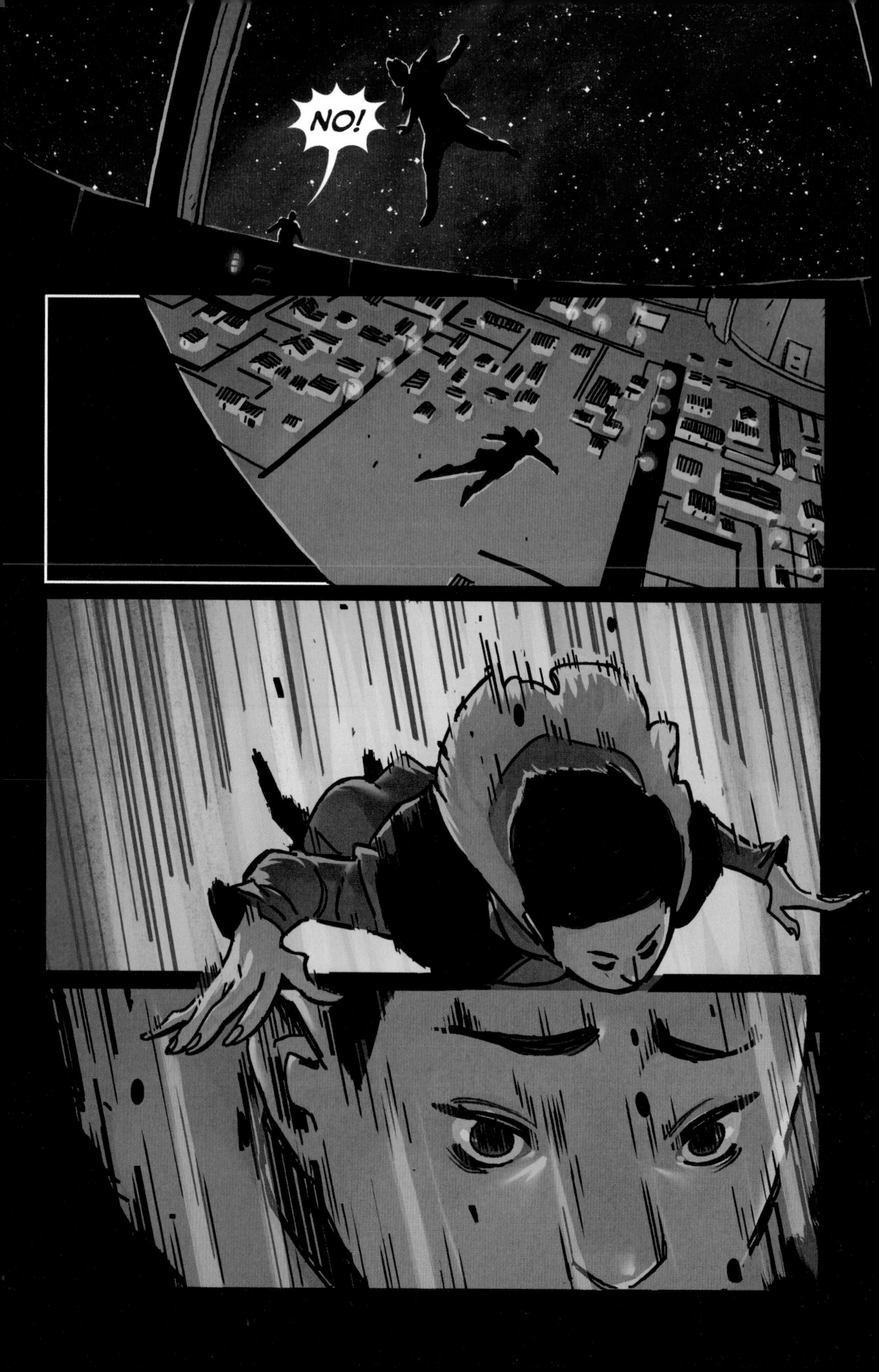
NO!

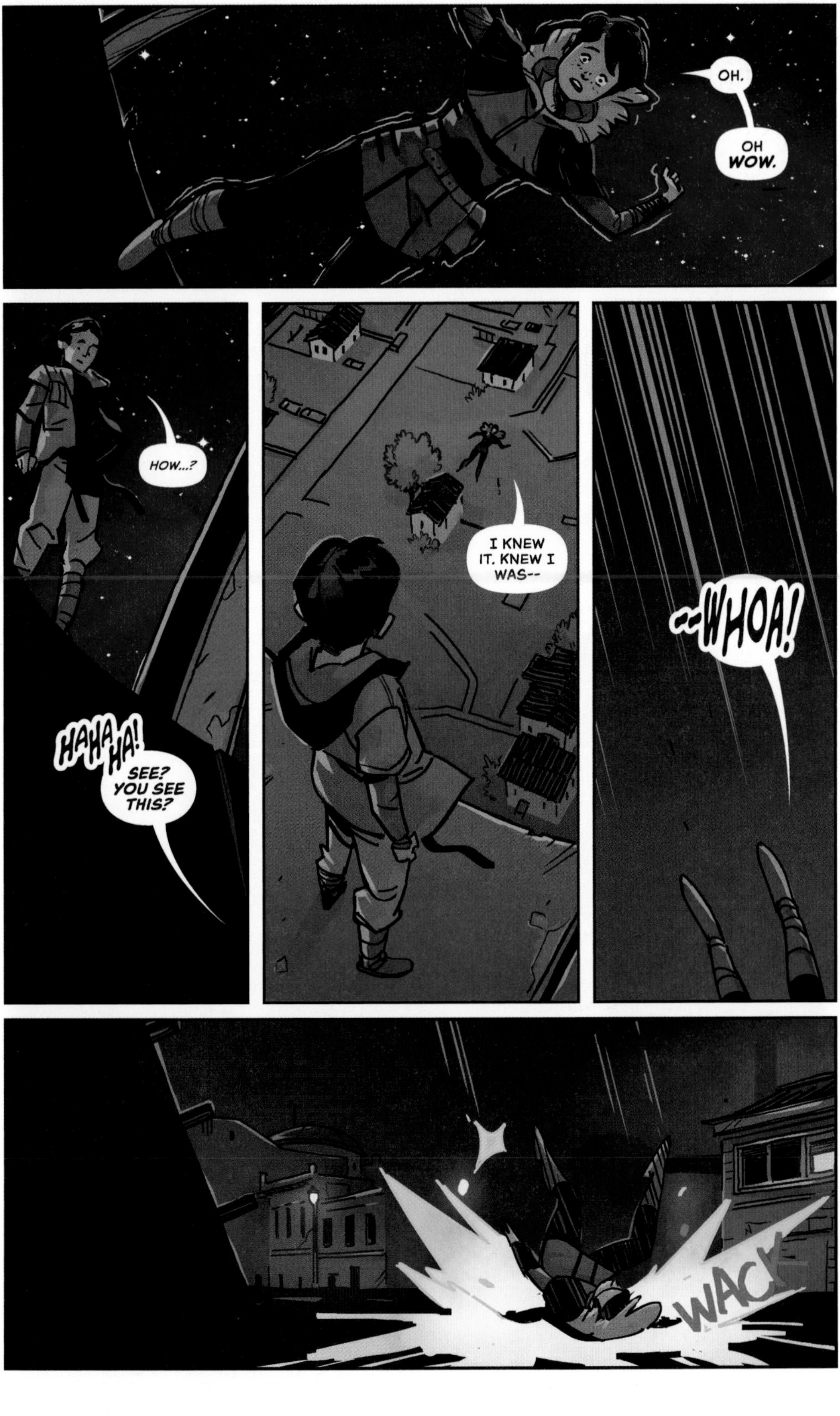
OH.
OH WOW.
HOW...?
I KNEW IT. KNEW I WAS--
HAHAHA!
SEE? YOU SEE THIS?
--WHOA!
WACK

ARE YOU OKAY?!

THINK I BROKE SOMETHING.

ALEA, I DON'T BELIEVE IT. WHEN YOU--

I THOUGHT YOU WERE--

BUT THAT--

THAT WAS INCREDIBLE. YOU WERE RIGHT.

I WAS *WRONG*.

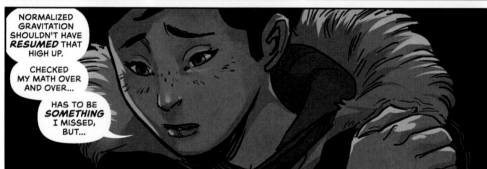

NORMALIZED GRAVITATION SHOULDN'T HAVE *RESUMED* THAT HIGH UP.

CHECKED MY MATH OVER AND OVER...

HAS TO BE *SOMETHING* I MISSED, BUT...

LOOK, JUST...

DON'T EVER DO SOMETHING LIKE THAT AGAIN, OKAY?

OKAY?

OKAY?

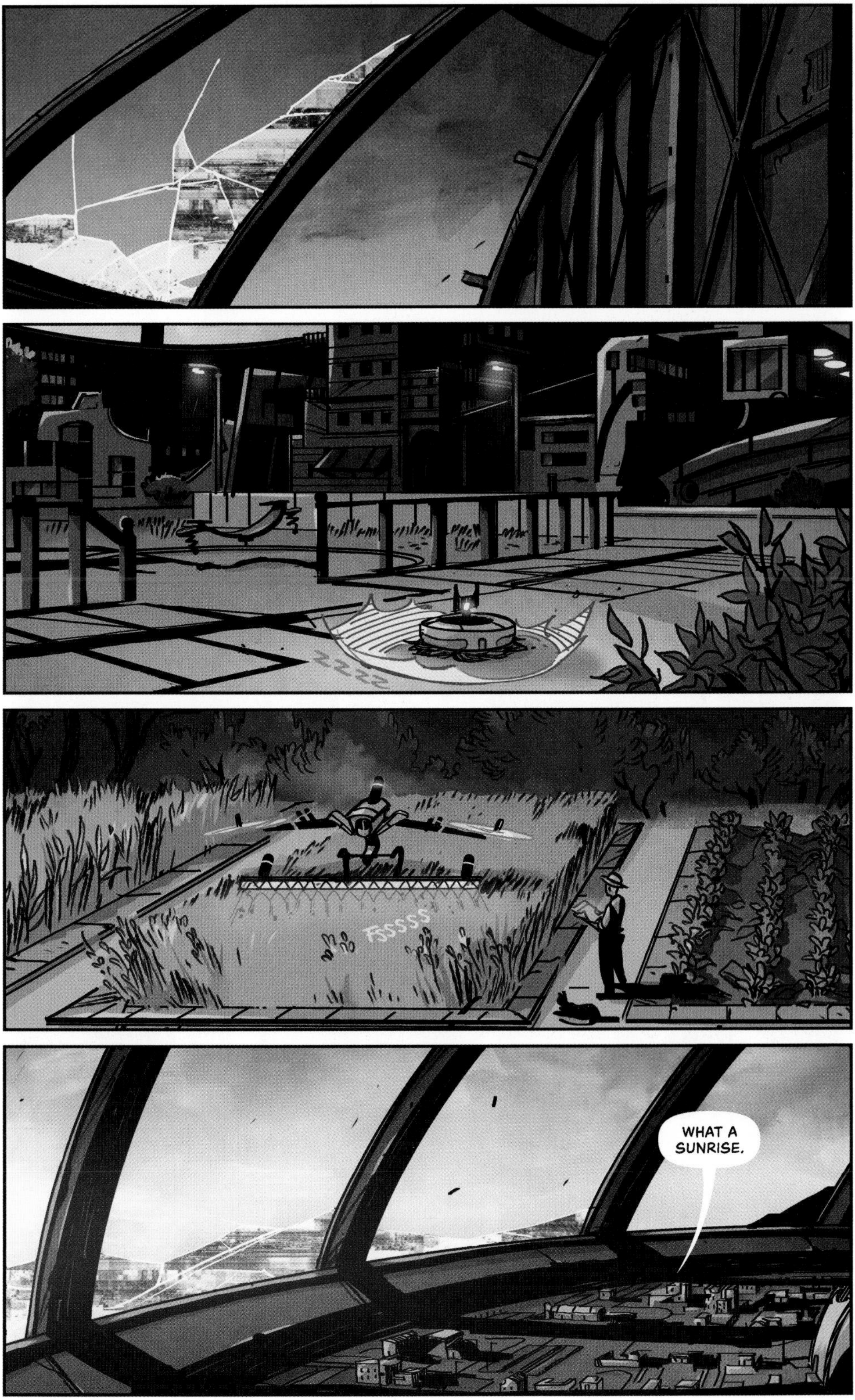
ZZZZZ
FSSSSS
WHAT A SUNRISE.

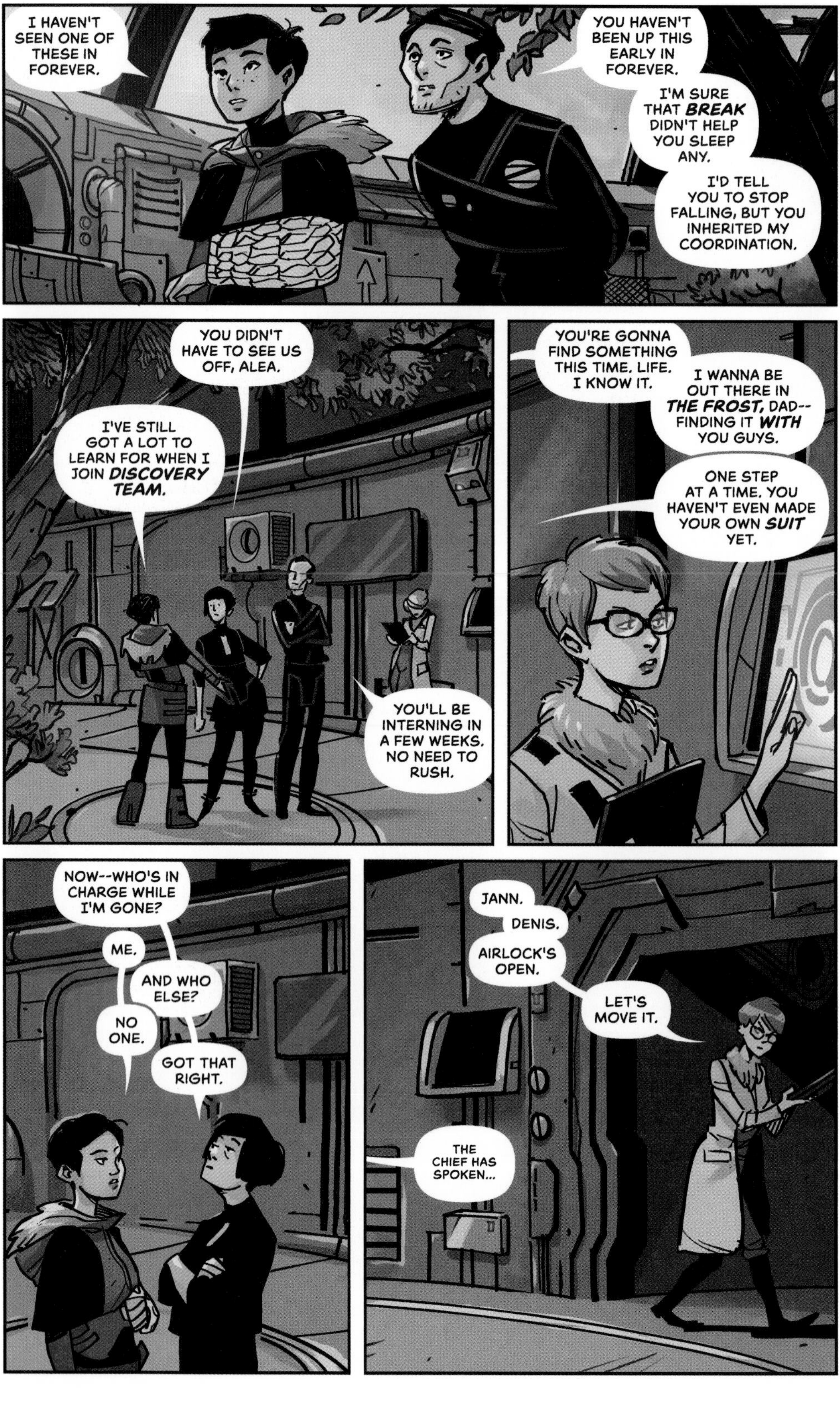
I HAVEN'T SEEN ONE OF THESE IN FOREVER.
YOU HAVEN'T BEEN UP THIS EARLY IN FOREVER.
I'M SURE THAT BREAK DIDN'T HELP YOU SLEEP ANY.
I'D TELL YOU TO STOP FALLING, BUT YOU INHERITED MY COORDINATION.
YOU DIDN'T HAVE TO SEE US OFF, ALEA.
I'VE STILL GOT A LOT TO LEARN FOR WHEN I JOIN DISCOVERY TEAM.
YOU'LL BE INTERNING IN A FEW WEEKS. NO NEED TO RUSH.
YOU'RE GONNA FIND SOMETHING THIS TIME. LIFE. I KNOW IT.
I WANNA BE OUT THERE IN THE FROST, DAD--FINDING IT WITH YOU GUYS.
ONE STEP AT A TIME. YOU HAVEN'T EVEN MADE YOUR OWN SUIT YET.
NOW--WHO'S IN CHARGE WHILE I'M GONE?
ME.
AND WHO ELSE?
NO ONE.
GOT THAT RIGHT.
JANN.
DENIS.
AIRLOCK'S OPEN.
LET'S MOVE IT.
THE CHIEF HAS SPOKEN...

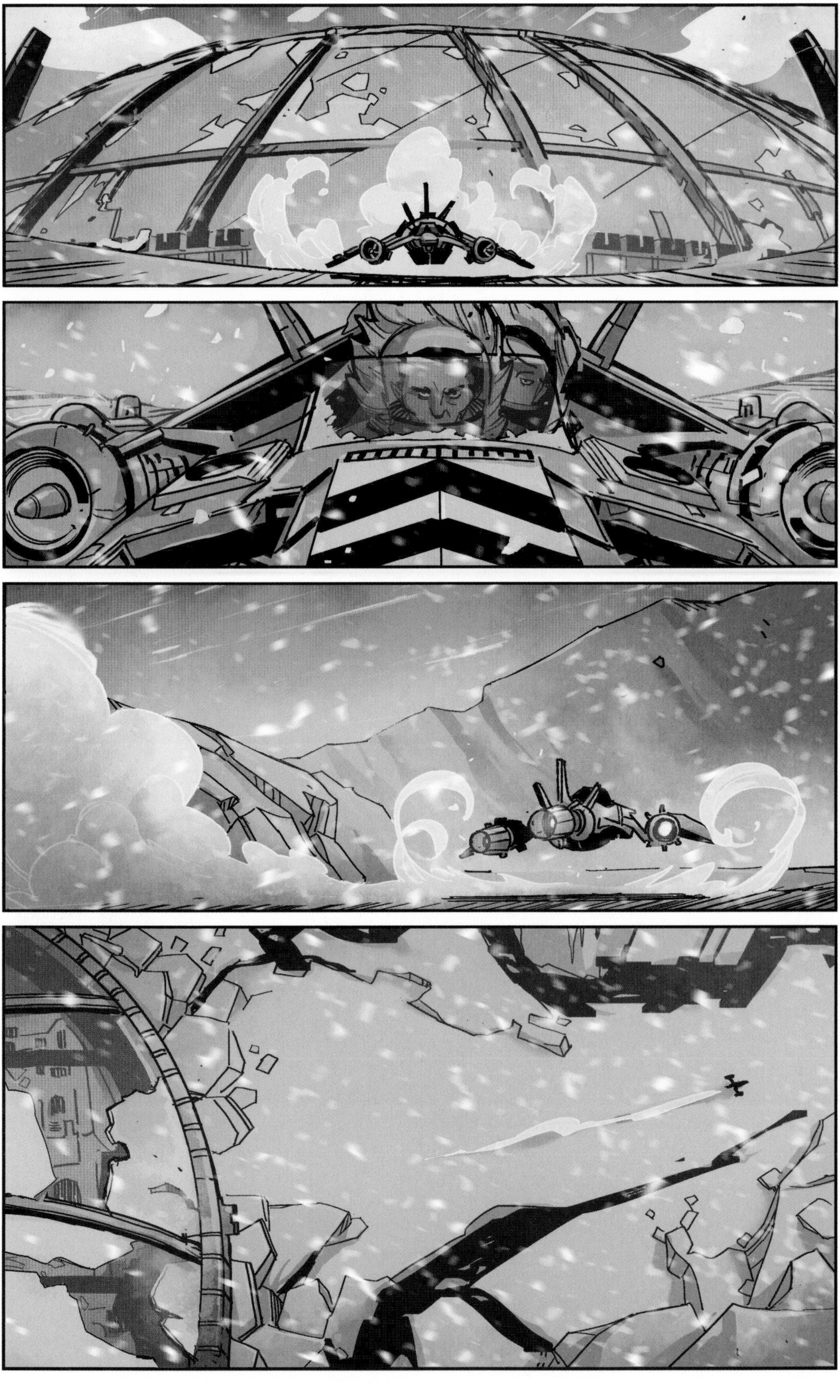

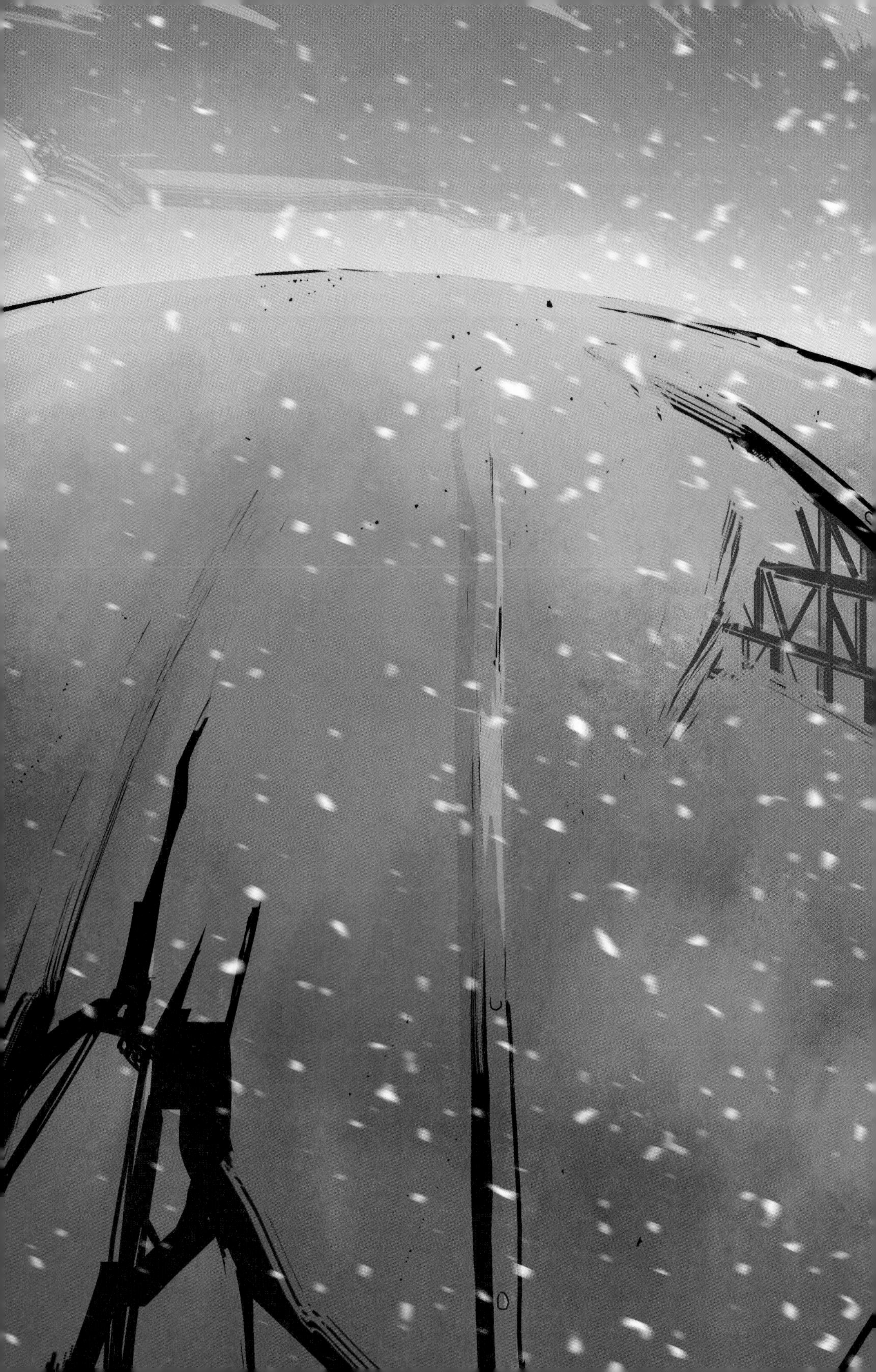

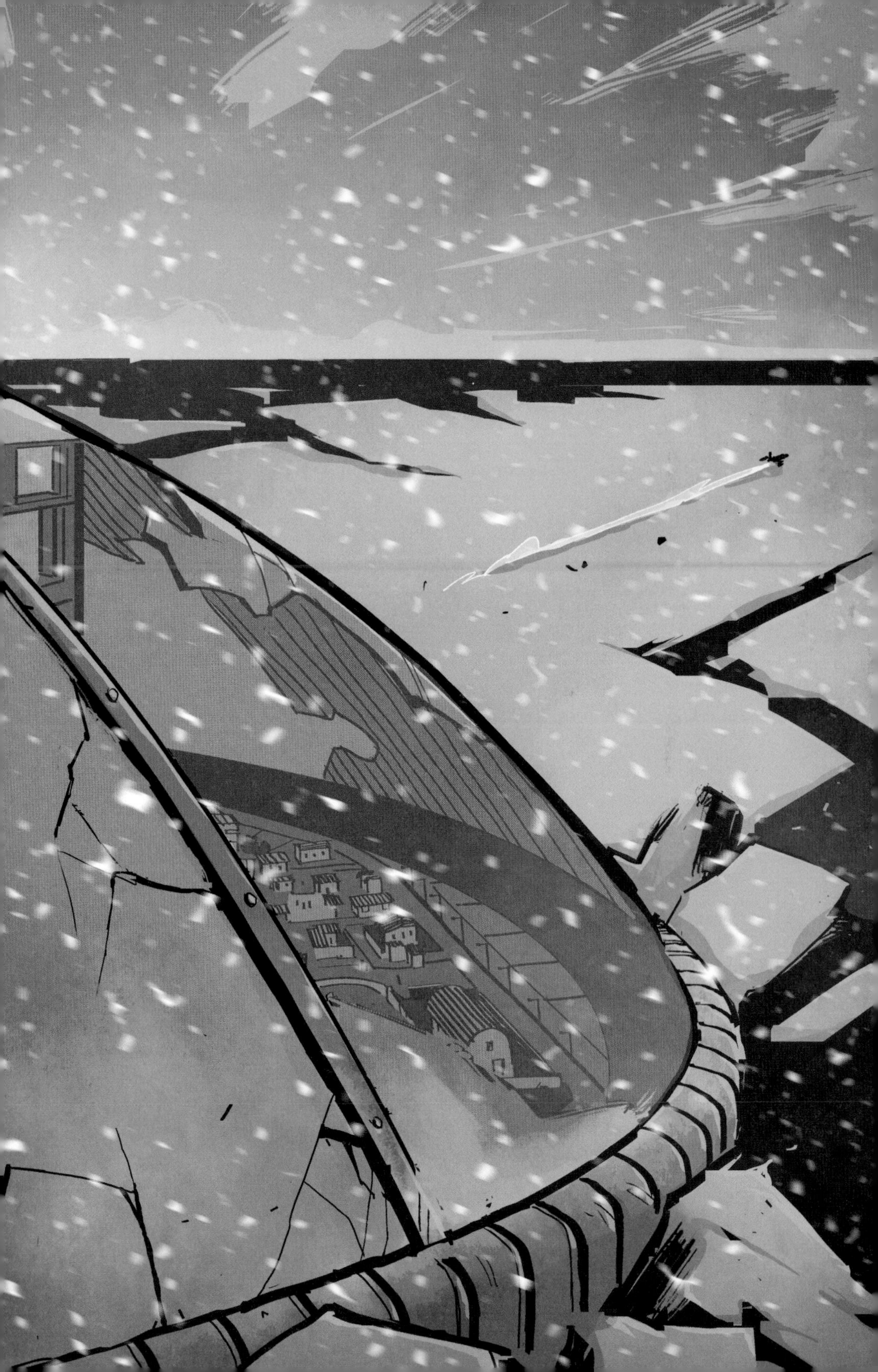

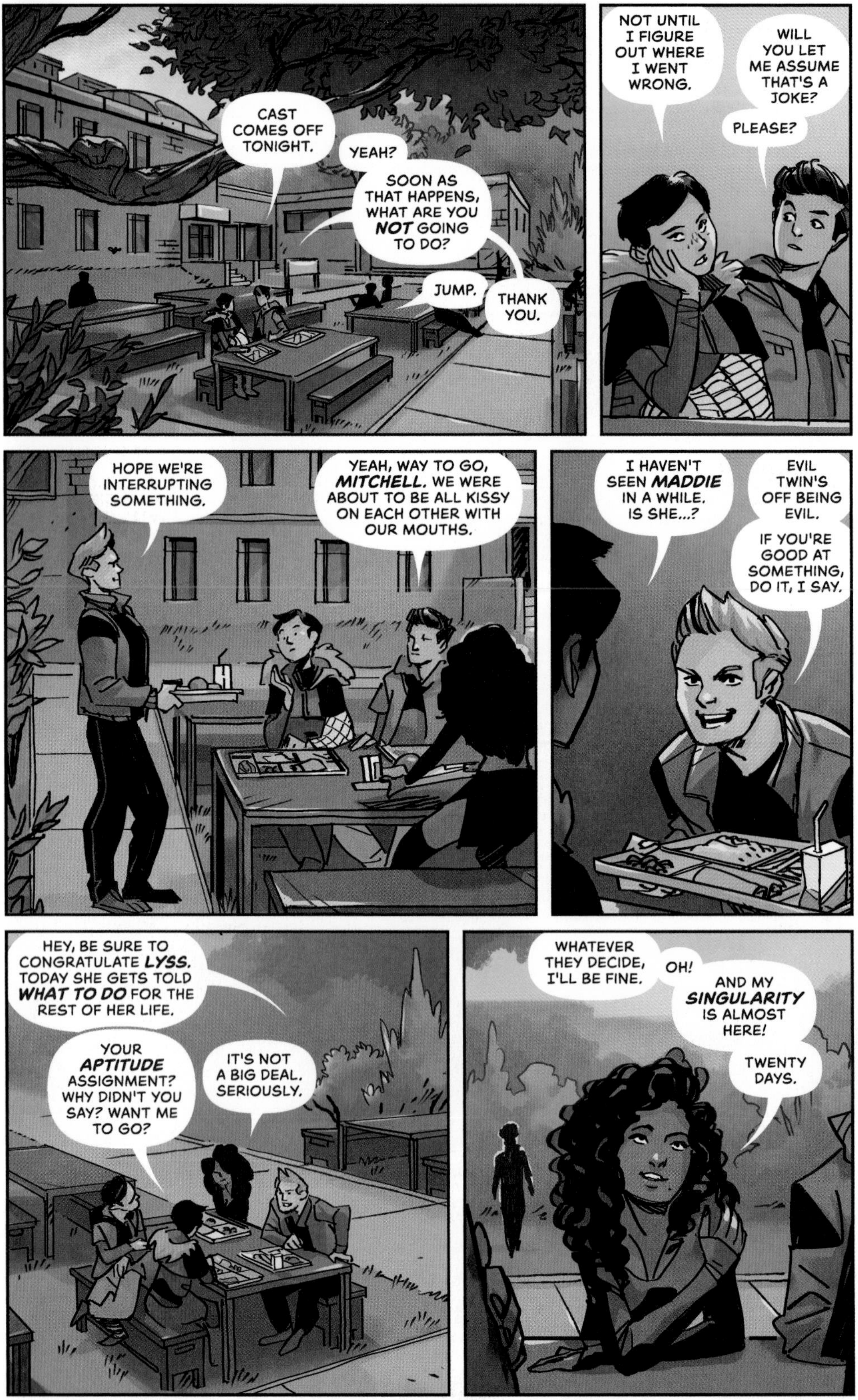
CAST COMES OFF TONIGHT.
YEAH?
SOON AS THAT HAPPENS, WHAT ARE YOU NOT GOING TO DO?
JUMP.
THANK YOU.
NOT UNTIL I FIGURE OUT WHERE I WENT WRONG.
WILL YOU LET ME ASSUME THAT'S A JOKE?
PLEASE?
HOPE WE'RE INTERRUPTING SOMETHING.
YEAH, WAY TO GO, MITCHELL. WE WERE ABOUT TO BE ALL KISSY ON EACH OTHER WITH OUR MOUTHS.
I HAVEN'T SEEN MADDIE IN A WHILE. IS SHE...?
EVIL TWIN'S OFF BEING EVIL.
IF YOU'RE GOOD AT SOMETHING, DO IT, I SAY.
HEY, BE SURE TO CONGRATULATE LYSS. TODAY SHE GETS TOLD WHAT TO DO FOR THE REST OF HER LIFE.
YOUR APTITUDE ASSIGNMENT? WHY DIDN'T YOU SAY? WANT ME TO GO?
IT'S NOT A BIG DEAL. SERIOUSLY.
WHATEVER THEY DECIDE, I'LL BE FINE.
OH!
AND MY SINGULARITY IS ALMOST HERE!
TWENTY DAYS.

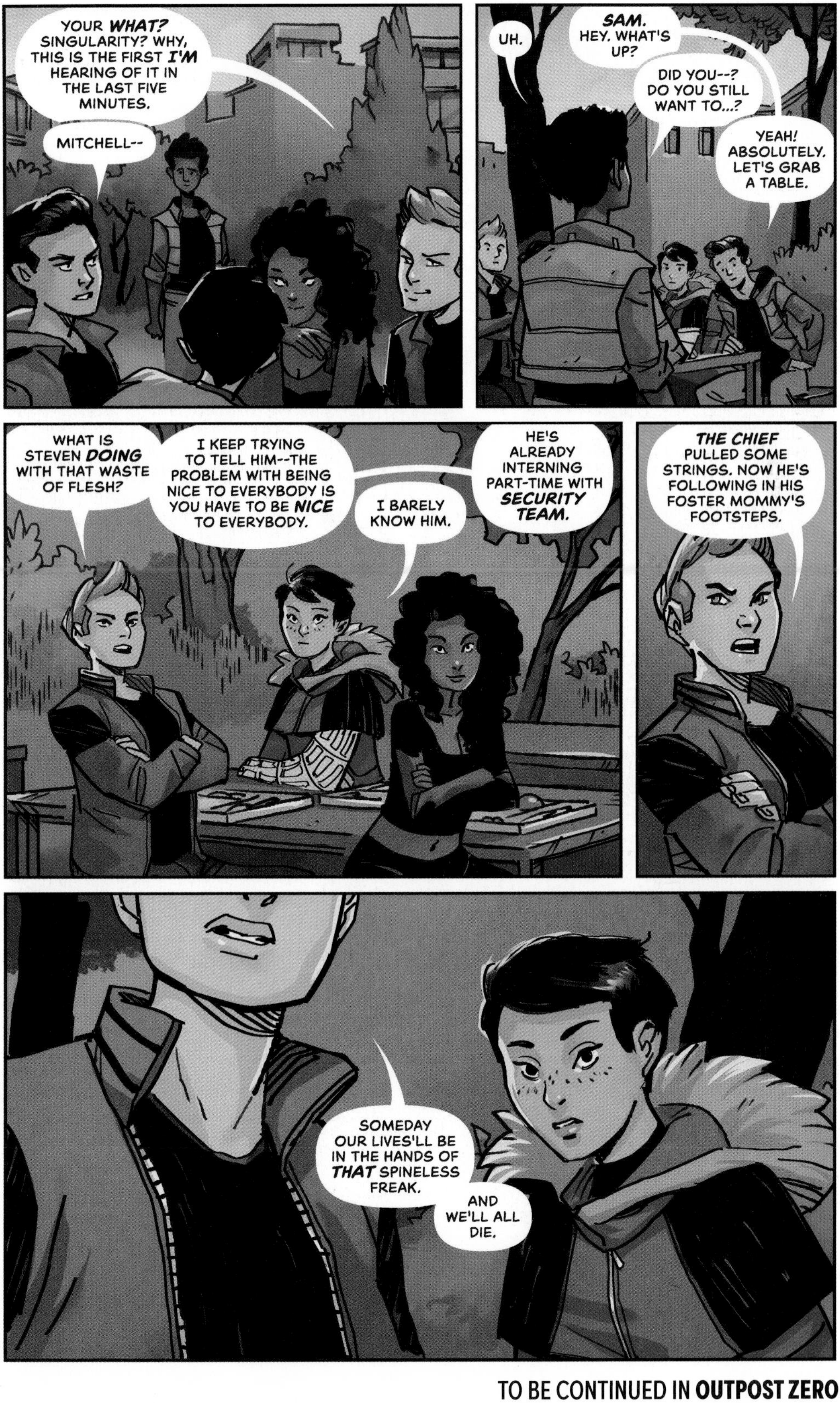
YOUR WHAT? SINGULARITY? WHY, THIS IS THE FIRST I'M HEARING OF IT IN THE LAST FIVE MINUTES.
MITCHELL--
UH.
SAM. HEY. WHAT'S UP?
DID YOU--? DO YOU STILL WANT TO...?
YEAH! ABSOLUTELY. LET'S GRAB A TABLE.
WHAT IS STEVEN DOING WITH THAT WASTE OF FLESH?
I KEEP TRYING TO TELL HIM--THE PROBLEM WITH BEING NICE TO EVERYBODY IS YOU HAVE TO BE NICE TO EVERYBODY.
HE'S ALREADY INTERNING PART-TIME WITH SECURITY TEAM.
I BARELY KNOW HIM.
THE CHIEF PULLED SOME STRINGS. NOW HE'S FOLLOWING IN HIS FOSTER MOMMY'S FOOTSTEPS.
SOMEDAY OUR LIVES'LL BE IN THE HANDS OF THAT SPINELESS FREAK.
AND WE'LL ALL DIE.

TO BE CONTINUED IN **OUTPOST ZERO**

EXPLORE NEW WORLDS

For Young Adult & Middle Grade Readers in SKYBOUND COMET

**Activate your heart.
Be an Everyday Hero!**

"Astro Boy meets The Iron Giant, a sweet, funny, action-packed story for every sci-fi loving young reader!"
-FAITH ERIN HICKS
(Avatar: The Last Airbender, The Nameless City)

IRMA KNIIVILA   TRI VUONG

AVAILABLE NOW!
ISBN: 978-1-5343-2130-4 • $12.99

**Tillie Walden enters the
world of Robert Kirkman's
THE WALKING DEAD!**

FROM THE EISNER & IGNATZ AWARD-WINNING AUTHOR OF "ON A SUNBEAM"
TILLIE WALDEN

AVAILABLE NOW!
ISBN: 978-1-5343-2128-1 • $14.99

**Tiny heroes,
epic adventures!**

MAC SMITH

ON SALE FEBRUARY 2023!
ISBN: 978-1-5343-2436-7 • $14.99

**Welcome to the smallest
town in the universe.**

SEAN KELLEY McKEEVER
ALEXANDRE TEFENKGI

ON SALE APRIL 2023!
ISBN: 978-1-5343-2437-4 • $17.99

**Will you make
the pact?**

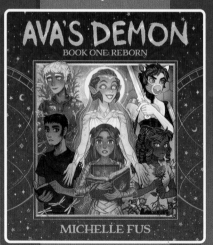

AVA'S DEMON
BOOK ONE: REBORN

MICHELLE FUS

ON SALE MAY 2023!
ISBN: 978-1-5343-2438-1 • $17.99

**SKYBOUND
COMET**

Visit **SkyboundComet.com** for more information,
previews, teaching guides and more!

image